Praise for Ben Bova and *The Hittite*

"Excellent. A thrilling and inventive retelling of the legend of Troy."   —David Hagberg,
New York Times bestselling author of
The Expediter

"Completely convincing and emotionally satisfying; the adventure and warfare were gripping enough to keep me awake to finish the book in a single night."
—Orson Scott Card,
New York Times bestselling author of
Ender's Game

"A cast of stars, all seen through the eyes of a Hittite warrior. With authentic battle scenes and the reality of siege warfare, *The Hittite* is an adventure you'll want to undertake."   —Barbara D'Amato,
Mary Higgins Clark Award–winning
author of *Foolproof*

"Bova gets better and better."
—Los Angeles *Daily News*

"Bova proves himself equal to the task of showing how adversity can temper character in unforeseen ways."
—*The New York Times* on *Venus*

"Exceptionally intelligent and absorbing."
—*Booklist* on *Mars Life*

Books by Ben Bova

FROM TOM DOHERTY ASSOCIATES

THE
HITTITE

BEN BOVA

TOR®

A TOM DOHERTY ASSOCIATES BOOK • NEW YORK

This is a work of fiction. All of the characters, organizations, and events portrayed in this novel are either products of the author's imagination or are used fictitiously.

THE HITTITE

Copyright © 2010 by Ben Bova

A Tor Book
Published by Tom Doherty Associates, LLC
175 Fifth Avenue
New York, NY 10010

www.tor-forge.com

Tor® is a registered trademark of Tom Doherty Associates, LLC.

ISBN 978-0-7653-6363-3

First Edition: April 2010
First Mass Market Edition: June 2011

Printed in the United States of America

0 9 8 7 6 5 4 3 2 1

To brave
and beautiful
Barbara;
and to
Harold Lamb,
who opened my eyes

Zeus now addressed the immortals: "What a lamentable thing it is that men should blame the gods and regard us as the source of their troubles when it is their own wickedness that brings them sufferings worse than any which Destiny allots them."

Homer, *The Odyssey*

I

▾

THE PATH TO TROY

1

The dreadful news reached us when we were less than a day's march from the capital, returning home after a long, hard campaign against the wily Armenians, in the mountains far to the north. The gods had turned their backs on our rightful emperor; he had been poisoned by his own scheming sons. Now, lusting for the power their father had wielded, the sons made war on one another.

The empire of the Hatti stretched from beyond the twin peaks of Mount Ararat in the northeast to the shores of the Great Sea. Our armies sacked Babylon and fought the prideful Egyptians at Qadesh and Megiddo in the gaunt lands of Canaan. With swords of iron and discipline even stronger we conquered all that we encountered.

Except ourselves.

Now Hattusas, our capital, had crumbled into chaos. Even before we reached its outer wall we could hear the tumult of terrified voices wailing to the gods for protection. It seemed as if the city's entire population was streaming out of the gates: white-bearded men, aged grandmothers, children wide-eyed with fear, whole families pushing carts loaded with their meager possessions, mothers with crying babies in their arms, all blindly fleeing. Smoke was rising from the citadel up on the hill in the center of the city, an ugly black plume staining the clouded sky.

I knew what each of my men was thinking: what's happened to my family, my wife, my children, my mother and father? I felt that fear clutch at my own heart as we reached the city's main gate.

"Stay together," I commanded my squad. "March in step."

I knew that we would need iron discipline now more than ever. They obeyed, good soldiers that they were. Instinct born of hard training made us move as one unit, spears at the ready.

Once inside the gates the stream of fleeing populace turned into a torrent of people ashen with panic, all rushing to get away from the city. And we saw why. Gangs of young men were marauding drunkenly through the twisting streets, breaking into houses and shops, stealing all that they could carry, brutally raping any women they found. Screams and pleas for mercy filled the air.

"Where are the constables?" one of my men cried.

Gone, I realized. With the emperor dead and his sons warring against each other, order and safety had collapsed into lawlessness.

A woman with a baby in her arms and two more little ones trailing behind her rushed up to me, her face twisted by fear.

"Soldiers! Help us! Protect us!"

My instinct was to fight these drunken looters, to safe-guard the defenseless people they were preying upon. But all I had was my squad of twenty. Twenty men against hundreds, one squad of soldiers against a city in anarchy. It was hopeless.

"Leave the city while you can," I told her. "Get away until this madness burns itself out."

She stared at me, disbelieving. Then she spat on me. My hand flew to the pommel of my sword. I told her through gritted teeth, "Get away while you can. Leave while you're still alive."

She turned and hurried to rejoin the stream of people fleeing for the city's gates.

"Stay in order," I shouted to my squad. "We can't fight them all."

The men grumbled but we marched on, eyes forward, shields on our arms and spears upright, up the narrow street that led to the citadel and to the home of my father, where my wife and sons lived. Three of my men had family in the city, I knew. The rest came from elsewhere in the empire.

"We're going to the citadel. From there you can go to your families or to the barracks," I told my men.

We marched toward the citadel, toward the house of my father.

The gangs gave us wide berth as we marched in step up the cobbled main street toward the citadel. Twenty men in the emperor's gear, each armed with a nine-foot spear and killing sword were enough to make most of them melt away from us. Someone threw a rock that bounced off my shield. When the twenty of us wheeled and leveled our spears in that direction, the looters scattered away like the vermin they were, scurrying for safety.

"Stay together," I repeated, resuming our march up the street. As usual, I stayed on the right end of our line, since I am left-handed and wear my shield on my right arm. Thus we presented a solid line of shields from end to end.

It was hard to watch the rioters looting and roaring, staggering from house to house, dragging out shrieking terrified women, and do nothing. Dead bodies lay in the street. Blood ran in the gutter down its middle. Young toughs in knots of four and five lurched from shop to shop, flagons of wine in their blood-soaked hands. I even saw bands of soldiers, still wearing the emperor's leather and iron, smashing and looting alongside the wild-eyed gangs.

"We'll tend to our own families," I repeated to my men. "There's nothing we can do for the others."

Truly, the city was in anarchy. Twenty soldiers would not be able to restore order. Twenty hundred were needed. The streets smelled of blood and panic. Smoke was thickening in the sky.

The stone tower of the citadel, up atop the hill, was in flames. Fire and death are ever the twin sons of war, and the black smoke rising from the royal palace told me that the gods had turned their backs on the Hatti. My home was hard by the high wall that encircled the citadel. My father, my wife, my two little sons were there. So I hoped.

"Stay in order," I called to my men. "I'll drub the man who breaks ranks."

We marched onward toward the burning citadel. None of the drunken looters came near us. Brave they were with their clubs and daggers against cringing women and quaking old men; against a disciplined squad of armed spearmen they made no opposition. We marched upslope along the cobbled street and everyone gave us a wide berth.

Most of my men were too young to be married. They lived in the barracks inside the citadel wall. The three who had homes to go to I released once we reached the wall, with orders to rejoin the squad before nightfall. The others milled about uncertainly.

"Stay together," I told them. "Go to the barracks and save what you can. Then form up again here, by this house."

It was the house of my father, the house where I had been born. And my sons, as well.

Like all the others along the street, my father's house was braced along the citadel wall. Built of well-fitted stone, it leaned slightly aslant. Its one window was tightly shuttered, but the door was ajar, leaning crookedly on its hinges. Not a good sign, I thought. The roof thatch was smoldering, probably from a spark wafted on the breeze. The very air was thickening with smoke from the burning citadel.

I stepped into the shadowy interior of the house, my eyes quickly adjusting to the gloom. My heart sank. The room had been ransacked; table overturned, chairs smashed to splinters. The fireplace was cold and dark. I looked up to the loft where the beds were; silent, empty. The bedclothes had been torn off and ripped.

Then, in the far corner where my father had often told me tales of war and conquest, I saw his withered body on the packed earthen floor, huddled beneath a bloodstained cloak.

I had seen dead bodies before, by the score, by the hundreds. Yet the sight of my father there in the shadows made my throat go dry. I sank to my knees beside him and gently, gently turned him so I could see his face.

They had battered him terribly. Yet his eyes fluttered, then focused on me.

"Lukka . . ." His voice was a tortured sigh.

"Don't try to speak. Let me—"

He clutched at my arm, his aged fleshless fingers still as strong as a hawk's talons. "I knew you would return." He coughed painfully. "I knew . . ."

"Quiet, Father. Quiet. I'll get a healer, a priest."

"No need. No use."

He coughed blood.

"Your sons," he gasped. "Gone . . ."

"Gone? Where?"

"They fled." He coughed again, his frail body spasming in my arms. "Your wife was mad with panic. Slavers were breaking into the houses . . ."

"Slavers?"

"She feared them . . . she took my grandsons . . ."

The third child of war, I thought. The poor wretches who were not killed or maimed were made into slaves.

"Find them!" my father commanded me. Gripping my arm even harder, he hissed, "Find them. My grandsons. They are my flesh. Find them, Lukka. Find them!"

Those were his last words to me. He died in my arms, his blood soaking into the earthen floor while smoke from the burning thatch made my eyes sting and water.

2

My sons. My wife. Find them.

I took a spade from the corner by the fireplace, where my father had always kept his tools. Coughing from the thickening smoke, I dug a shallow grave for him there in his house, the home of my ancestors. I tried to remember the words for the dead, but my mind would not recall them. All I could think of was his final command to me. Find his grandsons.

If the slavers have found them they're already dead, I thought. Slavers don't keep young children, especially boys. Mouths to feed, and too small to do any useful work.

I got up from my knees while choking smoke filled the room and eager flames licked across the timbers of the roof. I stepped out onto the street. The air was thick with smoke. More houses were burning, I could see, as swaggering gangs of looters put the torch to whatever they could not carry away with them, roaring with drunken laughter. Men can turn into beasts so easily, I realized. Take away the authority of the emperor and even trained soldiers become looting, raping animals.

I wanted to kill them. Kill them all. Slash their guts out and watch their eyes go wide with pain and shock. But that was nonsense, of course. I could kill five of them, ten, a dozen. But in the end I would be swarmed under and cut to pieces. What would that accomplish? So I stayed my hand and waited in the doorway of the house in which I had been born.

The sky seemed to be darkening; drops of rain began

to spatter the cobblestones. Not hard enough to stop the flames that were crackling on the roof, though.

My squad was nowhere to be seen. They'll be back, I told myself. At sundown, they'll return, just as I ordered them to.

But I wondered.

The world had split apart. The empire was in ashes and ruins. And my father had commanded me to find his grandsons, my little boys, and their mother, my wife: Aniti.

I had first met her on the day we were married in the temple of Asertu, nearly six years earlier. The two families had arranged the marriage while I was away on campaign with the army. A soldier's life is not his own. I had been a soldier since I was fourteen, like my father before me. I had no choice; he was accustomed to giving commands and having them obeyed. Before my beard was anything more than a wisp he led me to the barracks and entered me in his squad. Thus I spent most of my days in long campaigns far from home, carrying out the emperor's orders.

Aniti. I tried to remember how much time we had spent together in the years we had been married: a few months, all told. Enough to father two sons by her. She was a pleasant enough woman, not given to anger, never sullen. But I could not recall the color of her eyes, nor the sound of her voice.

The rain became heavier, making rivulets that flowed among the cobblestones. The roof of the house crashed down in a shower of sparks and flame, as if the gods honored my father's grave with sacred fire. I pulled my cloak tighter around me while I stood in the chilling rain and waited for my men to return.

As it grew darker they began to show up. One, then a pair of them, then another three. By the time it was fully dark eighteen of the twenty were standing in the rain-soaked street, their cloaks over their heads.

"Nerik isn't coming, Lukka," said Magro, usually the jokester among my men. He wasn't joking this day. He looked miserable beneath his dripping cloak. "I saw him go off with some of his friends from the barracks."

"And Hartu?" I called to them. "Anybody seen him?"

Head shakes and mumbles. Hartu had family in the city, I knew. He was the eldest son; his parents probably needed him more than I did—if they still lived.

We were eighteen men, eighteen soldiers of an army that no longer existed. As individuals we would be as helpless as any fleeing refugee. But if we stayed together we might be able to survive. As one lone man I could never hope to find my sons. But with my squad of disciplined spearmen . . .

I made a decision. "All right. Form up. We march."

"March?" asked big, slow-witted Zarton. "To where?"

"To find my sons," I told them.

3

For six months I led my squad of men westward, across the chaos and anarchy of the collapsed empire. We had to fight most of the way, against bandits, against villagers and farmers, against other desperate squads of former soldiers like ourselves.

Soon enough we discovered the remains of a refugee

caravan. It had been attacked by bandits. The dead were strewn across the ground like a child's broken toys. My wife and sons were not among them, thank the gods. I learned from one of the wounded guards who had been left to die that those who survived the attack were being herded to the slave market at Troy, far to the west, on the coast of the Aegean Sea.

Slaves. Slavers wouldn't keep two little boys, they'd kill them on the spot. Aniti, my wife, what of her? I wondered. A woman isn't responsible for what happens to her when she is in captivity, but still . . . a slave, powerless, defenseless. I had to squeeze my eyes shut to blot out the visions that came to my mind.

I thanked the dying guard and eased his way into the next life with a dagger to his throat. Then I searched the ground once again, until it was too dark to see, but my sons were not among the bodies scattered across the wreckage of the caravan.

So I pushed my men onward, toward Troy. They grumbled as soldiers always do, but they had no real choice. Together we were a formidable band of men, armed and disciplined. We lived off the land, became little better than bandits ourselves.

Bad dreams filled my sleep: dreams of my infant boys lying broken and dead in a roadside ditch. Dreams of my wife on the auction block of the slave merchants.

Some nights I dreamed of Hattusas, saw the city in flames while ravaging mobs looted and raped through the streets. In my dream I saw the old emperor die, poisoned by his own sons, and I was powerless to help my emperor. Try as I might I could not move, could not even shout a warning to him.

Then it wasn't the emperor who was dying, it was my

father, his life's blood seeping into the dirt floor of my house while choking smoke filled the room and eager flames licked across the timbers of the roof.

"Gone," my father moaned. "Taken by slavers . . . your wife, your sons . . . gone . . . Find them . . . Find my grandsons."

He died in my arms. The burning house crashed in on me.

I snapped awake and sat upright on the meager pallet of straw we had scraped together. Blinking the sleep away I slowly recalled where we were. A farmstead in the brown, scrubby hills off the royal road that led to Troy.

The farm wench beside me stirred slightly, then turned over, snoring.

I was soaked in sweat, like a weak woman instead of a Hatti soldier. In the gray light of early dawn I reached out my hand. My sword lay by my side. It had never been more than an arm's length away from me, not for these past six months.

Perhaps my wife and children were already dead; we had found corpses enough along the royal road. But not my sons. Not my wife. Not yet.

How long can they live under the slavers' lash? I wondered. My sons were little more than babies; the elder hardly five, his brother two years younger. How can she protect them, protect herself? I felt as if I had been thrown into the deepest of all the world's black pits, cut off from light and air and all hope. Suffocating, drowning, already dead and merely staggering through the motions of a living man.

Enough! I commanded myself. Don't let despair swallow you. Battles are lost before they begin when soldiers surrender themselves to despair.

Reaching out my hand, I lifted my naked sword. Its solid weight felt comforting in the predawn gray. A Hatti soldier. What does that mean when the empire no longer exists? When there is no emperor to give commands, no army to carry the might of the imperial will to the far corners of the world?

All that matters to me now is my two little boys, I told myself. And my wife. I will find them. I will free them, no matter what it takes. Or die in the trying.

I got to my feet and gathered up my clothes, my iron-studded leather jerkin, my helmet and oxhide shield. As I stepped outside the crude lean-to that passed for a barn I saw that the sun was already tingeing the eastern horizon with a soft pink light.

My troopers were beginning to stir. Twelve of us were left, out of the original twenty. We did not look much like a squad of Hatti soldiers now, a unit of the army that served as the emperor's mailed fist. Six months of living off the land, six months of raiding villages for food and fighting other marauding bands of former soldiers had transformed us into marauders ourselves.

I felt grimy. My beard itched as if tiny devils lived in it. There was a pond between the barn and deserted hut of a farmhouse. I waded into it. The water was shockingly cold, but I felt better for it.

By the time I had dried myself and pulled on my clothes, most of my men had risen from the blankets they had thrown on the ground and were stumbling through their morning pissing and complaining.

I waved to Magro, who had taken his turn as lookout, up on the big rock by the road. He came down and joined the men who were starting a cook fire. We had nothing but a handful of beans and a few moldy cabbages; the farmhouse and barn had already been picked clean, empty except for the sullen-faced wench we had found hiding in the dung pile.

I saw little Karsh sitting awkwardly on the ground, craning his neck to peer at the gash on his shoulder. He was a Mittani, not a true Hatti, but he was a good soldier despite his small size. More than a week ago he had taken a thrust by a screaming farmer who had leaped at us from behind a door, wielding a scythe. I myself had dispatched the wild-eyed old man, nearly hacking his head from his shoulders with one swing of my iron sword.

"How's the shoulder, little one?" I asked. Karsh had been a downy-cheeked recruit when he had first joined my squad. Now he looked as lean and grim as any of us.

"Still sore, Lukka."

"It was a deep wound. It will need time to heal completely."

He nodded and we both knew what he feared. Some wounds never heal. They fester and spread until the arm has to be lopped off. That would mean Karsh's death, out here with no surgeon, not even a priest to perform the proper rituals for keeping evil spirits out of his wound.

I went back inside the shadowy barn and nudged the sleeping woman with the toe of my boot. She stirred, groaned, and turned over to stare up at me: naked, dirty, smelling of filth.

"There must be a cache of food hidden somewhere nearby," I said to her. "Where is it?"

She clutched her rough homespun shift to her and replied sullenly, "Other soldiers took everything before you got here."

"I don't believe you."

"It's the truth."

"Would it still be the truth if we dangled your feet in the fire for a while?" I asked.

Her eyes went wide. "There's a village not more than half a league down the same road you came in on," she said quickly. "Many fine houses. More than all the fingers of both my hands!"

Yes, I thought. Fine houses will be guarded by armed men, especially if there are things in them worth stealing.

"Get yourself dressed," I told her. "But do not come out of the barn until we leave. My men might mistake you for Asertu."

Her heavy brows knit together, puzzled. "Who is Asertu?"

I had forgotten that we had come so far that these people did not know the Hatti gods. "Aphrodite," I answered her. The goddess of love and beauty in this part of the world.

She actually smiled, thinking I was complimenting her.

My men were gathered around the cook fire, passing a wooden cup of broth from one to the next. I could smell the reek of stale cabbage from where I stood.

Looking around, I noted, "No one's on watch."

"We're all awake, with our weapons to hand," Magro said, handing the cup up to me. I took a sip. It was bitter, but at least reasonably hot.

"There's a village less than a league down the road," I told them. "Should be food there."

"Where there's food, there's guards," Zarton muttered. He was the biggest of my men, but never eager to fight.

"Villagers," I said. "No match for trained Hatti soldiers."

They mumbled reluctant agreement. My humor had fallen flat again. What was left of my squad hardly resembled a unit of trained Hatti soldiers. They still had their spears and shields, their swords and helmets, true enough, but our clothes had worn out months ago, replaced by whatever ragged, lice-crawling garments we could find among the terrified farmers and villagers we raided.

I had started by trying to trade with the people we came across, but what do soldiers have to trade besides their weapons? Sometimes villagers willingly provided us with what we demanded, just to be rid of us without bloodshed. Farmers usually fled as we approached, leaving their livestock and stores of grain or vegetables to us, glad to escape with their lives and their daughters.

The wench we had found hiding at this farm was lame. She could not run. But her family's farmstead had already been picked clean by the time we got there. Which meant that there were other bandits in the area.

I formed up the men, reminded them that we might run across another band of raiders.

"But we're not raiders," said Magro, grinning mockingly. "We're Hatti soldiers."

The others all laughed. Yet I knew that only by keeping the discipline we had all learned under the empire could we hope to survive. It was what had kept us alive so far: twelve of us, at least, out of my original squad of twenty.

I marched them up onto the dusty meandering road, rutted from the wheels of oxcarts and wagons. The road led to the next village, the next fight, the next bloodletting. I told myself that it led to my wife and sons. It was the road that the slavers had taken, the road that ended in the great city at the edge of the sea, where the slave market auctioned off poor wretches to buyers from Thrace and Argos, from distant Crete and even mighty Egypt.

Troy. My wife and sons were being driven to the slave market at Troy. They were still alive, I was certain of it. And I knew that if I did not find them and free them there, I would lose them forever. They would be carried off to some foreign land, slaves for the rest of their lives.

I had to find them. My father had been right in that. In all this world of chaos and misery, my two sons were all that really mattered. I can't let them spend their lives in slavery. I will find them, no matter how long it takes or who stands in my way.

4

What the wench called a village was a miserable collection of huts at a fork in the road we had been following. Worse, another raider band was already there. Several of the huts were ablaze, sending foul-smelling black smoke billowing into the bright morning sky. Magro and I lay concealed in a stand of half-grown wheat on a terraced hillside overlooking the village. The rest of my men were hunkered down on the other side of the knoll, out of sight.

"They don't look like soldiers," Magro whispered to me.

"Neither do we," I answered.

"Bronze weapons," Magro pointed out.

I nodded. They were bandits, then, not former soldiers. Only soldiers of the old emperor were gifted with iron swords. Each one was worth a man's weight in silver.

"Looks like they're ready to leave," I whispered.

The bandits must have hit the village the previous day and spent the night, taking their fill of the food and wine and women. Now they had rounded up all the ragged, bedraggled people in the bare little patch of dirt that passed for a village square and methodically, one by one, slit the throats of any man young enough to fight. The women screamed and wailed, the white-bearded old men sank to their knees. The young men, their hands bound behind them, fell like sheep, unable to defend themselves. One of the women threw herself at the raiders but was knocked to the ground by a backhand cuff.

Once their grisly task was finished, the bandits piled as much loot as each of them could carry and staggered out onto the left fork of the road. The women ran to their slain sons and husbands, raking their faces with their nails to add their own blood to what was already soaking the ground.

"What now?" Magro asked me. "They've picked the place clean."

Still watching the backs of the departing bandits, I answered him, "They've done half our work for us. Now all we need to do is take the goods they've collected away from them."

"I counted twenty-seven of them."

I nodded. "Most of them will run at the sight of us."

"Twenty-seven," Magro repeated, unconvinced.

It was easy to overtake the bandits. They were still

half-drunk and encumbered with the loot they carried. We trailed them to a wooded area, where we could approach them unnoticed, screened by the trees and ground foliage, and fell on them savagely.

In a few moments it was all over. They were fatally surprised. I killed three of the louts myself. Zarton, our big farm boy from the Zagros Mountains, put away five of them—or so he claimed. I counted twenty-two bodies sprawled on the bloody ground. The others fled shrieking for their lives.

"Food, wine, clothing . . . they did well for themselves," said little Karsh as we picked over the bundles the bandits had dropped.

"That village was richer than it looked," Magro said.

"Pick it up, all of it," I told the men.

"There's too much! How can we carry all this?" Even Zarton, who towered over most of us, looked unhappy at shouldering such a burden.

"We won't be carrying it far," I told them. "We're bringing it back to the village."

"Bringing it *back*?"

"We don't need all this, and they'll be very grateful to us for returning even half of it."

They stared at me in disbelief. Only Magro seemed to understand what I was up to.

"You want to know which fork of the road leads to Troy," he said to me softly as we trudged back to the village, laden with their goods.

I answered him with a nod. The men were sweating and grumbling, but I had to know which road the slavers had taken. I could not rest while there was still a chance that I might find my sons and my wife.

Would I have come so far if it was only my wife the

slavers had taken? I wondered. She was a woman, and there are many women in the world. Yet she was the mother of my sons, and those two little boys were what drove me on. So I sought the fruit of my loins, driven by a dying old man's will, while my men trudged unhappily back to the village the raiders had looted.

The villagers were indeed grateful, once they realized we intended to return some of their goods to them, rather than cause them more harm. They were a sad and pitiful lot, their young men still sprawled on the blood-soaked earth, their women still kneeling over them, crying and keening. The biting iron stench of their blood filled the air; if the women and old men did not get the corpses buried soon, there would be even worse smells.

The village's white-bearded headman gladly told me that the right fork led toward Troy, but he had no idea how far the city might be.

"I have heard of it," he told me, trying to maintain some shred of dignity in his quavering voice. "No one from this village has ever gone there."

No one from this village has ever gone farther than the wheat fields and dung-spattered sheep pastures of the nearby hills, I thought.

I ordered my men to gather up enough food to feed us for a few days and enough trinkets and baubles to use as trade goods at the next village we came to. The villagers did not object. They could not, even if they desired to.

We left them standing there amid their dead, wailing to their gods.

5

The sun was high and hot as we climbed the wooded slope that led up to the next ridgeline. Suddenly Zarton dropped the loot he was carrying and rested his long spear against a tree.

"I'm going back," he announced.

The men all stopped. I had been in the lead, so I had to turn around to face our mountain man.

"What do you mean?" I asked, stepping past half a dozen of the men to stand before Zarton.

He shrugged, a big, slow-witted powerful young ox. "I'm going back to that village. I'm not going on with you."

I glanced at the men closest to me. Some seemed puzzled by Zarton's words, but a few were nodding with understanding. Why keep on this grueling trek across the ruins of the empire when we can settle down in that village and be welcomed by the widows and daughters who need men to protect them? I saw it in their eyes.

"You are a soldier, Zarton," I said evenly. "You follow orders just as the rest do. My orders."

He shook his head stubbornly. "There's no empire anymore, Lukka. Why keep up the pretense?"

They all knew why. We were fighting our way toward Troy to find my wife and sons. It was my will that drove us on now, not the emperor's, but I had to be just as hard and inflexible as he had been. Otherwise we would all be lost and I would never find my sons.

"Pick up your goods and get back on the march," I commanded.

He actually grinned at me. "I'm not a soldier anymore, Lukka. I quit."

"You can't quit. Not unless I allow you to."

Zarton stood up a little straighter. The other men edged away from us.

"I'm going back to the village," he repeated, slowly, stubbornly.

"No you're not."

Usually he was an easygoing, amiable sort. But like the ox he resembled, he could be obstinate. And dangerous. Yet I knew that if I allowed him to leave, several of the other men would go with him. Discipline would evaporate. My squad would disintegrate before my eyes and I would have no chance whatever of reaching distant Troy.

Zarton gripped his spear in one ham-sized fist. It was more than half again his own considerable height. He looked at me with real sadness in his ice-blue eyes.

"I don't want to hurt you, Lukka. Don't stand in my way."

"I don't want to kill you, boy, but if you don't obey me I'll be forced to."

I had no spear, only the sword in its scabbard by my side. Being left-handed is an advantage in a sword fight because most men are accustomed to fight against right-handers, and my left-handed stance confuses them. But this would not be a sword fight: Zarton hefted his spear.

Before any of the other men could make up their minds about which of us to back, I said loudly: "Stand back, all of you. This is between Zarton and me, no one else."

They gladly backed away.

"This is wrong, Lukka," said Zarton, his heavy brows knitting sullenly.

"Don't make me kill you," I said evenly. "Put the spear down and obey my orders."

Shaking his head in disbelief, Zarton closed his other hand around the haft of his spear. But before he could lower its iron point at me I leaped at him, drawing my sword in the same motion.

He staggered back against the tree, shocked, and I stuck the point of my sword into his gut, just below the breastbone, and rammed the full length of the blade up into his chest. He looked surprised, his eyes wide with astonishment that I had not waited for him to set himself. Then his expression faded to a bewildered confusion as his mouth filled with bright red blood and his legs no longer supported him.

With a feeble little gasp Zarton collapsed against the tree's rough bark and slid to the ground. His eyes stayed open but they went cold and dead.

Yanking my sword from his body, I turned to face the other men. They all seemed just as shocked as Zarton had been.

"We march to Troy. I don't care how far it is or how many battles we have to fight to get there. We march to Troy. Is that understood?"

They nodded and muttered.

"Troy is a great city. It rules the Dardanelles and the Aegean beyond the straits. We can find a place in the service of the Trojan king," I told them. "We can become true soldiers again, instead of marauding robbers."

Perhaps they believed me. Perhaps not. I didn't care, not at that moment with foolish young Zarton lying dead at my feet with the flies already buzzing about him. I knew only one thing for certain: I would reach Troy or die in the trying. I picked up his spear and pointed with it down the road toward Troy.

We marched.

Yet that night, after a long day's trek, I saw Zarton again in my dreams. He rose out of the grave I had dug for him and stared at me from the underworld beyond the Styx, shaking his head sadly, sadly, his eyes brimming with tears.

In his arms he held my two baby boys.

6

It was nearly sunset, two days after I had killed Zarton. We were picking our way slowly down a gradual slope, through the undergrowth of a forest that had once been thick with lofty, broad-boled trees. But now half the trees had been cut down, their stumps overgrown with ferns and twisting vines. In the distance we heard the sound of woodcutters chopping away methodically.

That meant a village had to be nearby, or perhaps a larger town. Without a word of command from me, the men spread out, hefting their spears and moving silently through the underbrush, schooled by long experience.

The chunking sound of the axes grew louder as we made our way through the woods. The trees thinned even more, and I motioned the men to drop to their knees. Through the screening underbrush I saw a team of half-naked ax men sweating away at their work in the lengthening shadows of the dying day. Four of them were cutting wood, six more were scurrying to pile the cut logs into a lopsided cart pulled by a big dun-colored bullock patiently munching his cud.

"Move! Move, you dogs!" bellowed a mean-faced taskmaster at the team. His accent was harsh, barely understandable. "You've got to get this cart loaded and back in camp before the sun goes down."

His men were bone-thin, ragged, staggering under the loads they carried.

"And you whoresons!" roared the taskmaster. "Swing those axes or by the gods you'll think Zeus' thunder-bolts are landing on your backs!"

He brandished a many-thonged whip. He was a big man with powerful bare arms, but a potbelly hung out through his leather vest. Shaved bald, he had a thick bushy beard the color of cinnamon and a livid scar running down one side of his ugly face.

The woodcutters were guarded by five spearmen in leather jerkins studded with bronze bolts. Their spear points were bronze, I saw. Probably the short swords hanging at their sides were, too. Each of them wore little conical helmets that looked, at this distance, to be leather rather than metal.

Off in the hazy horizon the setting sun was tinting the clouds with flaming red. Beyond the edge of the forest and a bare dusty plain that stretched on the other side of a meandering river, I could make out the battlements of a walled city.

Troy!

The city was built on a dark bluff, and beyond it I could see the glittering silver of the sea. It had to be Troy, it could be no other, I told myself. We had reached our destination at last.

Five armed soldiers keeping watch over fewer than a dozen woodcutters. The soldiers looked young, callow. I decided we could afford a peaceful approach.

"On your feet, all of you, and follow me," I said to my men in a low voice. "That's Troy there in the distance. We're almost there."

Magro huffed with disbelief. "Don't tell me we'll sleep under a roof tonight."

I grinned at him as I hefted Zarton's spear. "Come on."

The young spearmen stiffened with surprise as we stepped out of the foliage and presented ourselves. They gripped their long bronze-tipped spears and backed away from us a few steps. We were twelve to their five.

The loudmouthed whip master fell silent. The woodcutters stopped their work and gaped at us. They were sweating, filthy, bare to the waist, mostly emaciated old men barely strong enough to lift an ax. They stared about wildly, as if they would break and run at the slightest excuse.

"Is that city Troy?" I asked, pointing with my right hand. I gripped the spear in my left, of course.

"Who are you?" one of the spearmen demanded, his youthful voice cracking with surprise and fear. "What are you doing here?"

I barely understood him. He spoke a dialect that I had never heard before, heavy and guttural. It had been many months since anyone had spoken Hatti to us; we had learned the local language as we trekked across the land.

"We are Hatti soldiers, from far to the east. We seek the city of Troy."

It took some while, but gradually I made them understand that we meant them no harm. The young spearmen told me that Troy was under siege by a huge army of Achaians, kings and princes of a hundred cities from the far side of the Aegean, or so he claimed. They themselves were part of the besieging Achaian army, sent out to guard this pitiful band of foragers who were gathering firewood. A pretty poor army, I thought.

"You can't enter the city," the young leader of the spearmen told me. "The High King Agamemnon would never allow trained warriors to pass through his lines."

We had arrived in the middle of a war. Where my wife and sons might be was anyone's guess.

"Then I must see this Agamemnon," I said.

"See the High King?" the spearman's voice squeaked with awe.

"Yes, if he is the leader of your army."

"But he's the High King! He speaks only to princes and other kings."

"He will want to speak to me," I said, with a confidence I did not truly feel. "I am an officer in the army of the Hatti. I can be of great service to him."

In truth, the spearman was little more than a beardless youth. The thought of going before his High King seemed to fill him with terror. At last he called one of the wood-loaders, a scrawny, knobby-kneed old man with a mangy, unkempt dirty gray beard and bald head shining with sweat.

"Poletes," the youth commanded, his voice still fluttering slightly, "take these men to the camp and turn them over to the High King's lieutenant."

The old man nodded eagerly, glad to be free of his heavy work, and led us down toward the slow-flowing river.

"That's the plain of Ilios," said Poletes, pointing to the other side of the river as we followed its winding bank.

His voice was surprisingly strong and deep for such a wizened old gnome. His face was hollow-cheeked beneath its grime, with eyes that bulged like a frog's. He wore nothing but a filthy rag around his loins. Even in the fading light of the dying day I could see his ribs and the bumps of his spine poking out beneath his nut-brown skin. There were welts from a whip across his back, too.

"You are Hittites?" he asked me as we walked slowly along.

"Yes," I said. "In our tongue we call ourselves Hatti."

"The Hittites are a powerful empire," he said, surprising me with the knowledge. "Have you come to aid Troy? How many of your army are with you?"

I decided it was best to tell him nothing. "Such things I will tell your High King."

"Ah. Of course. No sense blabbing to a *thes*."

That word I did not know. "Where are you from?" I asked.

"Argos. And I wish I were there now, instead of toiling like a dog here in this doomed place."

"What brought you here?"

He looked up at me and scratched his bald pate. "Not what. Who. Agamemnon's haughty wife, that's who. Clytemnestra, who is even more faithless than her sister, Helen."

It must have been obvious to him that I did not understand, but he went right on, hardly drawing a breath.

"A storyteller am I, and happy I was to spend my days

in the agora, spinning tales of gods and heroes and watching the faces of the people as I talked. Especially the children, with their big eyes. But this war has put an end to my storytelling."

"How so?"

He wiped his mouth with the back of his grimy hand. "My lord Agamemnon may need more warriors, but his faithless wife wants *thetes*."

"Slaves?"

"Hah! Worse off than slaves. Far worse," Poletes grumbled. He jerked a thumb back toward the men we had left; I could still hear the distant chunking of their axes. "Look at us! Homeless and hopeless. At least a slave has a master to depend upon. A slave belongs to someone; he is a member of a household. A *thes* belongs to no one and nothing; he is landless, homeless, cut off from everything except sorrow and hunger."

"But weren't you a member of a household in Argos?" I asked.

He bowed his head and squeezed his eyes shut as if to block out a painful memory.

"A household, yes," he said, his voice dropping low. "Until Queen Clytemnestra's men booted me out of the city for repeating what every stray dog and alley cat in Argos was saying—that the queen has taken a lover while her royal husband is here fighting at Troy's walls."

I raised my hand to stop our march. Even though the sun was setting, the day was still broiling hot and the river looked cool and inviting. I sat down on the grassy bank and, leaning far over, scooped up a helmetful of clear water. The men did the same. A few even splashed into the river, laughing and thrashing about like boys.

I drank my fill while Poletes slid down the slippery

grass into the water and cupped his hands to drink. Watching the brown filth eddying from his legs, I was glad that I had filled my helmet first.

"Well," I said, wiping sweat from my brow, "at least the queen's men didn't kill you."

"Better if they had," Poletes replied grimly. "I would be dead and in Hades and that would be the end of it. Instead I'm here, toiling like a jackass, working for wages."

"That's something, anyway," I said.

His frog's eyes snapped at me. Still standing shanks-deep in the river, he grabbed at the soiled little purse tied to his waist and opened its mouth enough for me to peer in. A handful of dried lentils.

"My wages," he said bitterly.

"That is your payment?"

"For the day's work. Show me a *thes* with coin in his purse and I'll show you a sneak thief."

I shook my head, then got to my feet and motioned my men to do the same.

"Lower than a slave, that's what I am," Poletes grumbled as I lent him my arm and hauled him out of the water. "Vermin under their feet. They treat their dogs better. They'll work me to death and let my bones rot where I fall."

7

Muttering and complaining all the way, Poletes led us across a ford in the river and toward the camp of the Achaians, which stretched along the sandy shore of the restless sea. It was protected by an earthen rampart twice the height of a grown man running parallel to the shoreline. I saw sharpened stakes planted here and there along its summit. In front of the rampart was a deep ditch, with more stakes studding its bottom. There was a packed sandy rampway that led up to an opening in the rampart, which was protected by a wooden gate that stood wide open, defended by a handful of lounging spearmen. If this is a sample of Achaian discipline, I thought, a maniple or two of Hatti soldiers could take this gate and probably the whole camp with it.

We trudged up the ramp and through the open gate, unchallenged by the men who were supposed to be guarding it. Once inside the gate, I saw that what they called a camp looked more like a crowded, bustling noisy village than a military base, and smelled like a barn despite the breeze coming off the sea. People milled about, all of them talking at once, it seemed, at the top of their lungs. There was no hint of military organization or discipline among these Achaians.

They had pulled their long, pitch-blackened boats up onto the sandy beach and raised tents and even sizable huts of wood next to them. Between the boats stood roped-off corrals where horses neighed and stamped, and makeshift pens of slatted wood for stinking goats and sheep that bleated and shitted endlessly. Noise and filth were everywhere; the stench almost gagged me at first.

It grew chilly as the sun sank below the flat horizon of the dark blue sea. They have been here for some time, I realized, as we made our way through the confused jumble of the camp. Men were gathering around cook fires; pale smoke wafted away on the wind. Dirty-faced slave women in rags stirred big pots of bronze while men sat close by, cleaning weapons, binding fresh wounds, jabbing daggers into the pots to yank out steaming half-cooked chunks of meat. The noise of men shouting back and forth and beasts yowling was enough to make my head hurt; the stench of dung and animals and smoke hung in the air like a palpable cloud.

There were plenty of women in the camp: slaves tending their masters' cook fires, carrying heavy double-handled jugs of wine on their shoulders, polishing armor with the resigned, hopeless patience that slavery teaches.

As instructed, Poletes marched us to the camp of Agamemnon, High King among the Achaians. The old man pointed out the two dozen boats that Agamemnon had brought to Troy, all pulled far up on the sandy beach, side by side, each decorated with a golden lion painted on its prow. Agamemnon's quarters was the largest wooden lodge I had yet seen, its main door guarded by no less than six armed warriors in shining bronze armor and helmets.

Poletes spoke to one of the guards, who walked off into the lengthening shadows of the noisy, busy camp.

"How long has this war been going on?" I asked Poletes.

Clutching his thin arms over his bare chest to try to ward off the growing cold, Poletes told me, "For years, now. Of course, much of that time has been spent raiding the villages and farms nearby. It took awhile for these mighty warriors to work up the courage to attack Troy itself."

"The slave market . . ." I started to say.

But Poletes ignored me as he continued, "The city's

walls were built by Poseidon and Apollo, they say. No one can breach them. Yet Agamemnon and the other kings are determined to continue their siege until—"

"You there!" a haughty voice stopped Poletes as if his tongue had been ripped out.

I turned and saw a sour-faced man approaching us, with the guard Poletes had spoken to trailing a few paces behind him. The man wore no armor, but his straight back and sharp tone told me he was accustomed to giving orders. Even in a rough wool chiton he looked like a soldier.

Ignoring Poletes, he marched straight up to me, looked me up and down, then cast a baleful glance at my men.

"I am Thersandros, captain of the High King's guards. Who are you and what do you want?" he demanded of me.

My men snapped to attention, spears erect. I, too, straightened the spear in my hand and answered, "I am Lukka, commander of this squad of Hatti troops. I want to offer my services to your king."

The corner of his mouth ticked once. I could see there was gray in his thick beard and shaggy hair.

"Offer your services to the king, eh? More likely you're looking for a free meal."

"We are trained Hatti soldiers," I said evenly. "We can be of great help to your king."

He planted his fists on his hips. "A dozen more mouths to feed, that's all I see here."

I drew myself up to my full height, several fingers taller than he. "Are you going to announce our presence to your High King or not?"

He tried to outstare me, but soon blinked and looked

away. "To the High King? You must be mad. I'll tell his chief steward, he's the one who's always sending boats back to Argos for more warriors."

"Fair enough," I said, deciding to accept his decision.

"You, *thes*," he growled at Poletes. "Get back to the work gang, where you belong."

Poletes turned to me, his big frog's eyes silently begging, like a sorrowful puppy.

"He's with me," I heard myself say, even as I thought it was foolish to be so softhearted. A Hatti soldier should be made of sterner stuff.

"Him?" Thersandros guffawed. "He's nothing but a worthless *thes*."

"He's my servant," I said evenly.

"You can't—"

"He's my servant," I repeated, with more iron in it.

Thersandros shrugged and muttered, "Suit yourself, then. Find yourselves a fire for the night. Over there will do." He pointed to a handful of men sprawled around one of the cook fires. "Tell them Thersandros said they should share what they can with you."

I tried to hold back the anger that rose in me. Sending a pack of strangers to soldiers already huddling by their evening fire and ordering them to "share what they can" is an excellent way to start a fight.

Yet even as I stood before Thersandros, struggling to keep my temper, my eye chanced on the line of women who were carrying food and drink into Agamemnon's cabin.

They were slaves, I knew. Most of them were young and slim, some were even pretty.

The third one in the line was my wife.

8

I started to call out to her, but she disappeared into the cabin before I could gather my wits and utter a sound. I started toward the lodge, but Thersandros grabbed my arm.

"You can't go in there!" he snapped, frowning at me. "That's the High King's quarters."

"That woman is my wife," I said.

His frown changed into a look of sheer disbelief. "Those are slaves, Hittite. The High King's slaves, at that."

I pulled free of his grip. "She's my wife," I insisted.

Thersandros pointed to the guards in polished bronze armor standing on either side of the hut's doorway. "They'll spit you on your spears if you try to go in there."

"Then you go in and bring her out to me."

"Me?" He broke into a bitter, barking laugh. "The High King doesn't give up his slaves, Hittite. Not to me and certainly not to the likes of you."

He dragged me away from the cabin, back toward my men. "I'll ask about her for you," he said, grudgingly. "Don't expect a miracle."

My blood was hot. I gripped the pommel of my sword, thinking that I could slice this Thersandros' liver out of him before he knew what hit him. Then, with my squad of men, I could break past those guards and take my wife out of Agamemnon's lodge, out of slavery.

And then what? I asked myself. Twelve men against

the whole Achaian camp? Madness. And where were my sons? What would happen to them if I started a brawl here in the camp? How could I save them, protect them, if I were killed battling like a hotheaded fool?

So I forced myself to remain silent, to walk slowly away from Thersandros and back toward my waiting men, seething with rage, trembling with the effort to control myself.

Aniti is alive, I told myself. A slave, but still alive. Where are my sons? I wondered. A bitter voice in my mind answered. Already dead, most likely. I squeezed my eyes shut and tried to silence that voice.

Poletes broke my train of thoughts. Pointing to the Achaians gathering around their fire, he said, "Let's get something to eat before everything's gone. My stomach is as shriveled as a dried prune."

As boldly as a free man he walked up to the knobby-kneed Achaian standing by the cook pot and said loudly, "Thersandros says that you must share what you have with these men."

The Achaian didn't hesitate an instant. He cuffed Poletes with a backhand swat that sent the old storyteller sprawling.

I stepped up to him, Zarton's spear still in my hand. "This man is my servant. What you do to him you do to me."

With my free hand I hauled Poletes to his feet. His lip was cracked and bleeding.

The Achaian eyed me up and down, took note of my spear and the sword at my hip, the shield strapped to my back, my travel-stained leather jerkin and iron helmet. He wore only a ragged wool chiton, belted at the waist. His hair and beard were dark and thickly curled, matted with sweat and grime. His bare arms and legs were lean but wiry, roped with muscle.

"And who in the name of Hades are you?" His voice was low, gruff.

The men who had been eating out of wooden bowls were looking up at us. Several of them got slowly to their feet. I knew my own men were drawing themselves up behind me.

"I am Lukka, of the Hatti. Hittites, in your tongue. I've offered the services of my men to your High King."

The man blinked several times. He's trying to find a way to deal with us without humiliating himself, I reasoned. He doesn't want a fight, and neither do I.

"I can pay for whatever food you provide," I said.

"Pay?"

I held out the spear. "Take it. Its point is made of iron, far stronger than your bronze spearpoints."

He hesitated. "Bronze holds a sharper edge."

"And shatters where an iron point holds strong." With a nod, he took the spear from my hand. He hefted it, then allowed a slow smile to creep across his bearded face.

"Hittites, eh? You've come a long way, then."

"We have," I said, making myself smile back at him. "And we're hungry."

He nodded and turned to the stolid, thickset wench stirring the pot. With a kick to her rump he barked, "Find more meat for the stew! We have hungry mouths to feed."

It turned out that he was not a difficult man, after all. His name was Oetylos, and like the rest of the High King's men he was from Argos.

"Agamemnon is a mighty king," he said over his wooden bowl as we sat together. "Who else could have brought all these kings and princes together to bring Helen back to her rightful husband?"

I ate the hot, spicy stew slowly and let him talk. I needed to know more about this Agamemnon. I needed to know how I could get this mighty king to release my wife from slavery. And my sons, if they still lived.

9

I woke with the sun. A chill wind swept in from the sea as the first rays of light peeped over the high wall of the city, up on the bluff. My men, who had been sleeping on the ground wrapped in their cloaks as I had, stirred and began to sit up, coughing and complaining, as usual. Looking around for Poletes, I saw him huddled with several of the dogs, scratching fleas as he still slept.

Silent, sad-faced women brought us wooden cups and filled them with a thin barley gruel. My wife was not among them. We sat in a circle and sipped at our breakfast while the Achaian camp slowly came astir. Poletes joined us, grateful to be given a steaming bowl.

Then Thersandros came striding among us, fists on his hips. "Hittite!" he called to me.

I got to my feet. There was little sense of discipline that I could see. Instead of saluting him I merely walked over and stood three paces before his wary eyes.

"Do Hittite warriors know how to dig?" he asked me, almost in a growl.

"All soldiers learn to use a shovel," I replied. "My men have built—"

He cut me off with a curt gesture. Pointing to the top of the earthen rampart that protected the camp, he said, "Then take your men up there and do what you can to strengthen the wall."

I wanted to tell him that he would be wasting our abilities; we were soldiers, not laborers. Instead I said, "How soon can I see your High King? I want to offer—"

"Offer your backs to the shovels," Thersandros said. "My lord Agamemnon has other things on his mind this morning."

With that he turned and walked away from me.

A soldier learns to obey orders or he doesn't remain a soldier for long. I decided there was nothing I could do but bide my time.

My men were on their feet by now. Walking back to them, I told them that our task this fine, breezy morning was an engineering detail.

Magro saw through my words immediately. "They want us to dig for them?"

I nodded and smiled grimly.

Oetylos had shovels waiting for us. Grousing and frowning, my men took the tools and started trudging up the slope of the rampart.

"You, too, storyteller," Oetylos said to Poletes, and he threw the old man a filth-encrusted burlap sack: for carrying sand, I surmised.

We were not the only ones plodding up the rampart. Work gangs of slaves and *thetes* were also heading for the top, shovels on their shoulders, with whip-brandishing overseers behind them. At least we had no taskmaster to shout at us.

The rampart stretched along the length of the beach,

protecting the camp and the boats pulled up onto the sand. I could see only one opening in the sandy wall, protected by a ramshackle wooden gate and guarded by half a dozen lounging spearmen. In front of the rampart was a broad ditch, studded with wooden spikes, as was the top of the fortification itself.

Once at the top of the rampart we had a fine view of the plain and the city of Troy up on the bluff. Its walls were crenellated, its gates tightly shut. Inside the Achaian camp warriors were eating a breakfast of broiled mutton and thick flat bread, while their slaves and men-at-arms yoked horses to chariots and sharpened swords and spears.

"They're going to attack the city," I surmised aloud.

Poletes answered in his surprisingly strong voice, "They will do battle on the plain. The Trojans will come out this day to fight."

"Why should they come out from behind those walls?" I wondered.

Poletes shrugged his skinny shoulders. "It has been arranged by the heralds. Agamemnon offered battle and white-bearded Priam accepted. The princes of Troy will ride out in their fine chariots to fight the kings of the Achaians."

That didn't make much sense to me, and I wondered if the storyteller was trying to make up a dramatic scene out of whole cloth.

As the sun rose higher in the sparkling clear sky we worked at improving the rampart. I immediately saw that the best thing to do was dig sand out of the bottom of the ditch that fronted the defensive wall and carry it up to the top. That way the ditch got deeper and the rampart grew higher. It was hot work, and my men sweated almost as much as they grumbled and swore about their work.

I dug and sweated alongside them. I assigned Poletes to stay at the summit, watching over our weapons and shields and jerkins, which we had left there. We worked in our skirts, bare to the waist.

The morning was quite beautiful. Up at the top of the rampart the cool breeze from the sea felt good on my sweaty skin. The sky was a wondrously clear bowl of sparkling blue, dotted by screeching white gulls that soared above us. The sea was a much deeper blue where restless surges of white-foamed waves danced endlessly. Grayish brown humps of islands rose along the distant horizon. In the other direction Troy's towers seemed to glower darkly at us from across the plain. The distant hills behind the city were dark with trees, and beyond them rose hazy bluish mountains, wavering in the heat.

Slaves and *thetes* of the other digging crews scrambled up the slope lugging woven baskets filled with sand.

I saw that Poletes had wandered off a ways to talk with some of the others, his skinny arms waving animatedly, his eyes big and round. At length he returned to our cache of weapons and clothes and beckoned to me.

"All is not well among the high and mighty this morning," he half-whispered to me, grinning with delight. "There's some argument between my lord Agamemnon and Achilles, the great slayer of men. They say that Achilles will not leave his lodge today."

"Not even to help us dig?" I joked.

Poletes cackled with laughter. "The High King Agamemnon has sent a delegation to Achilles to beseech him to join the battle. I don't think it's going to work. Achilles is young and arrogant. He thinks his shit smells like roses."

I laughed back at the old man.

My men and I toiled like laborers while the sun climbed higher in the cloudless sky. Agamemnon and the other Achaian leaders must be very fearful of the Trojans, I thought, to put us to work on improving their defensive barricade.

Then a handful of *thetes* began pushing on the wooden gate. It creaked and groaned as they pushed it slowly, slowly open. The chariots began to stream out onto the plain, the horses' hooves thudding on the packed-earth ramp that cut across the trench running in front of the rampart. All work stopped. The men still down in the trench scrambled up to the top of the rampart so they could watch the impending battle.

10

Bronze armor glittered in the sun as the chariots clattered through the gate and arrayed themselves in line abreast. Most were pulled by two horses, though a few had teams of four. The horses neighed and stamped their hooves nervously, as if they sensed the mayhem that was in store. I counted seventy-nine chariots, a pitifully small number compared to the assemblages of the army of the Hatti.

I myself had seen more than a thousand chariots

assembled before the walls of Babylon. My grandfather claimed there were ten thousand at the battle of Megiddo.

Each of the Achaian chariots bore two men, one handling the horses, the other armed with several spears of different weights and lengths. The longest were more than twice the height of a warrior, even in his bronze helmet with its plume of brightly dyed horsehair.

Both men in each chariot wore bronze breastplates, helmets and arm guards. I could not see their legs but I guessed that they were sheathed in greaves, as well. Most of the chariot drivers carried small round targes strapped to their left forearms. Each of the warriors held a heavy hourglass-shaped shield that was nearly as tall as he was, covering him from chin to ankles. I caught the glitter of gold and silver on the hilts of their swords. Many of the charioteers had bows slung across their backs or hooked against the chariot rail.

A huge shout went up as the last chariot passed through the gate and down the heavily trodden rampway that crossed the trench. The four horses pulling it were magnificent matched blacks, glossy and sleek. The warrior standing in it seemed stockier than most of the others, his armor filigreed with gold inlays.

"That's the High King!" said Poletes over the roar of the shouting men. "That's Agamemnon."

"Is Achilles with them?" I asked.

"No. But that giant over on the left is Great Ajax," he pointed, excited despite himself. "There's Odysseos, and—"

An echoing roar reached us from the battlements of Troy. A cloud of dust showed that a contingent of chariots was filing out of the large gate on the right side of the city's wall and winding its way down the incline that led to the plain before us.

Foot soldiers were hurrying out of our makeshift gate now, men-at-arms bearing bows, slings, axes, cudgels. Down the ramp of packed sand they hurried and spread out behind the line of Achaian chariots. A few of them wore armor or chain mail, but most of them had nothing more protective than leather vests, some studded with bronze pieces. Squinting into the bright sunshine, I saw that Trojan footmen were lining up behind their chariots. None of the troops marched in order, on either side; they simply ambled out like a horde of undisciplined rabble.

The two armies assembled themselves facing each other on the windswept plain. It grew strangely quiet. The clouds of dust the chariots had raised eddied away on the breeze coming from the sea. The river we had forded the day before formed a natural boundary to the battlefield on our right, while a smaller meandering stream defined the left flank. Beyond their far banks the ground on both sides was green with tussocks of long-bladed grass, but the battlefield itself had been worn bare by chariot wheels and the tramping of horses and warriors.

For nearly the time it took to eat a meal, nothing much happened. The armies stood facing each other. The sun climbed higher in the nearly cloudless sky. Horses whinnied nervously. Heralds went out from each side and spoke with each other while the wind gusted in our ears.

"None of the heroes are challenging each other to single combat this day," explained Poletes. "The heralds are exchanging offers of peace, which each side will disdainfully refuse."

"They do this every day?"

He nodded. "Unless it rains."

A question popped into my mind. "Why are they fighting? What's the reason for this war?"

Poletes turned his wizened face to me. "Ah, Hittite, that is a good question. They say they are fighting over Helen, the wife of Menalaos, and it's true that Prince Paris abducted her from Sparta while her husband's back was turned. Whether she came with him willingly or not, only the gods know."

"Who is Prince Paris?"

"King Priam's youngest son. Sometimes he is called Alexandros." Poletes broke into a chuckle. "A few days ago Menalaos, the lawful husband of Helen, challenged him to single combat, but Paris ran away. He hid behind his foot soldiers! Can you believe that?"

I didn't know what to say, so I remained silent.

"Menalaos is King of Sparta and Agamemnon's brother," Poletes went on, his voice dropping lower, as if he did not want the others to overhear. "The High King would love to smash Troy flat. That would give him clear sailing through the Dardanelles into the Sea of Black Waters."

"Is that important?"

"Gold, my boy," Poletes whispered. "Not merely the yellow metal that kings adorn themselves with, but the golden grain that grows by the far shores of that sea. A land awash in grain. But no one can pass through the straits and get at it unless they pay a tribute to Troy."

I was beginning to understand the reason behind this war.

"Paris was on a mission of peace to Mycenae, to arrange a new trade agreement between his father, Priam, and High King Agamemnon. He stopped off at Sparta and ended up abducting the beautiful Helen instead. That was all the excuse Agamemnon needed. If he can conquer Troy he can have free access to the riches of the lands beyond the Dardanelles."

"Why don't the Trojans simply return Helen to her rightful husband? That would put an end to this war, wouldn't it?"

Poletes smiled knowingly. "It would indeed. But you have not seen the golden-haired Helen."

"Have you?"

He shook his head sadly. "No. But everyone who has agrees that she is the most beautiful woman in the world. Aphrodite's child, they claim."

"No woman could be so important that men would fight a war over her." But I remembered that the night before I was almost willing to attack Agamemnon's lodge to seize my wife and sons. Almost.

"Perhaps so, Hittite," said Poletes. "Helen is merely an excuse for Agamemnon's greed. But the Trojans won't give her up and here we are."

A series of bugle blasts erupted on the plain before us.

"Now it begins," Poletes said, suddenly grim, hard-eyed. "Now the fools rush to the slaughter once again."

11

Standing beside Poletes atop the rampart I watched as the charioteers cracked their whips and the horses bolted forward, carrying Achaians and Trojans eagerly toward each other.

I focused my attention on the chariot nearest us and saw the warrior in it setting his sandaled feet in a pair of raised sockets, to give him a firm base for using his spears. He held his body-length shield before him on his left arm and with his free hand plucked one of the lighter, shorter spears from the handful rattling in their holder.

"Diomedes," said Poletes, before I asked. "Prince of Argos. A fine young man."

Shrieks and screams filled the air as each warrior shouted out his battle cry. The horses pounded madly across the field, eyes bulging, nostrils wide.

The chariot approaching Diomedes swerved suddenly and the warrior in it hurled his spear. It sailed harmlessly past the prince of Argos. Diomedes threw his spear and hit the rump of the farthest of his opponent's four horses. The horse whickered and reared, throwing the other three so far off stride that the chariot slewed wildly, tumbling the warrior onto the dusty ground. The charioteer ducked behind the chariot's siding.

Other combats were turning the worn-bare battlefield into a vast cloud of dust, with chariots wheeling, spears hurtling through the air, shrill battle cries and shouted curses ringing everywhere. The foot soldiers seemed to be holding back, letting the noblemen fight their single encounters for the first few moments of the battle.

I could see no order to the battle, no judgment or tactics. The nobles in their chariots merely rushed into single combat against the enemy's chariot-riding noblemen. No formations of chariots, no organized plan of attack, nothing but chaos.

One voice pierced all the others, a weird screaming cry like a seagull gone mad with frenzy.

"The battle cry of Odysseos," Poletes said. "You can always hear the King of Ithaca above all the others."

I was still concentrating on Diomedes, eager to learn how these Achaians fought their battles. As his opponent sprawled in the dust, his charioteer reined in his team and Diomedes hopped down to the ground, two spears gripped in his left hand, his massive figure-eight shield bumping against his helmet and greaves.

"A lesser man would have speared his foe from the chariot," said Poletes admiringly. "Diomedes is a true nobleman. Would that he had been in Argos when Clytemnestra's men put me out!"

Diomedes approached the fallen warrior, who clambered back to his feet and held his shield before him while drawing his long sword from its sheath. The prince of Argos took his longest and heaviest spear in his right hand and shook it menacingly. I could not hear what the two men were saying to each other, but they shouted something back and forth.

Suddenly both men dropped their weapons and shields, rushed to each other, and embraced like a pair of long-lost brothers. I was stunned.

"They must have relatives in common," Poletes explained. "Or one of them might have been a guest in the other's household sometime in the past."

"But the battle . . ."

Poletes shook his gray head. "What has that to do with it? There are plenty of others to kill."

The two warriors exchanged swords, then each got back onto his chariot and they drove in opposite directions.

"No wonder this war has lasted for years," I muttered.

But although Diomedes' first encounter of the day ended nonviolently, that was the only bit of peace that I saw amid the carnage of battle. Chariots hurtled at each other, spearmen driving their long weapons into the entrails of their opponents. The bronze spear points were themselves the length of a grown man's arm. When all the power generated by a team of galloping horses was focused on the gleaming tip of a sharp spear point, nothing could stand in its way, not even many-layered shields of oxhide. Armored men were lifted off their feet, out of their chariots, when those spears hit them. Bronze armor was no protection against that tremendous force.

The noble warriors preferred to fight from their chariots, I saw, although here and there men had alighted and faced their opponents on the ground. Still the foot soldiers held back, skulking and squinting in the swirling clouds of dust, content to let the noblemen face each other singly. Were they waiting for a signal? Was there some tactic in this bewildering melee of individual combats? Or was it that the foot soldiers knew they could never face an armed nobleman and those deadly spears?

Here two chariots clashed together, the spearman of one driving his point through the head of the other's charioteer. There a pair of armored noblemen faced each other on foot, dueling and parrying with their long spears. One of them whirled suddenly and rammed the butt of his spear into the side of his opponent's helmet. The man dropped to the ground and his enemy drove his spear through his unprotected neck. Blood spurted onto the thirsty ground.

Instead of getting back into his chariot or stalking another enemy, the victorious warrior dropped to his knees and began unbuckling the slain man's armor.

"A rich prize," Poletes cackled. "The sword alone should buy food and wine for a month, at least."

Now the foot soldiers came forward, on both sides, some to help strip the carcass, others to defend it. A comical tug-of-war started briefly but quickly turned into a serious fight with knives, axes, cudgels and hatchets. The armored nobleman made all the difference, though. He cut through the enemy foot soldiers with his long sword, hacking limbs and lives until the few still standing turned and ran. Then his men resumed stripping the corpse while the nobleman stood guard over them, as effectively out of the battle for the time being as if he himself had been slain.

Many of the chariots were overturned or empty of their warriors by now. Armored men were fighting on foot with long spears or swords. I saw one nobleman pick up rocks and throw them, to good effect. Archers, many of them charioteers who fired from the protection of their cars' leather-covered side paneling, began picking off unprotected footmen. I saw an armored warrior suddenly drop his spear and paw, howling, at an arrow sticking in his beefy shoulder. A chariot raced by and the warrior in it spitted the archer on his spear, lifting him completely out of his chariot and dragging him in the dust until his dead body wrenched free of the spear's barbed point.

All this took but a few minutes. There was no order to the battle, no plan, no tactics. It was nothing more than a huge, jumbled melee. The noble contestants seemed more interested in looting the bodies of the slain than defeating the enemy forces. It was more like a game than a war, a game that soaked the ground with blood and filled the air with screams of pain and rage.

The one thing that stood out above all others was

that to turn and attempt to flee was much more dangerous than facing the enemy and fighting. I saw a charioteer wheel his team around to get away from two other
chariots converging on him. Someone threw a spear that
caught him between the shoulder blades. His team ran
wild, and while the warrior in the chariot tried to take
the reins from the dead hands of his companion and get
the horses under control, another spearman drove up
and killed him with a thrust in the back.

Foot soldiers who turned away from the fighting took
arrows in the back or were cut down by chariot-mounted
warriors who swung their swords like scythes.

It was getting difficult to see, the dust was swirling so
thickly. I coughed and blinked grit from my eyes. Then I
heard a fresh trumpet blare and the roar of many men
shouting in unison. The thunder of horses' hooves shook
the ground.

Through the dust came three dozen chariots heading
straight for the place where we stood atop the earthworks
rampart.

"Prince Hector!" shouted Poletes, his voice brittle
with awe. "See how he slices through the Achaians!"

Here was a man who understood battle tactics, I realized. Prince Hector had either regrouped his main chariot force or had held them back from the opening melee
of the battle. Whichever, he was now driving them like
the wedge of a spear point through the shocked
Achaians, slaughtering left and right. Hector's massive
long spear was stained with blood halfway up its
wooden shaft. He carried it lightly as a wand, spitting
armored noblemen and leather-clad foot soldiers alike,
driving relentlessly toward the rampart that protected
the beach, the camp, the boats.

For a few minutes the Achaians tried to fight back, but when Hector's chariot broke past the ragged line of their chariots and headed straight for the gate at the rampart, the Achaian resistance crumbled. Noblemen and foot soldiers alike, chariots and infantry, they all ran screaming for the safety of the earthworks.

Hector and his Trojan chariots wreaked bloody havoc among the panicked Achaians. With spears and swords and arrows they killed and killed and killed. Men ran hobbling, limping, bleeding toward us. Screams and groans filled the air.

An Achaian chariot rushed bumping and rattling to the gate, riding past and even over fleeing footmen. I recognized the splendid armor of the squat, broad-shouldered warrior in it: Agamemnon, the High King.

He did not look so splendid now. His plumed helmet was gone. His gold-inlaid armor was coated with dust. An arrow protruded from his right shoulder and blood streaked his arm.

"We're doomed!" he shrieked in a high girlish voice. "We're doomed!"

12

The Achaians were racing for the safety of the rampart with the Trojan chariots in hot pursuit, closely followed by the Trojan footmen running pell-mell, brandishing swords and axes. Here and there a Trojan would stop for a moment to sling a stone at the fleeing Achaians or drop to one knee to fire an arrow.

An arrow whizzed past me. Poletes ducked behind me for protection. I turned and saw my men edging back to where they had laid their spears and shields. We were alone along the length of the rampart's top now; the slaves and *thetes* had already fled down into the camp. Even the overseer with his whip had vanished.

A noisy struggle was taking place at the gate. It was a ramshackle affair, made of warped planks taken from some of the boats. It was not a hinged door but simply a wooden barricade that could be wedged into the opening in the earthworks. Some men were frantically trying to put the gate in place while others were struggling to hold them back and keep it open until the remainder of the fleeing Achaian chariots could wheel through. I saw that Hector and his chariots would reach the gate in a few moments. Once past it, I knew, the Trojans would slaughter everyone in the camp.

"Stay here," I said to Poletes, then called to my men, "Follow me!"

Without waiting to see if they obeyed me I dodged among the lopsided stakes planted along the rampart's crest, heading toward the gate. Out of the corner of my eye I saw a javelin hurtling toward me. It thudded into the ground at my feet; I stopped long enough to wrest it out of the ground, then started toward the gate again. Magro, Karsh and the others were a few paces behind me, spears in their hands, shields on their arms.

Hector's chariot was already pounding up the sandy ramp that cut across the trench in front of the rampart. There was no time for anything else so I leaped from the rampart's crest onto the ramp, where the panicked Achaians were still struggling over their makeshift gate. I landed directly in front of Hector's charging horses, naked to the waist, without shield or helmet. I yelled and, gripping the light javelin in both hands, pointed it at the horses' eyes. Startled, they reared up, neighing.

For an instant the world stopped, frozen as if in a painting on a vase. Behind me the Achaians were straining to put up the barricade that would keep the Trojans from invading their camp. Before me Hector's team of four nut-brown horses reared high, the unshod hooves of their forelegs almost in my face. I stood crouched slightly, the javelin in both my hands, pointed at the horses.

The horses shied away from me, their eyes bulging white with fear, twisting the chariot sideways along the pounded-earth ramp. I saw the warrior in the chariot standing tall and straight, one hand on the rail, the other raised above his head, holding a monstrously long blood-soaked spear.

Aimed at my chest.

He was close enough so that I could see his face clearly, even with his helmet's cheek flaps tied tightly under his bearded chin. I looked into the eyes of Hector, prince of Troy. Brown eyes they were, the color of rich farm soil, calm and deep. No anger, no battle lust. He was a cool and calculating warrior, a thinker among these hordes of wild, screaming brutes. He wore a small round shield buckled to his left arm instead of the massive body-length type most of the other nobles carried. On it was painted a flying heron, a strangely peaceful emblem in the midst of all this mayhem and gore.

My men were jumping to the ramp now, shields before them and spears making a small hedgehog of points. Just as Hector cocked his arm to hurl his spear at me, an arrow from behind us caught his charioteer in the throat.

Suddenly uncontrolled, the horses panicked and stumbled over each other on the narrow ramp. One of them started sliding along the steep edge of the trench. Whinnying with fear they backed and turned, tumbling the dead charioteer and Prince Hector both onto the sandy ground. Then they bolted off back down the ramp and toward the distant city, dragging the empty chariot with them.

Hector scrambled to his feet, his massive spear still in his hand. More Trojans were rushing up the ramp on foot, their chariots useless because Hector's panicked horses had scattered the other teams.

I glanced over my shoulder. My men had formed a solid line behind me, their spears forward. I stepped back and took my usual place on the right end of the line. I had no shield, but still I took my accustomed place.

The barricade was up now and Achaian archers were firing through the slits between its planks while others stood atop the rampart, hurling stones and spears. Hector held up his little shield against the missiles and backed away. A few Trojan arrows came our way but did no hurt.

The Trojans retreated, but only beyond the distance of a bowshot. There Hector told them to stand their ground.

The morning's battle was ended. The Achaians were penned in their camp behind the trench and rampart, with the sea at their backs. The Trojans held the corpse-strewn plain.

Panting from exertion, sweat streaming down my bare torso, I banged my fist on the flimsy wooden gate and a trio of grimy-faced youths opened it far enough for me and my men to slip through.

Poletes ran up to me. "Hittite, you must be a son of Ares! A mighty warrior to face Prince Hector!"

I said nothing, but glanced back at the plain, where Trojans were already dragging away their dead. How many of the proud lords on both sides of this war were now lying out there, stripped of their splendid armor, their jeweled swords, their young lives? I saw birds circling high above in the clean blue sky. Not gulls: vultures.

13

Others came up and joined Poletes' praise as my men and I stood just inside the gate in the hot noontide sun. They surrounded us, clapping our backs and shoulders, smiling, shouting. Someone offered us wooden bowls of wine.

"You saved the camp!"

"You stopped those horses as if you were Poseidon himself!"

Even the crusty, hard-eyed overseer looked on me fondly. "That was not the action of a *thes*," he said, eyeing me carefully. "Why are warriors working as laborers?"

I replied grimly, "Ask your High King."

They edged away from us. Their smiles turned to worried glances. Only the overseer had courage enough to stand his ground and say, "Well, the High King should be pleased with you this day. And the gods, too."

Poletes stepped to my side. "Come, Hittite. I'll find you a good fire and hot food."

I let the old storyteller lead us away from the gate, deeper into the camp, while we pulled on our shirts and leather jerkins.

"I knew you were no ordinary men," he said as we made our way through the scattered huts and tents. "Not someone with your bearing. This must be a nobleman, I told myself. A nobleman, at the very least."

"Only a soldier of the Hatti," I replied.

"Pah! Don't be so modest." Poletes chattered and yammered, telling me how my deeds looked to his eyes, reciting the day's carnage as if he was trying to set it firmly in his memory for future recall. Every group of men we passed offered us a share of their midday meal. The women in the camp smiled at us. Some were bold enough to come up to us and offer freshly broiled meats and onions on skewers.

Poletes shooed the women away. "Tend to your masters' hungers," he snapped. "Bind their wounds and pour healing ointments over them. Feed them and give them wine and bat your cow-eyes at them."

I smiled inwardly and wondered how much my men appreciated Poletes' "protection."

To me, the old storyteller said, "Women cause all the trouble in the world. Be careful of them."

"Are these women slaves or *thetes*?" I asked him.

"There are no women *thetes*, Hittite. It's unheard of! A woman, working for wages? Unheard of!"

"Not even prostitutes?"

"Ah! Yes, of course. But that's a different matter. And in the cities there are temple prostitutes, protected by Aphrodite. But they are not *thetes*. It's not the same thing at all."

"Then the women here in camp . . ."

"Slaves. Captives. Daughters and wives of slain enemies, captured in the sack of towns and farms."

My wife was a slave of the High King's. How can
I get her away from him? I asked myself. Are my sons
alive? Where are they?

We came to a group of men sitting around one of the
larger cook fires, down close beside the black-tarred
boats. They looked up and made room for us. Up on the
boat nearest us a large canvas of blue and white stripes
had been draped to form a tent. A helmeted guard stood
on the deck before it, with a well-groomed dog by his
side. I stared at the carved and painted figurehead on the
boat's prow, a grinning dolphin's face against a deep blue
background.

"The camp of Odysseos," Poletes explained to me in a
low voice as we sat and were offered generous bowls of
roasted meat and goblets of honeyed wine. "These are
Ithacans."

He poured a few drops of wine on the ground before
drinking, and made me do the same. "Reverence the
gods, Hittite," Poletes instructed me, surprised that neither I nor my men knew the custom.

The men around the fire praised me for my daring at
the barricade, then fell to wondering which particular
god had inspired me to such heroic action. The favorites
were Poseidon and Ares, although Athene was a close
runner-up and even Zeus himself was mentioned now
and then. They soon fell to arguing passionately among
themselves without bothering to ask me or my men
about it.

I was happy to let them quarrel. I listened, and as they
argued I learned much about this war.

They had been campaigning in the region each summer

for many years. Achilles, Menalaos, Agamemnon and the other warrior kings had been ravaging the coastal lands, burning towns and taking captives, until finally they had worked up the courage—and the forces—to besiege Troy itself.

But without Achilles, their fiercest fighter, the men thought their prospects were dim. Apparently Agamemnon had awarded Achilles a young woman captive and then had changed his mind and taken her for himself. This insult was more than the haughty young Achilles could endure, even from the High King.

"The joke of it all," said one of the men, tossing a well-gnawed lamb joint to the dogs hovering beyond our circle, "is that Achilles prefers his friend Patrokles to any woman."

They all nodded and muttered agreement. The strain between Achilles and Agamemnon was not over a sexual partner; it was a matter of honor and stubborn pride. On both sides, as far as I could see.

As we ate and talked the skies darkened and thunder rumbled from inland.

"Father Zeus speaks from Mount Ida," said Poletes.

One of the foot soldiers, his leather jacket stained with spatters of grease and blood, grinned up at the cloudy sky. "Maybe Zeus will give us the afternoon off."

"Can't fight in the rain," one of the others agreed.

Sure enough, within minutes it began pelting down. We scattered for whatever shelter we could find. Poletes and I hunkered down in the lee of Odysseos' boat. Through the driving rain I saw my men scurrying for the shelter of the tents scattered around Odysseos' boats.

"Now the great lords will arrange a truce, so that the

women and slaves can go out and recover the bodies of our dead. Tonight their bodies will be burned and a barrow raised over their charred bones." He sighed. "That's how the rampart began, as a barrow to cover the remains of the slain heroes."

I sat and watched the rain pouring down, turning the beach into a quagmire, dotting the frothing sea with splashes. The gusting wind drove gray sheets of rain across the bay, and it got so dark and misty that I could not see the headland. It was chill and miserable and there was nothing to do except sit like dumb animals and wait for the sun to return.

I crouched as close as I could to the boat's hull, smelling the sharp tang of the pitch they had smeared over the planks to keep the vessel watertight. My wife is among the slaves in Agamemnon's camp, I knew. Are my sons with her? Are they still living?

Suddenly I realized that a man was standing in front of me. I looked up and saw a sturdy, thick-torsoed man with a grizzled dark beard and a surly look on his face. He wore a wolf's pelt draped over his head and shoulders, dripping with the pounding rain. Knee-length tunic, a short sword buckled at his hip. Shins and calves muddied. Ham-sized fists planted on his hips.

"You're the Hittite?" he shouted over the driving rain.

I got to my feet and saw that I stood several fingers taller than he. Still, he did not look like a man to be taken lightly.

"I am Lukka," I replied. "My men are—"

"Come with me," he snapped, and started to turn away.

"To where?"

Over his shoulder he answered, "My lord Odysseos wants to see what kind of man could stop Prince Hector in his tracks. Now move!"

Poletes scrambled up and pranced happily in the mud beside me around the prow of the boat, through the soaking rain, to a rope ladder that led up to the deck.

"I knew Odysseos was the only one here wise enough to make use of you," he cackled. "I knew it!"

14

It was slippery going, clambering up the rope ladder in the wind-whipped rain. I feared that Poletes would fall. But, following Odysseos' man, we made it to the boat's deck and ducked under the striped canvas. The Ithacan opened a wooden chest and tossed a pair of large rags at us.

"Dry yourselves," he said curtly. We did, gladly, as he shucked the dripping wolf's pelt he'd been wearing and slung it to the deck with a wet slapping sound.

I threw my towel next to his sodden pelt. Poletes did the same. For long moments we stood there while the Ithacan looked us up and down.

"Presentable enough," he muttered, more to himself than to us. Then he said, "Follow me."

Thunder rumbled in the distance as we walked behind him around a wooden cabin. And there sat Odysseos, King of Ithaca.

He was sitting behind a bare trestle table, flanked on either side by two standing noblemen in fine woolen cloaks. He did not appear to be a very tall man; what I could see of legs seemed stumpy, though heavily muscled. His chest was broad and deep. Later I learned that he swam in the sea almost every morning. His thick strong arms were circled with leather wristbands and a bronze armlet above his left elbow that gleamed with polished onyx and lapis lazuli even in the gloom inside his shipboard tent. Puckered white scars from old wounds stood out against the dark skin of his arms, parting the black hairs like roads through a forest. There was a fresh gash on his right forearm, as well, red and still oozing blood slightly.

The rain drummed against the canvas, which bellied and flapped in the wind scant finger widths above my head. The tent smelled of dogs, musty and damp. And cold. I felt chilled and Poletes, with nothing but his ragged loincloth, hugged his shivering body with his bare arms.

Odysseos wore a sleeveless tunic, his legs and feet bare, but he had thrown a lamb's fleece across his wide shoulders. His face was thickly bearded with dark curly hair that showed a trace of gray. His heavy mop of ringlets came down to his shoulders and across his forehead almost down to his black eyebrows. Those eyes were as gray as the sea outside on this rainy afternoon, probing, searching, judging.

"You are a Hittite?" were his first words to me.

"I am, my lord."

"Why have Hittites come to Troy?"

I hesitated, trying to decide how much of the truth I should speak to him. Swiftly I realized that it had to be either everything or nothing.

"I seek my wife and two young sons who have been taken captive, my lord."

He rocked back on his stool at that. Clearly it was not an answer he had expected.

"Your wife and sons?"

"My wife is among the High King's slaves," I added. "If my sons live, they must be with her."

Odysseos glanced up at the nobleman standing on his left, whose hair and long beard were dead white. His limbs seemed withered to bones and tendons, his face a skull mask. He had wrapped a blue cloak around his chiton, clasped at the throat with a medallion of gold. Both noblemen appeared weary and drained by the morning's battle although neither of them bore fresh wounds as Odysseos did.

The King of Ithaca returned his attention to me. "Who is he?" he asked, pointing to Poletes.

"My servant," I answered.

Odysseos nodded, accepting the storyteller. Lightning flashed and he looked up, waiting for the thunder. When it came at last he muttered, "The storm moves away."

Indeed, the rain seemed to be slacking off. Its pelting on the canvas of the tent was noticeably lighter.

At last Odysseos said, "You did us a great service this morning. Such service should be rewarded."

The frail old whitebeard at his left spoke in an abrasive nasal voice, "You fought this morning like a warrior born and bred. Facing Prince Hector by yourself! Half naked, too! By the gods! You reminded me of myself when I was your age! I was absolutely fearless then! As far away as Mycenae and even Thebes I was known. Let me tell you—"

Odysseos raised his right hand. "Please, Nestor, I pray you forgo your reminiscences for the moment."

The old man looked displeased but sank back in silence.

"You say you seek your wife and sons," Odysseos resumed. "Then you are not here as a representative of your emperor?"

Again I hesitated. And again I decided there was nothing to tell him but the truth.

"There is no emperor, my lord. The lands of the Hatti are torn with civil war. The empire has crumbled."

Their jaws dropped open. Odysseos swiftly recovered, but he could not hide the smile that crossed his face.

Nestor blurted, "Then the Hittites are not sending troops to aid the Trojans?"

"No, my lord."

"You came here by yourself?" Odysseos asked.

"With the eleven men of my squad." Poletes coughed beside me, and I added, "And my servant."

Rubbing his beard with one hand, his eyes going crafty, Odysseos murmured, "Then Troy can expect no help from the Hittites."

Nestor and the other nobleman broke into happy smiles. "This is indeed good news," said Nestor. "Wonderful news!"

Odysseos nodded, then said, "But it doesn't change the situation we face. Hector is camped on the plain outside our rampart. Tomorrow he will try to break through and drive us into the sea."

That sobered the other two.

He looked up at me again. "We owe you a reward. What would you have?"

Immediately I replied, "My wife and sons."

"You say they are among Agamemnon's slaves."

"I saw my wife there, yes, my lord."

Odysseos breathed out a sigh. "Slaves are the property of he who owns them."

"They are my sons," I said firmly. "Little more than babies. And she is my lawful wife."

He rubbed at his beard again. "The High King is touchy these days about giving up his slaves. He's in the midst of a dispute with young Achilles about a slave woman."

"That's none of my affair, my lord."

"No, it isn't. But still . . ." He glanced up at Nestor again, who remained stone silent now. For long moments Odysseos sat there, saying nothing. It appeared to me that he was thinking, planning. At last he got to his feet and stepped around the table to clasp me on the shoulder.

"What is your name, Hittite?"

"I am called Lukka, my lord."

"Very well, Lukka," he said. "I will speak to Agamemnon—when the time is right. Meanwhile, welcome into the household of the King of Ithaca. You and your men." Poletes shuffled his feet slightly. "And your servant," Odysseos added.

I was not certain of what I should do until I saw Nestor frowning slightly and prompting me by motioning with both hands, palms down. I knelt on one knee before Odysseos.

"Thank you, great king," I said, hoping it was with the proper degree of humility. "I and my men will serve you to the best of our abilities."

Odysseos took the armlet from his bicep and clasped it on my arm. "Rise, Lukka the Hittite. Your courage and strength shall be a welcome addition to our forces." To the officer who had led us in, still standing behind Poletes and me, he said, "Antiklos, see that they get proper garb and all else that they require."

Then he nodded a dismissal at me. I turned and we marched away from Odysseos and the two others. Poletes was beaming at me, but I realized that my travel-worn clothes must look threadbare to the Achaians. Antiklos looked me up and down again as if measuring me, not for clothing, but as a fighter.

As we left the tent and went back into the weakening rain I could hear Nestor's piercing voice, "Very crafty of you, son of Laertes! By bringing him into your household you gain the favor of Athene, whom he undoubtedly serves. I couldn't have made a wiser move myself, although in my years I've made some very delicate decisions, let me tell you. Why, I remember when Dardanian pirates were raiding the coast of my kingdom and nobody seemed to be able to stop them, since King Minos' fleet had been destroyed in the great tidal wave. Well, the pirates captured a merchant boat bearing a load of copper from Kypros. Worth a fortune, it was, because you know that you can't make bronze without copper. No one knew what to do! The copper was . . ."

His voice, loud as it was, finally faded as we made our way through the faltering drizzle back down the rope ladder to the beach.

15

The rain petered out although the wind still gusted cold and sharp as I rounded up my squad. Antiklos said nothing until the dozen of us, plus Poletes, were standing before him with spears and shields.

"Are those helmets iron?" he asked.

"Yes," I replied. "The Hatti know how to work iron."

Antiklos gave a grudging grunt. "You'd better sleep lightly. There are thieves in camp."

I made a smile for him. "If I see any man wearing any piece of our equipment I'll give him an iron sword—in his belly."

He smiled back. "Follow me, then."

He led us past several Ithacan boats pulled up onto the beach. Then we came to a sizable hut made of logs and daubed with the same smelly black pitch that caulked the boats. It was the largest structure that I had seen in the Achaians' camp, taller than two men's height, big enough to house several dozen men or more, I estimated. There was only one doorway, a low one with a sheet of canvas tacked over it to keep out the rain and wind.

Inside, the shed was a combination warehouse and armory that made Poletes whistle with astonishment. Chariots were stored against the far wall, tilted up with their yokes nearly touching the beams of the ceiling. Stacks of helmets and armor were neatly piled along the wall on our right, while racks of spears, swords and bows lined the wall opposite. The ground was covered with rows of chests stuffed with clothes and blankets.

"So much!" Poletes gasped.

Antiklos made a grim smile. "Spoils from the slain."

Poletes nodded and whispered, "So many."

A wizened old man stepped across the sand floor from his hideaway behind a table piled high with clay tablets.

"What now? Haven't I enough to do without you dragging in a troop of strangers?" he whined. He was a lean and resentful old grump, his hands gnarled and twisted into claws, his back stooped.

"New ones for you, scribe," said Antiklos. "My lord Odysseos wants them outfitted properly." And with that, Antiklos turned and ducked through the shed's doorway. But not before giving me a wink and a grin.

The scribe shuffled over close enough almost to touch me, then squinted at Poletes and my men. "My lord Odysseos, heh? And how does he expect me to find proper gear for the dozen of you?"

"Thirteen," Poletes said.

The scribe made a gesture in the air with his deformed hands. "An unlucky number! Zeus protect me!"

He grumbled and muttered as he led me past tables laden with bronze cuirasses, arm protectors, greaves and plumed helmets. I stopped and picked up one of the fancy bronze helmets.

"Not that!" the scribe screeched. "Those are not for the likes of you."

I tossed the helmet back onto the table with a dull clunk. "We have our own arms and armor," I said. "What we require is clothes and blankets. And tenting."

Scowling as he replaced the helmet in its proper spot on the table, the scribe then sank one of his clawlike hands into my forearm and tugged me to a pile of clothes on the ground, close by the entrance to the shed.

"Here," he said. "See what you can find among these."

It took awhile. Poletes grumbled about fleas while my men rummaged among the pile, shaking out garments and blankets and joking among themselves about it.

"In finery like this," Harta said, grinning, "I'll make the women swoon when I walk up to them."

"They'll swoon from your stink," Magro answered

him. "Try taking a bath first. You won't smell so bad then."

At length we had dressed ourselves in linen tunics and leather skirts. They were stained and hardly new, but much better than the travel-worn togs we had arrived in. While the scribe glared and grumbled at us, I made certain that Poletes got a tunic and a wool shirt.

The scribe resisted with howls and curses but I made certain that each of my men took a good blanket, Poletes included. We also took canvas, poles and pegs for making tents. He squealed and argued and threatened that he would tell the king himself what a spendthrift I was. He wouldn't stop until I picked him off his feet by the front of his tunic and shook him a few times. Then he shut up and let us take what we needed. But his scowl would have curdled milk.

By the time we left the shed the rain had stopped altogether and the westering sun was rapidly drying the puddles along the beach. We found a clear space and settled down. The men began putting up tents. I sent Karsh and Tiwa to find wood for a fire; Poletes scampered off to dicker for food and a couple of slaves to do the cooking. He came back with a flagon of wine in his skinny arms— and two chunky, unwashed women who stared at us with frightened eyes.

Sitting down next to our little fire, Poletes opened the flagon and handed it to me. "There are benefits to being of the house of Odysseos," he said happily.

Yes, I thought. But how do I get to see my wife and sons, off in Agamemnon's part of the camp?

By the time we had eaten our sparse meal and drunk the wine, the sun had set. A pale sliver of a moon rose over the hills to the east, but the everlasting wind off the water turned even chillier. I watched as my men crawled into their newly built tents and prepared for sleep. Yawning, I realized that I was ready for sleep myself.

But I still thought of my wife and sons. I could go to Agamemnon's camp, I told myself. I could search for them there.

Then Poletes stepped to me, fell to his knees and grasped my right hand in both of his, tightly, with a strength I would not have guessed was in him.

"Hittite, my master, you have saved my life twice this day."

I wanted to pull my hand loose. I could see my men watching us in the deepening shadows.

"You saved the whole camp from Hector's spear and his vengeful Trojans, but in addition you have lifted me out of a life of misery and shame. I will serve you always, Hittite. I will always be grateful to you for showing mercy to a poor old storyteller."

He kissed my hand.

I felt my cheeks redden. Reaching down, I lifted him by his frail shoulders to his feet.

"Poor old windbag," I said gruffly. "You're the first man I've ever seen who's grateful for becoming a slave."

"*Your* slave, Hittite," he corrected. "I am happy to be that, indeed."

I shook my head, uncertain of what to do or say. Finally I muttered, "Well, get some sleep."

"Yes. Certainly. May Phantasos send you happy dreams."

I sat down on my blanket and drew up my knees, thinking that my wife was in this camp, hardly an arrow's shot away from me. And my sons. My boys. I decided that sleep could wait. I was going to find them. I got to my feet.

"Hittite?" a voice called softly.

I automatically grasped the hilt of my sword.

"Hittite, the king wants you." In the wan moonlight I saw that it was Antiklos standing before me, silhouetted against the starry sky.

"Bring your iron helmet and spear," Antiklos said. "Leave your shield."

"Why does the king summon me?" I asked.

Antiklos made a grunt. "He wants you to help him impress sulking Achilles."

16

Ordering Poletes to stay, I followed Antiklos past the tents of my men to the prow of Odysseos' boat. The King of Ithaca was standing on the beach. As I had suspected, he was almost a head shorter than I. The plume of his helmet reached no higher than my brows.

He nodded a greeting to me and said simply, "Follow me, Hittite."

The three of us walked in silence through the sleeping camp and up to the crest of the rampart, not far from the gate where I had won their respect that morning. Men stood guard up there, gripping their long spears and peering into the darkness nervously. Beyond the inky shadows of the trench the plain was dotted with Trojan campfires. Above them the crescent moon rode past scudding silvery clouds.

Odysseos gave a sigh that seemed to wrench his powerful chest. "Prince Hector holds the plain, as you can see. Tomorrow his forces will storm the rampart and try to break into our camp and burn our boats."

"Can we hold them?" I asked.

"The gods will decide, once the sun comes up."

I said nothing. I suspected that Odysseos was trying to hit upon a plan that might influence the gods his way.

A strong tenor voice called up from the darkness below us. "Odysseos, son of Laertes, are you counting the Trojan campfires?"

Odysseos smiled grimly. "No, Big Ajax. There are too many for any man to count."

He motioned to me and we went back down into the camp. Ajax was indeed something of a giant among these Achaians: he towered over Odysseos and even topped me by several fingers. He was big across the shoulders as well, his arms as thick as young tree trunks. I felt a sudden pang of remorse: he reminded me of Zarton, my stubborn young ox.

Ajax stood bareheaded beneath the stars, dressed only in a tunic and leather vest. His face was broad, with high cheekbones and a little pug of a nose. His beard was thin, new-looking, not like the thick curly growth of Odysseos and the other chieftains. With something of a shock I realized that Big Ajax could hardly be out of his teens, no older than Zarton was when I killed him.

A much older man stood beside him, hair and beard white, wrapped in a dark cloak that reached to the ground.

"I brought Phoenix along," said Ajax. "Maybe he can appeal to Achilles better than we can."

Odysseos nodded his approval.

"I was his tutor when Achilles was a lad," Phoenix said, in a frail voice that quavered slightly. "He was proud and touchy even then."

Ajax shrugged his massive shoulders. Odysseos said, "Well, let us try to convince mighty Achilles to rejoin the army."

We started off for the far end of the camp, where Achilles' Myrmidones had beached their boats. Half a dozen armed Ithacans trailed the three nobles and I fell in with them. The wind was blowing in off the water, cold and sharp as a knife. The sky above was clouding over. Perhaps it will rain tomorrow, I thought. Perhaps there will be no battle, after all.

Once we entered the Myrmidones' portion of the camp we passed several sentries on duty, fully armed and armored, with helmets strapped on tightly, heavy shields and long spears in their hands. They wore cloaks, which the wind plucked at and whipped around their gleaming suits of bronze. They recognized giant Ajax and the squat King of Ithaca, and allowed the rest of us to pass unchallenged.

Finally we were stopped by a pair of guards whose armor glittered in the light of a big bonfire, just before a large cabin built of planks.

"We are a deputation from the High King," said Odysseos, his voice deep and grave with formality, "sent to see Achilles, prince of the Myrmidones."

The guard saluted by clasping his fist to his heart and answered, "Prince Achilles has been expecting you and bids you welcome."

He stepped aside and gestured them to the open door of the cabin. Odysseos turned and beckoned me to accompany him, Ajax and Phoenix. The other Ithacan troops remained outside.

Mighty warrior that he was, Achilles apparently enjoyed his creature comforts. His cabin's interior was draped with rich tapestries and the floor was covered with carpets. Couches and pillows were scattered across the spacious room. In one corner a hearth fire smoldered red, keeping out the cold and damp. I could hear the wind moaning through the smoke hole in the roof, but inside the cabin it was reasonably snug and warm.

Three women sat by the fire, staring at us with great dark eyes. They were slim and young, dressed modestly in sleeveless gray chemises. Iron and copper pots stood on tripods at the hearth, faint wisps of steam rising from them. I smelled spiced meat and garlic.

Achilles himself sat on a wide couch against the far wall of the cabin, his back to a magnificent arras that depicted a gory battle scene. The couch was atop a dais, raised above the carpeted floor of the cabin like a king's throne.

My first sight of the fabled warrior was a surprise. He was not a mighty-thewed giant, like Ajax. His body was not broad and powerful, as Odysseos'. He seemed small, almost boyish, his bare arms and legs slim and virtually hairless. His chin was shaved clean and the ringlets of his long black hair were tied up in a silver chain. He wore a splendid white silk tunic, bordered with a purple key design, cinched at the waist with a belt of interlocking gold crescents. He wore no weapons, but behind him a half-dozen long spears rested against the arras, within easy reach.

His face was the greatest shock. Ugly, almost to the point of being grotesque. Narrow beady eyes, lips curled in a perpetual snarl, a sharp hook of a nose, skin pocked and cratered. In his right hand he gripped a jeweled wine cup; from the bleary look in his eyes it seemed to me that he had already drained it more than once.

At his feet sat a young man who was absolutely beautiful, gazing not at the four of us but up at Achilles. His tightly curled hair was reddish brown, rather than the usual darker tones of these Achaians. I wondered if it was his natural color. Like Achilles, he was beardless. But he seemed young enough not to need to shave. A golden pitcher of wine stood on the carpet beside him.

I looked at Achilles again and thought that I understood the demons that drove him. A small ugly boy born to be a king. A boy destined to rule, but always the object of taunts and derisive laughter behind his back. A young man possessed with fire to silence the laughter, to stifle the taunting. His slim arms and legs were iron-hard, knotted with muscle. His dark eyes were absolutely humorless. There was no doubt in my mind that he could outfight Odysseos or even powerful Ajax on sheer willpower alone.

"Greetings, Odysseos the Ever-Daring," he said in a calm, clear tenor voice that was close to mocking. "And to you, mighty Ajax, King of Salamis and champion of the Achaian host." Then his voice softened, "And to you, Phoenix, my well-loved tutor."

I glanced at the old man. He bowed to Achilles but his eyes were on the beautiful young man at Achilles' feet.

"You bring a stranger with you," Achilles said, his cold eyes inspecting me.

"A Hittite," Odysseos replied, "who has joined my household, together with his squad of men. They will make a fine addition to our forces."

"Indeed," Achilles said thinly.

Odysseos got down to the subject at hand. "We bring you greetings, Prince Achilles, from Agamemnon the High King."

"Agamemnon the bargain-breaker, you mean," Achilles snapped. "Agamemnon the gift-snatcher."

"He is our High King," Odysseos said, in a tone that suggested they were all stuck with Agamemnon and the best they could do was to try to work with him.

"So he is," admitted Achilles. "And well-beloved by Father Zeus, I'm sure." The sarcasm in his voice dripped like acid.

It was going to be a difficult parley, I could see.

"Perhaps our guests are hungry," suggested the young man in a soft voice.

Achilles tousled his curly mop of hair. "Always the thoughtful one, Patrokles. Always thoughtful."

He bade us sit and ordered the serving women to feed us and bring wine cups. Odysseos, Ajax and Phoenix took couches arranged near Achilles' dais. I stepped back, as befitted a common soldier. Patrokles got to his feet and filled all their cups from his pitcher of gold. The women passed trays of broiled lamb with onions among the noblemen. No one paid the slightest attention to me.

After a round of toasts and polite banter, Achilles said, "I thought I heard mighty Agamemnon bawling like a frightened woman earlier today. He breaks into tears quite easily, doesn't he?"

Odysseos frowned slightly. "Our High King was wounded this morning. A cowardly Trojan archer hit him in the right shoulder."

"Too bad," said Achilles. "I see that you did not escape

the day's fighting without a wound. Did it bring you to tears?"

Ajax burst out, "Achilles, if Agamemnon cries it's not from pain or fear. It's from shame! Shame that the Trojans have penned us up in our camp. Shame that our best fighter sits here on a soft couch while his comrades are being slaughtered by Hector and his Trojans."

"Shame is what he *should* feel," Achilles shouted back. "He's robbed me! He's treated me like a slave or even worse. He calls himself High King but he behaves like a thieving whoremaster!"

And so it went, for nearly an hour. Achilles was furious with Agamemnon for taking back a prize he had been awarded, some captive woman. He claimed that he did all the fighting while Agamemnon was a coward, but after the battle the High King parceled out the spoils to suit himself and even then reneged on what Achilles felt was due him.

"I have sacked more towns and brought the Achaians more captives and loot than any man here, and none of you can say that I haven't," he insisted hotly. "Yet that fat lard-ass can steal my rightful rewards away from me, and you—all of you!—allow him to do it. Did any of you stick up for me in the council? Do you think I owe you anything? Why should I fight for you when you won't even raise your voices on my behalf?"

Patrokles tried to soothe him, without much success. "Achilles, these men are not your enemies. They come to you on a mission of reconciliation. It isn't fitting for a host to bellow at his guests so."

"Yes, yes, I know," Achilles replied, almost smiling down at the young man. Turning to Odysseos and the others, he said, "It's not your fault. I'm not angry at you.

But I'll see myself in Hades before I help Agamemnon again. He's not trustworthy. You should be thinking about appointing a new leader among yourselves."

Odysseos tried tact, praising Achilles' prowess in battle, downplaying Agamemnon's failures and shortcomings. Ajax, blunt and straightforward as a shovel, flatly told Achilles that he was helping the Trojans to slay the Achaians. Old Phoenix appealed to his former student's sense of honor and recited childhood homilies to him.

Achilles remained unmoved. "Honor?" he snapped at Phoenix. "What kind of honor would I have left if I put my spear back into the service of the man who robbed me?"

Odysseos coaxed, "We can get the girl back for you, if that's what you want. We can get a dozen women for you."

"Or boys," Ajax added. "Whatever you want."

I thought of my sons and felt glad that they were still as young as they were.

Achilles got to his feet, and Patrokles scrambled to stand beside him. I was right, he was terribly small, although every inch of him was hard with sinew. Even slender Patrokles topped him by a few finger widths.

"When Hector breaks into the camp I will defend my boats," Achilles said. "Until Agamemnon comes to me personally and apologizes, and begs me to rejoin the fighting, that is all that I will do."

Odysseos rose, realizing that he was being dismissed. Phoenix stood up beside him and Ajax, after glancing around, finally understood and got ponderously to his feet also.

"What will the poets say of Achilles in future generations?" Odysseos asked, firing his last arrow at the warrior's pride. "That he sulked in his cabin while the Trojans slaughtered his friends?"

The shot glanced off Achilles without penetrating. "They will never say that I humbled myself and threw away my honor by serving a man who humiliated me."

They walked slowly to the doorway, speaking polite formal farewells. I fell in behind Odysseos, as befitted my station in his household. Phoenix hung back and I heard Achilles invite his old mentor to remain the night.

Outside, Ajax shook his head wearily. "There's nothing we can do. He just won't listen to us."

Odysseos clapped his broad shoulder. "We tried our best, my friend. Now we must prepare for tomorrow's battle without Achilles."

Ajax trudged off into the darkness, followed by his men. Odysseos turned to me, a thoughtful look on his face.

"I have a task for you to perform," he said. "If you are successful you can end this war."

"And if I am not?"

Odysseos smiled grimly. "No man lives forever, Hittite."

17

In less than an hour I found myself walking warily in the moonlight down the ramp before the gate in our rampart and heading toward the Trojan camp. A white cloth knotted above my left elbow proclaimed that I was operating under a flag of truce. The slim willow wand in my hand was the impromptu symbol of a herald.

"These should get you past their sentries without having your throat slit," Odysseos had told me. He did not smile as he spoke the words and I did not find his reassurances very reassuring. I carried neither shield nor weapons, except for a small dagger tucked into my belt.

"Go to Prince Hector and speak to no one else," Odysseos had commanded me. "Tell him that Agamemnon offers a solution to this war: if the Trojans will return Helen to her rightful husband, the Achaians will return to their own lands, satisfied."

"Hasn't that offer been made before?" I had asked.

Odysseos smiled at my simplicity. "Of course. But always with the demand for a huge ransom, plus all the fortune that Helen brought with her from Sparta. And always when we were fighting under the walls of Troy. Priam and his sons never believed that we would abandon the siege without breaking in and sacking the city. But now that Hector is besieging us, perhaps they will believe that we are ready to quit and merely need a face-saving compromise to send us packing."

He was crafty, this Odysseos. Far craftier than the other Achaian leaders. But I wondered, "Returning Helen is nothing more than a face-saving compromise?"

He looked at me curiously. "She is only a woman, Hittite. Do you think Menalaos, her husband, has been pining away in celibacy since the bitch ran off with Paris?"

Then he added, "Have you abstained from women while searching for your wife?"

That caught me squarely. I realized once again that it was my sons I truly sought. If we had been childless, would I have come all this way to find my Aniti?

Odysseos made me repeat his instructions and then,

satisfied, led me to the gate in the rampart, where I had earned my moment of glory earlier that day. I gazed out into the darkness. In the silvery moonlight a mist had risen, turning the plain into a ghostly shivering vapor that rose and sank slowly like the breath of some living creature. Here and there I could make out the glow of Trojan campfires, like distant stars in the shrouding fog.

"Remember," said Odysseos, "you are to speak to Prince Hector and no one else."

"I understand, my lord."

I walked carefully down the ramp, the inky shadows of the trench on either side of me, and finally made my way through the slowly drifting tendrils of the mist toward the Trojan camp, guided by the fires that flickered and glowed in the distance. The fog was cold, chilling against my bare arms and legs, like the touch of death.

A sharp wind began gusting in from the sea and shredding the mist covering the plain. In the distance I could make out the beetling towers of Troy hulking black and menacing against the moonlit sky.

A dog began barking, and a voice called out of the darkness, "You there! Hold!"

I froze and clenched the willow wand in my fist. It seemed much too slim to protect me.

A pair of sentries approached me warily, heavy spears in their hands. Two massive dogs skulked before them, growling at me. I gulped down a deep breath of chill night air and stood immobile.

"Well? Who are you?"

"I am an emissary from the High King Agamemnon," I said, slowly and carefully. "I have been sent to speak to Prince Hector."

The sentries were an unlikely pair, one short and

squat with a dirty tangled beard and a potbelly bulging his chain mail corselet, the other taller and painfully thin, either clean-shaved or too young to start a beard. I realized he was holding the growling dogs on a chain leash, and struggling to keep them under control.

"Prince Hector the Tamer of Horses he wants to see," said the potbelly. He laughed harshly. "So would I!"

The younger one grinned and showed a gap where a front tooth was missing.

"An emissary, eh?" Potbelly eyed me suspiciously. "With a cloak on his back long enough to hide a sword. More likely a spy. Or an assassin."

I held up my herald's wand. "I have been sent by the High King. I am not here to fight. Take my cloak if it frightens you. There's nothing hidden beneath it."

"Be a lot safer to ram this spear through your guts and feed you to the dogs," growled Potbelly.

The youngster put out a restraining hand. "Hermes protects messengers, you know. I wouldn't want to draw the anger of the Trickster."

Potbelly scowled and muttered, but finally lifted my cloak and satisfied himself that I was not hiding a weapon. He took my dagger, though, and tucked it into his own belt. Then the two of them led me to their chief.

They were Dardanians, allies of the Trojans who had come from several leagues up the coast to fight against the invading Achaians. Over the next hour, while the moon climbed higher in the starry sky and then began its descent toward the sea, I was escorted from the chief of the Dardanian contingent to a Trojan officer, from there to the tent of Hector's chief lieutenants, and finally past a stinking makeshift horse corral and rows of silently waiting chariots tipped over with their long yoke poles poking into the air, to the small plain tent and the guttering fire of Prince Hector.

At each stop I explained my mission again. Dardanians and Trojans alike spoke a dialect similar to the Achaians. Not one of them had the wit to notice that my words were differently accented, the speech of a stranger to their shores. I realized that Troy's defenders included contingents from many areas up and down the coast. The Achaians had been raiding their towns for years, and now they had all banded together under Trojan leadership to resist the barbarian invaders.

It must have been close to midnight when at last I was brought before Hector. His tent was barely large enough for himself and a servant. A pair of armed noblemen stood outside by the fire in bronze breastplates and fine helmets. Insects buzzed and darted in the firelight. No slaves or women were in sight. Hector himself stood at the entrance flap to his tent. I recognized those steady, grave brown eyes.

He was tall for these people, nearly my own height. Hector wore no armor, no badge of rank, merely a soft clean tunic belted at the waist, with an ornamental dagger hanging from the leather belt. He had no need to impress anyone with his grandeur. He possessed that calm inner strength that needs no outward decorations.

In the flickering light of the campfire he studied me for a moment. His face was handsome, intelligent, though there were lines of weariness around his eyes, furrows across his broad brow. Despite the fullness of his rich brown beard I saw that his cheeks were becoming hollow. The strain of war was taking its toll on him.

"You are the man at the gate," he said. His words were measured, neither surprise nor anger in them.

"I am, my lord."

He looked me over carefully. "Your name?"

"Lukka."

"From where?"

"From far to the east, the land of the Hatti."

His eyes widened. "You are a Hittite?"

"Yes, my lord."

He puzzled over that for a few moments, brow knitted. Then he asked, "What brings you to the plain of Ilios? Why are you fighting for the Achaians?"

I said nothing. Odysseos had commanded me to give Hector his message and nothing more.

"Well?" Hector demanded. "Troy has always been loyal to the Hittite empire. We appealed to the emperor for help. Is this his answer? Has the emperor sent his army to fight against us?"

"I cannot say, my lord. I am commanded by King Odysseos to give you High King Agamemnon's offer to end the war."

"I've heard Agamemnon's offers before," Hector growled.

"But my lord—"

"Why are you fighting against us?" Hector demanded, his voice iron hard.

"My lord, I arrived at the Achaian camp last night, with eleven spearmen."

"Hittite warriors."

"Soldiers, yes. We had never seen Troy before, we didn't know that you were at war. I was atop the rampart when the day's battle started. Suddenly, in the midst of the fighting, I acted on impulse. I don't know what made me jump in front of your chariot like that. It all happened in the flash of a moment."

Hector looked into my eyes, as if to judge the truth of my words. "Battle frenzy," he murmured. "A god took control of your spirit, Hittite, and inspired you to deeds no mortal could accomplish unaided. It has happened to me more than once."

I was happy to take that path. "Yes, perhaps that is what happened to me."

"Have no doubt of it. Ares or Athene seized your spirit and filled you with battle frenzy. You could have challenged Achilles himself in such a state."

He turned and stepped inside the tent, beckoning me to follow him. The two noblemen standing guard stirred momentarily, then returned to their positions beside the fire. Inside the tent there was only a rough cot of stretched ropes and a small table with a single chair bearing a bowl of fruit and a flagon of wine with two silver cups flanking it. Hector took an apple and gestured for me to help myself.

He sat and poured wine into both cups.

"Sit, Hittite. Sit and drink."

The quality of Trojan wine was far superior to that of the Achaians.

"You carry the wand of a herald and say that you are here as an emissary of Agamemnon." Hector leaned back tiredly in the creaking chair.

"I bring an offer of peace, my lord."

"We have heard such offers before. Is there anything new in what Agamemnon proposes?"

I wondered if Agamemnon knew what Odysseos was offering, but decided that it was not my station to get involved in such matters.

"The High King offers to leave Troy and return to the

lands of the Achaians if Troy will return Helen to her rightful husband."

Hector nodded wearily. "And?"

"Nothing else, my lord."

"Nothing?" He was suddenly alert. "No demand for ransom, or for the return of Helen's so-called fortune?"

"No, my lord."

Sitting up straighter in his chair, Hector ran a hand across his beard. "So now that we have him pinned against the sea, Agamemnon is willing to end the war if we return Helen to his brother."

"That is what I have been instructed to tell you, my lord."

Hector thought for several long moments, then began to speak slowly. "When he had us penned inside our city walls Agamemnon was not so generous. Now that we have the upper hand, he wants to run away."

"With Helen returned to her husband, my lord," I reminded him.

"Helen. She's nothing but an excuse to make war against us. If we let Agamemnon go, he'll be back next year with more fire and death."

There was nothing I could say to that.

"No," Hector muttered, more to himself than to me. "We have the upper hand now. We can drive them into the sea once and for all."

My mind immediately painted a picture of the Achaian boats burning, Trojans killing with their long spears, slaves and women put to the sword in the orgy of looting and raping that follows battle. My sons, my wife, torn to pieces.

To Hector I said, as calmly as I could, "My lord, the

Achaians believe your success in yesterday's fighting was helped greatly by the fact that Achilles did not enter the battle. He will not remain on the sidelines forever."

"One man," Hector countered.

"The best warrior among the Achaians," I pointed out. "And his Myrmidones are a formidable fighting unit, I am told."

Hector fixed me with those steady brown eyes again. "No, Hittite. It was you who stopped me at the gate. If not for you, those black boats would be smoldering piles of ashes this very night."

That staggered me.

"I hold no resentment against you. You were in the thrall of a god, and no man can undo what the gods bring forth."

"Perhaps the gods will favor the Achaians tomorrow."

"Perhaps."

"Then what am I to tell the High King, my lord?"

Hector slowly rose to his feet. "That is not my decision to make. I command the army, but my father is still king in Troy. He and his council must consider your offer."

I stood up, too.

"Polydamas," Hector called, "conduct this herald to the king. Aeneas, spread the word that we will not attack until King Priam has considered the latest peace offer from Agamemnon."

And suddenly I understood the subtlety of Odysseos. The Trojans will not attack the Achaian camp as long as I am dickering with their king. That will give Agamemnon and all the others a day's respite from battle, at least. A chance to rest, bind their wounds, perhaps even convince Achilles to come back to the fight. Odysseos had sent an expendable hero, me—a man that Hector would recognize and respect, yet not a man important to the Achaian strength—into the Trojan camp in a crafty move to gain a day's recuperation from the morning's disaster.

Marveling at Odysseos' cunning, I followed the Trojan nobleman called Polydamas through the moonlit night, across the scattered campfires dotting the plain and up to the walls of Troy.

18

I entered the besieged city of Troy in the dead of night. The moon was sinking toward the sea; it was so dark I could see practically nothing. The city wall loomed above me like a threatening shadow. I could see feeble lanterns by the gate as we passed a massive old oak tree, tossing and sighing in the night breeze, leaning heavily, bent by the incessant wind of Ilios.

To approach the gate we had to follow a road that led along the high wall. Very sound construction: troops attempting to storm the gate would have to go along the base of the wall, where defenders from above could fire arrows, stones, boiling water on them. Just before the gate a second curtain wall extended on the other side of the road, so attackers would be vulnerable to fire from both sides, as well as straight ahead, above the gate itself.

The gate was built of heavy oak, wide enough for two chariots to pass through side by side. It was slightly ajar and seemed only lightly defended at this hour of the night. Virtually the entire Trojan force was encamped down by the beach, I realized. A trio of teenagers were sitting by the open gateway, wearing neither armor nor helmets. Their shields and long spears rested against the stone wall. A few more stood on the battlements above, visible in the flickering of a fire they had going to keep themselves warm up there.

Inside, a broad packed-earth street meandered between buildings that seemed no more than two stories tall. The moon's fading light only made the shadows of their shuttered fronts seem deeper and darker. No one was stirring at this time of night along the main street or in the black alleyways leading off it, not even a cat.

My impression was that Troy was much smaller than Hattusas. Then I remembered that Hattusas was in ruin and ashes. Was that the fate that awaited this city?

Polydamas was not a wordy fellow. Unlike the Achaians, he spoke to me only when it was necessary. In almost total silence he led me to a low-roofed building and into a tiny room lit by the fluttering yellow-blue flame of a small copper oil lamp sitting on a wooden stool next to a narrow bed, covered by a rough woolen blanket. The only other furniture in the room was a chest made of cedarwood, its front intricately carved.

"You will be summoned to the king's presence in the morning," said Polydamas, his longest speech of the night. With not another word he left me, closing the wooden door softly behind him.

And bolting it.

With nothing better to do I undressed, pulled back the scratchy blanket, and sat out on the bed. It was springy: a thin mattress of feathers atop a webbing of ropes. Reaching under it, I found a chamber pot. After using it, I stretched out and quickly fell asleep.

I dreamed of my dying father again, and of Hattusas burning as drunken gangs of looters raged through its streets while I did nothing, nothing. Aniti was in my dream, but she was nothing more than a shadow, featureless, like a fragile, feeble wraith, already dead and in Hades.

I was jolted awake by the sound of the door bolt snapping back. I sat up, immediately alert, my hand automatically reaching for the sword that I had left with my men back at the Achaian camp along the beach.

A serving woman backed into the room, carrying a basin and an earthen jug of water. When she turned around and saw me sitting there naked, she dropped her eyes and made a little curtsy, then turned and deposited the pottery atop the cedarwood chest. She scurried out of the room and shut the door. Within a moment I heard the giggling of several women from beyond the door.

I washed hurriedly and pulled my clothes on. As I was awkwardly tying the white cloth of truce onto my arm, a Trojan man entered my room after a single sharp rap on the door. He seemed more a courtier than a warrior. He was fairly tall, but round-shouldered, soft-looking, with a bulging middle. His beard was quite gray, his pate balding, his tunic richly embroidered and covered with a long sleeveless robe of deep green.

"I am to conduct you to King Priam's audience chamber, once you have had your morning meal." His voice was high and soft, much like his stature.

Diplomacy moved at a polite pace, and I was glad of it. The Trojan courtier led me to the urinals in back of the house, then to the large kitchen that fronted it. Breakfast consisted of fruit, cheese, and flat bread, washed down with goat's milk. I ate alone, with the

Trojan courtier standing over me. No one else was in the room. Half the kitchen was taken up by a big circular hearth under an opening in the roof. It was cold and empty except for a scattering of gray ashes that looked as if they had been there a long time.

Through the kitchen's only window I could see men and women out on the street, going about their morning chores. Two serving women came in and sat patiently by the hearth while I ate in silence. The courtier ignored them, except to order them to bring a plate of figs and honey for himself.

Finally we walked out onto what seemed to be Troy's only major street, sloping gently uphill toward a majestic building of graceful fluted columns and a steeply pitched roof. Priam's palace, I guessed. Or the city's main temple. Perhaps both. The sun was not high yet, but still it felt much warmer here in the street than out on the windy plain.

"Is that where we're going?" I pointed toward the palace.

The courtier bobbed his head. "Yes, of course. The king's palace. A more splendid palace doesn't exist anywhere in the world—except perhaps in Egypt, of course."

I thought of the emperor's citadel in Hattusas. It made Priam's palace look like a toy. But it was gone now, gone. As we walked up the street, I saw how small Troy really was. And crowded. Houses and shops clustered together tightly. The street was unpaved, and sloped like a V so that water could run down its middle when it rained. Cart wheels had worn deep grooves in it. The city buzzed and hummed with voices talking, bargaining, calling out wares for sale. Somewhere a woman was singing, high and sweet. The men and women bustling about their morning's work seemed curious yet courteous. I received bows and smiles as we strolled up toward the palace.

"The royal princes such as Hector and Paris and their brothers live in the palace with the king." My courtier was turning into a tour guide. He gestured back down the street. "Near the Scaean Gate are the homes of the lesser nobility. Fine homes they are, nevertheless, far finer than you will find in Mycenae or even in Miletus."

We were walking through the market area now. Awning-shaded stalls lined the two-story brick homes here, although I saw precious little foodstuff for sale: dried vegetables, a skinny lamb that bleated mournfully. Freshly baked bread filled the street with its aroma, though.

The merchants, men and women both, seemed happy and smiling despite their lack of goods.

"You bring a day of peace," the courtier told me. "Farmers can bring their produce to market this morning. Woodcutters can go out to the forest and bring back fuel before night falls. The people are grateful for that."

"The siege has hurt you," I murmured.

"To some extent, of course. But we are not going hungry. There is enough grain stored in the royal treasury to last for years! The city's water comes from a spring that Apollo himself protects. And when we really need firewood or cattle or anything else, our troops escort the necessary people on a foray inland." He lifted his gray-bearded chin a notch or two. "We will not starve."

I said nothing.

He took my silence for agreement. "Look at those walls! The Achaians will never scale them."

I followed his admiring gaze down a crooked alley

and saw the towering walls that rose above the houses. They did indeed look high and strong and solid. But I had led Hatti troops past walls that were even higher and thicker, more than once.

"Apollo and Poseidon helped old King Laomedon build those walls, and they have withstood every assault made on them. Of course, Herakles once sacked the city, but he had divine help and still even he didn't dare try to breach those walls. He attacked over on the western side, where the oldest wall stands. But that was long ago."

I perked up my ears. The western wall was weaker? As if sensing he had said too much, my guide lapsed into a red-faced silence. We walked the rest of the way to the palace without further words.

Men-at-arms held their spears stiffly as we passed the crimson-painted columns at the front of the palace and entered its cool, shadowed interior. I saw no marble, which surprised me. Even in distant Hattusas, the peoples of the Aegean Sea were known for their splendid work in marble. Instead, the columns and the thick palace walls were made of a grayish, granitelike stone, polished to gleaming smoothness. Inside, the walls were plastered and painted in bright yellows and reds, with blue or green borders running along the ceilings.

The interior of the palace was actually cold. Despite the heat of the morning sun those thick stone walls insulated the palace so well that I almost imagined I could see my breath frosting in the shaded air.

The hall beyond the entrance was beautifully decorated with painted landscapes on its plastered walls: scenes of lovely ladies and handsome men in green fields rich with towering trees. No battles, not even hunting scenes. No proclamations of royal power or fighting prowess.

Statues lined this corridor, most of them life-sized, some smaller, several so huge that their heads or outstretched arms scraped the polished beams of the high ceiling.

"The city's gods," my courtier explained. "Most of these statues stood outside our four main gates, before the war. Of course, we brought them in here for safe-keeping from the despoiling Achaians. It wouldn't do for them to capture our gods! What fate would befall us then?"

"Indeed," I muttered.

Some of the statues were made of marble, most of wood. All were brightly painted. Hair and beards were deep black, tinged with blue. Gowns and tunics were mostly gold, and real jewels adorned them. The flesh was delicately colored, and the eyes were painted so vividly they almost seemed to be watching me.

I could not tell one of their gods from another. The males were all broad-shouldered and bearded, the goddesses ethereally beautiful. Then I recognized Poseidon, the sea god, a nearly naked, magnificently muscled figure who bore a trident in his right hand.

We stepped out of the chilly entrance hall and into the warming sunlight of a courtyard. A huge statue, much too large to fit indoors, stood just before us. I craned my neck to see its face against the crystal-blue morning sky.

"Apollo," said the courtier. "The protector of our city."

We started across the sunny courtyard. It was decked with blossoms and flowering shrubs. Potted trees were arranged artfully around a square central pool where fish swam lazily. These people are not warriors, I realized. Not like the Hatti or the Achaians. Artists and tradesmen, I thought, content to control the straits that led into the Sea of Black Waters and the rich lands beyond.

"We also have the Palladium, our statue of Athene," the courtier said, pointing across the pool to a smaller wooden piece, scarcely five feet tall. "It is very ancient and very sacred."

It certainly looked very ancient. Its face and draperies had been worn smooth from years of weathering. It seemed to be the image of a woman, but she was wearing a warrior's helmet and carried spear and shield. A female warrior? I had heard of such but always dismissed the tales as mere legend.

We quickly crossed the courtyard and entered the other wing of the palace. As we stepped into the shade of its wide entrance hall, the temperature dropped instantly.

More guards in polished armor stood in this hallway, although their presence seemed more a matter of pomp and formality rather than security. The courtier led me to a small chamber comfortably furnished with chairs of stretched hide and a gleaming polished table inlaid with beautiful ivory and silver. There was one window, which looked out on another, smaller courtyard, and a massive wooden door reinforced with bronze strapping. Closed.

"The king will see you shortly," my guide told me, looking nervously toward the closed door.

I took a chair and tried to relax. I did not want to appear tense or apprehensive in front of the Trojan king. The courtier, whom I assumed had spent much of his life in this palace, paced the floor anxiously. He seemed to grow more apprehensive with each passing moment.

At last he blurted, "Do you truly bring an offer of peace, or is this merely another Achaian bluff?"

So that was it. Beneath his confidence in the walls built by gods and the food and firewood gathered by their army and the eternal spring that Apollo himself protects, he was avid to have the war ended and his city safe and at peace once more.

Before I could reply the heavy wooden door creaked open. Two men-at-arms pushed it, and an old man in a green cloak similar to my courtier's motioned me to come in. He leaned heavily on a long wooden staff topped with a gold sunburst symbol. His beard was the color of ashes, his head almost totally bald. As I ducked through the doorway and approached him he squinted at me nearsightedly.

"Your proper name, herald?"

"Lukka."

"Of?"

I blinked, wondering what he meant. Then I replied, "Of the House of Ithaca."

He frowned at that, but turned and said, "Follow me."

19

I walked behind the old man into a spacious chamber crowded with people. Five steps into it, he stopped and banged his staff on the floor three times. I saw that the stone floor was deeply worn at that spot.

He called out, in a voice that may have once been rich and deep but now sounded like a cat yowling, "Oh

Great King—Son of Laomedon, Scion of Scamander, Servant of Apollo, Beloved of the gods, Guardian of the Dardanelles, Protector of the Troad, Western Bulwark of the Hatti, Defender of Ilios—an emissary from the Achaians, one Lukka by name, of the House of Ithaca."

The chamber was wide and high-ceilinged. Its middle was open to the sky above a circular hearth that smoldered a dull red and sent up a faint spiral of gray smoke. Dozens of men stood among the painted columns on the far side of the hearth: the nobility of Troy, I supposed, or at least the noblemen who were too old to be with the army. And their ladies! There were women among them, in robes that were rich with vibrant colors and flashing jewels. That surprised me. Women were never allowed in the emperor's audience chamber in Hattusas, I knew.

I stepped forward and beheld Priam, the King of Troy, sitting on a splendid throne of carved ebony inlaid with gold. It was set on a three-step-high dais. He was flanked on his right by Hector, who must have come up from his camp on the plain, sitting in a high-backed chair of carved wood. On the king's left sat a younger man and standing behind him was a woman who could only be Helen.

My breath caught in my throat. She was truly beautiful enough to cause a war. Helen's blond, golden curls fell past her shoulders. She had a small, almost delicate figure except for magnificent breasts covered only by the sheerest blouse. A girdle of gold cinched her waist, adding emphasis to her bosom. Her face was incredible, sensuous lips and alabaster skin, yet wide-eyed with an appearance of innocence that no man could resist.

The young prince on Priam's left had to be Paris, I thought. Helen leaned against the intricately carved back of Paris' chair, resting one hand on his shoulder. It took an effort for me to look away from her and study Paris. He was almost prettily handsome, darker of hair than his older brother, his neatly trimmed beard seemed new, thin. He looked up at her and she smiled dazzlingly at him. Then they both turned their gaze toward me as I approached the throne. Helen's smile disappeared the instant Paris looked away from her. She regarded me with cool, calculating eyes.

Priam was older even than aged Nestor, and obviously failing. His white beard was thin and ragged, his long hair also, as if some wasting disease had hold of him. He seemed sunk into his robe of royal purple as he sat slumped on his gold-inlaid throne, too tired even this early in the morning to sit upright or lift his arms out of his lap.

The wall behind his throne was painted in a seascape of blues and aquamarines. Graceful boats glided among sporting dolphins. Fishermen spread their nets into waters teeming with every kind of fish.

"My lord king," said Hector, dressed in a simple white tunic, "this emissary from Agamemnon brings another offer of peace."

"Let us hear it," breathed Priam, as faintly as a sigh.

They all looked to me.

I glanced at the assembled nobility and saw an eagerness, a yearning, a clear hope that I carried an offer that would end the war. Especially among the women I could sense the desire for peace, although I realized that the old men were hardly firebrands.

I had never been presented to the emperor in Hattusas, but I had a vague idea of how to behave in the presence of royalty. I bowed deeply to the king, then to

Hector and Paris, in turn. I caught Helen's eye as I did so, and she seemed to smile slightly at me.

"Oh great king," I began, "I bring you greeting from High King Agamemnon, leader of the Achaian host."

Priam nodded and waggled the fingers of one hand, as if urging me to get through the preliminaries and down to business.

I did. "Great king, the Achaians are willing to leave your shores if you will return Helen to her rightful husband."

It seemed as if nobody in the wide chamber breathed. The very air went still.

Then Priam wheezed, "And?"

"Nothing further, my lord. Return Helen and the war will end."

Hector fixed me with a hard gaze. "No demand for tribute? No demand for Helen's fortune to be returned?"

"No, my lord."

Priam's wizened face broke into a slow smile. "No demands except the return of Helen?"

"Yes, my lord."

The old king turned toward Hector. "This is indeed a new and better offer."

Hector frowned slightly. "Yes. With our army camped at their rampart. They know that we'll be storming their camp and driving them into the sea."

"At what cost?" Priam asked softly.

"I will never surrender my wife," Paris snapped. "Never!"

"My lord," I said, "I am a newcomer to this war. I know nothing of your grievances and rights. I have been instructed to offer you the terms for peace, which I have done. It is for you to consider them and make an answer."

Paris was clearly angry. "We refused their insulting terms when Agamemnon and his host were pounding on our gates. Why should we even consider returning my wife to them, now that we have the barbarians penned up on the beach? In a day or two we'll be burning their boats and slaughtering them like the cattle they are!"

Ignoring his son's outburst, Priam asked me, "A newcomer, you say? Yet you claim to be of the House of Ithaca. When you ducked your head past the lintel of our doorway I thought you might be the one they call Great Ajax."

I replied, "King Odysseos has taken me into his household, my lord king. I arrived on these shores only a few days ago."

"And singlehandedly stopped me from storming the Achaian camp," Hector said, somewhat ruefully. "Too bad Odysseos has adopted you. I wouldn't mind having such a fearless man at my side."

Surprised by his offer, I answered merely, "I fear that would be impossible, my lord."

Priam stirred on his throne, coughed painfully, then said, "We thank you for the message you bring, Lukka of the House of Ithaca. Now we must consider before making answer."

He gestured a feeble dismissal. I bowed again and backed away from the throne. The courtier who had brought me escorted me back to the door of the anteroom. The guards closed the heavy door behind me and I was alone in the small chamber. I went to the window and looked out at the colorful garden, so peaceful, so bright with flowers and humming bees intent on their morning's work. No hint of war there. I found myself wondering what my wife was doing, and where my sons might be.

Useless daydreaming, I told myself. But still my thoughts wandered and my fears rose, dark and troubling.

Then a different picture formed in my mind: Agamemnon and his warriors raging through this palace, destroying this beautiful garden, slaughtering Hector and aged Priam and all the rest.

And Helen? What would they do with Helen? Return her to her husband, Menalaos? Would he take her back after her willing marriage to Paris? Or would she be killed along with all the others?

I clenched my fists and squeezed my eyes tight. I tried to regain the vision of my wife and sons.

"Lukka of the House of Ithaca."

I wheeled from the window. A single soldier stood at the doorway, bareheaded, wearing a well-oiled leather harness rather than armor, a short sword at his hip.

"Follow me," he commanded.

I went with him down a long hallway and up a flight of steps, then through several rooms that were empty of people, although richly furnished and decorated with gorgeous tapestries. They would burn well, I found myself thinking. Up another flight of stairs we went, and finally he ushered me into a comfortable sitting room with wide undraped windows that looked out onto a broad terrace and the distant dark blue sea. Lovely murals decorated the walls, scenes of peaceful men and languid women in a pastel world of flowers and gentle beasts.

The soldier closed the door and left me alone. But not for long. Through the door on the opposite side of the room, a scant few moments later, stepped the beautiful Helen.

20

S he was breathtaking, there is no denying it. She wore a flounced skirt of shimmering rainbow colors with golden tassels that tinkled as she walked toward me. Her corselet was now as blue as the Aegean sky, her white blouse so gauzy that I could see the dark circles of the areolae around her nipples. She wore a triple gold necklace and more gold at her wrists and earlobes. Jeweled rings glittered on her fingers.

Behind her, standing just inside the doorway, stood an older, darker woman, in a hooded black robe that reached to the floor. Dark and silent as a specter, she watched me with eyes that seemed to glow from within the shadow of her hood. A servant, I thought, although she looked more like Death itself to me. I tried to ignore her, reasoning that Helen would not be alone with a man, especially an emissary from Agamemnon, the brother of her true husband.

Helen was tiny, almost delicate despite her hourglass figure. Her skin was like cream, unblemished and much lighter than the women I had seen in the Achaian camp. Lighter even than my wife's, she who had been born in the mountains of the Hatti homeland. Helen's eyes were as deeply blue as the Aegean, her lips lush and full, her hair the color of golden honey, with ringlets falling well past her delicate shoulders. One stubborn curl hung down over her forehead. She wore a scent of flowers: light, clean, yet beguiling.

She smiled at me and gestured toward a chair as she took a cushioned couch, her back to the open windows.

I sat and waited respectfully for her to speak. She was a woman, of course, but she had been Queen of Sparta and was now a princess of Troy. No ordinary woman, she.

"You say you are a stranger to this land." Her voice was low, melodious. I could understand how Paris or any other man would dare anything to have her. And keep her.

I nodded and found that I had to swallow once before I could speak. "My lady, I arrived here only two days ago."

"You are a traveler, then?"

"Not by choice."

She looked at me with a hint of suspicion in those clear blue eyes. "A warrior?"

"I have been a soldier in the army of the Hatti, my lady."

She blinked with surprise. "You are a Hittite?"

"Yes, my lady."

Suddenly Helen was filled with happiness. "The Hittites are sending troops here to help us!"

"I fear not, my lady. I am here to find my wife and young sons, who have been taken into slavery."

She looked genuinely surprised. "How can that be?"

With a shake of my head, I replied, "It is a long tale, my lady. Best not to bore you with it."

"I see." She hesitated, then asked, "What gods do the Hittites worship?"

I was the surprised one now. I thought a moment. "Tesub, the Storm God, of course—"

"Zeus," she murmured.

"Asertu, the goddess of love. Arina, the sun goddess. Kusa, goddess of the moon."

"You have no warrior goddess?"

"A warrior goddess?" The idea seemed ridiculous to me. Men are warriors, not women. "No, my lady."

"Then you do not serve Athene, under any name."

I shook my head.

"Athene despises me. She is the enemy of Troy."

I remembered the weathered little wooden statue in the garden courtyard. "The Trojans honor her image, though."

"You cannot fail to honor so powerful a goddess. No matter how much Athene hates me, the people of this city must continue to placate her as best they can. Certain disaster will overtake them if they do not."

"I was told that Apollo protects the city."

She nodded, her lips pressed into a tight line. "Yet I fear Athene." Helen looked beyond me, looking into the past, perhaps. Or trying to see her future.

I began to feel uneasy. The black-robed servant had not moved from where she stood in the doorway, her eyes boring into me from beneath her hood.

"My lady, is there some service you wish me to perform for you?"

Helen's gaze focused on me again. A faint smile dimpled her cheeks. "You wonder why I summoned you."

"Yes."

The smile turned impish. "Don't you think I might want a closer look at such a handsome stranger? A man so tall, with such broad shoulders? A man who stood against Hector and his chariot team and turned them away?"

She was teasing me. Taunting, almost. And I felt a stirring in my blood. I realized that Helen could melt stone with those blue eyes of hers.

It took me an effort of will to refrain from reaching

out to her. I bowed my head slightly. "May I ask you a question, my lady?"

"You may—although I don't promise to answer it."

"The Achaians argue among themselves: did Paris actually abduct you or did you leave Sparta willingly?"

Her smile faded. She lowered her eyes, as if thinking hard about what answer to make. At last she replied, "Lukka, you don't understand the ways of women, do you?"

"That's true enough," I admitted.

"Let me tell you this much," Helen said. "No matter how or why I accompanied Paris to this great city, I will not willingly return to Sparta."

I thought, But you will return, willingly or not, if Priam accepts the offer of peace that I gave him.

Helen spread her arms. "Look about you, Lukka! You have eyes, use them! What woman would willingly live as the wife of an Achaian lord when she could be a princess of Troy?"

"But your husband Menaleos is a king."

"And an Achaian queen is still regarded less than her husband's horses and dogs. A woman in Sparta is a slave, be she wife or concubine, there is no real difference. Do you think there would be women present in the great hall at Sparta when an emissary arrives with a message for the king? Or at Agamemnon's Mycenae or Nestor's Pylos or even in Odysseos' Ithaca? No, Lukka. Here in Troy women are regarded as human beings. Here there is civilization."

She seemed really angry.

"Then your preference for Paris is really a preference for Troy," I said.

She put a finger to her lips, as if thinking over the words she wished to use. Then, "When I was wed to Menalaos I had no choice. The young lords of Achaia all wanted me . . . and my dowry. My father made the decision. If the Achaians should win this war, the gods forbid, and force me to return to Sparta with Menalaos, I will again be chattel."

Before I could reply she added, "That is, if Menalaos allows me to live. More than likely he will slit my throat."

The servant back at the doorway stirred at that, the first sign of life I had seen from her.

"Would you agree to return to Menalaos if it meant that Troy would be spared from destruction?"

"Don't ask such a question! Do you think for one instant Agamemnon fights for his brother's honor? The Achaians are intent on destroying this city. I am merely their excuse for attacking."

"So I have heard in the Achaian camp."

"Priam is near death," Helen went on, her voice lower. "Hector will die in battle, that is foretold. But Troy itself need not fall, even if Hector dies."

I thought, And if Hector dies Paris will become king. Making Helen the Queen of Troy.

She turned and beckoned to the older, black-robed woman. "Apet, come here."

Still like a dark phantom, the older woman glided silently to her mistress's side.

"Lukka, I wish my maidservant to deliver a message to Menalaos. Will you promise to protect her in the Achaian camp?"

I looked from Helen's wide blue eyes to the coal-black

eyes of the older woman, then back again. "My lady, I am only a common soldier, bound to the House of Ithaca."

"Do you promise to protect my servant?" Helen repeated, with some iron in her voice.

I nodded once. "I will do my best, my lady."

"Good." Turning to the servant, Helen said, "Apet, you will tell Menalaos that if he wants me to return to him he will have to win me on the field of battle. I will not go willingly to him as the consolation prize for losing this war."

I took a deep breath. Helen was far more daring than any woman I had ever heard of. And much more astute. I realized that she unquestioningly wanted Troy to win this war, wanted to remain in this city and one day become its queen. Yet she wanted her servant to tell her former husband that she will come back to him—if he wins! She wanted to tell him, through her servant, that she will return to Sparta and be a docile Achaian wife—if and when Troy is burned to the ground.

Clever woman! No matter who loses this war, she will protect her own lovely skin.

Helen rose to her feet, signaling that our meeting was ended. "Lukka, my servant Apet will go with you when you return to the Achaian camp. You will bring her to Menalaos, then see that she is returned safely to me."

If Menalaos doesn't cut her head off, I thought, for such a message. And mine with her. But I said nothing as I bowed to Helen and went to the door by which I had entered.

"May the gods protect you, Lukka," Helen said to me as I pulled the door open.

"And you, my lady," I replied. I stepped through the doorway, feeling the glittering eyes of Helen's servant on my back like a pair of daggers. The guard who had brought me to this chamber was still waiting outside to escort me back to the king's audience hall.

As the door swung shut behind me, I heard Helen telling her servant, "Apet, you will leave with Lukka and give my message to Menalaos. Speak to no one else. He will recognize you and know that you speak my words."

"But my nursling . . ." The older woman began, in a voice dry and harsh with age. The door closed, and I heard no more.

And then it struck me. Helen had called me by my own name. All the others called me "Hittite" and nothing more. But she knew my name and used it.

I marveled at that.

21

The gray-bearded courtier who had escorted me earlier was waiting for me in the audience hall, still in his ceremonial long green robe, when the guard and I got back there. Otherwise the columned chamber was empty, silent except for our footsteps padding softly on the stone floor.

"The king and royal princes are deliberating on your message, Hittite," the courtier told me, nearly whispering. "You are to wait."

He left and I waited, wondering how and when Helen's servant would meet up with me. The guard went to the far door and stood there, immobile, except for his eyes watching me. I studied Priam's throne. I had never seen the throne of the emperor back at Hattusas, but it could hardly be grander than this magnificent chair of midnight-black ebony and its filigreed inlays of gold, I thought. Troy is rich, that is clear. No wonder Agamemnon and the other Achaians want it.

"Hittite."

I turned to see Hector approaching me. And berated myself for not being alert enough to hear his footsteps.

"Prince Hector," I said.

"Come with me. We have an answer for Agamemnon."

I followed him into another part of the palace. As before, Hector wore only a simple tunic, almost bare of adornment. No weapons, except for the ornamental dagger. No jewelry. No proclamation of his rank. He carried his nobility in his person, and anyone who saw him instinctively knew that here was a man of merit and honor.

Yet, as I matched him stride for stride through the palace's maze of halls and chambers, I saw again that the war had taken its toll of him. His bearded face was deeply etched by lines around the mouth and eyes. His brow was creased and a permanent notch of worry had worn itself into the space between his eyebrows.

We walked in tight silence to the far side of the palace and up a steep narrow stairway that was deep in gloomy darkness lit only by occasional slits of windows. Higher and higher we climbed the steep, circling stone steps, breathing hard, around and around the stairwell's narrow confines until at last we squeezed through a low square doorway onto the platform at the top of Troy's tallest tower.

"Paris will join us shortly," said Hector, walking over to the giant's teeth of the battlements. It was almost noon, and hot in the glaring sun despite the stiff breeze from the sea that gusted at us and set Hector's brown hair flowing.

From this vantage I could see the Achaian camp, scores of long black boats drawn up on the beach behind the sandy rampart and trench. The Trojan forces were camped on the plain, tents and chariots dotting the worn-bare soil, cook fires sending up thin tendrils of smoke that were quickly blown away by the wind.

‘ Beyond the gentle waves rolling up onto the beach I saw an island near the horizon, a brown hump of a worn mountain, and beyond it another hovering ghostlike in the blue hazy distance.

"Well, Brother, have you told him?"

I turned and saw Paris striding briskly toward us. Unlike Hector, his tunic looked as soft as silk and he wore a handsome royal-blue cloak over it. A jeweled sword was at his hip and more jewels flashed on his fingers and at his throat. His hair and beard were carefully trimmed and gleamed with sweet-smelling oil. His face was unlined, though he seemed not that many years younger than his brother.

"I was waiting for you," said Hector.

"Good! Then let me give him the news."

"Wait," Hector said, raising one hand to hold back his brother. "I have a question to ask this man."

I thought I knew what he was going to ask me.

Sure enough, Hector fixed me with a stern gaze and said, "You say you are a Hittite."

"Yes, my lord."

"A soldier of the emperor?"

I nodded mutely.

"Is your emperor sending troops to aid us? We asked

for help many moons ago. Are you the first contingent to arrive here?"

"And if you are," Paris interrupted sharply, "what are you doing in the Achaian camp? Fighting against us? Claiming to be of Odysseos' House of Ithaca?"

I kept my eyes focused on Hector. "My lord, the emperor of the Hatti is not sending troops to help you. He cannot even help himself. He is dead, murdered. The empire is racked by civil war. I brought my squad of men here seeking my wife and sons."

Hector studied my face for long moments, as if trying to determine if I was telling the truth or not. I looked back into his steady brown eyes.

At last he murmured, "We'll get no help from the Hittites, then."

"So much for being the western bulwark of their empire," Paris sneered. "When we need them, they have no strength to help us."

Shaking his head, Hector said to his brother, "It changes nothing. At least the Hittites aren't coming to fight against us."

Paris looked surprised at that idea.

"Very well," Hector said, with a tired sigh, "give him our father's reply."

Smiling nastily, Paris said to me, "You may tell fat Agamemnon that King Priam rejects his pathetic offer. Moreover, by this time tomorrow our chariots will be riding through his camp, burning his boats and slaying his white-livered Achaians until nothing is left but ashes and bones. Our dogs will feast well tomorrow night."

I kept my face frozen, impassive.

Hector made the tiniest shake of his head, then laid a restraining hand on his brother's blue-cloaked shoulder. "Our father is not feeling well enough to see you again, Hittite. And although my brother's hot words may seem insulting, the answer that we have for Agamemnon is that we reject his offer of peace."

"And any offer that includes returning my wife to the barbarian!" Paris snapped.

"Then we will have war again tomorrow," I said.

"Indeed we will," said Paris.

I asked, "Do you really think you are strong enough to break through the Achaian defenses and burn their fleet?"

"The gods will decide," Hector said calmly.

"In our favor," added Paris.

22

Hector gave me a four-man guard of honor to escort me out of the same gate that I had entered the night before. And Apet was standing at the gate waiting for me in her hooded black robe. Still as silent as Death, she fell in with my escort as we passed through the walls of Troy. The guards took no notice of her; it was as if she were invisible to them.

They called it the Scaean Gate, and I learned that it was the largest of four gates to the city. In the daylight I could see the massive walls of Troy close-up. Almost I could believe that gods had helped to build them.

Immense blocks of stone were wedged together to a height some five times more than the tallest man. High square towers surmounted the walls at each gate and at the corners. The walls sloped outward, so that they were thickest at ground level.

Since the city was built on the bluff overlooking the plain of Ilios, an attacking army would have to fight its way uphill before ever reaching the walls.

I returned to the Achaian camp to find old Poletes waiting at the makeshift gate for me.

"Who is this?" he asked, staring at Apet.

"A messenger from Helen," I replied.

Poletes' eyes brightened. "What news does she bring?"

"Nothing good," I said. "There will be battle tomorrow."

Poletes' skinny shoulders slumped beneath his threadbare tunic. "The fools. The bloody fools."

"Where are my men?" I asked.

With a gesture, he replied, "At the Ithacans' camp, by the boats."

I nodded, then headed for Odysseos, with Poletes skipping beside me, his knobby legs working overtime to keep pace with me, and Apet plodding along after us. All through the camp men were busily sharpening swords, repairing battered shields, wrapping wounds with fresh strips of cloth soaked in olive oil. Soldiers and noblemen alike stared at us, reading in my grim face the news I carried from Troy. The women looked, too, then turned away, knowing that tomorrow would bring more blood and carnage and terror. Most of the slaves were natives of this land and hoped to be freed from their bondage by the Trojan soldiery. But they knew, I think, that in the frenzy and bloodlust of battle their chances of being raped and put to the sword were much more likely than their chances of being rescued and returned to their rightful households.

I had to find my wife and sons before tomorrow's battle, I knew. I had to get Odysseos to fulfill his promise to me.

Once we reached my men, hard by Odysseos' boats, I instructed Poletes, "Take care of this woman. She bears a message for Menalaos from Helen."

He nodded agreement and I left them with my men while I went to Odysseos' boat to deliver my news.

There was only one guard on the deck, and he didn't even have a spear. He was sitting on the boat's gunwale, honing his sword with a whetstone.

"The king?" he replied when I asked for Odysseos. Pointing to the sea, he told me, "He's out there with the dolphins, Hittite. Every morning he swims in the sea."

I followed his outstretched arm and saw Odysseos moving purposefully through the waves, his arms swinging up rhythmically, his bearded face turning upward for a gulp of air and then sliding down into the water once more. I had never seen a man swimming before; it looked strange, unnatural.

But when Odysseos clambered back onto the deck, naked and dripping, he was smiling and invigorated. Servants appeared with towels and clothing in their arms.

"Hittite," he said as he rubbed himself briskly with one of the rough towels. "You delivered my message to Prince Hector?"

"I did, sire. He had me repeat it to Priam and his court."

Odysseos dismissed his servants to hear my report. Sitting on a three-legged stool, he rested his back against the boat's only mast. The musty canvas that had served as a tent when it had been raining was folded back now that the hot sun was shining, but his bearded face was as dark and foreboding as any storm cloud when I told him that Priam and his sons rejected the Achaian peace terms.

"They offered no counter terms?" he asked.

"None, my lord. Paris said he would never surrender Helen under any circumstances."

"Nothing else?"

I hesitated, then said, "Helen has sent one of her maidservants with me to give a message to Menalaos. She says that she will return with him to Sparta only if he conquers Troy and she has no other choice."

Almost smiling, Odysseos said, "If *he* conquers Troy. Agamemnon would be very surprised to hear that."

I added, "Hector and Paris seemed quite certain that tomorrow they will break into this camp and burn the boats."

Odysseos tugged at his beard, muttering, "They know they have the upper hand."

I looked out across the rows of beached boats. Each of them had its mast in place and its sail furled, ready to be opened at a word of command. The crews were making ready to sail, I realized. The day before, most of the masts had been down.

Finally, Odysseos rose to his feet and called for his servants to dress him. "You will come with me, Hittite," he said urgently. "Agamemnon must hear of this."

"My lord, you said that you would return my wife and sons from the High King to me. I want to take them to a place of safety before tomorrow's battle starts."

Odysseos almost laughed at me. "A place of safety? Where?"

I had no answer.

"No, Hittite," he said as two women brought him a clean tunic and sandals. "I'm going to need you and your men behind me tomorrow. We'll talk of your family after the battle." Then he added, "If we still live."

Odysseos bade me wait until Agamemnon called a meeting of his council to discuss the news I brought. I asked him to allow me to bring Apet to Menalaos' hut but he said only, "After the council meeting."

So I waited with my men—and Helen's maidservant—by our campfire while the slave women prepared the midday meal. My mind was in turmoil. My wife and sons were in Agamemnon's part of the camp. I had to see them, had to find out for myself if they were alive.

I found myself walking through the camp, ignoring the men sitting around their cook fires spearing meat from their steaming kettles. Perhaps somehow I could get my family away from the High King's men and bring them here to Odysseos' camp, under my protection. If they still lived, after all these months. If they still lived.

How can I get them away from Agamemnon's men? I wondered. I had no answer. Of course, discipline in the camp was practically nonexistent. These Achaians seemed to have no idea of military authority, no concept of correct order. Perhaps I could bluff my way through whatever guards I encountered.

Soon enough I came to the boats with Agamemnon's golden lions painted on their prows. Several plank huts had been built here and the area teemed with men in armor and slaves in rags.

No one stopped me or even seemed to notice a stranger in their midst. I still wore the leather harness and iron-studded jerkin of the Hatti. I had left my spear and shield back at Odysseos' camp, but my iron sword was strapped to my side and my helmet tied tight on my head. As elsewhere in the camp, most of the men were circled around the cook fires, jabbing at their midday meat. I saw dozens of women serving them, but not my Aniti.

A pair of men stood lounging in front of one of the black-hulled boats, leaning on their long spears and gesticulating with their free hands as they talked animatedly together. The Achaian version of guards, I thought.

They abruptly stopped their conversation as I approached them and stared questioningly at me.

Before they could ask, I said, "I am Lukka, the Hittite."

Both of them were almost a full hand shorter than I, their skins dark, their beards shaggy, their heads bare.

"You're the one who stopped Hector yesterday," said one of them. He had a scar across his forehead.

"Yes," I said. "I'm looking for a woman—"

"Who isn't?" the other one joked.

"My wife," I said.

Their heavy brows went up.

"She's a Hittite. Pale skin. Almost as tall as I am. Her hair is lighter than yours. Her name is Aniti."

Recognition dawned in their eyes. "Oh. You mean the whore."

23

I must have blinked with shock. Without conscious decision, my hand shot out and I grabbed the Achaian by the front of his tunic.

"What did you say?"

His eyes widened. I saw his companion grip his spear with both hands.

"The Hittite woman," sputtered the man I was holding in my fist. "She . . . she's a . . ."

"Don't start trouble, Hittite," said the other one, hefting his spear.

"She's my wife," I snapped.

The one I held pointed with a shaking finger. "She's probably back there, beside the boat."

"Aniti, the Hittite," the other one said.

I let go of the man and strode past them, toward the nearest boat. Raging fury burned inside me. A whore? My wife, a whore? Bad enough to be a slave, a captive who has no choice but to obey her master. But a whore? To willingly give herself to men for gain? I was infuriated enough to kill. I saw nothing either to my right or left, only the boat with a group of raggedly clad women huddled under its curving prow.

And in their midst, two little boys playing in the sand. My sons!

I rushed up to them. The women scattered, the boys looked up with sudden fear in their faces. They looked all right otherwise, unharmed, unmarked, faces dirty and perhaps thinner than other children I'd seen, but certainly not starving, not injured.

They bolted and ran away from me, wailing. Into the arms of their mother.

Aniti dropped to her knees and scooped them up in her arms. "What's wrong?" she asked. "What's—"

Then she looked up and saw me.

"Lukka," she gasped.

"Aniti."

She got to her feet slowly. The boys hid behind the skirt of her filthy chemise. She looked somewhat heavier than I remembered her, her face smeared with grime, her eyes staring disbelievingly.

"I . . ." she seemed stunned with surprise. And fear. And shame, I thought. "You're here."

"I came from Hattusas to find you and my sons."

"All that way . . ."

"You . . ." I felt just as tongue-tied as she. "They made you a slave."

She nodded bleakly. "And worse."

"A whore?"

"To protect the babies. When the slavers attacked our caravan, I did what I had to do to protect them."

"A whore?" I repeated, miserable in every bone of my body. The anger was gone; I felt ashamed, humiliated.

Aniti's face hardened. "How do you think I kept them alive? All the way from Hattusas to here. How do you think I kept the slavers and these dogs of barbarians from spitting your sons on their spears?"

I couldn't find words. There was nothing to say.

"*You* didn't protect me!" she snapped, her voice rising. "Your fine army and all the emperor's men didn't protect me! Or your sons! I had to do it the only way I could, the only way you men would allow!"

She was blazing with fury. The boys looked wide-eyed, frightened.

I heard myself say—mutter, really—"I'll get you back from Agamemnon. You and the boys."

"No you won't. The High King doesn't give away his slaves. Especially those he enjoys having."

I slapped her face. I didn't mean to, my hand flashed out on its own. Aniti stood there in shocked silence, the mark of my fingers white on her reddened skin. My sons both burst into tears.

I turned and stalked away from them.

24

Feeling utterly miserable, furious with Aniti and even more so with myself, I made my way back to Odysseos' camp. My men were sitting around the embers of their midday fire, honing their swords, checking their shields, doing the things soldiers do the day before battle.

Apet sat off to one side, silent and dark. I sat on the sand beside her, silent and dark myself. Dark as a thundercloud. My men took one look at my face and knew enough to steer clear of me.

My sons are alive, I told myself. That's the important thing. No matter what Aniti has become, she has kept the boys alive and well. I'll have to take them from her. They can't remain with a whore, even if she's their mother. Better she were dead! I'll take them from her after tomorrow's battle. If I live through it. If any of us live through it.

But what will I do with her? I can't take her back, not now. I thought that perhaps what she had become was not her fault; she did what she had to do to protect my sons. Yet how could I take her back? Giving herself willingly to other men. How could I even think of taking her back?

For hours I sat there in silence, my mind spinning. Almost I hoped that tomorrow's battle would bring my death. That would be a release. Yet who would protect my sons if I died? Who would shield them from the blood lust that turns men into beasts during battle? And Aniti? What will become of her? I knew I shouldn't care, yet somehow I did.

It was nearly sunset when Odysseos strode up, dressed in a fine wool chiton, and ordered me to come with him to the meeting. I welcomed his command; I needed something to do to take my mind off my sons.

"Leave your sword," the King of Ithaca told me. "No weapons are allowed in a council meeting."

I unstrapped my sword and handed it to Magro for safekeeping, then fell in step beside Odysseos.

"Agamemnon will be unhappy," he told me as we walked through the camp toward the cabin of the High King. "I did not inform him beforehand that I was sending you to Hector."

I thought the King of Ithaca should have looked worried, even grim, at the prospect of displeasing Agamemnon. Instead, he seemed almost amused, as if the prospect of defending himself before the council did not trouble him one bit.

Despite myself I longed for a glimpse of my wife and

sons as we made out way toward Agamemnon's cabin in the lengthening shadows of sunset. They were nowhere in sight. I tried to blot out of my mind the images of what Aniti did in the night. I tried to focus my thoughts on the boys instead. I tried.

The High King's cabin was larger than Achilles', but nowhere near as luxurious. The log walls were bare except for shields hung on them as ornaments, although the king's bed was hung with rich tapestries. For all his bluster, Agamemnon kept no dais. He sat on the same level as the rest of the council members. The loot of dozens of villages was scattered around the cabin: armor, jeweled swords, long spears with gleaming bronze points, iron and bronze tripods, chests that must have contained much gold and jewelry. The High King had cleared the cabin of women and other slaves. None were there except the council and a few servants. And me, as Odysseos' chosen emissary to the Trojans.

As soon as we all were seated in a circle around the gray ashes of the hearth, Agamemnon squawked in his high piping voice, "You offered them peace terms?" He leveled a stubby finger at Odysseos. "In my name? Without asking me first?"

The High King looked angry. His right shoulder was swathed in strips of cloth smeared with blood and some smelly poultice. He was broad of shoulder and body, built like a squat turret, round and thick from neck to hips. He wore a sleeveless coat of gilded chain mail over his tunic, which was cut away at the right shoulder for the bandaging. Over the mail was a harness of gleaming leather, with silver buckles and ornaments. A jeweled sword hung at his side. His sandals had gold tassels on their thongs. All in all, Agamemnon looked as if he were dressed for a parade rather than a council of his chief lieutenants, the kings and princes of the various Achaian tribes.

Perhaps he thought to overawe them with his panoply, I thought, knowing their penchant for argument.

I counted thirty-two men sitting in a rough circle around the glowing hearth fire in Agamemnon's hut, the leaders of the Achaian contingents. Every tribe allied to Agamemnon and his brother Menalaos was there, although the Myrmidones were represented by Patrokles rather than Achilles. I sat behind Odysseos, who was placed two seats down on the High King's right, near enough to give me the opportunity to study Agamemnon closely.

There was precious little nobility in the features of the High King's fleshy face. Like his body, his face was broad and heavy, with a wide stub of a nose, a thick brow, and deep-set eyes that seemed to look out at the world with suspicion and resentment. His hair and beard were just beginning to turn gray, but they were well combed and glistening with fresh oil perfumed so heavily that it made my nostrils itch, even from where I sat.

He held a bronze scepter in his left hand; his right rested limply on his lap. The one rule of sanity and order in the council meeting, apparently, was that only the man holding the scepter was allowed to speak.

"Well?" he demanded of Odysseos. "How dare you offer peace terms in my name?"

Odysseos reached for the scepter. Agamemnon let him take it, grudgingly, I thought.

"Son of Atreos, it was nothing more than a ruse for gaining a day's rest from the Trojan attack. A day the men are using to strengthen our defenses."

"And to prepare the boats to sail," muttered Big Ajax, sitting farther down the circle. Agamemnon glared at him.

Odysseos continued, "I knew that Hector and prideful Paris would not accept peace terms while their forces are camped at our gates."

Before anyone could object, he went on, "And what if they did? Menalaos would have his wife returned to him and we could leave these shores with honor."

Agamemnon snatched the scepter back. "Leave without razing Troy? What honor is there in that? I have sacrificed my own daughter to tear down Troy! I will not leave until that city is reduced to ashes!"

Odysseos reached for the scepter again, but Menalaos, sitting between him and Agamemnon, took it first. "If Helen is returned to me, we could sail for home and then come back next year, with an even bigger army."

He was younger than his brother, but they shared the same pugnacious look to their faces.

Agamemnon shook his head hard enough to make his beefy cheeks quiver. "And how will we raise a bigger army, with Helen returned? Who will come to Troy with me once the bitch is back in Sparta?"

White-bearded Nestor, sitting at Agamemnon's left, raised his voice. "High King, you do not hold the scepter. You have no right—"

"I'll speak whenever I want to!" Agamemnon shrilled.

They argued back and forth, then finally commanded me to tell them exactly what the Trojan princes had said to me. I accepted the scepter, then got to my feet and repeated the words of Paris and Hector.

"Paris said that?" Menalaos spat on the sandy floor. "He is the prince of liars."

"Pardon me, King of Sparta," said old Nestor, "but you do not have the scepter and therefore are speaking out of turn."

Menalaos smiled scornfully at the whitebeard. "Neither do you, King of Pylos."

Nestor got to his feet and reached for the scepter. I handed it to him willingly. He remained standing as he said, "If this Hittite is reporting truly, Hector expects to storm our ramparts in the morning. Hector is an honest man, not given to deception"—he eyed Odysseos as he said that—"and a great warrior. Tomorrow we will face a battle that could well determine the fate of this war. I have seen such battles before, you know. In my youth . . ."

On and on Nestor rambled, secure in his possession of the scepter. Odysseos looked bored, Menalaos and the others of the council fidgeted in their chairs. Agamemnon's face slowly reddened.

At last the High King grabbed the scepter from Nestor's hand. Startled, the old man gaped at Agamemnon, then slowly sank back onto his chair.

"We face disaster!" Agamemnon cried, his narrow little eyes actually brimming with tears. "Hector could overrun our camp and slaughter us all!"

Odysseos leaned across and took the scepter from the High King's hand. Holding it aloft, he proclaimed loudly, "We must not give way to despair! We must show Hector and his Trojans what metal we are made of. We will defend our camp and our boats. We will drive Hector away from our ramparts. Think of the songs the bards will sing of us when we are victorious tomorrow!"

A murmur went around the council circle. Heads nodded.

Odysseos turned to Patrokles, sitting almost exactly

opposite to Agamemnon's place. "Noble Patrokles, tell mighty Achilles that tomorrow he will have the chance to gain great glory for himself."

Patrokles nodded solemnly. "Glory is what he lives for. But if he refuses, perhaps I could convince him to let me lead the Myrmidones—"

"You?" Agamemnon laughed aloud. "You're too soft for anything but serving tidbits. Stay by your master's side and let the men tend to the fighting."

Patrokles' face burned red. I thought Agamemnon had just thrown away whatever slight chance we might have had to get the Myrmidones to fight alongside us, with or without Achilles.

25

By the time the council meeting ended it was growing dark outside. I left Agamemnon's lodge with Odysseos, as befitted my station. A considerable bonfire was crackling out there, casting a fitful red glare across the sand. The King of Ithaca waited outside the door of the lodge until Menalaos came out.

"Son of Atreos," he said, reaching out to clasp Menalaos by the shoulder, "the Hittite tells me that Helen has sent one of her maidservants with a message for you."

Menalaos' heavy brows lifted with surprise. "She sends me a message?"

"Apparently so," replied Odysseos, nodding.

"Bring her to my cabin then."

Odysseos turned to me. "Do so."

I left the two kings as they ambled toward Menalaos' cabin and hurried to the campfire where my men were sitting with their evening meal, their swords and spears resting on the ground beside them, atop their shields. Apet sat with the slave women, her black robe pulled around her, its hood down across her shoulders, as she spoke animatedly to them. She's not so silent with other women to listen to her, I said to myself.

Magro spotted me first and scrambled to his feet. The others quickly rose, also.

"Where's my sword?" I asked them. I felt naked here in camp without it.

"We're going to fight in the morning?" asked little Karsh as he picked my sword from the pile of weapons on the ground.

"Yes," I said, taking the sword from his hand. "We'll stand with Odysseos at the gate and show them what trained Hatti soldiers can do."

"On foot, against chariots?"

"We'll hold the gate," I said flatly.

Magro laughed. "While the Trojan footmen scramble up the palisade and outflank us."

I shrugged. "There will be plenty of Achaian footmen to defend the length of the palisade."

Magro spat onto the sandy ground, showing what he thought of the Achaian footmen.

"Eat well and get some sleep," I told them. "Tomorrow you'll earn your keep."

Before they could reply I walked over to the huddle of women. "Apet," I called. "Menalaos wants to hear what you have to say."

She pulled up her hood and rose to her feet like an offering of black smoke. Her features were shadowed by the hood, but if she felt any fear of facing her former master she showed nothing of it. Without an instant of hesitation she fell in step alongside me.

Odysseos was still in Menalaos' cabin when we got there. The two of them were sitting at a trestle table, spearing broiled chunks of lamb from a large oval platter with their daggers, flagons of wine at their elbows. The King of Sparta ordered all his servants out of the cabin once his guard allowed Apet and me inside. I got the feeling he wanted Odysseos to leave, too, but he said nothing to the King of Ithaca.

Apet pulled down the hood of her robe as she walked beside me to the table. My stomach rumbled, reminding me I had not eaten since the morning, in Troy.

"You are Helen's servant, the Egyptian," Menalaos said truculently. "I remember you from Sparta."

Apet bowed stiffly and said "Aye, my lord" in a low whispering tone.

"You went with Helen when Paris spirited her away."

"Aye, my lord."

"Why shouldn't I have you nailed to a tree and burned alive?" he spat.

"Mighty king," she said, with just a trace of mockery in her voice, "I have been Queen Helen's faithful slave since she was a babe in arms. Her father brought me from distant Egypt to be her nurse and attendant. It was his command that I never leave her side."

Menalaos snorted with disdain. "Your loyalty should have been to me. I am her husband."

Apet bowed her head slightly, but said nothing.

Menalaos fidgeted in his chair and glanced uncomfortably at Odysseos, who focused his eyes on Apet.

At last Menalaos burst out, "Well, Egyptian, what message do you bring from my wife?"

Apet's coal-black eyes never left his. "My mistress commands me to tell you that she will willingly return to Sparta with you only after you have conquered Troy. She will not accompany you as the consolation prize for losing the war."

Menalaos jumped to his feet. "Consolation prize?" he roared.

"So says my mistress, your wife."

He snatched his dagger from the table. "I'll cut out your insolent tongue!"

Odysseos stood up and reached for his arm. I stepped in front of Apet.

"My lord king," I said, "I have been charged by your wife to protect this slave and return her safely to Troy." I rested my hand lightly on the hilt of my sword.

Odysseos made a smile and said, "Come, come, Menalaos. It does you no honor to kill a slave. A woman, at that."

Menalaos contained his fury, just barely. Through gritted teeth he said to Apet, "Return to your mistress and tell her that I will pluck her from the funeral pyre that was once Troy. Then she will learn the fate that befalls a faithless woman."

Apet nodded once, pulled up the hood of her robe, and turned to leave the cabin. I walked beside her, my hand still on my sword hilt.

When we reached Odysseos' camp it was fully dark. The moon's waxing crescent threw cool silver light across the beach, the boats and the tents that dotted the sand. Several of my men were sitting in front of the tents they had put up for themselves. Magro scrambled to his feet as I approached with Apet beside me.

"The others are wrapped in their blankets, snoring," Magro told me.

"Poletes?" I asked.

"He's snoring with the rest of them."

I nodded as I glanced at the dying embers of our campfire. "Get some sleep yourself. Tomorrow will be a hard day."

"And you?" he asked.

I forced a smile. "I'm hoping you oafs left some supper for me to eat."

"I will bring you food, Hittite," said Apet, surprising me. Without another word she moved off to where the women were lying in their meager blankets on the sandy ground.

I watched her bend over and rouse them, then turned back to Magro. "Get to sleep."

"Yes, sir," he said. "Enjoy your supper."

I sat on the sand and gazed up at the bright shining stars. By this time tomorrow I might be dead, I thought, but the stars will still be there, fixed in their places by the gods themselves.

Apet returned with two of the slave women trudging along behind her, one bearing an iron pot, the other an armload of firewood. Within a few minutes they had the fire blazing beneath the pot. I smelled a stew of meat and onions and spices that were strange to me.

I began to think about my wife and sons again, in Agamemnon's camp. Could I steal them away this night? Take them and my men with me out of this camp, away from this death trap? Would Aniti come with me? I realized that I couldn't leave her here, in the degradation she had sunk to. Despite everything, I had to bring her, too. Could I get them past the sentries at the gate?

And go where? I wondered. Where?

Then I realized that Apet was bending over me, a steaming wooden bowl in her hands. I put it to my lips: the stew was burning hot but delicious.

"Take a bowl for yourself," I told her. "Sit here beside me."

She went to the cook fire and returned in moments. She sighed as she lowered herself to the sand; it was almost a groan. I realized she must be very old.

"I thank you, Hittite," she said, her voice grating like a rusty hinge.

"I don't like to eat alone," I replied.

"I thank you for protecting me against that barbarian lout when he was angry enough to murder me."

I looked into her face for the first time. The moonlight showed clearly that her skin was parched and wrinkled with age.

"I promised your mistress that I would protect you."

"And you kept your promise."

We ate in silence for a few moments. Then I heard myself ask her, "You have known Helen for many years?"

"Since she was a nursling, Hittite, long before all these evils befell her."

"She brought them on herself, didn't she?"

Apet did not reply for several heartbeats. At last she said slowly, "If you only knew, strong warrior. If you only knew how the gods have wronged her."

"Tell me, then."

And there, in the moonlit night, with the cook fire slowly dying and the wind sighing in from the sea, while two armies waited for tomorrow's battle, Apet told me of Helen and how she had come to Troy.

II

▼

HELEN'S STORY

1

Men have said—Apet told me—that Helen is the most beautiful woman in the world. If that is true it is not her own doing, but the work of the gods, and must be accepted. Yet it has caused her nothing but grief.

Helen is the daughter of Tyndareos, King of Calydon, and Leda, his queen. Some say that mighty Zeus himself begat her, in human guise. Her mother never told her of it, but only smiled knowingly when Helen asked her what the other children meant by that.

Even as a baby—Apet went on—Helen was sweet and happy. Her laughter could make your heart soar. So beautiful. So delightful.

Years before, I had been captured by her father, Tyndareos, in a raid on my village in the Nile delta and taken to Calydon as a slave. I served the barbarians faithfully, and when Helen was born her mother made me her nursemaid.

Before she was twelve years old, word of Helen's

beauty spread so widely that princes from every king-dom in Achaia sought her hand in marriage. She was introduced to each of them as they visited her father's palace to court her. Most of them were older men, twice Helen's age, although not as old as her father or his brothers. Still, she held her breath and said not a word to these huge bearded men while they looked her over like butchers inspecting a heifer.

I stayed at her side always, and after a brief few moments with each visiting prince I was bade to take Helen back to the women's quarters, where she could remove the stiff gold-worked corselet and gown that her father insisted she wear—and breathe again.

Helen tried to tell her mother of her fears, but her mother told her to be grateful that she was sought after by the richest and most powerful families in the land. It was only to me that she could confide her fears.

"Apet, they're so *old*! And the way they look at me . . . it frightens me."

"Come, come, my nursling," I would say, soothing her. "The gods have graced you with great beauty, and men are dazzled by such."

"Their eyes . . . they stare at me so."

"Don't be afraid of the princes, my sweetest. Learn to use your beauty to get them to bring you gifts and do your bidding."

Gradually, while the royal visits continued, I explained how she must think like a woman and use a woman's strengths to make the best of her life. She began to understand; she had seen the barnyard animals in rut and once, while her parents were away, had even gone out to the stables and watched a stallion mount a mare before I caught her and whisked her back inside the palace.

Among those barbarians women have no say in their own destinies; daughters are exhibited to prospective suitors, then bargained for and decided upon by their fathers or other male kin.

The suitors besieging her father's house were many and powerful. Helen's father favored Menalaos, King of Sparta, because his own ancestry was rooted there. When Menalaos came to the palace Helen was allowed to have dinner with him and his companions. While I watched from the kitchen doorway, she sat next to her father, quaking inside through every moment without me by her side. Menalaos was more than fifteen years older than she, already past thirty; flecks of gray showed in his hair. He jabbed at his food with a dagger and dripped wine into his beard. She was terrified of him.

Her father, Tyndareos, had different worries. He feared that whichever one of the besieging suitors he chose, the choice would antagonize all the others. They were hot-tempered men, powerful and quick to make war, each of those who sought Helen's hand; they would make deadly enemies. Yet the longer her father hesitated, the more the eager princes pressed him for a decision. Helen waited in an agony of suspense, wishing that she could run far away.

I had told her about the splendor of Egypt since she'd been a baby, of the magnificent cities and great pyramids that had been erected before the beginning of time.

"I wish we could go to Egypt," Helen said to me, more than once during those nerve-stretching days.

"Ah, there is a land where a beautiful princess is treated properly," I told her. "There is a land of true civilization."

She sighed and pined for glorious Egypt while her father struggled over his decision about her fate.

Then ever-shrewd Odysseos, her father's friend, suggested a solution. Upon a visit to Calydon Odysseos listened to Tyndareos' fears, then told him to make all the suitors take a solemn oath that they would accept his choice and support her betrothed, should the need ever arise. They all agreed soon enough, each man hoping to be the one favored above all the others, each fearful that winning Helen would also win the jealousy of all the other princes. Thus they swore their pledge.

As he had planned to do all along, Tyndareos wed Helen to the King of Sparta: Menalaos, of the house of Atreos, brother to mighty Agamemnon. It seemed a good match to her father, but Helen was not happy with it. And she feared the anger of Athene, for Helen had dedicated herself to Aphrodite, the goddess of love and beauty, and the omens told of Athene's displeasure with her.

To doubly assure his safety, her father also wed Helen's older sister, Clytemnestra, to Menalaos' brother Agamemnon of Argos, King of lion-gated Mycenae. His house was thus doubly bound to the house of Atreos and the two most powerful kingdoms in Pelops.

Sparta was a crushing disappointment to Helen. She had dreamed of a well-built citadel, with many servants for the new queen, and a kind and loving husband. Instead, Menalaos' house was like a cold, dreary stone dungeon; its floor was bare earth and the smoke from its hearth fire made your eyes sting. The serving people were dull, surly. Her husband and his noble kinfolk talked of nothing but hunting and war. She was a queen, yet she was expected to spin and weave and serve her lord without question. She was his possession, his chattel. Helen felt that even Aphrodite had abandoned her.

All that she knew of the arts of love was what I had told her.

"Your duty is to please your husband," I instructed Helen on the day of her wedding in Sparta. "Your own pleasure is not so important as his."

I knew Helen had heard tales of married women who had taken lovers. And of what happened to them when their husbands found out.

"Should I expect no pleasure at all from my husband?" she asked me tearfully.

I grasped her chin gently. "Light of my days, women are vessels for men's passion, and we must be satisfied to please them. A woman's happiness comes from the children she bears. Think of them when making love with your husband."

Her wedding night was no surprise, then. While her husband drank and caroused with his male relatives and friends, I helped Helen out of her gold-embroidered wedding dress and into a shimmering nightgown that clung to her young body. When Menalaos lurched through the bedroom door, Helen flinched with terror, yet she dutifully stepped to the well-draped bed and waited with wide, fearful eyes for him to strip while I went to the next room and shut the heavy oaken door with troubled, trembling hands.

And listened.

More than half drunk from the feasting, Menalaos used her, took her virginity, then rolled over and fell asleep. No surprise, but still Helen felt bitterly dissatisfied.

Helen's life in Sparta fell into a wearying, dull routine. Most of the time she was kept inside the citadel, like a royal captive, closely watched and guarded against the eyes of other men. Yet her husband allowed her to attend the feasts when important visitors came to the citadel. Menalaos would sit her at his side and grasp her wrist possessively. Thus she met ambassadors from Athens and Thebes and even far-off Crete. They all remarked wonderingly of her beauty.

"Am I not the most fortunate of men?" her husband would boast to his noble kinfolk and the visiting dignitaries, leering at Helen between cups of honey-sweetened wine. "Gaze upon my wife and see for yourselves how the gods have favored me."

Yet when they were in bed together he barely spoke a word to her beyond the grunting of his clumsy, pawing passion. In truth, Helen had little to say to him, for whenever she did try to speak to him he either ignored her or commanded her to be silent. Helen fell into long, tearful bouts of desperation, seeing nothing in her life but dreary, meaningless years of misery.

"Be steadfast, my nursling," I would tell her. "Soon enough you will have children to cheer your days."

Yet she did not conceive, and I began to wonder if the gods had indeed marked her to be barren. Or was it Menalaos that the gods were punishing?

If I had not been there to comfort Helen, I fear she would have gone mad. She prayed to Aphrodite and to

Hera, patroness of motherhood, that bearing Menalaos a child would change his attitude toward her. And her prayers were answered! She became pregnant at last. But when she gave birth, her baby was a daughter and Menalaos was furious.

"I want a son," he snarled at her as she lay exhausted and sweaty in her labor bed.

He would not even look at their daughter. He ordered her taken from Helen and given to a wet nurse. When she tried to protest he sneered, "You can suckle me, instead."

For days Helen begged him for her baby. Even when she was strong enough to get up from bed he refused to let her see her daughter. Then I discovered why, listening to the whispers of the serving women by the well in the citadel's courtyard.

I rushed to Helen's side, tears streaming from my eyes.

"Apet, what is it?" she asked.

I could not speak. Instead I raked my cheeks with my fingernails and flung myself on the stones of the hearth.

Helen dropped to her knees beside me, her whole body trembling. "Apet, what is wrong?"

I could only utter a strangled groan.

And she knew. "My baby!"

"Dead," I choked out. "Left on the mountaintop for the wolves and crows."

Helen screamed and tore her hair. The two of us wept uncontrollably, huddled together at the hearth, until long after the sun went down and the chill of night filled the bedchamber.

Menalaos did not come to her that night. Nor the next. When at last he did Helen stood by their bed fully dressed as I hid behind the half-shut door to her dressing closet with a dagger in my hand, ready to kill her husband if he struck her.

"Where is my daughter?" Helen demanded of Menalaos.

"She was sickly," he said, avoiding her eyes. "Too weak to live."

"Where is my daughter?" she repeated.

"I want a son."

"Then go make a bastard with one of your serving wenches," she said coldly. She seemed to be a statue of ice, showing no fear, no emotion whatever except hatred as hard as stone. Go ahead and strike me, she challenged him wordlessly. Beat me senseless. It makes no difference.

Menalaos raised his hand and took half a step toward her, then stopped. I gripped my dagger hard and held it at the ready. Then his shoulders slumped. Saying nothing, Menalaos turned about and left the bedchamber. I stepped into the room, the dagger still in my hand.

"Put that away," Helen commanded me. "It won't be needed."

So she lived as a dutiful wife while Menalaos spent most of his days hunting with his companions and most of his evenings drinking with them. He visited Helen's bedchamber a few times; each time she rebuffed him. Often the dog raised his hand to hit her, but she stood before him without flinching.

"I am not a helpless infant," she said. "If you strike me I will return to my father and his brothers."

He glowered at her. "You will remain here in Sparta! You are my wife."

"Yes," she said. "And the mother of your daughter."

He fled from her room.

As the months dragged on the servants gossiped about the slaves he slept with instead of his wife. Helen cared not. Her life was ruined, what did it matter what her husband did or how the servants prattled? There were rumors of bastard babies; always daughters. I told Helen that Hathor and mighty Isis had put a curse on Menalaos for murdering her baby.

"He will never have a son," I whispered to her, my eyes burning like coals.

"How can you be sure?" she asked me.

"I have invoked the power of the goddess," I told her. "He will never father a son."

"Perhaps," she said. "But if he does, he will want to marry the mother and make his son a legitimate prince."

I shook my head. "To do that he will have to kill you."

"Yes," she answered, and I realized the truth of it as she spoke. My eyes went wide. Helen understood the fate that lay in store for her better than I did.

For the first time in my life I felt fear for my sweet one, like a chill wave of sickness rising within me.

"If ever Menalaos has a son," she said to me numbly, "our days are numbered."

"Your father . . ."

"My father will never know," she said, seeing the reality of it. "Menalaos will tell him that I died of a fever, or some such."

"I will slay the dog first," I growled.

Helen put her hand on my shoulder. "No, Apet. No. This life is not so lovely that I would cling to it."

I felt shocked. "Don't speak like that, my nursling! Don't dwell on death!"

"Why not? What have I to live for?"

"The gods will protect you," I promised. "The old goddess, she who shaped the world even before your Hera and Aphrodite came to be . . ."

"But what of Athene?" Helen asked in a low, sad voice. "She is the one goddess that Menalaos honors, the warrior goddess who had been jealous of me since my birth. She would be glad to see me dead and in Hades."

So with ever-mounting dread we lived the cold days and long, empty nights in dismal, gloomy Sparta, waiting for the inevitable day when Menalaos came to Helen with a son and a new wife and a sword thrust for her throat.

Then came a visitor to her husband's court: Alexandros, known as Paris, a prince of mighty Troy, come to collect the annual tribute that all the Achaian kingdoms paid to Priam, the Trojan king.

3

Helen would never have met Paris, would not even have seen him, had not her husband been called away to Crete to attend the funeral of Catreos, his grandfather. Even so, she was kept well away from the visitor. Her husband's kinsmen guarded her closely.

But I made it my business to see this Trojan prince with my own eyes. No one paid any attention to another serving woman in the great hall where the men took their meals. I slipped in with the other servants and took a good look at this prince of Troy. He was young, with a dazzling smile and eyes that gleamed like stars in the sky.

I rushed to tell Helen of him. "He looks like a godling, my precious: as handsome as Apollo, by the gods."

The maidservants chattered of little else except Paris' splendid appearance, his flashing smile and ready wit. Every serving girl in the palace dreamed of sharing his bed, and several of them claimed that they did.

"You must meet this royal visitor," I told Helen.

"How can I?" she asked, gazing out the window of her chamber into the dung-dotted courtyard below. "I am a prisoner in this citadel of stone."

"You are the queen, and your husband is away," said I. "Your husband's kinsmen are duty-bound to obey you."

She turned and stared at me. "Do you think I could?" she wondered aloud. "Would it be possible?"

"You are the queen, are you not? Use your power, my lamb. Use your beauty to dazzle this prince of Troy."

"What are you saying, Apet?"

I smiled at my lovely one. "Troy is a fine, noble city. And it is far from Sparta."

It was a fantasy, a dream. We both knew that. Yet the idea of leaving Sparta, leaving this hopeless dismal life, seemed to lift the misery that had engulfed Helen, filled her with eager expectation.

"At the very least, my heart's love," I said, "you will know a few hours of civilized conversation and gracious charm. Is that not worth the frowns of your husband's kinsmen?"

"Yes!" she answered. "Yes, it is!"

Thus Helen became determined to at least cast her

eyes on this charming visitor, desperate for some way to break the monotony of life in wretched Sparta. I learned from the servants that Paris went riding every morning. A woman did not ride in Sparta, not even the queen was allowed to. But I arranged to have Helen walking by the stables—well escorted, of course, by myself and a handful of young, chattering Spartan ladies—as noble Paris returned from his morning's canter.

He and six of his Trojan guards rode into the stable grounds, past the open gate, their horses neighing and stamping up dust from the bare earth. The horses were well-lathered, I saw. Paris must have ridden them hard. I saw Helen shiver despite the warm morning sunlight. She told me later that at that instant Aphrodite sent a vision into her mind of what it would be like to have him riding her, to bear his weight upon her body.

Standing at the far end of the dusty ground that fronted the stables, with me close beside her, Helen forgot the smells of the horses and dung, forgot the stares of the stable hands at the sight of their queen, forgot even the cooing and whispering of her escorting ladies. All at the sight of Paris, prince of Troy.

He was stunning. Young, clean-shaven, with dark eyes that sparkled at Helen as soon as he caught sight of her. His midnight-black hair had been tousled carelessly by the wind. His shoulders and torso seemed slim, yet his legs, bare below the hem of his tunic, were strong and graceful. The tunic itself was a work of art, beautifully embroidered and shaped to his form.

He slid off the sweaty horse and walked straight to Helen, ignoring the grooms and his own men who had ridden with him and were now dismounting.

Dropping to one knee before her, Paris said, "You

must be golden-haired Helen, Queen of Sparta. I have heard that you are the most beautiful woman in the world and now I can see that it is true."

Had he not been a royal visitor and under the protection of not only the rules of hospitality but the power of distant Troy, Menalaos' kinsmen would have whipped him out of the palace and sent him on his way home. But none of those frowning old men were at the stables that morning, thank the gods.

Helen could barely speak, his words and his beauty had taken her breath away. At last she managed to say graciously, "Rise, prince of Troy."

He got to his feet and stood before her, smiling a smile so brilliant that the sun itself seemed dimmed.

"I had hoped to meet you, Queen Helen," he said. "The gods have been kind to me on my last day here in Sparta."

"Your last day?" she blurted.

He nodded, and his smile turned sad. "Yes. I have waited for your royal husband for many days."

"He was called away to Crete, his grandfather's funeral . . ."

"I know. But I can wait for his return no longer. I must start back to Troy tomorrow."

Helen's legs seemed to go weak; she leaned on me for support. I knew the thoughts racing through her mind: she had finally met this prince and now he was going to leave her! I could almost hear her calling to Aphrodite, begging the goddess to help her.

"Must you go?" Helen asked, her voice a breathless whisper.

"I would stay longer if I could," Paris said to her, "just to gaze into your blue eyes."

Helen's cheeks burned red and she had to look away from him.

Paris went on, "But my ship is ready and your husband's tribute has been counted and loaded onto the wagons. Besides," he glanced back over his shoulder, "his kinsman would not be pleased if I remained here to woo you."

Speechless, Helen merely stood there quaking like a helpless girl facing a lion—a lion she wanted to embrace, even if he would rend her limb from limb.

Then Paris said, "The nobles feast me tonight in the great hall. Afterward I take leave of Sparta and ride to my swift ship at sunrise tomorrow."

Helen stood tongue-tied until I whispered in her ear. She repeated my words aloud.

"I will join you at the feast, then," she said, looking surprised to hear her own voice saying it.

His radiant smile returned. "Then at least I will have one last memory of the most beautiful woman in the world to carry back to Troy with me."

And I could tell the thoughts whirling through Helen's mind: would that he could have more than a memory to bring back to Troy with him!

As if he could read Helen's mind, Paris said in a half-whisper, "If I were not a prince, with the responsibilities my father has laid on my shoulders, I would steal you away from Sparta."

With that, he turned and strode away, back to his men, leaving Helen standing there half-fainting.

4

Despite the warnings of the noble Spartan ladies, Helen summoned the royal chamberlain and told him she would attend the evening's feast in her husband's place. He looked stunned, and left Helen's chambers as fast as his legs could carry him. Within minutes Menalaos' three closest cousins were scratching at her door. When I admitted them, they told Helen flatly that women were not allowed at the men's feasting unless the king himself permitted it.

"I am not a mere woman," she said, as haughtily as she could. "I am the queen and you will do as I command. Only my husband can gainsay me."

Good, my nursling, I cheered silently. But I knew that inwardly Helen was trembling like a leaf in a windstorm. She looked past the bearded, sour-faced men, to me, who stood behind them. I smiled encouragement to her. The noblemen grumbled and argued for a while but Helen stood firm. At last they bowed to her demand, grudgingly. As soon as the door closed behind them, she bade me summon all her servants. She was going to see Paris again! She wanted to look her absolute best for him.

All that day we prepared. It was high summer, yet even though the sun was bright, a cold wind swept down from the mountains like a chilling omen. I paid it no heed as Helen selected her best gown of pure white linen and a gold corselet that cinched her waist, modest yet

flattering. Three serving women spent the whole afternoon oiling and curling her hair and then pinning it up
demurely.

"You don't want to look *too* alluring for the visitor,"
one of the maids said, giggling.

Another added, "Especially with your husband away."

They laughed like carefree girls, thinking forbidden
thoughts of romance and seduction. Little did any of us
realize what was to befall us.

"I hear the Trojan prince is as handsome as Apollo,"
the third maid said.

"And how would you know that?" I demanded,
growing irritated at their simpering.

"Oh, the word has spread throughout the palace,
Apet. They say that in bed he makes love like Zeus!"

"And he's as big as Herakles."

"Be silent!" I commanded, fearful that they would see
how Helen's face was flushed with desire.

Menalaos' palace was a sorry place to host a prince of
Troy. Rough gray stone walls and dirt floors. For deco-
ration there was little more than shields and spears
adorning the rooms. Even Helen's own chamber had
only one small mirror, which she herself had brought in
her dowry. Troy was a magnificent city, we had both
heard: rich and cultured.

"It is not as glorious as the cities of the Nile, such as
Memphis or Thebes," I told her, "but it is as far above
Sparta as a palace is to a pigsty."

I could see Helen picturing in her mind's eye the
graceful columns and fine draperies and silks that graced
the palace in Troy where Paris lived.

At last the time arrived. Quaking with fear and a

yearning passion, Helen took her husband's place at the farewell feast for Alexandros. I accompanied her into the dining hall, such as it was, and stood behind her high-backed chair, silently watching and listening.

The old men of the court frowned and muttered in their beards, shaking their heads as Helen sat at the head of Menalaos' feasting table that evening, next to his empty chair. They were all kin to her husband, and shocked that a woman would present herself alone at the men's meal. Yet none of them had the strength to contradict the queen.

The dining hall was the largest room in the palace. It was already filled with the high and mighty of her husband's court. Menalaos' kinsmen seated themselves along the heavy oaken table, looking like a scowling, grumbling collection of graybeards, whispering among themselves and clucking their tongues like any clutch of gossiping old women. Paris was not yet present.

The old men got to their feet, grudgingly, I thought, as Helen took her place at the head of the long plank table. They were shocked at her effrontery, of course, but Helen cared not. She was burning to see this handsome young man from far-off Troy one final time before returning to the dismal fate that awaited her as Queen of Sparta.

The fire in the circular hearth, off in the farthest corner of the hall, was banked down to proper cooking heat and a boar from the afternoon's hunt was roasting on the slowly turning spit, the odor from its dripping juices filling the hall with a delicious aroma. For once, the smoke from the fire rose obediently through the roof hole and was borne away by the twilight breeze.

All of Sparta's nobles were at the table; servants were already pouring wine into their cups. Yet the chair to Helen's right remained empty.

"Where is our guest?" she asked.

"Washing his dainty feet, I suppose," said the grizzled old man sitting beside the empty chair.

"The afternoon's hunt must have fatigued him," said the noble across the table, with heavy sarcasm. He had lost an eye in battle years ago and wore a stained black patch over the empty socket.

"He's probably perfuming his curly locks and trying to decide which cloak he should wear," added a third of the seated nobles.

They all laughed heartily. Their opinion of the Trojan prince was not high.

Just then the court crier stamped his staff on the stone flagging by the great door and called:

"Prince Alexandros of Troy, known as Paris!"

He had dressed magnificently, in a splendid cloak of royal blue and a chiton embroidered with flowers around the neck. His midnight-dark hair had been curled and gleamed with oil. Yet it was his smile, his sparkling eyes, that made even my old heart leap.

Helen scarcely could speak to him once he took his place at her right hand. He was polite to her and chatted amiably with the elders at the table. They addressed him with deference, as befitted a prince of powerful Troy, and kept their disdain well hidden.

"I am very flattered that you have granted me the honor of your company this day," he said to Helen. "You look even more beautiful now than you did this morning."

I knew that Helen's heart was racing like a foolish

girl's. Her breath caught in her throat. His smile was dazzling. His eyes seemed to be searching hers, trying to read her spinning thoughts.

"The prince of Troy is very kind," she managed to say.

"Not at all. Anyone with even a single eye in his head can see that your beauty rivals Aphrodite's." He winked outrageously at the one-eyed nobleman sitting across from him.

A wintry chill fell along the entire length of the dining table. The old men did not approve of a handsome young prince speaking to their lord's wife, nor did they appreciate jokes made at their expense. And even the dullest among them must have known by now that the two of them had met by the stables earlier in the day.

If Paris was aware of their displeasure, he gave no sign of it. He turned back to Helen, his smile still radiant.

"Truly, I am honored that you chose to take your husband's place this evening."

Helen's voice caught in her throat. She could do nothing but stare at Paris like a moonstruck girl.

"The gods spin out our fates," said Paris. "Zeus himself has given me this chance to see you, and I should be content."

"But you are not content?" Helen managed to utter.

"How should I be? I have been granted a vision of paradise and now I must leave and never see you again."

What could Helen reply to that? She lowered her eyes and felt the warmth of his smile upon her—and the murderously cold angry stares of her husband's kin.

Paris turned from her and began to describe Troy to the men along the table, the city's many towers, the splendors of the royal palace with its gardens and beautiful tapestries and floors of polished stone. He seldom glanced at Helen, but I knew he was speaking to her, not the rough-bearded men who cared little for such elegance. Helen longed to see Troy, to see for herself the beauty and delight that he described. Paris was wooing her with words, in front of her husband's kinsmen. My own heart raced at his audacity.

The meal finished all too soon. Helen rose from her chair and bade Paris farewell, knowing that he would leave on the morrow with the grudgingly given tribute that he was to carry back to Troy.

"Perhaps someday I can visit Troy," she said, never realizing what thoughts it stirred in his breast.

Paris smiled his brightest. "Perhaps," he murmured.

Then she left the dining hall and went to her bedchamber, with me beside her. Her face was downcast, her heart empty and sad that she would never see this handsome, exciting man again.

As soon as we stepped into her bedchamber and closed the door behind us, I told Helen, "You have won his heart, my lamb. He is smitten with your beauty."

"What good is that now?" she asked, forlorn.

"You will see," I replied, smiling. "You will see."

I brought out her best nightgown and insisted that she wear it. When Helen realized what I expected she sat on the edge of the bed, so stunned was she with surprise and sudden hope.

"It cannot be!" she protested. "Apet, he would have to be mad to come here."

"He is mad," I replied happily. "Your beauty has driven him insane with desire."

She was about to shake her head, but instead she whispered, "Could it be? Could it truly be?"

"I have prayed to the old goddess that you might be

delivered from Sparta," I told her as I slid the gown over her head. "And I have done more than pray, my nursling."

"What do you mean?" Helen demanded. "What have you done, Apet?"

I smiled mischievously. "There will be no guard at your door this night, my lovely. No servants will linger in your quarters."

Helen could do nothing but stare at me, knowing that I was risking my life for her. There were no secrets that could stand against palace gossip.

"Apet, by tomorrow—"

I placed a silencing finger against my lips. "By tomorrow the world will be changed, my pet. You will see."

Helen went to bed, almost reluctantly, but she could not sleep, could not even close her eyes. I stood in the closet next to her room, waiting. But I fingered the Cretan dagger I always carried beneath my robe, just in case my dear one needed my protection.

Long after all the palace was quiet and dark, I still stood there while Helen lay awake, staring into the shadows. Then the door creaked softly. Someone entered her room. I knew who it was. I knew who I wanted it to be. Helen dared not speak or move or even breathe.

A crescent moon cast dim silver light through the bedchamber's only window, past the fitfully billowing curtains. He sat on the bed beside her, his form a black shadow against the breeze-stirred drapery. My heart raced madly.

"Helen," he whispered.

"Prince Alexandros," she found the courage to whisper back.

"Paris," he said.

"Paris."

"I can't leave without making love to you, Helen. Your beauty has enchanted me."

"But the servants . . ."

"No one will bother us. Your maidservant has seen to that."

"If anyone in the palace—"

"I don't care."

"This is madness!"

"Yes, of course it is," he replied, with a soft laugh. "I am mad about you."

"No," she said, so softly I barely heard it.

"How could any man set eyes upon you and not want to love you?" he whispered, bending over her so close she could feel his warm breath against her throat.

"I am married to Menalaos. He will kill us both."

"Then we will die," sighed Paris as he lay down on the bed beside her and slowly began to undo her nightgown.

Helen did nothing to resist him. His hands caressed her naked flesh, his lips covered hers.

For the first time in her life Helen felt truly aroused. Paris knew how to stroke her, how to pleasure her with touch and tongue and soft, whispered words. She was drowning in delight, all thoughts, all fears, all cares washed away in throbbing tides of ecstasy. At the last, she jammed her fist into her mouth to keep from screaming aloud with sheer rapture.

There was nothing in Helen's world except Paris. She had no husband, no daughter, no father or mother or night or day. She surrendered herself to Aphrodite completely and knew at last the meaning of her mother's smile when she asked if all-powerful Zeus had fathered her.

The moon sank behind the dark hills and the first rose-tinged fingers of dawn began to light the sky.

"Go quickly," she said to Paris. "Go and forget me and this night. Go and pray that Menalaos never finds out what we have done."

He leaned close to her, so close that their lips almost touched. "I can't," he said.

"You must go!" she insisted. "And quickly, before anyone else arises."

"I can't leave you."

"Menalaos will kill us both!"

He smiled down at her. "Not if you come with me to Troy."

"To Troy?" The thought seemed to stun her.

"Come with me and be my wife. You will be a princess of the mightiest city of the Aegean."

A princess of Troy. Wife of Paris in the many-towered city by the Dardanelles. A city of gentility and beauty, fabled throughout the world. It was impossible. It could never be. Yet to be a princess in civilized Troy would be far better than being a queen in Menalaos' Sparta.

Paris jumped to his feet and reached for his clothes. "Quickly," he said. "My men are waiting at the palace's main gate. Get dressed!"

In a daze, hardly believing what was happening to her, Helen did as he commanded. It was as if her true self was far away, watching this bewildered young woman obeying the bidding of the handsome prince of Troy. I came in and helped her to dress, then Paris wrapped her in his own brilliant blue cloak and pulled its hood over her head.

Like children playing a game the two of them stole through the still-sleeping palace and out to the mounted men waiting impatiently for their prince, while I roused a pair of slumbering slaves to quickly stuff as much of Helen's clothes as they could into a pair of large wooden chests while I packed all her jewelry into a large woolen sack. It was almost too heavy for me to carry, but I would not let the slaves touch it.

They loaded the chests onto a mule cart as Paris lifted Helen up onto his horse and seated her behind him. She clutched his strong body and rested her head against his back. I climbed by myself onto the cart that one of Paris' men drove. Then we were away, leaving Sparta, leaving her husband and her life, riding into a new dawn. How we got past the gates I do not know; Paris' Trojan companions either bribed the guards or slew them, I never asked even later, when I wondered about it.

I felt weak with relief. Paris would take care of Helen. He would sweep her across the sea to a new life and make certain that everything was right. Menalaos was already fading into a distant, hateful dream.

With the sky brightening into a new day we galloped down the rutted road to the distant harbor. The cart I rode in jounced and groaned so badly I thought it would fall apart long before we reached the water's edge. But soon enough we saw the square sail of Paris' boat, with its sign of a white heron painted upon it.

Thus we left Sparta and headed for Troy, while the gods and goddesses atop Olympos watched and took sides for Helen and against her. Grim Ares, god of war, smiled at the thought of the blood that would be spilled over her. Athene, ever her enemy, began to plot her downfall.

5

Apet fell silent at last. For long moments I stared at her lean, withered face while the ever-constant wind from the sea swept across the Achaian camp along the beach.

In the dying embers of the campfire the aged Egyptian woman looked like a statue carved out of old, dried-out wood. The moon had set, but the skies were spangled with thousands of bright glimmering stars.

"So she came to Troy willingly with Paris, or Alexandros, or whatever he calls himself," I muttered.

"Willingly, aye," said Apet, her voice low and heavy with memories. "She feared for her life in Sparta, feared that if Menalaos sired a son he would murder her and install the bastard's mother as his new queen."

I nodded with understanding. Helen chose the path that offered her safety. Did she actually love Paris, or did she flee with the young prince of Troy to find safety for herself? Both, I supposed. Women seldom do anything for one reason alone, I told myself.

"The Spartan nobility welcomed her cautiously," Apet continued. "Queen Hecuba was very gracious. Paris was her favorite son, and he could do no wrong in her eyes."

"And Priam, the king?"

Apet let out a sigh. "He was kind to her and ordered a royal wedding for her. Only the Princess Cassandra dared to say openly that Helen would bring disaster to Troy."

"What of Hector and the other princes?"

"Oh, they expected Menalaos to demand his wife back.

They thought that perhaps Menalaos would enlist the aid of his brother, Agamemnon. None of them dreamed that all the Achaian kings and princes would band together to make war on Troy."

How could they have foreseen that? I asked myself.

"It was the old pact that Tyndareos had made all of Helen's suitors swear to," Apet said. "Agamemnon demanded that all of them come to his brother's aid. It had been Odysseos' idea to keep the peace among the Achaian lords. But now Agamemnon used it to make war on Troy."

"So that he could wipe out Troy," I said, "and end its command of the entry to the Sea of Black Waters."

Apet shrugged. "Whatever their reasons, the Achaians sailed against Troy and devastated the lands of Ilios."

I looked up at the starry sky. Almost, I felt the eyes of the gods upon us.

"Tomorrow the war begins again," I said, starting to get to my feet. "I'd better get some sleep."

"But you have only heard part of Helen's story," Apet said to me, holding out a lean, emaciated hand to keep me from standing.

"Part of her story?"

"There is more," she said. "The real tragedy of her life was yet to unfold."

"What do you mean?" I demanded. "Isn't this war tragedy enough? Thousands of Achaian warriors assailing the walls of the city? Men dying on that worn-bare plain every day? What more tragedy could there be?"

"More, Hittite," said Apet. "More. For Helen, the ultimate tragedy."

Despite my awareness of the battle that would begin in a few short hours, I sat down on the sand again and listened as Apet unfolded the rest of Helen's tale.

6

So the barbarians brought their black boats to these
shores—Apet renewed her tale—ravaging coastal
villages and even striking deeper inland. At last they
camped here on the beach by the plain of Ilios and besieged Troy itself. Prince Hector led the Trojan troops
into battle on the plain, day after day. More than once
the Achaians drove his men to the city's gates, but Troy's
high strong walls always held the barbarians at bay.

The fateful morning came only a few days ago.

I accompanied Helen as she climbed up to the battlements of many-towered Troy to take her place with the
other royal women atop the Scaean Gate. Outside the
gate, on the plain, the Trojan warriors were assembling
in their chariots, with their footmen behind them. From
their camp along the beach the Achaian chariots were
wheeling into formation. Another day of blood and
mayhem was beginning.

But this day would be different. This day Helen would
feel her heart break within her. This day it would become clear to her at last that her Trojan husband was a
coward. And that she loved the one man in all the world
she could never obtain.

For many months Helen had thrilled to see the men
riding out to do battle on the plain of Ilios in their magnificent war chariots, splendid in their bronze armor
and plumed helmets, the morning sun glinting off the
points of their tall spears. She endured the stares and
whispers of the other women; what of it? She was a

princess of Troy, wife of handsome Paris, well loved by his mother, Hecuba, the queen.

Like a giddy child she watched Paris, Hector and all the other princes of Troy as they rode across the bare, dusty battlefield to meet the besieging Achaians. Paris was the handsomest of them all, although his older brother Prince Hector commanded the most respect.

With the foot soldiers and archers trailing behind them, the Trojan chariots advanced across the wind-swept plain toward the shoreline, where the Achaian invaders had drawn up their black ships.

In the distance, the Achaians came forward in their own chariots and brightly plumed helmets. We could not make out their faces, they were too far from the city walls, but I recognized the red eagle emblem on the heavy shield of Menalaos, Helen's former husband, and the golden lion of his brother, proud Agamemnon, High King among the Achaians. Beside them was the chariot of Odysseos, wise and faithful friend to Helen's father, with its blue dolphin painted on his man-tall shield.

The charioteers reined their horses to a halt in the middle of the battlefield, two long lines of armored warriors facing one another while the horses snuffled and stamped nervously. Swirling dust obscured them for several moments, but the never-failing breeze from the sea soon cleared the air.

Heralds advanced from each army, old graybeards in long robes. With their stentorian voices they hurled the usual insults back and forth while the foot soldiers on each side trudged up to the chariot lines and the archers knelt behind them.

Then the chief herald among the Achaians called out,

clear and strong enough for the wind to bear his words to us watching on the high wall:

"Menalaos, King of Sparta, whose wife, the fair Helen, has been stolen from him, challenges Paris, prince of Troy, to single combat, spear to spear, the outcome of this combat to decide which man Helen belongs to."

Helen's hands flew to her lips. Menalaos was willing to risk everything in single combat against Paris. The long war could be ended this very day. Yes, and at the end of the day she would be handed back to her former husband, she feared. Menalaos was a hardened warrior; he would spit her handsome Paris on his spear. The realization made her tremble.

The Trojan heralds withdrew back to Hector's chariot, where they conferred for a seeming eternity with Hector, Paris and the other princes. Why were they arguing among themselves? They were too far away for us to hear.

Hecuba and her daughters and serving women stood near; the proud queen seemed alarmed. Paris was her youngest son, her favorite, and she feared for him each time he rode out to battle. Wild-eyed Cassandra looked back and forth from her brother Hector's distant chariot to Helen, while she absently twirled a lock of her long curled hair, like a child.

Further along the wall, old Priam the king gazed out at the battlefield, his tired ancient eyes squinting painfully beneath shaggy white brows. His bodyservant, a stripling lad too young to be a warrior, spoke into his ear, relating what Priam's own eyes and ears were too weak to gather for themselves.

At last the Trojan heralds went back to the open

space between the lines of facing chariots. I recognized the berobed graybeard who would answer the Achaians: he also served as court announcer when Priam sat on his throne and received guests. Helen could hardly catch her breath; her fate would soon be decided. And Paris'. And the fate of mighty Troy itself.

The herald spoke: "Prince Alexandros, also known as Paris, declines to do battle against Menalaos this day."

Helen was so shocked her knees almost buckled. The women gasped with surprise. Even I gaped with wide eyes. I knew what feelings were running through Helen: she looked as if she wanted to run away, to hide, to die. She did not want to see Paris killed, but to refuse a challenge, to show cowardice in the face of the barbaric invaders . . . that was worse than dying.

Queen Hecuba and the other royal women turned to stare at Helen. There were tears in the queen's eyes; the other women looked at her with pity, or even scorn.

As we watched, unbelieving, Paris had his charioteer wheel his four sleek roan mares out of the Trojan battle line and head back toward the gate.

The Achaian kings and princes, even their common archers and foot soldiers, raised a din of jeering, hooting mockery while Hector and the other Trojans stood silent and mortified.

With a sinking heart Helen watched the man who had taken her from Menalaos' bed, the man for whom she had abandoned her family and her honor, flee shamefully to the safety of the city's walls. His chariot's metal-shod wheels clattered on the stone paving of the gate beneath us, echoing in our ears with the sound of humiliation.

Queen Hecuba drew herself to her full height and

said firmly, "And why should my son honor that Achaian barbarian by accepting his challenge? Paris wouldn't soil his spear on the dog."

She spoke too loudly, as if she were trying to convince everyone crowded along the crenellated walls watching the battlefield below. As if she were trying to convince herself.

To Helen she commanded, "Daughter, retire to your chamber. My son will be weary from the morning's exertion. He will need your ministrations."

Hecuba had always been kind to Helen. When Paris had brought her to Troy she accepted Helen as her newest daughter without a question about her first husband. When Menalaos and his cruel brother Agamemnon led an Achaian war fleet of swift black ships to the shore of Troy and laid siege to the city, the queen did not blame Helen for the war.

The other royal women dared not contradict the queen, so Helen was treated with courtesy and respect. Only Cassandra, Hecuba's half-mad daughter, pointed her trembling finger at her.

"You will bring destruction to Troy," Cassandra had said, that first evil morning when the black ships began to arrive. "You will cause the fall of this house."

Helen feared she was right, I knew. More, she feared being dragged back to uncouth Sparta by a triumphant Menalaos, or worse, slain by him as a faithless wife.

As we turned from the battlements to obey the queen's order I heard Prince Hector's strong, vibrant voice shout from the distant battlefield:

"Menalaos, I will accept your challenge! Pit your spear against mine and we will see who is the stronger."

Helen stopped, her mouth agape. She glanced back

over her shoulder and saw Menalaos climb back up onto his chariot.

"No, Hector, not you," Menalaos shouted back. "I challenged your wife-stealing brother."

Helen could breathe again. Menalaos ordered his charioteer to drive him back to the Achaian camp, along the shore where they had beached their black ships. The armies dispersed. There would be no fighting this morning.

I trailed silently behind Helen, down to the lower platform and across it through the high double doors that led into the palace grounds. The royal courtyard was quiet and empty in the morning sunlight; all the men of fighting age were outside, defending the city. The boys and older men, led by King Priam, were on the walls watching. The women, of course, had their separate place along the battlements.

Swiftly we crossed the courtyard. Helen dared not look at the Palladium, the ancient life-sized statue of ivory and wood that stood weathered and worn in its shrine among the flower beds at the far end of the courtyard. Some believed that the statue was a likeness of Athene, others that it had been carved by the goddess herself. As long as the Palladium remained within Troy's walls, it was said, the city would never fall.

Helen stayed well clear of it. Athene was her enemy, and she knew that this war was the goddess's doing as much as her own. She feared that the Trojans' faith in the goddess was misplaced, that Athene would betray the city to the Achaians one day.

With a nod she bade me to remain in the anteroom. I stayed by the door, silent and still as befitted my duty. Helen knew I would wait for her until my old legs could no longer hold me, if need be. Through all her life I had been her steadfast companion, her childhood nurse, her devoted servant, her loyal friend and guide.

Paris was waiting for Helen in her bedchamber, standing by the open doorway that led onto the balcony, gazing out at the plain of Ilios and, beyond, to the sea. He still wore his bronze breastplate and greaves. His tall shield of seven-layered ox hide stood in the corner. His plumed helmet had been thrown carelessly on the bed.

He was beautiful, her Trojan husband, with flashing dark eyes and a thickly curled mane of midnight-black hair. Standing there by the doorway, framed against the bright blue morning sky, he looked like a young god come down from Olympos.

But for the first time his beauty failed to rouse Helen. Instead of the godlike man who had swept her away from her life as queen of rude, dull Sparta, she saw a spoiled self-centered princeling, a man who had always gotten his way with a smile and the indulgence of his doting mother. She saw a coward who had run away from honorable combat in fear for his life.

It was as if Helen had suddenly awakened from a long, lovely dream. Her eyes were open now, and they did not like what they saw.

"There you are," said Paris, turning from the doorway to smile at her.

She knew that he expected her to unbuckle his breastplate. That would be the beginning that would end with both of them undressed on the bed.

Instead Helen went to the carved wooden chair in the chamber's far corner and stood by it, leaning on its back for a strength she did not feel within herself.

His smile turned rueful. "You are displeased with me."

"Yes," she admitted, her voice trembling. Within her she did not know if she was angry or hurt or ashamed.

"Because I refused Menalaos' challenge?" Paris sounded almost amused at the idea.

"Yes," she repeated, unable to say more without wounding him.

"But I did it for you," he said.

"For me?"

"Of course! Why else?"

Helen did not know what to say, how to reply.

"Dearest Helen," Paris said, "Menalaos would never dare to challenge me unless one of the gods inspired him to such bravery. In all the months that he and his brother have besieged us, has he once called me out for single combat?"

"No," she had to admit.

"You see? This morning a god was in him. Probably Ares, who thrives on men's blood. Or perhaps mighty Zeus himself."

"Do you believe that?" she asked, her voice low, her spirits even lower at the excuse her husband was inventing.

He was smiling his brightest at her. "What would have happened if Ares or Zeus or one of the other Olympians, in the guise of Menalaos, had spitted me on his spear?"

"Don't even speak of that!" Helen blurted. "Please!"

"But suppose it happened," Paris insisted. "You would be returned to your former husband. You would go back with Menalaos to dingy old Sparta."

"Or be slain by him."

"You see? That's why I refused to face him, or whichever god it was inhabiting his body. I couldn't allow that to happen to you."

Almost he convinced her. "It might have been Athene," she murmured, more to herself than to him.

Paris nodded, smiling. "Yes, perhaps it was Athene. What better way to hurt you than by slaying me?"

He stepped closer to her and spread out his arms. Numbly, Helen began to unbuckle his bright bronze breastplate. Paris placed his hands on her slim shoulders, and I saw her flinch at his touch. He scowled briefly, but said nothing.

Someone scratched at the door.

"Who would dare?" Paris grumbled.

"Perhaps it is the king," Helen whispered.

Paris gave her a disappointed frown, then called out, "Enter!"

The stout oak door swung inward and Prince Hector strode into the room. He had removed his armor and was clad only in the knee-length linen chiton beneath it. I could see the creases the straps had made on his broad, strong shoulders.

"I thought I'd find you here," Hector said to his brother. His voice was low yet strong, edged with iron.

"Where else?" Paris said carelessly.

"You disgraced yourself this morning," Hector said. "You disgraced all of us."

Paris was slightly taller than his older brother, although Hector was built more sturdily. Hector's face was stronger, too; not as beautiful as Paris' but steadfast, with a broad brow and dauntless brown eyes that never wavered. His hair and neatly cropped beard were reddish chestnut, almost auburn.

Paris stood up to his brother. "Why should I risk my wife's fate on a lucky spear thrust? You may think me a coward, but I love her much too dearly to give Menalaos a chance to take her away."

Brave, honest Hector had no response to his brother's words. His clear brown eyes glanced at Helen, then returned to face Paris. The stern expression on his face eased a little; some of the tension seemed to ebb out of his body.

"I suppose I can't blame you," he said at last, his voice so soft I could barely make out his words.

Paris laughed and clapped Hector on the shoulder. "Send out the heralds to tell the barbarians we'll meet them on the battlefield this afternoon. After a good meal and a bit of rest we'll chase them back into the sea."

Hector's taut lips relaxed into a slight smile. "Very well," he said. "This afternoon."

He nodded to Helen and left us, closing the door gently behind him. Paris stretched out his arms again, waiting for Helen to begin unstrapping his armor, knowing that he would soon be undressing her.

Yet even as Helen stepped toward her husband her head turned toward the door. I could see from the troubled look on her face that her thoughts were on Hector. It was he who shouldered the burden of this war, not Paris. As the eldest son of aged Priam, it was Hector who directed the defense of Troy, Hector who led the chariots each day into the dust and blood of battle. Except for the invincible Achilles, Hector was the most feared warrior of them all.

He never complained, never blamed his younger brother for bringing this calamity to Troy. He was strong and faithful and valiant. Nor did he blame Helen. Indeed, he hardly ever glanced at her. But she stared at the door that he had closed behind him.

It was at that moment, even as Helen began to undress her husband, that I realized she had fallen in love with Hector, crown prince of Troy, her husband's brother. The realization shocked me like the searing agony of a branding iron.

Helen loved Hector! He had no way of knowing that she loved him, and even if he did find out he would spurn her. Even if he were not already married and a father he would never glance at his brother's wife.

I saw that Helen's eyes were filling with tears. And I could hear the goddess Aphrodite whispering, Beautiful Helen, whom every man desires, it is your fate to fall in love with the one man on earth who will never love you.

7

As soon as Paris left Helen for the afternoon's fighting, donned once more in his gleaming armor, she summoned me to her. Since childhood I had been the one person she could confide in.

I knew what was tearing at her heart. I should have realized it sooner; perhaps then I could have done something to help my dearest. Helen gazed at me with all the pain and bewilderment she felt brimming from her eyes. I could do nothing except hold out my arms to her. She burst into tears and ran to me.

Burying her face in the warmth of my embrace, Helen blurted, "Oh, Apet, Apet, I love him but he doesn't love me. He *can't* love me, not now or ever. How can I live?

How can I watch him risk his life day after day because of me?"

"Prince Hector," I murmured.

"What can I do?" she pleaded. "Where can I turn?"

I wrapped my arms around her and rocked her softly as I had done when she was a baby. The only wisdom that I could think of was, "You must go to the goddess and ask her aid."

"To Aphrodite?"

"She is your protectress and guide. She will give you the strength to find the right path."

"Yes," Helen agreed, wiping her tears with the back of her hands. "Aphrodite."

As we walked hurriedly through the empty corridors of the palace I could hear the city's populace roaring and cheering from up on the walls, their shouts like the howls of a wild beast. The queen was up there with all the royal women, I knew, including Hector's wife, Andromache. I could not bear the thought of letting them see Helen so unhappy.

The temple was dark and chill. At Helen's command the five priestesses who tended the votive fire beneath the goddess' statue removed themselves to the outer chamber. I alone went with Helen to stand before the altar. The graceful marble likeness of beautiful Aphrodite rose three times taller than my own height, and still it only hinted at the goddess' power and splendor.

Aphrodite had ever been Helen's guide, her protectress. Even now she defended Troy against the jealousy of Athene before almighty Zeus atop lofty Mount Olympos, the home of the gods. In the dimly lit temple her face was in shadow, but I felt her painted eyes gazing down upon Helen as she sank to her knees at the goddess' feet, miserable and confused.

"Beautiful Aphrodite, guardian of my heart, how can I live in such wretchedness?" Helen breathed, so softly that I could barely hear her words. "How can I remain married to Paris when it is Hector whom I truly love?"

I dared not look up at the goddess' face. The temple felt cold, silent and empty. What Aphrodite imparted to my dear one I know not, but I know what was in my heart, the sad truth of her fate: Helen, your path has ever been difficult. Great beauty such as yours stirs the passions of mortals and even the jealousy of goddesses.

8

All that long afternoon Helen spent in the temple of Aphrodite, remembering the past, waiting and yearning for the goddess to inspire her with wisdom. I grew tired, standing there in the shadows of the silent temple. My eyes grew heavy and I felt empty, exhausted, a desperate sense of dread crowding around me like the shadows of night or the shades of the dead who had already been slain on the battlefield outside the city's walls. My tired old legs throbbed with pain. Quietly, while Helen prayed to the goddess, I stretched out on the polished stone floor and closed my eyes.

I must have drowsed off, for the next thing I remember is Helen nudging me gently with the toe of her sandal.

I sat up, my face burning with shame. "I . . . I am sorry,

my precious. You were at the altar such a long time. Look, night is falling."

Through the columned entrance of the temple we could see in the courtyard beyond that the sky was violet with the last dying moments of sunset. A chill breeze was wafting in from the sea.

Helen helped me to my feet. "Oh, Apet, you have been my faithful servant as long as I can remember, since I was a baby suckling at your breast."

"Aye, my nursling. And I will serve you until death parts us."

In the deepening shadows of the temple I saw Helen's face grow pensive. "My own baby daughter must be watching me from the dim shadows of Hades. I will be with her soon. I will join her in death."

"No, don't say that! Don't even think it!"

"Apet, I cannot let Hector die: not for me, not to keep me from the hands of Menalaos."

"Hector fights to defend Troy against the barbarians," I told her. "And his death has been foretold; there is nothing you can do to change his destiny."

"The goddess thinks otherwise."

Standing on the cold stone floor I gazed up at the statue of Aphrodite, towering above us in the shadows of the silent temple. The golden glow from the oil lamps that were never permitted to go out did not reach as high as her painted face. Yet I sensed the goddess watching over us.

My blood ran cold. "The goddess spoke to you?"

"Not in words that I could hear," said Helen, her eyes also on Aphrodite. "She spoke in my heart."

Almost afraid to doubt her, still I heard myself ask, "What . . . did the goddess tell you?"

Her voice hardly more than a breathless whisper, Helen replied, "She told me that there is neither joy nor love in the path I must follow."

"No . . ."

"Responsibility. That is what the goddess spoke of to me, Apet. I must accept my responsibilities just as Hector has, unflinchingly, without complaint. I must cease behaving like a foolish girl and start to act as an adult woman. Only then can I save Hector from the death that awaits him."

"A hard path to follow," I said.

Helen nodded cheerlessly.

"And what of Paris?"

Her eyes flared. "He must never know! Hector himself must never know! I will do what I must to end this war."

Pulling her cloak around her shoulders, Helen started toward the temple's entrance.

"I will speak with the king," she said, as I hurried to follow her.

"The king?"

"Yes," she said. "I must see Priam."

It was simple enough to arrange. The day's fighting was over, the men were back inside the city walls. The lad who was stationed as a token guard outside the door to Helen's chambers served as a messenger. He was very impressed with his own importance when she gave him her message for Priam.

"Tell the king that I seek a private audience with him," Helen said to the boy. "As quickly as he can find time to see me."

"I will fly to the king like an eagle," he said, his eyes shining.

I leveled a finger at him. "Better to fly like a bee, lad. They go straight to their destination instead of circling as the birds of prey do."

He ran off.

Paris was not in Helen's bedchamber when we entered. Instantly, Helen looked fearful. Had he been killed? Wounded? No, I thought; someone would have told us. Helen's fear quickly turned to guilt, because she realized that if Paris were dead it would simplify the decision she had to make.

She hurried across the chamber and quietly opened the door that led into his. Paris was sprawled on his bed, snoring softly. His face was smeared with dirt runneled by rivulets of sweat. His lovely dark hair was tangled and matted. His hands and bare arms bore fresh scratches but no true wounds.

A month ago, even a day ago, she would have gone to his side and wakened him with soft kisses and honeyed words. Now she could not. She could not make herself step to her husband's side and offer him the love that she should have felt for him. I could see that it made Helen feel sad, as if a part of her life had been lost. Yet we both knew that even worse was to come.

While twilight deepened into dark night Helen remained there in the doorway, watching her sleeping husband, tormented by guilt and hopeless love and the pressing weight of responsibility.

I heard a scratching at the outer door. Opening it, I saw the lad we had sent to the king, accompanied now by a grown man, one of the palace guards decked in a stiff leather jerkin studded with bronze.

I bowed them into the anteroom, then went to Helen.

"My lady," I whispered to her. "The king's messenger is here."

Helen pulled herself away from the sight of her sleeping husband and turned to see the messenger.

"The king will see you immediately, my lady," he said, once she had quietly shut the door to Paris' chamber. "I am sent to escort you to him."

9

I followed behind Helen and the tall, dark-bearded guard through the corridors of the palace. Men and women both greeted Helen courteously as we passed. If they blamed her for the war and the harpies of death that plucked their loved ones from them, they made no show of it. Queen Hecuba had made it clear that her son's wife was not to be reproached. What the queen expected, the king enforced. The people of Troy's royal palace may not have loved Helen, but they dared not show her disrespect.

The walls of the corridors were decorated with graceful paintings of flowering green meadows and peaceful horses, with birds soaring among the soft clouds scattered across a gentle blue sky. No such scenes had occurred at Troy since Helen had arrived, I realized. She had destroyed the peace and tranquillity of this beautiful city.

"How went the day's fighting?" Helen asked our escort.

"Well enough," he said. "The barbarians pressed us

almost back to the Scaean Gate at first, but Prince Hector rallied our warriors and drove them back to their own ramparts. By then it was growing dark, so both sides agreed to end the battle and wait for the morrow."

"Was Prince Hector hurt?" Helen blurted.

"Not he!" the guard replied proudly. "He took men with his spear the way a cook spits chunks of meat."

The guard led us not to the royal reception hall, but to Priam's private quarters. He opened the oaken door, then stepped aside to let Helen and me through. He shut the door softly behind us, remaining outside in the corridor.

Priam was standing by the window, gazing out into the darkening night. He wore a simple wool chiton, dyed deep blue, and a heavy shawl over his shoulders to ward off the night chill. His only adornment was the royal signet ring on his gnarled finger. I doubted that he could take it off, even if he wanted to. He was very old, bent with years, his white beard halfway down his chest. This war was killing him, I could tell.

It was too dark outside to see anything. Whatever he was staring at was inside his mind, I thought. The little room was lit by two oil lamps ensconced on either side of the door. Their fitful flames threw flickering shadows between us. There was no one else in the room, not even a servant to wait upon the king. Had he guessed what Helen was about to say? Did he realize that she wanted complete privacy?

He turned toward Helen with hardly a glance at me. I was her maidservant, her silent shadow, not a real person as far as the king was concerned.

"It went well this afternoon," he said at last.

"I am pleased," she said.

Gesturing to the circular table in the middle of the room, he said, "Please, sit and be comfortable. Would you like some refreshment? Something to eat?"

"No, thank you. Nothing."

I stood by the door as Helen took one of the carved wooden chairs and the king sank slowly, painfully, into another. "I believe I'll take some wine," he said, reaching for the pitcher on the table, beaded with condensation.

"Allow me, please," Helen said. He smiled and leaned back in his chair as she poured a cup of wine for him.

"You were not on the wall to watch this afternoon," the king said gently. It was more of a question than a reproach.

"I was in the temple of Aphrodite, seeking guidance," she replied.

"Ah." Priam smiled at her, a pleased expression on his wrinkled face. "And did the goddess enlighten you?"

She had to swallow down a catch in her throat before she could choke out her reply. "Yes."

The door suddenly swung open and Hector stepped in. "You called for me, Father?" Then he recognized Helen sitting there and said merely, "Helen."

With his broad shoulders and straight back, Hector seemed to fill the room. Priam pointed to the chair next to him as he said, "Helen's message was to the effect that she had something important to say. About the war, I presume."

Suddenly Helen could not speak. She merely nodded, her tongue locked inside her mouth.

Hector poured himself a cup of wine as they both waited for Helen to say something. She had not wanted him here, had not asked for his presence. Yet Priam had summoned him. More and more, the old king was turning the responsibilities of leadership to his eldest son. Even now he chose to have Hector listen to what Helen had to say.

At last she forced myself to speak up. "This is not easy for me."

Hector nodded understandingly.

"This war is my fault," she started to say.

Hector smiled easily at her. "My passionate brother had a little to do with it, too."

"If I had refused to come here to Troy with him there would be no war," Helen said.

"No, that is not true at all," Priam objected. "Our lives are determined by the fates and not even the gods themselves can undo what Destiny has chosen for us."

"Still," she said, her voice sinking even lower, "Agamemnon and Achaians besiege Troy in order to return me to Menalaos."

"My dearest daughter," said Priam, "it may be true that you are the excuse for this war. But you are not the reason for it."

I could see the confusion on Helen's face. "What do you mean?"

Hector explained, "Agamemnon and the other Achaian princes have long sought a way to break Troy's hold on the Dardanelles. He wants to be able to sail into the Sea of Black Waters without paying tribute to us."

"But Agamemnon could never get the other kings and princes of Achaia to join him in war against us," Priam added.

"Until my brother gave him the excuse he needed," Hector said.

"It is not Paris' fault alone," Helen said quickly, as if

someone else spoke the words for her. "I bear as much responsibility as he. More, even."

They both shook their heads. I knew what was in their minds. A woman cannot be responsible for such mighty affairs of state. A woman could only be a pawn, an object of desire, a passive onlooker, helpless before the strength of men. An excuse, not a reason. Men make decisions. Men make wars.

"You must not blame yourself for this war," Priam said gently. "It is not your fault, Helen. It is the gods who have brought this calamity upon us."

Her eyes were on Hector, though.

He returned her gaze in thoughtful silence. At last he said, "Paris was wrong to take you from Menalaos. If there is any fault here, it is his."

It was useless to argue with them. Instead, Helen insisted, "Even if I am not the cause of the war, I can stop it."

Hector's eyes were locked on hers. "You cannot . . ."

"I can," she said firmly. "I can return to Menalaos. Then Agamemnon and all the others will have to leave."

Priam shook his white-maned head. "I doubt that they will."

"They will have to," she said. "What reason can Agamemnon give the other Achaian kings once I have returned to Menalaos?"

Hector snapped out a single word. "Loot."

Helen was not convinced. "Ask for Odysseos to come into the city to discuss ending the war. He is wise—"

"Crafty," Hector said.

"He is my father's firm friend. And he is high in the councils of the Achaians. Tell him that I will willingly return to Menalaos and see what he thinks of it."

Hector stretched out his hand toward her, then drew it back as if he suddenly realized that he was reaching for a thing forbidden.

"What do you think my brother will say to your proposal?" he asked her.

Helen longed for him to tell her that *he* did not want her to leave Troy. But she knew he never would, never could.

"Paris will object, of course," she answered. Then she turned to Priam. "But he cannot overrule the king."

Priam sank his bearded chin into his hands, as if the weight of this decision was too much for him.

"If only the Hatti would answer my call for help," he murmured.

"The Hatti?" she asked.

"A mighty empire," replied Hector, "far to the east. They have been our allies for generations."

"I sent an emissary to them when the Achaians first drew up their black boats on our shore," Priam said. "Their army should come to our aid soon."

Helen glanced at Hector. Gently, Hector said to his father, "If the Hatti have not come in all the time since we sent our emissary to them, Father, they are not coming at all."

"Not so," argued the king, his brow wrinkling. "Their capital is far to the east. They will come . . . any day now . . . they *must* come!"

Hector smiled sadly and said nothing more to disillusion his father.

Priam shook his white head. "The Achaians send back to their homeland for fresh warriors. We have only the villagers nearby to help us. The Hatti are our only chance to win this war."

Both men looked at Helen. The brief surge of hope she had felt sank away like water seeping into sand.

"Call Odysseos," she said. "Arrange a truce and offer to make peace."

Priam blinked his watery eyes at her. I could see the conflict in his soul.

Hector said to his father, "Once we try to negotiate they will think we are weakening. It would be better to drive the Achaians away in fair battle than to barter for peace. Otherwise they will take Helen and then continue the war."

"Yes, I agree," Priam said, with a sigh. "But we have not been able to drive them away, have we?"

"Achilles was not on the field of battle this afternoon, Father. Perhaps he is hurt, or ill."

Priam's red-rimmed eyes flashed with sudden hope. "Their camp has been struck by disease more than once."

"Let us beat them off and drive them into the sea before Achilles returns to the battle," Hector urged. "Then there will be no need to send Helen to them."

Priam seemed lost in thought.

"What guarantees have we that they will leave us in peace once Helen has been returned to them?" Hector asked. "Agamemnon wants to break our power! He's come too far to sail meekly back home without destroying us."

Hector did not want Helen to leave Troy! He was adamantly against the idea! I could see her cheeks flush with emotion. She knew it was foolish, but she could not help but think that he cared for her, perhaps without even realizing it in his conscious mind.

Then Hector added, "It would break Paris' heart to part with Helen. Just as it would break mine to part with Andromache. No man willingly gives up his wife."

Helen's face sank. Hector was thinking of his brother, of his city, not of her.

Priam gazed at Helen for long moments. I held my breath.

Finally the king said, "If Achilles does not come out to fight tomorrow morning, we will do our utmost to drive the Achaians into the sea. But if he is in their battle line, we will ask Odysseos for a truce to discuss terms of peace."

Hector glanced at Helen once more, then turned back to his father. "Agreed," he said.

Helen fled the room as quickly as she decently could, fighting to hold back her tears as she ran through the corridors of the dark and silent palace.

III

▼

THE DOWNFALL
OF TROY

1

"I t was three days ago," said Apet to me, "when Helen realized that she loved Hector, not his brother. That was the day that she fled to the temple of Aphrodite to seek the goddess' help."

"When she told King Priam she would return to Menalaos to stop the war," I said.

The fire was down to nothing but cold ashes by the time Apet finished her tale. The sky to the east was beginning to turn milky white with the coming dawn.

Apet stared at me with her coal-black eyes. "I wonder, Hittite, if you are the answer to her prayer."

"Me?" I scoffed at the idea.

"Perhaps Aphrodite has sent you to Helen," Apet murmured. "The gods move in strange paths, far beyond our poor powers of understanding."

I shook my head, refusing to accept the possibility. The old crone had told me too much, especially about Prince Hector. It's a mistake to know your enemies too well, I thought. Better that they be faceless, soulless figures to be cut down without thinking about their loves, their fears, their hopes.

"Now you know how Helen came to Troy," Apet said, her voice dry and hoarse. "Now you know how her heart aches."

I nodded and got slowly to my feet. My legs were stiff from sitting for so long. I reached down and helped her to get up.

"What do you intend to do, Hittite?" the old woman asked me.

"What I must, Egyptian," I replied. "My wife and children are in this camp, among Agamemnon's slaves. I must save them."

Her dark eyes lit with understanding. "Then you will fight against Hector."

"Yes."

"Perhaps you will be the instrument the fates have chosen to deal him his death."

I didn't answer, but I thought it more likely that I would be one of those to die in the morning's battle.

"Come," I said at last, "I'll escort you to the gate. From there the Trojans can take you back to the city."

I took up my spear and shield. Apet pulled up the hood of her robe and followed me, silent as a shadow again, to the ramshackle gate in the parapet. A team of men were working in the dawn's pale light to reinforce the gate with additional planks. I thought it would be better to tear down the ramp leading up to the gate, so that the Trojan chariots couldn't rush up on it. But these Achaians seemed to have no head for engineering, or any other military finesse.

We squeezed through the planks of the gate while the workmen hammered away and their foreman frowned at us. Out beyond, the plain was dotted by hundreds of tiny points of light: the last smoldering remains of the Trojans' campfires.

I walked Apet down the rampway and out onto the bare earth of the battleground perhaps a hundred paces before a Trojan sentry cried, "Halt! You there! Stop!"

He was alone, armed with a spear as I was. He held his shield before him as he slowly, reluctantly, approached us.

"This woman is a servant of Princess Helen," I said, keeping my voice firm and even. "She is to be returned to the city."

Without waiting for him to reply I turned and headed back toward the gate. Apet will be safe enough, I told myself. The lad will take her to his officer who will see to it that she gets back to her mistress.

I saw men up atop the rampart, silhouetted against the brightening sky: archers sticking handfuls of arrows into the sand, skinny wide-eyed youths piling up javelins and stones for slinging. Footmen were gathering behind the gate now, stacking up spears in preparation for battle. Servants were strapping armor onto their lords, who looked grim and tense as I walked alone past them. By the time I got back to my own men, the sky was turning pink. The dawn bugle sounded. I would get no sleep at all before the battle started.

Odysseos clambered down from his boat in bronze breastplate, arm guards and greaves. Behind him came four young men bearing his helmet, his heavy oxhide shield and spears of various lengths and weights.

"Bring your men and come with me, Hittite," he commanded, smiling grimly. "Mighty Agamemnon has given us the honor of defending the gate."

I gestured to my men to follow me. As we paced briskly toward the gate I asked Odysseos, "My lord, may I make a suggestion?"

He nodded as he took the helmet from one of his men and pulled it over his curly dark locks.

"It's not enough to defend the gate, sire. You must be prepared for Hector to break through it."

He gave me a sidelong glance as he fastened his helmet strap beneath his chin. With the nosepiece down and the cheek flaps pulled tight, there was little I could see of his face except for eyes and curly beard. "Don't you think we can hold the gate?"

"That's in the hands of the gods, my lord. But we should be prepared for the worst."

"You don't have a very high opinion of us, do you, Hittite?" With his helmet strapped on tightly, I could not see the expression on Odysseos' face, but I thought I heard the ghost of a smile in his voice.

We were at the gate now. It looked flimsier than ever in my eyes, despite the extra planks the work crew had hammered onto it. There weren't even any sizable logs or tree trunks bolstering it; all the trees inside the camp had been cut down long ago and used for fuel. Armed and armored men milled around behind it. I thought that they expected to lean against it and hold it in place with their weight when the Trojans tried to push it open.

Pointing to the ramshackle pile of boards, I explained, "My lord, if Hector breaks through this gate his chariots will run wild through the camp."

Odysseos nodded grimly. "So what would you do?"

"I would take as many men as could be spared and erect a wall of shields on either side of the gate. If the Trojans break through they will be trapped between the two walls."

"And our men could spear them from behind their wall of shields!"

"Archers could fire at them point-blank," I added.

"Yes," he said. "I see." Turning, he called to one of his servants. "Find Antiklos. Hurry!"

It was a good plan, I was convinced. And it would have worked well . . . if we'd had the time to put it into action.

But suddenly the early-morning air was split by the blast of dozens of horns. I looked up and saw the men atop the rampart pointing, wild-eyed.

"Here they come!"

2

Through the gaps between the gate's boards I saw a formation of chariots pouring out of Troy's Scaean Gate and boiling across the plain, raising an enormous cloud of dust as they raced toward us.

Odysseos pushed me aside and peered through the gate. With a shake of his helmeted head he muttered, "They won't get through the gate with chariots. The horses will bolt halfway up the ramp."

The horses have more sense than the men, I thought.

"They'll have to dismount and charge the gate on foot," Odysseos said.

But I wondered why Hector was leading such a wild charge toward the gate. What did he have in mind? The crown prince of Troy was no vainglorious fool. He knew that his chariot horses would not gallop blindly into a barrier, especially a barrier that now bristled with spears.

I had never seen such a cloud of dust before. Even considering that there were scores of chariots racing across the worn-bare plain, the dust they raised was enormous, choking, impenetrable. I pitied any foot soldiers trying to follow those chariots.

The formation of chariots plunged ahead, racing closer to us, closer. They were spread out in a broad line, I saw, not the kind of wedge formation that we Hatti used to break an enemy's line. It seemed to me that each chariot was dragging something: a collection of brush, dead limbs from trees and bushes. That's what was raising the thick cloud of dust, I realized.

And then, in an instant, Hector's wily plan became clear.

Just as the chariots approached to within an arrow's shot of the ramp they swerved to right and left. Out of that cloud of blinding dust raced a team of six powerful horses, blindfolded, three of them on each side of a massive tree trunk. Young men rode atop each horse, flattening themselves on their backs and necks, flogging them with slim whips to urge them on. The tree trunk that the team carried bobbed and jounced as the horses pounded blindly toward us. The youngsters guiding the horses wore kerchiefs over their noses and mouths; their faces and bodies were caked with gray dust.

A battering ram, I realized. A battering ram driven by six wildly charging horses.

The men up atop the rampart started firing arrows and hurling javelins. A few struck the horses but they kept plunging wildly ahead, spittle flying from their gasping mouths. One of the youths guiding the horses took an arrow between the shoulder blades and slid off his mount to be trampled by the others behind him.

And then the battering ram smashed into the gate, shattering it to splinters. The horses plowed on blindly across the beach and splashed into the foaming sea while Hector's chariots streamed up the ramp and into the heart of the camp.

Footmen and nobles alike scattered, screaming for their lives, as Hector and other Trojans speared left and right from their wheeling chariots.

"Stand fast!" I shouted to my men. We formed a line behind our shields and leveled our spears at the chariots racing past us. The Trojans kept their distance from us, driving deeper into the camp, toward the boats lining the beach.

I had lost sight of Odysseos. Footmen were running down from the crest of the rampart, staggering and tumbling in their haste. A few knelt here and there to fire arrows at the chariots.

A dozen men cannot stop an army, even if they are disciplined Hatti soldiers. But I ordered my little squad forward as the chariots poured through the shattered gate in a blur of madly charging horses and armored spearmen.

"Kill the horses!" I shouted to them.

Some of the footmen behind us must have heard my command. Arrows began to fly at the horses. Several were hit, stumbling to the ground, spilling the warriors in the chariots. My men and I made short work of them before they could struggle to their feet.

But Trojan footmen were climbing over the rampart now and firing down at us. Little Karsh took a javelin through his throat and fell face-first, spewing blood. We would soon be overwhelmed, I saw, if we remained where we stood.

"Forward!" I roared, and the eleven of us charged into the Trojan footmen swarming down the rampart. They scattered before us like leaves blown on the wind.

Screams and curses filled the air. Blood was everywhere. An arrow nicked my bare calf, a pinprick that I ignored. Another one of my men went down, but we closed ranks behind our shields and continued pressing forward.

Ahead of us the Trojan chariots were wheeling and careening in a melee of killing and bloodlust. All semblance of order and control was gone now. The beach was too narrow for organized maneuvers, each chariot was operating on its own. The armored noblemen didn't step down from their chariots this day; they fought from inside them, spearing Achaians while their charioteers drove the maddened horses deeper into the camp.

There was little dust in the air, there on the sandy beach. In the distance I could see the boats of Agamemnon, with their proud golden lions emblazoned on their prows. The Achaians seemed to be making a stand there, of sorts. Other boats were already burning. Giant Ajax stood huge and grimacing on the prow of his own boat, hurling benches and paddles down on the Trojan chariots.

I led my men toward Agamemnon's boats. I could see a mass of women huddled against the side of a boat, practically in the lapping waves of the sea. My sons must be there, I thought. With Aniti. Terrified. Awaiting death.

We cut our way through the Trojan footmen, heading toward that boat. A ragged line of Achaians was forming there, behind their man-tall shields. I heard Odysseos' high-pitched battle cry from somewhere in the struggle. Trojan chariots were milling about, the warriors jabbing at the Achaians with their long spears.

Like a machine we marched toward the boat and the chariots attacking it. We were a wall of shields, with bristling spears taking the blood of any man foolish enough to come near us. A chariot wheeled about, the warrior in it looking surprised at the sight of us advancing upon him. His charioteer urged the matched pair of roans at us, but they balked at our spear points. He swerved them to our right and I led my men into a charge. We killed the closer horse and slammed into the chariot with our shields. I myself dispatched the warrior with a spear thrust to his unprotected side. The charioteer leaped out of the chariot and ran away into the milling, roaring, fighting mass.

With our backs to the boat's curving black hull, we joined the defensive line and killed any fool who came within the length of our spears. But their sheer numbers forced us back, slowly, inexorably, until my feet were splashing in the water.

The women were behind us, screaming and wailing. The Trojan chariots dared not approach us as long as we held our line of shields with our blood-soaked spears leveled. Even the footmen kept their distance, pelting us with javelins and arrows. Two more of my men went down. It was only a matter of time before we were all killed.

And then a roar shook the camp.

"Achilles!"

"The Myrmidones!"

The Trojans looked to their right, their faces white with sudden fear. I urged my men forward and the footmen before us melted away. As we rounded the prow of the boat I saw down the beach that a formation of chariots was charging against the Trojans. Standing in the foremost chariot was a man in splendid golden armor who could only have been Achilles.

The Trojans ran. They broke before the spearpoints of Achilles and his Myrmidones and ran like mice. Footmen scrambled back over the palisade. Chariots raced for the gate. One of the Trojan warriors tried to rally the chariots and make a stand but it was useless: Hector himself could not stop the sudden panic that raced through them.

"It's Achilles!" said a joyful voice. I turned and saw Odysseos standing beside me, his helmet and armor grimed with dust and blood, his shield split and battered, a broken spear in his free hand.

"Achilles has saved us," Odysseos said gratefully.

But the battle was not yet over. The retreating Trojans were still hurling arrows and javelins at us as they scrambled up the rampart. A chariot raced past us and I recognized Hector standing in it, spattered with the blood of his victims. He half-turned and looked straight at me.

The world seemed to slow down. Even the roar and groans of battle dwindled as if my head had been ducked under water. Time itself seemed to stretch out like soft taffy. I could see Hector standing in his chariot, his eyes focus on me; see him raise his heavy, bloody spear; see him hurl it at me. I tried to raise my shield but it was as if it weighed a hundred times its normal weight. Hector's heavy spear soared languidly through the air, directly at me.

I ducked, but everything went black.

3

When I opened my eyes again I saw nothing but the clear blue sky. Am I dead? I wondered.

Then Poletes' scrawny face slid into my view, with his mangy beard and bulging eyes. I realized that I was lying flat on my back.

I heard myself ask, "What happened?" My throat felt raw, burning.

Poletes grinned at me and held out my helmet in both his bony hands. I saw a dent in it that had not been there before.

"Your iron helmet saved your life," he said, looking amused at it all. "Not even mighty Hector's spear could penetrate it."

I tried to sit up, but the world went spinning and I sagged back onto the sand. I waited until the spinning stopped, then tried again.

"You took a hard knock," Poletes said, helping me to a sitting position.

My head thundered. I looked around. The battle seemed to be over, or at least it had moved away from Agamemnon's boats. The beach was littered with the bodies of the slain. I saw several of my men sitting not far off. Magro was awkwardly winding a strip of gray cloth around his sword arm; it seeped blood.

Sitting there, still feeling woozy, I called him to me.

He sank to his knees beside me, looking grim. I realized that it had been a long time since our squad's clown had cracked a joke. Or even a smile.

"I saw Karsh go down," I said.

"He's dead. The Hurrian, too."

"Your arm?"

"Took an arrow. It's not deep."

"Any others killed?"

He shook his head. "Nicks and cuts, that's all. The gods were with us."

But not with little Karsh, I thought. Not with the quiet, uncomplaining Hurrian.

"The battle?"

"It's over. The Trojans are back behind their own walls again." Yet Magro did not look happy.

"What happened?"

Poletes interrupted Magro. "A fantastic day! A day that even the gods will long remember."

Before I could shut him up, the old storyteller exclaimed, "The Myrmidones came boiling out of their camp like a stampede of stallions and slew hundreds, thousands of the Trojans!"

I knew he was exaggerating, but I heard myself say, "They were terrified of Achilles."

"And well they should be," Poletes went on, "but it was not Achilles who led the charge."

"Not Achilles?"

"Even with Hector and his brothers ravaging through the camp, the mighty Achilles stayed in his hut and refused to fight."

"But who—"

"Patrokles!"

"That tender-faced boy?"

Nodding eagerly, Poletes said, "Patrokles put on his master's golden armor and led the Myrmidones in the counterattack. Hector and his brothers must have thought it was Achilles, the magnificent slayer of men. The Trojans were shocked and ran out of the camp, back to the very walls of Troy."

"They thought they faced Achilles," I muttered.

"Of course they did. A god filled Patrokles with battle fury. Everyone in the camp thought he was too soft for fighting, yet he drove the Trojans back to their own gates and slew dozens with his own hand."

I cocked an eyebrow at "dozens." War stories grow larger with each telling, and this one was already becoming overblown, scarcely an hour after it happened.

Magro spoke up, "But then the gods turned against Patrokles. Hector spitted him on his spear, in front of the Trojan gates."

"And stripped Achilles' golden armor from his dead body," Poletes added. "The Myrmidones retreated back to camp while the Trojans slipped behind their high walls and barred their gates."

My head was buzzing as if some muffled drum was thumping away in my ears. The gods play their games, I thought. They give Patrokles a moment of glory but then take their price for it.

"Now Achilles sits in his hut and covers his head with ashes. He swears a mighty vengeance against Hector and all of Troy."

"So now he'll fight," I said.

"Tomorrow morning," Magro said. "Achilles will

meet Hector in single combat. The heralds have arranged it."

Single combat between Hector and Achilles. Hector was much the bigger of the two, an experienced fighter, cool and intelligent even in the fury of battle. Achilles was no doubt faster, though smaller, and fueled by the kind of rage that drives men to impossible feats. Only one of them would walk away from the combat, I knew. And I remembered Helen telling me that Hector's death had been foretold.

Then I realized that the humming in my head was really the distant wailing and keening from the Myrmidones' camp. I knew it was a matter of form for the women to mourn. But there were men's deep voices among the cries of the women, and a drum beating a slow, sorrowful dirge.

I got slowly to my feet, still feeling shaky. Down the beach, where the Myrmidones' camp was, a huge bonfire suddenly flared up, sending a cloud of sooty black smoke skyward.

"Achilles mourns his friend," Poletes said. I could see that the excess of grief unnerved him slightly.

I realized that we were still in front of Agamemnon's line of boats. My wife and sons must be nearby.

To Magro I said, "Take the men back to Odysseos' area. I'll join you before the sun sets."

My head still spun slightly, and the Myrmidones' mournful drumbeat was painful to my ears. I walked somewhat unsteadily toward the group of women gathered around wounded warriors, tending them with salves and cloth windings.

Suddenly my stomach heaved. I staggered to the shoreline and, one hand on the sticky tar of the boat, doubled over and retched into the sea. One of the women came to me, her eyes questioning.

"I'm all right," I told her, wiping my mouth with the back of my hand.

She handed me a cloth soaked in cool water. I dabbed it on my lips, then cleaned my hands with it.

"Your leg is injured," she said.

I looked down and saw that a slice on my calf was oozing blood. "It's nothing," I said.

"You're one of the Hittites?" she asked.

"Yes. Where is Aniti?" Before she could say anything I added, "My wife."

Her eyes went wide for an instant, then she pointed to the next boat, up the beach. "I saw her over there with her children."

I thanked her and, splashing through the ankle-deep water, headed for the next boat.

Aniti was sitting on the sand while my two boys were at the water's edge, splashing in the ripples running up the beach. She saw me approaching and jumped to her feet.

"You're all right?" I asked.

She nodded wordlessly.

"I can see the boys are unharmed."

"I kept them aboard the boat, so that they couldn't see the killing."

I nodded back at her.

"You're hurt."

"A scratch. I took a knock on the head, also. From Prince Hector himself."

"You sound proud of it."

I made myself smile. "It's not many men who can say they took a blow from Hector and lived to tell of it."

She looked away from me, toward the boys, then said in a low voice, "I'm glad you weren't killed."

"Aniti . . . I . . ." My tongue refused to work properly.

"You want to take the boys from me, I know."

"I want to take them out of slavery. You, too," I heard myself say. "I'm trying to get Agamemnon to release you. The three of you."

She smiled bitterly. "The boys he will give you without quarrel. But not me. He values me too highly."

My fists clenched. But I held my temper and said merely, "We'll see."

Then I turned away from her and headed back to where my men were readying themselves for their evening meal.

4

Despite the mourning rites among the Myrmidones, the rest of the camp was agog about the impending match between Achilles and Hector. There was almost a holiday mood among the men. As I made my way back to Odysseos' area, they were placing bets, giving odds. They laughed and made jokes about it, as if the bout had nothing to do with blood and death. I realized that they were trying to drive away the dread and fear they all felt. And trying to keep the flicker of hope within them from blossoming into a flame that would be snuffed out if Hector killed Achilles.

I had my own worries. I knew I could take my sons from Agamemnon: the High King owed me that much, at least, and Odysseos would plead my case for me. But Aniti. Somehow, no matter how I told myself to be done with her, I couldn't let her go. How could I get Agamemnon to give her up? Why should I even try?

My head was spinning again, but this time with the emotions that seethed within me. Aniti was my wife, despite all that had happened to her, despite all she herself had done, she was still my wife and my possession. I told myself that if I took the boys, I would need their mother to tend them.

But the truth was that I could not leave Aniti in the hands of Agamemnon or any other man. I could not leave her in slavery and simply walk away from her. I realized that she was not only my wife, my property. She was my responsibility. I wished it were not so, but it was. I could not leave her to remain in slavery.

The wailing lamentations from the Myrmidones' camp continued unabated. It sent shivers up my spine. But slowly it came to me that the others felt that this battle between the two champions could settle the war, one way or the other. They thought that no matter which champion fell, the war would end tomorrow and the rest of us could go home.

I wondered if that was true. If Achilles dies tomorrow, I thought, most of these Achaians will pack up their boats and sail away. But if Hector is killed, the Trojans could still button themselves inside their high walls and defy Agamemnon's host. The Achaians had no hope of overtopping those walls; they knew nothing of siege engines and scaling ladders.

But I did.

Once I reached our section of the camp and saw that my men, what was left of them, were settled by their tents, I went to Odysseos' boat and climbed the rope ladder to its deck.

A young guard was sitting on the gunwale, staring wistfully out to sea, when I clambered up on the opposite side. The sun was nearing the flat horizon of the sea, turning the sky to flaming reds and oranges. Puffy clouds were turning violet, rimmed with gold. The guard jumped to his feet once I slapped my boots on the deck's planks.

"I wish to see the king," I said, before he could question me.

"You are the Hittite," he replied respectfully.

"I am."

"Wait here."

He hurried off behind the cabin. I stood and waited, my head still throbbing. It took several moments, but at last the youngster reappeared and beckoned to me.

"My lord Odysseos will speak to you, Hittite." He gestured toward the far end of the cabin.

Odysseos was sitting on a plank bench, alone, dressed in nothing more than a rough wool chiton. A flagon of wine stood on the table before him, beaded with condensation. It looked deliciously cool. I saw only one cup.

"Hittite," said Odysseos. "You're still alive."

"Two of my men were killed, my lord."

"But we survived. The camp is still here and the Trojans are locked behind their walls once again. Only a few of the boats were burned."

I stood before him and saw that he had fresh cuts on his forearm, his shoulder, even a slight nick above his brow.

"My wife and sons survived also," I said.

Odysseos eyed me. "You want them back."

"I do, my lord."

He reached for the flagon and poured himself a cup of wine. "You'll have to ask the High King for them."

"Yes, I know."

Breaking into a rare smile, Odysseos said, "This would be a good time for it. Agamemnon should be happy that Achilles has returned to the fight."

I understood the logic of it.

"But the High King does not give gifts so easily," he added, bringing the cup to his lips. His eyes stayed fixed on mine.

"The woman is my wife, my lord. She belongs to me."

"Still . . . it might be better to wait until tomorrow, after Achilles slays Hector. He'll be in a more giving mood then."

"But what if Hector slays Achilles?"

Odysseos shrugged. "That would make things . . . difficult."

I asked, "Do you think the Trojans will surrender if Hector falls?"

His brows knit; he hadn't thought of what would happen after the battle between the two.

"Surrender? No, I suppose not. The Trojans won't let us inside their walls willingly, no matter how many of their champions fall."

I heard myself say, "I can get you inside their walls."

"You?"

I pointed toward the city up on the bluff, bathed now in reddish gold by the setting sun. "See the course of the wall, where it is lower than the rest?" It was the western side of the city, where the garrulous courtier had told me that the defenses were weaker.

"Still twice the height of a grown man," Odysseos muttered.

"My men can build siege towers and wheel them up to that part of the wall so that your warriors can climb up inside them and step from their topmost platforms right onto the battlements of the wall."

"Towers?" Odysseos asked. "Taller than the wall? How can that be?"

"We have done it before, my lord. We build the towers of wood, and place them on rollers so that we can bring them up against the wall."

For a long moment Odysseos said nothing. Then, "But the Trojans would destroy the towers as you approached the wall."

"With what?" I challenged. "Spears? Arrows? Even if they shoot flaming arrows, we'll have the towers covered with wetted horsehides."

"But they'll concentrate their men at that one point and beat you off."

I realized that Odysseos was no fool. He grasped the concept of the siege towers even though he had never seen one in his life. And he immediately understood the weak point of my plan.

"Usually we build three or four towers and attack several spots along the fortifications at the same time. Or we create some other diversion that keeps the enemy's forces busy elsewhere."

"You've done this before?"

"Many times, my lord. Our army cracked the walls of Babylon that way."

"Babylon!"

"A much bigger city than Troy, my lord. With higher walls."

Odysseos scratched at his thick black beard. "The High King must hear of this."

Yes, I said to myself. This is the gift I offer to Agamemnon in exchange for my wife and sons.

5

Odysseos bade me wait with my men while he changed into clothing more fitting for a visit to the High King. And he sent a messenger to Agamemnon to tell him of his desire for an audience.

I went down to our little camp, where Magro and the others were gathering around the evening cook fire. Poletes scrambled to his feet, eager to know what had transpired with Odysseos.

"We're going to Agamemnon," I said, perhaps a bit pompously, "to tell the High King how to win this war." And get my sons and wife back, I added silently.

Once I outlined the idea of the siege towers, Poletes shook his head. "You're too greedy for victory, my master. You want to win everything and leave nothing for the gods to decide."

He seemed almost angry.

I asked, "But men fight wars to win, don't they?"

"Men fight wars for glory, for spoils, and for tales to tell their grandchildren. A man should go into battle to prove his bravery, to face a champion and test his destiny. You want to use tricks and machines to win your battle." Poletes actually spat into the sand to show his displeasure.

I reminded him, "Yet you yourself have scorned these warriors and called them bloodthirsty fools."

"That they are! But at least they fight fairly, champion to champion, as men should fight."

I laughed. "Windy old storyteller, all's fair in love and war."

For once Poletes had no answer. He grumbled to himself and turned back to the fire and the kettle with supper simmering in it.

Odysseos came down from his boat, dressed in a clean robe and a deep blue cloak. Two young men in leather vests and helmets walked a respectful three paces behind him.

"Come, Hittite, we go to Agamemnon."

As we walked through the camp, Odysseos asked me, "You can put wheels on these towers and pull them up to the walls?"

"Yes, my lord."

"While under fire?"

"Yes, my lord."

"And these men you have with you know how to build such towers?"

"We have done it before, sire. We'll need a team of workers: axmen, carpenters, workmen."

He nodded. "No problem there."

As we walked toward the cabin of Agamemnon, I wondered that none of these Achaians had thought of building siege towers earlier. Then I realized that these barbarians weren't real soldiers. These kings and princelings might fancy themselves to be mighty warriors, but my own squad of troops could beat five times their number of these fame-seeking simpletons. It was as Poletes said: these Achaians fight for glory—and loot.

The High King seemed half asleep when we were ushered into his cabin. Odysseos' two guards stayed outside in the gathering night. Agamemnon sat drowsily in a camp chair, a jewel-encrusted wine goblet in his right hand. Apparently the wound in his shoulder did not prevent him from lifting his arm to drink. No one else was in the cabin except a pair of women slaves, dark-eyed and silent in thin shifts that showed their bare arms and legs.

Odysseos took a stool facing the High King. I squatted on the carpeted ground at his side. He was offered wine. I was not.

"A tower that moves?" Agamemnon muttered after Odysseos had explained it to him twice. "Impossible! How could a stone tower be made to move?"

"It would be made of wood, son of Atreos. And covered with hides for protection."

Agamemnon looked down at me blearily and let his chin sink to his broad chest. He seemed almost asleep. Still, the lamps casting long shadows across the room made his heavy-browed face seem sinister, even threatening.

"I had to return the captive Briseis to that young pup," he grumbled. "And hand over a fortune of booty. Even with his loverboy slain by Hector the little snake refused to reenter the war unless his 'rightful' spoils were returned to him." The scorn that he put on the word *rightful* could have etched granite.

"Son of Atreos," Odysseos soothed, "if this plan of mine works we will sack Troy and gain so much treasure that even overweening Achilles will be satisfied."

Agamemnon said nothing. He waved his goblet slightly and one of the slave women came immediately to fill it. Then she filled Odysseos' golden cup.

"Achilles," Agamemnon growled. I could hear the

hatred in his voice. "If he slays Hector tomorrow the bards will sing his praises forever."

"But the walls of Troy will still stand between us and the victory you deserve, High King," said Odysseos.

Agamemnon smiled slyly. "On the other hand, Hector might kill Achilles. Then I'll be rid of him."

Lower, Odysseos repeated, "But the walls of Troy will still stand."

"Three more weeks," Agamemnon muttered. He slurped at his wine, spilling much of it over his already stained tunic. "Three more weeks is all I need."

"Sire?"

Agamemnon let the goblet slip from his beringed fingers and plonk onto the carpeted ground. He leaned forward, a sly grin on his fleshy face.

"In three more weeks my ships will bring the grain harvest from the Sea of Black Waters through the Dardanelles to Mycenae. And neither Priam nor Hector will be able to stop them."

Odysseos made a silent little "oh." I saw at that moment that Agamemnon was no fool. If he could not conquer Troy, he would at least get his ships through the straits and back again, loaded with golden grain, before breaking off the siege. And if the Achaians had to sail away from Troy without winning their war, at least Agamemnon would have the year's grain supply in his own city of Mycenae, ready to use it or sell it to his neighbors as he saw fit.

Odysseos had the reputation of being cunning, but I realized that the King of Ithaca was merely careful, a man who considered all the possibilities before choosing a course of action. Agamemnon was the crafty one: greedy, selfish and grasping.

Recovering quickly from his surprise, Odysseos said, "But now we have the chance of destroying Troy altogether. Not only will we have the loot of the city and its women, but you will have clear sailing through the Dardanelles for all the years of your kingship!"

Agamemnon slumped back on his chair. "A good thought, son of Laertes. A good thought. I'll consider it and call a council to decide upon it. After tomorrow's match."

With a reluctant nod, Odysseos said, "After we see whether Achilles remains among us or dies on Hector's spear."

Agamemnon smiled broadly.

6

He's a fool," I muttered as we walked away from Agamemnon's cabin.

Odysseos laid a hand on my shoulder. "No, Hittite. He is the High King and you could have your tongue cut out for speaking that way."

The sun had set. The stars were coming into sight. That everlasting chill wind was again blowing in from the sea, through the camp and across the plain of Ilios, toward the dark brooding walls of Troy. The camp seemed quiet, subdued; the betting and excited anticipation over the coming bout between Achilles and Hector seemed to be over now. Men were crawling into their tents or making up their bedrolls for the night's sleep. Some were pairing off with slave women, I saw. I wondered what Aniti was doing. Was she with Agamemnon? The thought made my stomach turn.

"The High King is many things," Odysseos said to me, his voice low, grave, "but he is no fool. If Achilles wins tomorrow, the Trojans will be so demoralized they might agree to return Helen and end the war. If Hector wins, then Agamemnon is rid of a thorn in his flesh."

Understanding dawned in me. "Either way, he wins."

It was too dark to see the expression on Odysseos' face, but I heard the iron hardness in his voice. "Either way."

"But my sons," I said. "My wife."

"Too soon to ask for them, Hittite. You saw how angry he was over returning the slave to Achilles. You can imagine how he'd react to your request."

"But he has no right to them!"

Very softly, Odysseos replied, "He is the High King. That is all the right he needs."

I had no answer for that.

"Tomorrow, Hittite. Be patient for a few more hours."

My teeth clenched hard enough to snap an iron blade.

Odysseos seemed to be lost in thought as we walked in silence the rest of the way back to the Ithacans' section of the camp. All was quiet. Most of the men were already asleep.

At last he said, "I have another task for you, Hittite."

"Sire?"

"You will be a herald again and return to Troy. With a message for Helen. From me."

Wearing a white armband and carrying the willow reed of an emissary, I once again headed for Troy's Scaean

Gate, across the blood-soaked plain of Ilios, lit by the fattening crescent of the moon and the glittering stars that spangled the night sky. There were no troops camped on the plain this night; I walked alone and unchallenged until I stood before the city's high walls.

The guards at the gate were fully grown warriors in bronze armor, their shields and spears resting within an arm's reach. As before, I carried only a slim dagger tucked into my belt. As before, they took it from me before sending me under escort to Prince Hector.

He received me in the armory, a long hall filled with shields and weapons and empty chariots. The place rang with voices and the hum of work. Slaves and warriors alike were polishing, sharpening, mending wheels, stacking sheaves of arrows. Hector was inspecting a suit of bronze armor, checking its leather straps, pointing out to a slave scratches that he wanted buffed away by morning.

Paris was nowhere in sight. I was glad of that; the young prince would get angry if he knew the message I bore.

Hector looked up as I stopped before him, flanked by my two armed escorts.

"You again," he said.

I made a small bow. "My lord Odysseos has sent me—"

"With another offer of peace?"

"No, my lord. I bear a message for Helen."

"From Odysseos?"

"Yes, my lord."

"Tell it to me, I'll see that she gets it."

I drew myself up a bit taller. "My instructions are to give the message to Helen and no one else."

Hector fell silent for a moment, appraising me with those steady brown eyes of his. If he felt anxious about the morning's duel against Achilles, he gave no sign of it.

"We could force the message from you, Hittite," he said calmly.

"Perhaps," I replied.

For several moments more he said nothing, obviously thinking over the situation. At last he said to my escorts, "Take this emissary to Princess Helen, then escort him back to the Scaean Gate and send him on his way."

They clenched their fists on their breasts and started to turn.

"My lord Hector," I heard myself say. "May the gods be with you tomorrow." I had no idea why I blurted out those words, except that I thought Hector was a far better man than vainglorious Achilles.

Hector almost smiled. "The gods will do as they wish, Hittite. As usual."

Those were the last words I heard from Hector, prince of Troy.

If Hector was calm, Helen was in a frenzy. She burst into the little sitting room that my escorts brought me to, her eyes red and puffy. Apet lingered at the doorway, again in her black Death's robe.

"What does Odysseos want to tell me?" Helen fairly shouted. "Can he prevent tomorrow's fight?"

Her golden hair was disheveled, she wore a plain shift belted at the waist. It was obvious she had been crying. Yet still she was so beautiful that it took a conscious effort of will not to reach out to her and try to comfort her.

"Nothing can prevent tomorrow's fight, my lady," I said. "Or, rather, no one will take a step to prevent it."

She sank onto the sofa against the little chamber's far wall. "No. It's ordained by the Fates. Hector will die tomorrow. It's foretold. Troy is doomed. I'm doomed." She bowed her head and began to sob softly.

Still wondering where Paris was, I knelt on one knee before her. "My lady, Odysseos wants me to tell you how to survive."

Helen looked at me, her soft cheeks runneled by tears. "How can I survive if he dies?" she demanded. "Why should I survive? I'm the cause of his death!"

Apet hurried to her side. "Not so, my dear one. Hector is doomed, truly, but it's not your fault. It's his destiny and there's nothing anyone can do to avoid it."

Helen shook her golden-tressed head and broke into more sobs.

Kneeling at her feet, I told her, "My lord Odysseos instructed me to tell you that if the worst happens, if the Achaians break into Troy, you are to flee to the temple of Aphrodite and take sanctuary there. He will seek you there, in the temple of Aphrodite."

Helen's sobbing eased. "Odysseos will seek me?"

"So he told me. He will protect you while the city is being sacked."

Her face went cold. "And then return me to Menalaos."

"Yes, my lady."

"I'd rather die."

"No!" I urged. "You must live."

"Not as Menalaos' wife. He'd probably kill me, after

he's had his fill of beating me, raping me, humiliating me in front of his kinsmen."

Apet said, "Fly to Egypt, my pet! You'll be safe in the Land of the Two Kingdoms."

Egypt? I was stunned. The old woman must be insane. Egypt was a thousand leagues distant. Farther.

Helen echoed my thoughts. "How can we get to Egypt? How can we get away from Troy when the city falls? What good is anything if he's killed?"

She had lost all hope. And suddenly I felt pity for beautiful Helen. She had nothing to look forward to if Troy fell; nothing but pain and humiliation and ultimately death. Hector had been her real hope, her one chance for survival. If he died . . .

But it was more than that, I realized. She loved Hector. More than her girlish infatuation with Paris. She truly loved Hector. She was terrified that he would be killed by Achilles. That frightened her more than her own fate at the hands of Menalaos.

I found myself wondering what love truly is. How can one person be willing to die so that another could live? With a shock of surprise, I found myself envying Hector.

But such thoughts were not for me. I was a soldier; she was a queen, and a princess of Troy. Slowly I got to my feet. "My lady, that is Odysseos' message. If the Achaians enter the city, fly to the temple of Aphrodite. Not even the barbarians would despoil the temple of so powerful a goddess. He will find you there and protect you."

Helen nodded bleakly. "And then turn me over to Menalaos."

I spread my hands. "I have nothing to say about that, my lady." Yet I wished that I did.

Helen breathed a long, shuddering sigh. Then she stood up and said to me, "Thank you, Lukka, for bringing me Odysseos' message. Now you must return to your master and give him my thanks for offering me his protection."

"It's better than nothing," Apet said, in a half-whisper.

"Is it?" Helen asked. Then she dismissed me.

The same two young men escorted me to the Scaean Gate. I left Troy, my mind in a turmoil over Helen. She was too beautiful to die, to be killed by Menalaos. Even though he was her rightful husband and had the power of life and death over her . . . I shook my head and tried to clear away such thoughts. I squeezed my eyes shut and tried to picture my Aniti in my mind. Would she cry for me if I were killed? Would I cry for her?

It wasn't until I was halfway back to the Achaian camp strung out along the beach, trudging alone beneath the moon as it glided among clouds of silver, that the full import of Odysseos' message to Helen suddenly struck me.

He expected the Achaians to break through Troy's walls. He knew that if Achilles killed Hector the Trojans would shut themselves inside those walls and defy the invaders. He knew that the only way to get past those walls was to build the siege towers that I had described to him.

Haughty Agamemnon might not believe that the towers could work, but Odysseos did. He believed in them! He believed in me!

I wished that Helen did, too.

7

I slept fitfully that night, my dreams filled with visions of Helen and Aniti, Hector and Achilles, all in a confusing, troubling whirlwind. I awoke with the sun. The morning dawned bright and windy.

Although the single combat between Hector and Achilles was what everyone looked forward to, still the whole army prepared to march out onto the plain. Partly they went because a single combat between champions can degenerate into a general melee easily enough. Mostly they went to get a closer look at the fight.

Odysseos came to me as my men were tugging on their leather jerkins and strapping their helmets under their chins.

"I want you and your Hittites to stand close behind my chariot," said the King of Ithaca to me. "If a battle arises you must follow my chariot."

"I understand, my lord," I said. Then I added, "But we could be starting to fell trees for the siege towers. There's plenty of timber on the other side of the river."

"Not today," Odysseos said. "If all goes well, we may not need your towers."

I had no choice but to accept his decision.

Virtually the entire Achaian force marched out through the gate and drew itself up, rank upon rank, on the windswept plain before the camp's sandy rampart. By the beetling walls of the city the Trojans were drawing themselves up likewise, chariots in front, foot soldiers behind them. Swirls of dust blew into the cloudless sky and quickly dissipated. I could see pennants fluttering along the battlement of the city's walls. I even imagined I saw Helen's golden bright hair at the top of the tallest tower, by the Scaean Gate.

Odysseos ordered us to stand at the left side of his chariot. "Protect my driver if we enter the fray," he said. So I stood with my men, each of us clasping our heavy shields that extended from chin to ankle. Five plies of hides stretched across a thin wooden frame and bossed with iron studs, our shields would stop almost anything except a spear driven with the power of a galloping chariot behind it.

Poletes was up on the rampart with the slaves and *thetes*, straining his old eyes for a view of the fight. He would interrogate me for hours this night, I knew, dragging every detail of what I had seen out of my memory. If either of us still lives after this day's fighting, I told myself.

As I stood on the windy plain, squinting into the morning sun, a roar went up among the Trojans. I saw Hector's chariot, pulled by four magnificent white stallions, kicking up a cloud of dust as it sped from the Scaean Gate and drove toward the front of the arrayed ranks of Trojan soldiery. Hector stood tall and proud, his great shield at his side, wearing the gleaming bronze armor I had seen him with the previous night in the armory. A clutch of spears stood in their holder on the chariot, their points aimed heavenward.

For many minutes nothing more happened. Muttering started among the Achaian footmen. I glanced up at Odysseos standing in his chariot. The King of Ithaca merely smiled tolerantly. Achilles was behaving like a self-appointed idol, making everyone anxious for his appearance. I thought that it would have been a good trick against any opponent except Hector. That man will use the time to study every rock and bump on the field, I said to myself. He is no child to be frightened by waiting.

At last an exultant roar sprang up among the Achaians. Turning, I saw four snorting, spirited, midnight-black horses, heads tossing, groomed so perfectly that they seemed to glow, pounding down the earthen ramp that cut across our trench. Achilles' chariot was inlaid with ebony and ivory, and his armor—only his second-best since Hector had stripped Patrokles' dead body—gleamed with burnished gold.

With his plumed helmet on, there was little of Achilles' face to be seen. But as his chariot swept past us I saw that his mouth was set in a grim line and his eyes burned like furnaces.

He did not stop for the usual prebattle formalities. He did not even slow down. His charioteer cracked his whip over the black horses' ears and they plunged forward at top speed as Achilles took a spear in his right hand and screamed loud enough to echo off the walls of Troy: "PATROKLES! PA . . . TRO . . . KLES!"

His chariot aimed straight for Hector's. The Trojan driver, startled, whipped his horses into motion and Hector hefted one of his spears.

The chariots pounded toward each other. Both warriors cast their spears simultaneously. Achilles' struck Hector's shield and staggered him. He almost tumbled out of the chariot, but he regained his balance and reached for another spear. Hector's shaft struck between Achilles and his charioteer, splintering the wooden floor of the chariot.

A chill went through me. Achilles had not raised his shield when Hector's spear drove toward him. He had not even flinched as the missile passed close enough to shave his chin. Either he did not care what happened to him or he was mad enough to believe himself invulnerable.

The chariots swung past each other and again the two champions hurled spears. Hector's bounced off the bronze shoulder of Achilles' armor. Again he made no move to protect himself or to avoid the blow. His own spear caught Hector's charioteer in the face. With an awful shriek he toppled over backward, both hands pawing at the shaft that had turned his face into a bloody shambles.

The Achaians shouted and surged a few steps forward. Hector, knowing he could not control his horses and fight at the same time, jumped lightly from his chariot, two spears gripped in his left hand. The horses raced on, their reins slack, heading back for the walls of the city.

Achilles had the advantage now. His chariot drove around Hector, circling the stranded prince of Troy again and again, seeking an advantage, a momentary dropping of his guard. But Hector held his massive hourglass-shaped shield firmly in front of him and pivoted smoothly to present nothing more to Achilles than a bronze plumed helmet, the body-length shield and the greaves that protected his lower legs.

Achilles cast another spear, but it went slightly wide. Hector remained in place, or seemed to. I noticed, though, that each time he wheeled to keep his front to Achilles' chariot, he edged a step or two closer to his own ranks.

Achilles must have noticed this, too, and jumped out

of his chariot. A great gusting sigh of expectation went through both armies. The two champions now faced each other on foot, at spear's length.

Hector advanced confidently toward the smaller Achaian. He spoke to Achilles, who spat out a reply, but they were too far away for me to make out their words.

Then Achilles did something that wrenched a great moaning gasp from the Achaians. He threw his shield down thumping on the bare ground, then unstrapped his helmet and tossed it atop the shield. With the wind tousling his shoulder-length locks, he faced Hector with nothing but his body armor, his sword, and his last remaining spear.

The fool! I thought. He must actually believe he's invincible. Achilles gripped his spear in both hands and faced Hector without a shield.

Dropping the lighter of his two spears, Hector drove straight at Achilles. He had the advantage of size and strength, and of experience, and he knew it. Achilles, smaller, faster, seemed to be absolutely crazy. He did not even try to parry Hector's spear thrusts or run out of their reach. Instead he dodged this way and that, avoiding Hector's spear by scant finger widths, keeping his own spear point aimed straight at Hector's eyes.

It is a truth that in any kind of hand-to-hand combat you cannot attack and defend yourself at the same time. The successful fighter can switch from attack to defense and back again in the flick of an eye. Hector knew this; his obvious aim was to keep the shieldless Achilles on the defensive. But Achilles refused to defend himself, except for dodging Hector's thrusts. I began to see a method in Achilles' madness: his greatest advantages were speed and daring. The heavy shield would have slowed him down.

He gave ground and Hector moved steadily forward, but even there I saw that Achilles was edging around, maneuvering to place himself between Hector and the Trojan ranks, moving Hector closer and closer to our side of the field.

I saw the look on Achilles' face as they sweated and grunted beneath the hot sun. He was smiling. Like a little boy who enjoys pulling the wings off flies, like a man who was happily looking forward to driving his spear through the chest of his enemy, like a madman intent on murder.

Hector realized that he was being maneuvered. He changed his tactics and tried to engage Achilles' spear, knowing that once he made contact with it his superior strength could force his enemy's point down, and then he could drive his own bronze spearhead into Achilles' unguarded body.

Achilles danced away from Hector's spear, his long hair flowing, then dashed slightly forward. He feinted and Hector followed the motion of his spear for a fraction of an instant. It was enough. Launching himself completely off his feet like a distance jumper, Achilles drove his spear with all the strength in both his arms into Hector's body. The point struck Hector's bronze breastplate; I could hear the screech as it slid up along the armor, unable to penetrate, and then caught under Hector's chin.

The impact knocked Hector backward but not off his feet. For an instant the two champions stood locked together, Achilles ramming the spear upward with both his hands white-knuckled against its haft, his eyes blazing hatred and bloodlust, his lips pulled back in a feral snarl. Hector's arms, one holding his long spear, the other with his great shield strapped to it, slowly folded forward, as if to embrace his killer. The spear point went deeper into his throat, up through his jaw, and buried itself in the base of his brain.

Hector went limp, hanging on Achilles' spear point. Achilles wrenched it free and the Trojan prince's dead body slumped to the dusty ground.

"For Patrokles!" Achilles screamed, holding his bloodied spear aloft.

8

A triumphant roar went up from the Achaians, while the Trojans seemed frozen in gaping horror.

Achilles threw down his bloody spear and pulled his sword from its scabbard. He hacked at Hector's head once, twice, three times. He wanted the severed head as a trophy.

The Trojans screamed and charged at him. Without a word of command the Achaians charged, too. In the span of a heartbeat the single combat turned into a wild, brawling battle.

My men and I ran after Odysseos' chariot. I couldn't help but think that the very men who had hoped so dearly that this fight between the two champions would end the war were now racing into battle themselves, unthinking, uncaring, driven by bloodlust and blind hatred.

Then there was no more time for thought. My sword was in my hand and enemies were charging at me, blood and murder in their eyes. My iron sword served me well.

Bronze blades and spearpoints chipped or broke against it. Its sharp edge slashed through bronze armor. We caught up with Odysseos' chariot. He and several other mounted noblemen had formed a screen around the body of Hector as Achilles and his Myrmidones stripped the corpse down to the skin. I saw the brave prince's severed head bobbing on a spear and turned away in disgust. Then someone tied his ankles to a chariot's tail and tried to fight through the growing melee and force his way with the body back toward the Achaian camp.

Instead of being unnerved by these barbarities the Trojans seemed infuriated. They fought with a rage born of desecration and battled fiercely to recover Hector's body before it could be dragged back behind our rampart.

While the struggle grew wilder I realized that none of the Trojans were protecting their line of retreat or even thinking about guarding the gate from which they had left their city.

I rushed to Odysseos' chariot and shouted over the cursing and clanging of the battle, "The gate! They've left the gate unprotected!"

Odysseos' eyes gleamed. He looked out toward the city walls, then back at me. He nodded once.

"To the gate!" he called in a voice that roared across the plain. "To the gate before they can close it."

Screaming his blood-curdling battle cry, Odysseos fought his way clear of the struggle around Hector's corpse, followed by two more chariots. I ran after them, slashing my way clear until there was nothing between us and the walls of Troy but empty bare ground.

"To the gate!" I heard another voice bellow, and a chariot clattered past, its horses leaning into their harnesses, nostrils blowing wide, eyes white and bulging.

Within moments Hector's corpse was forgotten. The battle had turned into a race for the Scaean Gate. Odysseos led the Achaians who were trying to get there before the Trojans could close it. The Trojan army streamed toward it so they could get inside the protection of the city's walls before the gate was closed and they were cut off.

Achilles was back in his chariot, cutting a bloody path through the Trojans, hacking with his sword until the foot soldiers and chariot-riding noblemen alike gave him a wide berth. Then he snatched the whip from his driver's hands and lashed his horses into a frenzied gallop toward the city gate.

I saw Odysseos fling a spear into the chest of a Trojan guarding the gate. More Trojans appeared in the open gateway, graybeards and young boys armed with light throwing javelins and bronze swords. From up on the battlements that flanked the gate others were firing arrows and hurling stones. Odysseos was forced to back away.

But not Achilles. His long hair streaming in the wind, he drove straight for the gate, oblivious to the bombardment from above. The rear guard scattered before him, ducking behind the massive wooden doors. From behind, someone started to push them closed. Seeing that the gap between the two doors was too small for his chariot to pass through, Achilles jumped to the ground, his bloodstained great spear in his hands, and charged at the gate while his charioteer tried to regain control of the frightened horses. Achilles met a hedgehog of spear points but dived at them headlong, jabbing and slashing two-handed with his own spear.

Odysseos and another chariot-mounted warrior rushed

up to help him, their great shields strapped to their backs to protect them from neck to heel from the stones and arrows being aimed at them from above. I saw the main mass of the Trojans not far behind us, a wild tangled melee battling with the rest of the Achaians, fighting to reach the protection of the city's walls.

I pushed my way between Achilles and Odysseos' chariot, hacking with my sword at the spears sticking out from the gap between the doors. I grabbed a spear with my right hand and pulled it out of the hands of the frightened boy who had been holding it. Flinging it to the ground, I reached for another. I grasped the spear and pulled on it, dragging the graybeard holding it until he was within reach of my sword. He saw the blow coming and released the spear, raising his arms over his head and screaming, as if that would protect him. I hesitated for just a heartbeat, but that was long enough for the old man to drop to his knees and scrabble away from me.

A teenager thrust his spear at me. I dodged it and swung at the youth, but there was little purpose in my swing except to scare him off. He backed away slightly, then came at me again. I did not give him a second chance.

The struggle at the gate seemed to go on endlessly, although common sense tells me it took only a few moments. The rest of the Trojans came up, still battling furiously with the main body of the Achaians. Chariots and foot soldiers hacked and slashed and cursed and screamed their final cries in that narrow passage between the walls that flanked the Scaean Gate. Dust and blood and arrows and stones filled the deadly air. The Trojans were fighting for their lives, desperately trying

to get inside the gate, just as the Achaians had been trying to escape Hector's spear only a few days earlier.

Despite our efforts the Trojans still held the gate ajar
and kept us from entering it. Sometimes a few determined men can keep an army at bay, and the Trojan rear
guard at the gate had the determination born of sheer
desperation. They knew that if we forced that gate their
city was finished: their lives, their families, their homes
would be wiped out. So they held us at bay, new men
and boys taking the place of those we killed, while the
main body of their army slipped through the open
doors, fighting as they retreated to safety.

Then I saw the blow that ended the battle. Still fighting at the narrow entrance to the gate, I had to turn to
face the Trojan warriors who were battling their way to
the doors in their effort to get inside the city's walls. I
saw Achilles, his eyes burning with battle fury, his mouth
open with wild laughter, hacking any Trojan who dared
to come within his spear's reach. Up on the battlements
one of the Trojans leaned out with a bow in his hands
and fired an arrow toward Achilles' unprotected back.

As if in a dream, a nightmare, I shouted a warning
that was drowned out in the cursing, howling uproar of
the battle. I pushed past a half-dozen furiously battling
men to reach Achilles as the arrow streaked toward its
target. I managed to get a hand on his shoulder and push
him out of the way.

Almost.

The arrow struck him on the back of his leg, slightly
above the heel. Achilles went down with a high-pitched
scream of pain.

9

For an instant the world seemed to stop.

Achilles, the seemingly invulnerable champion, was down in the dust, writhing in pain, an arrow jutting out from the back of his left ankle.

I stood over him and took off the head of the first Trojan who came at him with a single swipe of my sword. Odysseos and another Achaian lord jumped down from their chariots to join me. Suddenly the battle had changed its entire purpose and direction. We were no longer trying to force the Scaean Gate; we were fighting to keep Achilles alive and get him back to our camp.

Slowly we withdrew, and in truth, after a few moments the Trojans seemed glad enough to let us go. They streamed back inside their gate and swung its massive doors shut. I picked up Achilles in my arms while Odysseos and the others formed a guard around us and we headed back to the camp.

For all his ferocity and strength, he was as light as a child. His Myrmidones surrounded us, staring at their wounded prince with shocked, disbelieving eyes. Achilles' unhandsome face was bathed with sweat, but he kept his lips clamped together in a painful white line as I carried him past the huge windblown oak just beyond the Scaean Gate.

"I was offered a choice," he muttered, his teeth clenched with pain, "between long life and glory. I chose glory."

"It's not a serious wound," I said.

"The gods will decide how serious it is," he replied, in a voice so faint I could hardly hear him.

Halfway across the body-littered plain six men ran up to meet us, puffing hard, carrying a stretcher of thongs laced across a wooden frame. I laid Achilles on it as gently as I could. He grimaced, but did not cry out or complain.

Odysseos put a heavy hand on my shoulder. "You saved his life."

"You saw?"

"I did. That arrow was meant for his heart."

"How bad a wound do you think it is?"

"I've seen worse," said Odysseos. "Still, he'll be out of action for many days."

We trudged across the blood-soaked plain side by side. The wind was coming off the water again, blowing dust in our faces, forcing us to squint as we walked toward the camp. Every muscle in my body ached. Blood was crusted on my sword arm, my legs, spattered across my leather jerkin. I could see swarms of flies already crawling over the dead bodies that littered the field.

"You fought well," Odysseos said. "For a few moments there I thought we would force the gate and enter the city at last."

I shook my head wearily. "We can't force a gate that is defended. It's too easy for the Trojans to hold a narrow opening."

Odysseos nodded agreement. "Do you think your men could really build a tower that will allow us to scale their wall?"

"We've done it before. At Ugarit and elsewhere."

"Ugarit," Odysseos repeated. He seemed impressed. "I will speak to Agamemnon and the council. Until

Achilles rejoins us we have little hope of storming their gate."

"And little hope even with Achilles."

He looked at me sternly. Odysseos didn't like hearing that, but he said nothing.

"My sons," I reminded him. "My wife."

He closed his eyes briefly. "I will speak to Agamemnon about them."

"I want them."

"I understand." Then Odysseos smiled wryly. "I have a wife, too. And a son. Back at Ithaca."

Perhaps he did understand.

Poletes was literally hopping up and down on his knobby legs as we entered the camp, following Achilles on his stretcher.

"What a day!" he exclaimed. "What a day! The bards will sing of this day for all time!"

As usual, he milked me for every last detail of the fighting. He had been watching from the top of the rampart, of course, but the mad melee at the gate was too far away from his old eyes and too confused for him to make out.

"And what did Odysseos say at that point?" he would ask. "I saw Diomedes and Menalaos riding side by side toward the gate. Which of them got there first?"

I could do nothing more than shake my head. "I was too busy keeping Trojan spear points off me to take notice of such things, storyteller."

"Who fired the arrow that wounded Achilles? Could it have been Prince Paris? He has a reputation as an archer, you know."

The women set out a meal of thick barley soup, roast lamb and onions, flat bread still hot from the clay oven and a flagon of unadulterated wine. Poletes kept asking questions with every bite.

I saw that my men were eating as I tried to satisfy the old storyteller's curiosity. The sun dipped below the western sea's edge and the island mountaintops turned gold, then violet, then faded into darkness. The first star gleamed in the cloudless purple sky, so beautiful that I understood why it was named after Asertu.

There was no end to Poletes' impatient questions, so I finally sent him to the Myrmidones' camp to learn for himself of Achilles' condition. Then I stretched out on my blanket, glad to be rid of the old man's pestering.

Magro came over and squatted on the sand beside me. "A hard day."

I sat up and asked him, "How's your arm?"

"It's nothing. A little stiff, that's all."

"Good."

He hesitated a heartbeat, then asked, "What do you think of today's battle?"

"Hardly a battle," I replied. "They're more like a bunch of overgrown boys tussling in a playground."

"The blood is real."

"Yes. I know. But they'll never take a fortified city by storming defended gates."

"They don't know anything about warfare, do they?"

"Not much."

Magro lifted his eyes. "There're enough good trees on the other side of the river to build six good siege towers, maybe more."

"We need the High King's permission first," I said.

Magro spat, "The High King. He's a fathead."

"But he's the High King."

Hunching closer to me, Magro whispered, "Why

don't we just get up and leave? Why should we get ourselves killed for them?"

Before I could answer, he went on, "We could march into Agamemnon's camp tonight and take your wife and sons. They'll only have a couple of sleepy teenagers on guard. We could slit their throats before they utter a sound and get away from here with your family."

I suddenly realized that the same thought had been hovering in the back of my mind. But then I wondered, "And go where?"

"Anywhere but here!" Magro said fervently. "This place is a death trap. Nothing good will come from this fighting."

I thought he was right. But then I thought of Helen. She would be at the mercy of her former husband if the Achaians conquered Troy. Or she could become Queen of Troy if they could drive the Achaians away.

"We're pledged to Odysseos," I heard myself tell Magro. "We have joined the House of Ithaca. We've eaten his bread and we'll fight his battles."

In the flickering light of the campfire I could make out a twisted smile on Magro's face. "Even though it's stupid?"

"Loyalty isn't stupid."

He gusted out a sigh. "That's what I thought you'd say."

As Magro started to get to his feet, Poletes came rushing to us and dropped to his knees before me, his face solemn in the light of our dying fire, his great owl's eyes grave.

"What's the news of Achilles?" I asked him.

"The great slayer of men is finished as a warrior," said Poletes, his voice low, somber. "The arrow cut the tendon in the back of his heel. He will never walk again without a crutch."

I felt my mouth tighten grimly.

Poletes glanced at the jug of wine by the fire, then looked back at me questioningly. I nodded. He filled cups for Magro and me, then poured himself a heavy draft and gulped at it.

"Achilles is crippled, then," I said.

Wiping his mouth with the back of his hand, Poletes sighed. "Well, he can live a long life back in Phthia. Once his father dies he will be king and probably rule over all of Thessaly. That's not so bad, I think."

I nodded, but I wondered how Achilles would take to the life of a cripple. He had chosen glory, he'd told me, over a long life.

As if in answer to my thoughts a loud wail sprang up from the Myrmidones' end of the camp. Magro and I jumped to our feet. Poletes got up more slowly.

"My lord Achilles!" a voice cried out. "My lord Achilles is dead!"

I glanced at Poletes.

"Poison on the arrowhead?" he guessed.

I threw down the wine cup and started off for the Myrmidones' tents. All the camp seemed to be rushing in the same direction. I saw Odysseos' broad back, and Big Ajax outstriding everyone with his long legs.

Spear-wielding Myrmidone guards held back the crowd at the edge of their camp area, allowing only the nobles to pass through. I pushed up alongside Odysseos and went past the guards with him. Menalaos, Diomedes, Nestor and almost every one of the Achaian leaders were gathering in front of Achilles' cabin.

All but Agamemnon, I saw.

We went inside, past weeping soldiers and women

tearing their hair and scratching their faces as they screamed their lamentations.

Achilles' couch, up on the raised platform at the far end of the cabin, was spattered with bright red blood. The young warrior lay on it, left ankle swathed in oil-soaked bandages, a dagger still gripped in his right hand, a jagged red slash just under his left ear running halfway across his windpipe still dripping blood. His eyes stared sightlessly at the mud-chinked planks of the ceiling. His mouth was open in a rictus that might have been a final smile or a grimace of pain.

Facing the long life of a cripple, mighty Achilles had killed himself. His final act of glory.

Odysseos turned to me. "Tomorrow you start your men building the siege towers."

10

Odysseos and the other nobles headed for Agamemnon's cabin for a council of war. I went back to my tent and tried to sleep. Tomorrow we would begin to build the siege towers. We will put an end to this war. We will cross Troy's high walls and destroy the city. I knew the fire and blood that awaited the Trojans. Battle is hard and bloody. Sacking a city is dirty and murderous. The men will run wild. Looting and raping are their rewards for winning, for surviving long enough to win. I remembered Hattusas in flames and agony. And other cities that we proud Hatti soldiers had taken and looted.

I thought of my wife and sons. They'll be safe enough here in camp. The troops will all be in the city, burning, raping, slaughtering in a frenzy of release.

And Helen will be in the temple of Aphrodite, waiting for the fate that will overtake her.

I didn't sleep well that night.

The camp's roosters raised their raucous cry of morning. I went to the latrine trench, then washed and shared a bowl of lentil soup with my men. Poletes was jabbering away. He had learned that the Trojans had sent a delegation to ask for the return of Hector's dismembered body. Try as they might to keep the news of Achilles' death a secret, the Achaians were unable to keep the Trojan emissaries from finding out the news. The whole camp was buzzing with it, although none but Odysseos and a few other nobles knew that Achilles had committed suicide.

Agamemnon's council met with the Trojan delegation, and after some gruff negotiating agreed to return Hector's body. The Trojans suggested a three-day truce so that both sides could properly honor their slain and Agamemnon's council swiftly agreed.

We used the three days of truce to build the first siege tower. My men and I camped among the trees on the far side of the Scamander River, screened from Trojan eyes by the riverbank's line of greenery. Odysseos, who above all the Achaians appreciated the value of scouting and intelligence-gathering, spread a number of his best men along the riverbank to prevent any stray Trojan woodcutters from getting near us. The wind usually blew past the city and farther inland, but occasionally it changed briefly and I feared that the Trojans could hear our hewing and hammering and sawing. I hoped they would take it as a shipbuilding chore and nothing more.

We commandeered dozens of slaves and *thetes* to do the dogwork of chopping down the trees and hauling loads of timber. My men commanded work crews with stern efficiency, but even so, by the end of the third day we had only one tower ready for use.

Odysseos, Agamemnon and the other leaders came across the river that evening to inspect our work. We had built the tower horizontally, of course, laying it along the ground, partly because it was easier to do it that way but mainly to keep it hidden behind the still-standing trees. Once it got dark enough, I had several dozen slaves and *thetes* haul on ropes to pull it up to its true vertical position.

Agamemnon scowled at it. "It's not as tall as the city walls," he complained.

Odysseos shot me a questioning glance.

"This first one is tall enough, my lord king," I said, "to top the western wall. That is the weakest point in the Trojan defenses. Even the Trojans admit that that section of their walls was not built by Apollo and Poseidon."

Nestor bobbed his white beard. "A wise choice, young man. Never defy the gods, it will only bring grief to you. Even if you seem to succeed at first the gods will soon bring you low because of your hubris. Look at poor Achilles, so full of pride. Yet a lowly arrow has been his downfall."

As soon as Nestor took a breath I rushed to continue, "I have been inside the city, my lords. I know its layout. The west wall is on the highest side of the bluff. Once we get past that wall we will be on high ground inside the city, close to the palace and the temples."

Odysseos agreed. To Agamemnon he said, "I, too, have served as an emissary, if you recall, and I have studied the city's streets and buildings carefully. The Hittite speaks truly. If we broke through the Scaean Gate we would still have to fight through the city's streets, uphill every-step of the way. Breaking in over the west wall is better."

"Can we get this thing up the bluff to the wall there?" Agamemnon asked.

I replied, "The slope is not as steep at the west wall as it is to the north and east, my lord. The southern side is easiest, but that's where the Scaean and Dardanian Gates are located. It's the most heavily defended, with the highest walls and tall watchtowers alongside each gate."

"I know that!" Agamemnon snapped. He poked around the wooden framework, obviously suspicious of what to him was a new idea.

Before he could ask, I explained, "It would be best to roll it across the plain at night, after the moon goes down. On a night when the fog comes in from the sea. We can float it across the river on the raft we've built and roll it across the plain on its back so that the mist will conceal us from any Trojan watchmen on the walls. Then we raise it—"

Agamemnon cut me off with a peevish wave of his hand. "Odysseos, are you willing to lead this . . . this maneuver?"

"I am, son of Atreos. I plan to be the first man to step onto the battlements of Troy."

"Very well then," said the High King. "I don't think this will work. But if you're prepared to try it, then try it. I'll have the rest of the army ready to attack at first light."

"Tonight?" I blurted.

"Tonight," Agamemnon said, glaring at me.

"But my lord, one tower isn't enough. We should have four, perhaps six, so we can attack the walls at different points."

"You have one," said Agamemnon. "If it works, all to the good. If it fails, so be it. The gods will decide."

With that, he turned and strode away.

We got no sleep that night. I doubt that any of us could have slept even if we had tried. Nestor organized a blessing for the tower. A pair of aged priests sacrificed a dozen rams and goats, slitting their throats with ancient stone knives as they lay bound and bleating on the ground, then painting their blood on the wooden framework.

Poletes fretted that they offered no bulls or human captives to sacrifice.

"Agamemnon doesn't think enough of your tower to waste such wealth upon it," he told me in the dark shadows. "When he started out for Troy and the winds blew the wrong way for sailing for weeks at a time, he sacrificed a hundred horses and dozens of virgins. Including his own daughter."

"His daughter?" That stunned me.

Nodding grimly, Poletes said, "He wants Troy. The High King will stop at nothing to get what he wants."

I had seen massive sacrifices at Hattusas and elsewhere. Human captives were often put on the altar. But his own daughter! It made me realize how ruthless the High King really was.

Fortune was with us that night. A cold fog seeped in from the sea. We rafted the tower across the river, crouched in the chilling mist with the tower's framework looming above us like the skeleton of some giant beast. The moon disappeared behind the black humps of the islands and the night become as dark as it would ever be.

I had hoped for cloud cover, but the stars were watching us as we slowly, painfully, pulled the tower on big wooden wheels across the plain of Ilios and up the slope that fronted Troy's western wall. Slaves and *thetes* strained at the ropes while others slathered animal grease on the wheels and axles to keep them from squeaking.

Poletes crept along beside me, silent for once. I strained my eyes for a sight of Trojan sentries up on the battlements, but the fog kept me from seeing much. Straight overhead I could make out the patterns of the stars: the Bears and the Hunter, facing the V-shaped horns of the Bull. The Pleiades gleamed like a cluster of seven blue gems in the Bull's neck.

The night was eerily quiet. Perhaps the Trojans, trusting in the truce the Achaians had agreed to, thought that no hostilities would resume until the morning. True, the *fighting* would start with the sun's rise. But were they fools enough to post no lookouts through the night?

The ground was rising now, and what had seemed like a gentle slope felt like a steep cliff. We all gripped the ropes in our hands and put our backs into it, trying not to grunt or cry out with the pain. I looked across from where I was hauling and saw Magro, his face contorted with the effort, his booted heels digging into the mist-slippery grass, straining like a common laborer, just as all the rest of us were.

At last we reached the base of the wall and huddled there, panting. I sent Poletes scampering to the corner where the wall turned, to watch the eastern sky and tell me when it started to turn gray with the first hint of dawn. We all sat sprawled on the damp ground, letting our aching muscles relax until the moment for action came. The tower lay lengthwise along the ground, waiting to be pulled up to its vertical position. I sat with my back against the wall of Troy and counted the time by listening to my heartbeat.

I heard a rooster crow from inside the city, and then another. Where is Poletes? I wondered. Has he fallen asleep or been found by a Trojan sentry?

Just as I was getting to my feet the old storyteller scuttled back through the mist to me.

"The eastern sky is still dark, except for the first touch of faint light between the mountains. Soon the sky will turn milky white, then as rosy as a flower."

"Odysseos and his troops will be starting out from the camp," I whispered. "Time to get the tower up."

The fog was thinning slightly as we pushed on the poles that raised the tower to its vertical position. It was even heavier than it looked, because of the horse hides and weapons we had lashed to its platforms. Teams of men braced the tower with more poles as it rose. There was no way we could muffle the noise of the creaking and our own gasping, grunting exertions. It seemed to take forever to get the thing standing straight, although only a few strenuous moments had passed.

Still, just as the tower tipped over and thumped ponderously against the wall in its final position, I heard voices calling confusedly from up atop the battlements.

I turned to Poletes. "Run back to Odysseos and tell him we're ready. He's to come as fast as he can!"

The plan was for Odysseos and a picked squad of fifty of his Ithacans to make their way across the plain on foot, because chariots would have been too noisy. I began to wonder if that had been the smartest approach.

Someone was shouting from inside the walls now and I saw a head appear over the battlements, silhouetted for a brief instant against the graying sky.

I pulled out my sword and swung up onto the ladder that led to the top of the tower. Magro was barely a step behind me, and the rest of my squad started swarming up the tower's sides, unrolling the horse hides we had placed to protect the tower's sides against spears and arrows.

"What is it?" I heard a boy's frightened high-pitched voice from atop the wall.

"It's a giant horse!" a fear-stricken voice answered. "With warriors inside it!"

11

I reached the topmost platform of the tower, sword in hand. Our calculations had been almost perfect. The platform reared a shin's length or so higher than the wall's battlements. Without hesitation I jumped down onto the stone parapet and from there onto the wooden platform behind it.

A pair of stunned Trojan youths stood barely a sword's length before me, their mouths agape, eyes bulging, long spears in their trembling hands. I rushed at them and cut the closer one nearly in half with a swing of my sword. The other dropped his spear and, screaming, jumped off the platform into the dark street below.

The sky was brightening. The city seemed asleep, but across the angle of the wall I could see another sentry on the platform, his long spear outlined against the gray-pink of dawn. Instead of charging at us he turned and ran toward the square stone tower that flanked the Scaean Gate.

"He'll alarm the guard," I said to Magro. "They'll all be at us in a few moments."

Magro nodded, his battle-hardened face showing neither fear nor anticipation.

It was now a race between Odysseos' Ithacans and the Trojan guards. We had won a foothold inside the walls; now our job was to hold it. As my men swiftly broke out the spears and shields that we had roped to the tower's timbers, I glanced over the parapet. Fog and darkness still shrouded the plain. I couldn't see Odysseos and his men in the shadows—if they were there.

A dozen Trojan guards spilled out of the watchtower, and I saw even more Trojans rushing toward us from the far side of the tower, running along the south wall, spears leveled. The battle was on.

My men had faced spears before, and they knew how to use their own. We formed a defensive wall by locking our shields together and put out a bristling hedgehog front with our long spears. I took a spear and butted my shield next to Magro's, at the end of our line. I could feel my heart pounding; my palms were slippery with sweat.

The Trojans attacked us with reckless fury, practically leaping on our spear points. They fought to save their city. We fought for our lives. There was no way for us to retreat without being butchered. We either held our foothold on the wall or we died.

Our shield wall buckled under their ferocious attack. We were forced a step back, then another. A heavy bronze spear point crashed over the top of my shield, missing my ear by a finger's width. I thrust my spear into the belly of that man: his face went from shocked surprise to the final agony of death in the flash of a heartbeat.

More Trojans were scrambling up the ladders to the platform, strapping armor over their nightclothes as they ran. These were the nobility, the cream of their fighting strength. I could tell from the gaudy plumes of the helmets they were putting on and the burnished bronze of their breastplates glinting in the light of the new day.

Farther off, archers were kneeling as they fired flaming arrows at our tower. Others fired at us. An arrow chunked into my shield. Another hit Harkan, two men down from me, in his leg. He staggered backward and let his shield drop. Instantly a Trojan drove his spear through Harkan's unprotected chest.

Their archers began lofting their shots to get over our wall of shields. Flaming arrows fell among us. Men screamed and fell to the wooden flooring, their clothes and flesh on fire.

The barrage of arrows would quickly break our shield wall and what was left of my men would go down under the weight of Trojan numbers. I felt a burning fury rise inside me, a rage against those archers who knelt a safe distance away and tried to kill us at their leisure. Call it battle fury, call it bloodlust, I felt a flame of hatred and rage that I had never experienced before.

"Hold here," I shouted to Magro. Before he could do more than grunt I drove forward, surprising the Trojans in front of me. Grasping my spear in two hands, level with the floor, I pushed four of them off their feet and slipped between the others, dodging their clumsy thrusts as they half-turned to slash at me. I killed one of them;

Magro and the rest of my men pushed forward and killed several more. The Trojans quickly turned back to face my advancing men.

I dashed toward the archers. Most of them turned and ran, although two of them stood their ground and managed to get off a pair of arrows at me. They thudded into my shield as I ran at the archers. I caught the first one on my spear, a lad too young to have more than the wisp of a beard. His companion dropped his bow and tried to pull out the dagger at his waist but I knocked him spinning with a swipe of my shield. He toppled off the platform screaming to the street below.

The other archers had retreated down the platform that ran along the battlements. The men of my squad were fighting the Trojan guards who had rushed them. For the span of a heartbeat I was alone. But only for that long. The Trojan nobles were charging along the platform toward me, a dozen of them, with more climbing the ladder behind them.

I hefted my long spear in one hand and threw it at the nearest man. Its heavy weight drove it completely through his shield and into his chest. He staggered backward into the arms of his two nearest companions.

I threw my shield at them to slow them down further, then picked up the bow from the archer I had slain. It was a beautiful, gracefully curved thing of horn and smooth-polished wood. But I had no time to admire its workmanship. I fired every arrow in the dead youth's quiver as rapidly as I could, forcing the nobles to cower behind their body-length shields, holding them at bay for a precious few moments more.

Once the last arrow was gone and I threw down the useless bow, the leader of the nobles facing me lowered his shield enough for me to recognize his face: handsome young Paris, a sardonic smile on his almost-pretty face.

"So the herald is a warrior after all," he called to me, advancing toward me with leveled spear.

Sliding my sword from its sheath, I replied, "Yes. Is the stealer of women a warrior as well?"

"A better one than you," Paris taunted.

Stalling for time, I said, "Prove it. Face me man to man, your spear against my sword."

He glanced past me, at my men battling at the top of our siege tower. "Much as I would enjoy that, today is not the day for such pleasures."

"Today is the last day of your life, Paris," I said.

As if on cue, a piercing, blood-curdling war cry screeched from behind me. Odysseos!

Paris looked startled for a moment, then he yelled to his followers, "Clear the wall of them!"

The Trojans charged. They had to get past me before they could reach Magro and my men. A dozen spears against my one sword. I shifted to my left, wishing I hadn't been foolish enough to throw away my shield. I barely avoided the first spear point aimed at my belly and hacked at another spear, cutting its haft almost in two with my iron blade. I backed away another step and then stepped back once more—onto empty air.

As I tottered on the edge of the platform another spear came thrusting at me. I banged its bronze head with the metal cuff around my right wrist, deflecting it enough to save my skin. But the motion sent me tumbling off the platform. I turned a full somersault in midair and somehow managed to land on my feet. The impact buckled my knees and I rolled on the bare dirt of the street. A spear thudded into the ground scant fingers' widths from me. I saw a pair of archers aiming their arrows at me and ducked behind the corner of a house before they could fire.

Looking up, I could see, against the brightening morning sky, Paris and his men rushing along the wall toward the spot where the siege tower stood. My undersized squad of Hatti soldiers were battling the Trojans while Odysseos and his men clambered over the wall's battlements and joined the struggle. But dozens more Trojans, roused so rudely from their sleep, were scurrying up ladders and rushing along the platform to overwhelm them. We needed a diversion, something to draw off the Trojan reinforcements.

I sprinted down the narrow alley between houses until I found a door. I kicked it open. A woman screamed in sudden terror as I stamped in, sword in hand. She cowered in a corner of her kitchen, her arms around two small children who huddled against her, wide-eyed with fright. As I strode toward them they all shrieked and ran along the wall, screeching and skittering like mice, then bolted through the open door. I let them go.

A small cook fire smoldered in the hearth. I yanked down the flimsy curtains that separated the kitchen from the next room and tossed them into the fire. It flared into open flame. Then I smashed a wooden chair and fed it into the blaze. Striding into the next room, I grabbed straw bedding and threadbare blankets and added them to the fire.

Two houses, three, and then a whole row of them I set ablaze. People were screaming and shouting. Men and women alike raced toward the fire sloshing buckets of water drawn from the fountain at the end of the street.

Satisfied that the fire would grow and occupy more and more of the Trojans, I started up the nearest ladder to return to the battle on the platform. Achaians were pouring over the parapet now and the Trojans were giving way. I leaped at them from the rear, yelling out to Magro. He heard me and led what was left of my men to my side, cutting a bloody swath through the defending Trojans.

"The watchtower by the Scaean Gate," I shouted, pointing with my reddened sword. "We've got to take it and open the gate."

We fought along the length of the wall, meeting the ill-prepared Trojans as they came up in knots of five or ten or a dozen and driving away those we didn't kill. The fire I had started was spreading to other houses now; a pall of black smoke hid the palace from our sight.

The watchtower was only lightly guarded: most of the Trojans were fighting against Odysseos and his Ithacans on the western wall. We broke into the guard room, using spear butts to batter down the door, and slaughtered the few men there. Then we raced to the ground and started to lift the heavy beams that barricaded the Scaean Gate. A wailing scream arose, and I saw that Paris and a handful of other nobles were racing down the stone steps of the tower toward us.

We had them on the horns of uncertainty now. If they allowed Odysseos to hold the western wall, the rest of the Achaians would enter the city that way. But if they concentrated on clearing the wall, we would open the gate and allow the Achaian chariots to drive into the city. They had to stop us at both places, and stop us quickly.

Archers began shooting at us, but despite them my men tugged and pushed to open the massive gate. Men fell, but the three enormous beams were slowly lifting, swinging up and away from the doors.

I ducked an arrow and saw Paris running toward me across the open square behind the gate.

"You again!" he shouted at me.

Those were his last words. He charged me with his spear. I dodged sideways, forced it down with my right forearm, and drove my iron sword through his bronze breastplate up to its hilt. As I yanked it out, bright red blood spattered over the golden inlays of his armor and I felt a mad surge of pleasure, battle joy that I had taken the life of the man who had caused this war.

Paris sank to the ground. I saw the light go out of his eyes. At that moment an arrow struck me on my left shoulder. I felt a sudden flare of pain. More annoyed than injured, I yanked it out and flung it to the ground.

Even as I did so, more Trojans came at me. But they stopped in their tracks as a great creaking groan of bronze hinges told me that the Scaean Gate was swinging open at last. A roar went up and I turned to see chariots plunging through the open gate, bearing down directly on me.

The Trojans scattered and I dived out of the way. Agamemnon was in the first chariot, spear raised triumphantly over the plume of his helmet. His horses pounded over Paris' dead body and the chariot bumped, then clattered on, chasing the fleeing Trojan warriors.

I stepped backward, dust from the charging chariots stinging my eyes, coating my skin, my clothes, my bloody sword. The battle lust in me began to ebb as I watched

Paris' mangled body tossed and crushed by chariot after chariot. Magro came up beside me, a gash on his cheek and more on both his arms. None of them looked serious, though.

"The battle's over," he said. "Now the slaughter begins."

12

Suddenly I was bone weary. I leaned my back against the rough stone wall of Troy.

"You're hurt," Magro said.

"It's not serious." My shoulder was covered with blood, but the wound had already clotted.

The rest of my men gathered around me, each of them bleeding from wounds. There were only six of us now. They looked uneasy. Not frightened, but edgy, nervous.

"Now's the time when soldiers collect their pay," Magro said tightly.

Loot, he meant. Stealing everything you can carry. Raping the women and then putting the city to the torch.

"Go," I said, realizing that I myself had set the first fire. "I'll be all right. I'll see you back at camp when the sun goes down."

Magro touched his fist lightly to his chest, then turned to the four remaining men. "Follow me," he commanded. "And remember: don't take any chances. There are still plenty of armed men left alive. And some of the women will try to use knives on you."

"Any bitch who tries to cut me will regret it," growled Manetho, the oldest man of my squad.

"Any bitch who sees your ugly face will probably use her knife on herself!" Magro jeered.

They all laughed and marched off together. Five men. Out of my original twenty.

For a while I stood near the wall and watched the Achaian chariots and foot soldiers pour through the open, undefended gate. The smoke was getting thicker. I squinted up at the sky and saw that the sun had barely topped the wall. It was still early in the morning.

So it is done, I said to myself. The city has fallen. Whatever gods the Trojans prayed to have done them no good. I felt no exultation, no joy at all. Killing a thousand men and boys, burning down a city that had taken so many generations to build, raping women and carrying them off into slavery—this is not triumph.

Slowly I pulled myself erect. The square before the gate was empty now, except for the mangled bodies of Paris and the other slain men. Up the rising main street, behind the first row of columned temples, I could see flames soaring into the sky, smoke billowing toward heaven. A sacrifice to the gods, I thought bitterly.

I looked down at what was left of Paris. We all die, prince of Troy. Your brothers have died. Your father is probably dying at this very moment.

But my sons still live. And my wife. I'll take them tonight. Whether Agamemnon agrees or not I will reclaim my sons and my wife and leave this cursed city.

Then I thought of Helen. Beautiful Helen who was the cause for this slaughter, the woman who used me as a messenger, who used all the men around her to do her bidding. But what else could she have done? How else would she have survived? She was fighting for her life, using the only weapons the gods had allowed her.

Where is she? Is she waiting in the temple of Aphrodite, as Odysseos told her to do?

I decided to find out.

13

I strode up the main street of burning Troy, sword in hand, through a morning turned dark by the acrid smoke of fires I had started. Women's screams and sobs filled the air, men bellowed and laughed raucously. The roof of a house collapsed in a shower of sparks. I thought of my father's house, where he lay buried beneath its ashes.

Up the climbing central street I walked, my face blackened with dust and smoke, my shoulder caked with my own blood. The gutter along the center of the cobbled street ran red.

A pair of children ran shrieking past me, and a trio of drunken Achaians lurched laughingly after them. I recognized one of them: Giant Ajax, lumbering along with a wine jug in one huge hand.

"Come back!" he yelled drunkenly. "We won't hurt you!"

I climbed on, toward the palace and the temples, past the market stalls that now blazed hot enough to singe the hairs on my arms, past a heap of bodies where some of the Trojans had tried to make a stand. Finally I reached the steps in front of the palace. They too were littered with fallen bodies.

Sitting on the top step, his head in his hands, was Poletes. Weeping.

"How did you get here?" I was stunned with surprise.

He looked up at me with tear-filled eyes. "I rode on the back of a chariot. I had to see for myself . . ." His voice choked with anguish.

Sheathing my sword, I asked, "Are you hurt?"

"Yes," he said, bobbing his bald head. "In my soul."

I almost felt relieved.

"Look at the desolation. Murder and fire. Is this what men live for? To act like beasts?"

I grasped him by his bony shoulder and lifted him to his feet. "Sometimes men act like beasts. They can build beautiful cities and burn them to the ground. What of it? Don't try to make sense of it, just accept us as we are."

Poletes looked at me through eyes reddened by tears and smoke. "So we should accept the whims of the gods and dance to their tune when they pull our strings? Is that what you tell me?"

"What else can we do?" I replied. "We do what we must, old moralizer. We obey the gods because we have no choice."

Poletes shook his head.

"Go back to the camp, old man. This is no place for you. Some drunken Achaian might mistake you for a Trojan."

But he didn't move, except to lean his frail body against the pillar behind him. Its once-bright red paint was blackened by smoke and someone had scratched his name into the stone with a sword point: Thersites.

"I'll see you back at camp, tonight," I said.

He nodded sadly. "Yes, when mighty Agamemnon divides the spoils and decides how many of the women and how much of the treasure he will take for himself."

"Go to the camp," I said, more firmly. "Now. That's not advice, Poletes, it's my command."

He drew in a long breath and sighed it out.

"Take this sign." I handed him the armlet Odysseos had given me. "It will identify you to any drunken lout who wants to take off your head."

He accepted it wordlessly. It was much too big for his frail arms, so he hung it around his skinny neck. I had to laughed at the sight.

"Laughter in the midst of the sack of a great city," Poletes said. "You are becoming a true Achaian warrior, my master."

With that he started down the steps, haltingly, like a man who really didn't care which way he went.

I walked through the columned portico and into the hall of statues, where Achaian warriors were directing slaves to take down the gods' images and carry them off to the boats. Into the open courtyard that had been so lovely I went. Pots were overturned and smashed, flowers trampled, bodies strewn everywhere staining the grass with their blood. The little statue of Athene was already gone. The big one of Apollo had been toppled and smashed into several pieces.

One wing of the palace was afire. I could see flames crackling through its roof. I closed my eyes for a moment, trying to picture in my mind the chamber where Helen had spoken to me. It was where the fire blazed, I thought.

From a balcony overhead I heard shouts, then curses.

The clash of blade on blade. A fight was going on up there.

"The royal women have locked themselves in the temple of Aphrodite," a man behind me yelled. "Come on!" He sounded like someone rushing to a feast, or hurrying to get to his seat before the opening of the final act of a drama.

I snatched my sword from its scabbard and rushed up the nearest stairs. A handful of Trojans was making a last-ditch defense of a corridor that led to the royal temples, fighting desperately against a shouting, bellowing mob of Achaian warriors. They were holding the narrow corridor, but being pressed back, step by bloody step.

I realized that behind the locked doors at the Trojans' backs must be the temple of Aphrodite. Aged Priam must be waiting for the final blow in there, together with his wife, Hecuba, and their daughters and grandchildren.

And Helen.

I saw Menalaos, Diomedes and Agamemnon himself thrusting spears at the few remaining Trojan defenders, laughing at them, taunting them.

"You sell your lives for nothing," shouted Diomedes. "Put down your spears and we will allow you to live."

"As slaves!" roared Agamemnon.

The Trojans fought bravely but they were outnumbered and doomed, their backs pressed against the doors they were trying so valiantly to defend. More and more Achaians rushed up to join the sport.

I sprinted down the next corridor and pushed my way through rooms where soldiers were tearing through chests of gorgeous robes, grabbing jewels from their gold-inlaid boxes, pulling beautiful tapestries from the walls. This wing of the palace would also be in flames soon, I knew. Too soon.

I found a balcony, climbed over its balustrade and, leaning as far forward as I dared, clamped one hand on the edge of a window in the rear wall of the temple wing. I swung out over thin air and pulled myself up onto my elbows, then hoisted a leg onto the windowsill. Pushing aside the beaded curtains, I peered into a small, dim inner sanctuary. The walls were niched with small shrines, each lit by a flickering candle. The tiles of the floor were so old they had been worn to dullness. The small votive statues in the niches were decked with rings of withered flowers. The room smelled of incense and old candles.

Standing by the door, her back to me, was Helen.

14

A pet, standing in a shadowy corner, saw me and hissed, "The Hittite."

Helen whirled to face me, her fists pressed against her mouth, her body tense with terror.

"Lukka," she whispered.

She stood there for an uncertain moment, dressed in her finest robe, decked with gold and jewels, more beautiful than any woman has a right to be. She ran to me and pressed her golden head against my grimy, blood-stained chest. Her hair was scented like fragrant flowers.

"Don't let them kill me, Lukka! Please, please! They'll

be crazy with bloodlust. Even Menalaos. He'll take my head off and then blame it on Ares or Athene! Please, please protect me!"

"That's why I came to you," I said. As I spoke the words I realized that they were true. It was the one decent thing I could do in the midst of this mad, murderous day. I had broken past Troy's lofty walls. I had killed the man who had abducted Helen. Now I would see that she herself would not be slain, not even by her rightful husband.

"Priam is dead," she said, her voice muffled and sobbing. "His heart broke when he saw the invaders coming over the wall."

"The queen?" I asked.

"She and the other royal women are in the main temple, just on the other side of that door. The guards outside have sworn to go down to the last man before allowing Agamemnon and his brutes to enter here."

I held her and listened for the clamor of the fight out in the corridor. It didn't last long. A final scream of agony, a final roar of triumph, then a thudding as the Achaians pounded against the locked doors. A splintering of wood, then silence.

"It would be better if you went in there," I suggested, "rather than forcing them to break in and find you."

Helen pushed herself away from me and glanced at Apet, still hovering in the shadows. Visibly struggling for self-control, Helen lifted her chin like the queen she had hoped to be. At last she said, "Yes. I am ready to face them."

I went to the connecting door, unlatched it, and opened it a crack. Agamemnon, his brother Menalaos, and dozens of other Achaian nobles were crowding into the temple, goggling at the gold-covered statues taller than life that lined its walls. The floor was gleaming marble. At the head of the temple, behind the alabaster altar, loomed a towering statue of Aphrodite, gilded and painted, decked with flowers and offerings of jewels. Hundreds of candles burned at its base, casting dancing highlights off the gold and gems. The victorious Achaians focused their attention on the richly draped altar and the old woman lying upon it.

I had never seen Hecuba before. The aged, wrinkled woman lay on the altar, arms crossed over her breast, eyes closed. Her robes were threaded with gold; her wrists and fingers bore turquoise and amber, rubies and carnelian. Heavy ropes of gold necklaces and a jewel-encrusted crown had been lovingly placed upon her. Seven women, dressed in the ash-gray robes of mourning, stood trembling around the altar, facing the sweaty, bloodstained Achaians, who gaped at the splendor of the dead Queen of Troy.

One of the older women was speaking to Agamemnon. "My mother took poison once the king died. She knew that Troy would not outlive this evil day, that my prophecy had finally come true."

"Cassandra," whispered Helen to me. "The queen's eldest daughter."

Agamemnon turned slowly from the corpse on the altar to the gray-haired princess. His narrow little eyes glared anger and frustration.

Cassandra said, "You will not bring the Queen of Troy back to Mycenae in your black boat, mighty Agamemnon. She will never be a slave of yours."

A leering smile twisted Agamemnon's lips. "Then I'll

have to settle for you, Princess. You will be my slave in her place."

"Yes," Cassandra said. "And we will die together at the hands of your faithless wife."

"Trojan bitch!" He cuffed her with a heavy backhand swat that knocked her to the marble floor.

Before any more violence erupted, I swung wide the door of the sanctuary. The Achaians turned, hands gripping the swords at their sides. Helen stepped through with regal grace and an absolutely blank expression on her beautiful face. It was as if the most splendid statue imaginable had taken on the glow of life.

She went wordlessly to Cassandra and helped the princess to her feet. Blood trickled from her cut lip.

I stood by the side of the altar, my hand resting on the pommel of my sword. Agamemnon and the others recognized me. Their faces were grimy, their hands stained with blood. I could smell their sweat.

Menalaos seemed to be stunned with shock. Then he suddenly stepped forward and gripped his wife by her shoulders.

"Helen!" His mouth twitched, as if he was trying to say words that would not leave his soul.

She did not smile, but her eyes searched his. The other Achaians watched them dumbly.

Every emotion a human being can show flashed across Menalaos' face. Helen simply stood there, in his grip, waiting for him to speak, to act, to make his decision on whether she lived or died.

Agamemnon broke the silence. "Well, Brother, I promised you we'd get her back! She's yours once again, to deal with as you see fit."

Menalaos swallowed hard and finally found his voice. "You are my wife, Helen," he said, more for the ears of Agamemnon and the others than for hers, I thought. "What's happened since Paris abducted you was not of your doing. A woman captive is not responsible for what happens to her during her captivity."

I thought grimly that Menalaos wanted her back so badly that he was willing to forget everything that had happened. For now.

Agamemnon clapped his brother on the back gleefully. "I'm only sorry that Paris didn't have the courage to face me, man to man. I would have gladly spitted him on my spear."

"Where is Paris?" Menalaos growled.

"Dead," I answered. "His body is in the square by the Scaean Gate."

The women started to cry, all except Helen. They sobbed quietly as they stood by their mother's bier. But Cassandra's eyes blazed with unconcealed fury.

"Odysseos is going through the city to find all the princes and noblemen," said Agamemnon. "Those who still live will make a noble sacrifice for the gods." He laughed at his own pun.

I left Troy for the final time, marching with the Achaian victors through the burning city as Agamemnon led the seven Trojan princesses back to his camp and slavery. Menalaos walked side by side with Helen, which somehow stirred a simmering anger in me. His wife once more. Thanks to me. I brought them this victory and she goes back to him.

I shook my head, trying to clear such thoughts away.

Tonight I claim my sons and my wife. Tomorrow we leave Troy forever.

And go where?

A guard of honor escorted our little procession, spears held stiffly up to the blackened sky. Wailing and sobs rose all around us; the air was filled with the stench of blood and smoke.

I trailed behind and noted that Helen never touched Menalaos, not even to take his hand. I remembered what Apet had told me, that being a wife among the Achaians, even a queen, was little better than being a slave.

She never touched Menalaos, and he hardly glanced at her after that first emotion-charged meeting in the temple of Aphrodite at dead Hecuba's bier.

But she looked back at me over her shoulder more than once, looked at me, as if to make certain that I was not far from her.

IV

▾

HELEN'S FATE

1

The Achaian camp was one gigantic orgy of feasting and roistering all that long afternoon and into the evening. There was no semblance of order and no attempt to do anything but drink, wench, eat and celebrate the victory. Men staggered about drunkenly, draped in precious robes pillaged from the burning city. Women cowered and trembled—those that were not beaten or savaged into insensibility.

Fights broke out. Men quarreled over a goblet or a ring or, more often, a woman. Blood flowed and many Achaians who thought they were safe now that the war had ended learned that death could find them even in the midst of triumph.

Above it all rose the plume of black smoke that marked Troy's funeral pyre. The whole city was blazing now, up on its bluff. Even from the beach we could see the flames soaring through the roofs of the citadel and temples.

It was nearly sunset by the time I arrived back where

Odysseos' boats were lying on the sand. My men were nowhere in sight, although Poletes was sitting there glumly by the cook fire, still with my armlet hung ridiculously around his scrawny neck.

"Have you seen Odysseos?" I asked as I took it from him and fitted it back on my bicep.

"He and the other kings have gone to Agamemnon's cabin. Tonight the High King will offer solemn sacrifices of thanksgiving to the gods," he said. "Many men and beasts will be slaughtered and the smoke of their pyres offered to heaven. Then Agamemnon will divide the major spoils."

I looked past his sad, weatherbeaten face to the smoldering fire of the city, still glowing a sullen red against the darkening shadows of the evening sky.

"You will be a rich man before this night is over, Master Lukka," said the old storyteller. "Agamemnon cannot help but give Odysseos a great share of the spoils and Odysseos will be generous with you—far more generous than the High King himself would be."

I shook my head wearily. "All I want are my sons and my wife."

He smiled bitterly. "Ah, but wait until Odysseos heaps gold and bronze upon you, tripods and cooking pots of precious iron. Then you will feel differently."

There was no point arguing with him, so I said merely, "We'll see."

I decided to go to Agamemnon's part of the camp and get Odysseos to ask that my family be returned to me. But before I could go more than a few steps Magro and the other four remaining men of my squad came staggering drunkenly across the sand toward me, followed by more than a dozen slaves tottering under loads of loot: fine blankets and boots, beautiful bows of bone and ivory, colorful robes. And behind them came a half-dozen women who huddled together, clinging to one another, staring at their captors with wide fearful eyes.

Magro halted his little procession when he saw me standing there, my fists on my hips.

"Is this what you've taken from the city?" I asked him.

He wasn't so drunk that he couldn't stand at attention, although he weaved a little. "Yes sir. Do you want to pick your half now or later?"

It was customary for the leader of a squad to take his choice of half the spoils, then allow the men to divide the remainder among themselves.

I shook my head. "No. Divide it among yourselves."

Magro gaped with astonishment. "All of it?"

"Yes. You've done well to stick together like this. Tonight Agamemnon divides the major spoils. The Achaians may want a share of your booty."

"We've already put aside the king's share," he said. "But your own . . ."

"You take it. I don't want it."

"Not even a woman or two?"

I scowled at him. "I'm going to find my wife, Magro. And my two sons."

He nodded, but the expression on his face made it clear that he thought I was being foolish. And I realized that there was only one woman in the camp that I wanted: beautiful, forbidden Helen.

Shaking my head at my own madness, I left them there by the water's edge and started again toward the part of the beach where Agamemnon's boats rested on the sand.

Before I got halfway there I saw scores of slaves and *thetes* toting armfuls of driftwood, timber, broken pieces of furniture from the looted city toward three tall pyres that they were piling up in the center of the camp, each one taller than the height of a man.

From the other side of the pyres Nestor led a band of priests decked in fine robes taken from Troy in a procession through the camp, followed by Agamemnon, Odysseos and all the other chiefs—all in their most splendid armor and carrying long glittering spears that seemed to me more ornamental than battle weapons.

"They are preparing to make their sacrificial offerings to the gods," said Poletes. I hadn't realized he had tagged along behind me until he spoke. His face looked solemn, gloomy.

"Then Agamemnon should be in a mood to reward me," I said.

Poletes shrugged. "Who knows what mood the high and mighty king will be in?"

I watched as Nestor led the parade through the camp, singing hymns of praise to Zeus and the other immortals. The sacrificial victims were being assembled by the pyres: a whole herd of smelly goats and bulls and sheep, hundreds of them. Horses, too. They kicked up enough dust to blot out the sullen embers of burning Troy up on the bluff. Their bleatings and bellowings made a strange counterpoint to the chanting and singing of the Achaians.

Standing off to one side of them were the human sacrifices, every man over the age of twelve who had been captured alive, their hands tightly bound behind their

backs, their ankles hobbled. I recognized the old courtier who had escorted me to Priam's palace. The victims
stood silently, grimly, knowing full well what awaited
them but neither begging for mercy nor bewailing their
fate. I suppose they each knew that nothing was going
to alter their destiny.

Then I saw a different group, women and boys: slaves
from the camp. They were going to be sacrificed, too, I
realized. Agamemnon had no intention of bringing them
back across the sea with him. Gold, yes. Fine robes and
weapons and jewelry that would add to his treasury. But
not the slaves he had kept at camp, except for the royal
Trojan women.

I ran toward them, seeking Aniti and my sons. A cor-
don of Achaian guards surrounded them, armed with
spears.

"My wife!" I shouted at the nearest one. "I've got to
find my wife."

Like any soldier, he bucked me to his commanding
officer, a stumpy, thickset Achaian named Patros. He
listened to me with some impatience and told me to get
one of the High King's servitors to bring an order releas-
ing my wife and sons.

"Let me find them," I pleaded. "Let me see them so
they know I'll save them."

Patros looked me over. He was a grim-faced old vet-
eran with a dark bushy beard and a no-nonsense attitude.

"I'll hold your sword while you search," he said.

Gladly I gave him my iron sword and plunged into
the crowd of women and boys, shouldering through
them, looking for Aniti.

At last I found her, sitting on the ground amid a sad,
bedraggled group of other women, mostly older than she.

She looked surprised to see me. Scrambling to her feet, she said, "Lukka! You're here!"

"Where are the boys?" I demanded.

"The boys? What of me? They're going to kill me!"

"I'll get them to release you. Where are my sons?"

"Back at Agamemnon's boats. I left them with one of his serving women."

"Good." I turned and started toward the guards ringing the victims.

Aniti grabbed at my arm with both hands, sinking her nails into my flesh. "Wait! Take me with you!"

"The guards won't let you pass."

She was suddenly frantic. "Take me with you! Don't leave me! They'll kill me!"

Other women began to crowd around us, each of them pleading, beseeching. I swatted the nearest with a backhand that knocked her to the sand and the others cringed backward.

To Aniti I said, "I'll be back with one of the High King's men. I'll get them to free you."

"No!" she screamed. "Don't leave me here!"

Pulling free of her, I repeated, "I'll be back in time to free you."

At that instant one of the pyres lit up with a roar. Flames shot skyward. I could feel the blast of heat on my face.

Aniti sank to the ground, sobbing. "Don't leave me, Lukka. Please, please, take me with you."

I knew it was fruitless, but I bent down and lifted her to her feet. "Come on, then," I said, as gently as I could.

Several of the other women followed behind us. Sure enough, Patros, still holding my iron sword, stopped us.

"You can go, Hittite. She cannot."

Two of his spearmen moved toward us. One of them jabbed the butt of his spear at the crowd of women that was gathering behind us and they gave way.

"This one is my wife," I said to Patros.

He shook his head. "Orders. The sacrificial offerings are to stay here until the priests come for them."

Aniti seemed frozen with shock. She stood at my side, eyes wide, mouth half open, clutching my arm.

I said to Patros, "You can keep my iron sword. Just let me take my wife with me."

He was a decent enough man. He knew he couldn't back down from his orders, not even for a sword of iron. But he sent one of his spearmen to find a priest. I waited impatiently. I could see that Aniti was trembling, her eyes darting everywhere, panting with fear.

The spearman brought a priest, a young, apple-shaped fellow with smooth cheeks and oiled locks hanging down to his shoulders. His robe of sea-green was richly embroidered with gold thread: spoils from Troy, I reckoned.

Before Patros could say a word, I fixed the chubby young priest with my sternest glare. "This woman is my wife. I am a Hittite and so is she. She was included in the sacrifice by mistake. I'm taking her with me."

He looked shocked. "Take one of the victims intended for the gods? Sacrilege! Be off with you!"

"The High King was to return her to me," I insisted. "She's here among the victims by mistake."

"The gods don't make mistakes," he answered smugly. "You must accept their judgment."

My hands clenched at my sides. I held my temper, but

just barely. No sense starting a brawl when my sword was in the hands of the guard and he had a pair of spearmen backing him.

"I'll be back with the king's messenger," I said to the priest. "If anything happens to my wife I'll hold you responsible."

The flames of the pyre cast flickering red highlights across his bloated face. "I serve the gods," he said, his voice quavering slightly. "What happens is their doing, not mine."

"And I'll serve you on a spit if my wife isn't here and unharmed when I return."

With that I grabbed my sword out of Patros' hand and headed off for Agamemnon's cabin.

Aniti wailed, "Lukka, wait! Take me with you!"

I lowered my head and broke into a trot. There was no time to waste.

The second pyre burst into flame, and the ritual slaughter began. First came the animals, from a few doves to raging, bellowing bulls that thrashed madly even though their hooves were firmly lashed together, arching their backs and tossing their heads until the priest's ritual stone ax cut through their throats with showers of hot blood. Horses, sheep, goats, all were being led to the sacrificial altars.

As the sun went down the pyres blazed across the darkening beach, sending up smoke to the heavens that the Achaians thought was pleasing to their gods. Before long the priests were covered with blood and the camp stank of entrails and excrement.

2

I reached Agamemnon's boats. It seemed that the whole camp was gathering there. The spoils of Troy had been piled into a gigantic heap, gleaming and glittering in the fires of the pyres. Hundreds of captives were now being marched toward the altars that had been built by the pyres, guarded by solemn-faced warriors.

Agamemnon was sitting on a beautifully carved chair that had been pillaged from the city, up atop a make-shift platform that served as a rough sort of throne. He had already started to divide the spoils, so much for each chieftain, starting with white-bearded old Nestor.

The Achaian nobles were crowding around, greed and envy shining in their eyes. I searched for Odysseos and saw him standing off to one side of Agamemnon's impromptu throne.

As I made my way toward the King of Ithaca, Agamemnon parceled out bronze armor and weapons, gold ornaments, beautiful urns and vases, porphyry and onyx, glittering jewels; kitchen implements of copper, iron tripods and cooking pots; robes, silks, blankets, tapestries— and women, young boys and girls. I thought of my sons. Were they safe? Would the High King hand them over to one of his heroes?

Half of everything Agamemnon kept for himself: the High King's prerogative. But as I pushed past some of the chieftains and nobles I heard them complain about his tightfisted ways.

"He's got the generosity of a dung beetle," grumbled one grizzled old warrior.

"He knows we did the hardest fighting, up on the wall," said an Ithacan. "And what do we get for it? Less than his wine steward."

"Those women should have been ours, I tell you. The fat king is too greedy."

"What can you do? He takes what he wants and we get his leavings."

I thought that even Odysseos looked less than pleased as I neared him. The pyres lit his darkly bearded face with flickering lurid red.

I went around behind the assembled kings. A ragged line of guards in armor stood there, leaning on their spears. The Ithacans recognized me and let me through. I came up behind Odysseos and called softly, "My lord Odysseos."

He twitched with surprise and turned to face me. "Hittite, what are you doing here?"

"My wife has been placed among the sacrificial victims."

He frowned at me. "I can't get Agamemnon's attention now. Later, after the spoils have been meted out."

"But that will be too late! They've already started slaughtering the human sacrifices."

Odysseos glanced at Agamemnon, glorying in his conquest atop his makeshift throne. Then he pulled off the copper band from his wrist. It was studded with glittering jewels. Handing it to me, he said, "Find a priest, show him this and tell him that the King of Ithaca commands him to release your wife."

It was as much as he would do, I realized. I thanked him and sprinted away to search for a priest. In the back of my mind I wondered if my sons were truly safe, but I knew that Aniti was in imminent danger.

It was maddening. The boys must be nearby, I thought. But I had no time to search for them. I pushed through the men crowded around Agamemnon and the pile of spoils, looking for a priest. They were all gathered at the altars that had been set up next to the three pyres, where guards were dragging old men and boys to their deaths.

I raced to the nearest altar, so close to the blazing pyre that the heat of the flames felt like an oven. A lad of ten or eleven was struggling madly as a pair of guards hauled him twisting and screaming to the waist-high stone they were using as an altar. Even with his hands tied behind his back and his ankles hobbled the boy put up enough of a fight for one of the guards to club him with the hilt of his sword. Then they hefted him up, moaning and half-conscious, and draped him across the altar. Three priests stood there, their robes and beards so soaked in blood that they looked black and evil in the flaming light of the pyre.

The boy's eyes opened wide as the oldest priest raised his stone knife. He started to screech but the priest sliced the boy's throat open in a shower of blood that silenced him forever.

There were several other priests, younger men, standing by the altar watching. Their robes were also stiff and black with victims' blood. They looked tired from the work they had been doing. I clutched at the first one I could reach.

"What?" He seemed startled.

Showing him Odysseos' bejeweled wristband, I said, "The King of Ithaca commands the release of one of the women. She was put in among the victims by mistake."

He stared down at the jeweled copper band, then looked up into my face. "You're no Ithacan."

"I serve Odysseos," I said, gesturing to the armband I wore.

The priest was young enough so that his beard was still dark. But his eyes were shrewd, suspicious.

"How do I know that you didn't steal these trinkets?"

I slid my sword from its sheath. "I am a Hittite. My sword is iron. I serve the King of Ithaca."

"I'm only a junior priest, fit only to slaughter animals. I can't—"

"You'll do what I ask or I'll make a sacrifice of you."

Strangely, he smiled at me. "So this sacrificial victim you want to save is a woman, eh?"

"My wife."

That made his dark brows go up. "Your wife?"

"Come with me," I said, clutching his shoulder once again. "I'll explain on the way."

Dragging the priest by his arm, I hurried across the sand to the crowd of victims that were now being herded slowly by their guards toward the sacrificial altars. I quickly told the priest my story, not caring if he believed me or not. The victims shuffled reluctantly toward their doom, some of the women wailing and moaning, but most of them silent and hollow-eyed, beyond hope. The guards prodded them along with their spears.

I couldn't find Patros. The whole mass of victims was moving like a reluctant herd of cattle toward the blazing pyres and the blood-soaked altars. I could smell the iron tang of blood in the air, and the stink of fear: sweat and piss.

"You can't pass through!" said one of the guards as we approached them. He waved his spear angrily.

"The Hittite woman," I shouted at him. "She's to be released."

"What Hittite woman?" the guard shouted back, frowning. Three of his companions came edging toward us.

"My wife, dammit!" I snapped. "I've got to find her before she's killed!"

The guard glanced uneasily at his cohorts, then turned back to me. "Our orders are to feed these people to the altars."

The priest spoke up. "If one of the prisoners is among the victims by mistake . . ." He shrugged his shoulders, unwilling to say more.

"We can't let prisoners go," the guard said. "It's hard enough keeping them moving. I've had to clout some of 'em."

"I serve Odysseos, the King of Ithaca," I said, thrusting the wristband under his nose. "He sent me to save my wife."

He goggled at the band. "King Odysseos? Really?"

"Really. Now let me through. I've got to find her!"

He glanced at the other spearmen again, then looked questioningly at the priest.

"The gods don't need a victim who's offered by mistake," the priest said.

"I guess not," said the guard. He seemed more confused than unwilling. Finally he told me, "All right, go ahead and get her. If you can find her in this crowd."

"I'll find her," I said, pushing past him and plunging into the throng of wailing victims.

I was growing frantic myself. Tugging the young priest along with me, I bulled through the throng of women and children, searching for Aniti.

The soldiers kept urging the crowd forward, toward the altars and blazing pyres. They prodded the victims with the butts of their spears, angry at anyone who was too slow to suit them. A few of them jabbed at the women with their spear points, laughing cruelly even when they drew blood.

One youngster—no more than twelve or thirteen, I thought—stumbled and fell to her knees. A guard kicked her, then pulled her by her hair, screeching, to her feet.

"Keep moving!" he demanded. "Keep moving."

Up at the altars the priests were working in shifts, one man slitting throats until his arms grew tired, then another stepping into his place.

Aniti! I kept telling myself. She's got to be in here someplace!

Where are you? I called silently as I elbowed my way through the sobbing, terrified women and children.

And another fear clutched at my heart. I dreaded the thought that I might find my own sons among the victims. The vision of their being tossed into the flames made me shake with anger.

Finally I made it to the head of the crowd, to the blood-crusted flat stone they were using as an altar. The women screamed and struggled as guards seized them, twisting their arms behind their backs and forcing them to bend over the reeking altar stone. Four priests stood wearily by, while a fifth slashed throats again and again with his ritual stone knife. The victims' screams turned into gurgling death rattles, then the guards dragged the bodies off to the blazing pyres.

The priests looked tired, their faces set in weary resignation. The one who was doing the slaughtering straightened up and handed the knife to another, then stepped back, rubbing his aching arms. The killing went on, one after another, as mechanical as a blacksmith hammering out a sword blade.

The gods know I've killed men and never thought twice about it. But that was in battle, facing men who were armed and doing their best to kill me. What I saw now was nothing more than slaughter, butchery, gods or no gods.

I stepped up to the nearest priest, a shaggy-bearded old man, still dragging the young priest in my grip. The old man went wide-eyed.

"How dare you . . . ?"

"I seek my wife," I said, and I shook the young priest's arm.

"He serves Odysseos," the young priest said, his voice high and shaking. "He says his wife was put in with the victims by mistake."

The older priest scowled at me. "The gods—"

"She's a Hittite!" I interrupted him. "She doesn't belong here. She's tall, with light brown hair. Her name—"

"A Hittite woman?" The priest searched my eyes.

"My wife!"

He shook his head, then turned toward the blazing pyre and the oily black smoke rising thickly from it. "She is one with the gods, Hittite."

3

I stared at the black smoke rising into the darkening sky.

"Had we known . . ." the old priest began. But he saw the look on my face and lapsed into silence.

My young priest looked horrified. But he swallowed hard and managed to say, "The gods have taken her."

The gods. Fat Agamemnon and these brutish warriors. Despoilers of Troy, killers and rapists. And I had
helped them. I had helped them to kill my own wife. I
know I should have felt hot, surging anger: rage, a killing fury. But instead I felt nothing. Nothing. I was numb.
It was as if I had been plunged into the icy waters of the
sea, sinking to the bottom. I heard nothing. I saw nothing. I wanted to scream. I knew I should wreak vengeance on these slaughtering barbarians. But I simply
stood there, paralyzed, as cold as a block of stone.

I had caused this. I had helped them to kill Aniti. She
had depended on me to save her and I had failed.

Then I thought about my sons. I had to find them
before these Achaian butchers took them, too.

Abruptly I turned from the priests and their blood-
caked altar and headed back toward Agamemnon's boats.
My sons would be there, if they lived.

If they lived.

I went from boat to boat, searching for them. A few
remaining serving women huddled next to the curving
hulls, on the side away from the fires, hoping that the
black shadows would hide them from roving drunken
Achaians, trembling and wide-eyed at the slaughter going
on. Many were sobbing, hiding their faces in their hands.
More than one had clapped her hands over her ears, trying to blot out the screams of the sacrificial victims.

A few young boys sat among them, equally terrified.
Lads of ten or so, they seemed. Not my sons. Not my
boys.

They all jumped with surprise at the sight of me, edging away at the sight of an armed warrior. I went from
boat to boat, but my sons were nowhere in sight.

Then one of the older women, her white hair hanging

limply past her shoulders, called to me: "Hittite? You are the Hittite?"

She was short and round; her wrinkled face looked like a crushed piece of parchment in the flickering red light of the fires. An aged grandmother, I thought. She belonged in a farmhouse with her children around her, not here on this blood-soaked beach before the ruins of Troy.

I stepped to her. "I am the Hittite," I said.

"Aniti said you would come," she said, in a voice cracked with age. "When they . . . when they took her she told me to . . . to protect the boys . . . until you came for them."

"Where are they?"

She turned and walked slowly down the length of the boat. Near the steering oar, barely a dozen paces from the lapping water of the sea, two little boys were sleeping soundly beneath a single threadbare blanket.

Asleep. They've slept through it all, I realized. All the blood and fire, all the carousing and screaming. They looked so calm, so relaxed. Their hair was tousled, their eyes softly closed. The smaller of them had his thumb in his mouth.

I sank to my knees beside them. They're alive. They're unhurt. Thank the gods, they're alive.

And then I thought of Aniti. Their mother. My wife. I couldn't protect her, couldn't save her. The last moments of her life must have been terrible. Being dragged away from her babies. Herded in with the other victims. Pushed closer and closer to the blazing pyres. Then forced down on the altar. The last thing she must have seen was that damnable stone knife.

I cried. The tears leaked from my eyes unbidden. I hardly knew Aniti, yet I felt a sadness, a sorrow beyond words. She didn't deserve this fate. I should have done better for her. I had failed her.

But she had not failed her babies. Even as they dragged her off to the sacrificial fires, she had left the boys with this doughty old grandmother and told her that I would come for them.

How long I knelt there sobbing I don't know. But at last I wiped my eyes and focused on my sons. I had failed to protect their mother, but I would die before I'd let any harm fall on them.

I rose to my feet. The old woman stood in the shadows, watching me.

"Thank you, Grandmother," I said. Taking Odysseos' bracelet from my wrist, I handed it to her.

"No!" she gasped. "I couldn't."

"Take it," I said. "It's not a gift. It's payment for protecting my sons."

Reluctantly, with trembling hands, she reached for the bracelet. Even in the shadow of the black boat's hull its gems glittered.

She helped me lift the two boys into my arms. Lighter than my shield, they stirred sleepily but neither of them opened his eyes. Carrying the two of them, I strode past the boats of Agamemnon, determined to leave this camp, this beach, this accursed band of barbarian cutthroats.

And go where? I didn't know, not then. Nor did I care. All I wanted at that moment was to take my sons away from Troy and the victorious Achaians.

Away from Helen, a voice within me whispered. And I loathed myself for the thought.

As I came to the Ithacan boats, where my men were

happily dividing their spoils, Magro saw me approaching. He scrambled to his feet and ran to me.

"You've got them!"

"I've got them."

"And your wife?"

I looked toward the flames still crackling at the pyres. My voice caught in my throat, but at last I was able to croak out, "I was too late."

He shook his head. "Well, there are other women."

I said nothing. Magro helped me to gently lay the boys on a blanket and cover them.

As we straightened up he said, "You'd better look after your servant."

"Poletes?"

"He swilled down a flagon of wine and now he's off telling stories that could get him in trouble."

"Stories?"

"He's mocking Agamemnon and his generosity."

I felt my brows knit. "Isn't everyone?"

"Yes, but he's also talking about Queen Clytemnestra, back in Mycenae. If the High King hears about what he's saying . . ." Magro ran a finger across his throat.

4

"Where is the old windbag?" I asked.

Magro waved in the direction away from the pyres. "He tottered off in that direction. I warned him to keep his mouth shut, but he's full of wine."

I pulled in a deep breath. "I'll find him. Watch over my sons."

Magro glanced down at the sleeping boys. "They'll make good soldiers," he said, grinning.

"What?"

"If they can sleep through this night, they'll be able to sleep anywhere. That's an important gift for a soldier."

"You just make certain no one disturbs them," I said.

Magro tapped his fist to his chest. I turned and started along the beach once more, searching for Poletes. I passed a stream of Achaians toting away their loot, many of them disgruntled with the share of booty Agamemnon had parceled out to them. The fire from the pyres was slowly dying, but off in the distance I could see the city still glowing red with flames behind its high walls.

I found Poletes sitting on the sand by a small campfire, practically under the nose of one of Menalaos' boats, surrounded by a growing mob of squatting, standing, grinning, laughing Achaians. None of them were of the nobility, as far as I could see. But off in the shadows I noticed white-bearded Nestor standing with his skinny arms folded across his chest, frowning in Poletes' direction.

"... and do you remember when Hector drove them all back inside our own gates here, and he came scurrying in with an arrow barely puncturing his skin, crying like a woman, 'We're doomed! We're doomed!' "

The crowd around the fire roared with laughter. I had to admit that the old storyteller could mimic Agamemnon's high voice perfectly. He was in good fettle, the gloom and melancholy of only an hour or so earlier seemed entirely gone now. Perhaps it was the audience surrounding him that had changed his mood. More likely it was the wine; I saw an empty flagon resting on its side an arm's length from his squatting figure.

"I wonder what Clytemnestra will do when her brave and noble husband comes home?" Poletes went on. "I wonder if her bed is high enough off the ground to hide all her lovers?"

Men rolled on the ground with laughter. Tears flowed. I started to push my way through the crowd to get him.

Too late. A dozen armed men tramped in. Poletes' audience scrambled out of their way like leaves blown by the wind. I recognized Menalaos at their head.

"Storyteller!" he roared. "The High King wants to hear what you have to say. Let's see if your scurrilous tales can make *him* laugh."

Poletes' eyes went wide with sudden fear. "But I only—"

Two of the armed soldiers grabbed him under his armpits and hauled him to his feet.

"Come along," said Menalaos.

I stepped in front of them. "This man is my servant. I will deal with him."

Before Menalaos could reply, Nestor bustled up. "The High King has demanded to see this teller of tales. No one can interfere!" It was the shortest speech I had ever heard the old man make.

With a grim shrug, Menalaos headed off toward Agamemnon, his guards dragging Poletes after him, followed by Nestor, me and many of the men who had been rollicking at the storyteller's gibes.

Agamemnon still sat on his slightly tilted throne, fat, flushed with wine, flanked by the treasures of Troy. His chubby fingers gripped the arms of his chair as he watched Poletes being hauled before him. Jeweled rings glittered in the firelight on each finger and both his thumbs.

The old storyteller sagged to his knees, trembling before the High King, who glared down at his skinny, shabby presence.

"You have been telling lies about me," Agamemnon snarled.

Somehow Poletes found enough courage to lift his chin and face the High King. "Not so, your royal highness. I am a professional storyteller. I do not tell lies, I speak only of what I see with my own eyes and hear with my own ears."

"You speak filthy lies!" Agamemnon bellowed. "About me! About my wife!"

"If your wife were an honest woman, sire, I would not be here at all. I'd be in the marketplace at Argos, telling stories to the people, as I should be."

"I'll listen to no calumnies about my wife," Agamemnon warned.

But Poletes, still on his knees, insisted, "The High King is supposed to be the highest judge in the land, the fairest and the most impartial. Everyone knows what is going on in Mycenae—ask anyone. Your own captive Cassandra, a princess of Troy, has prophesied—"

"Silence!" roared the High King.

"How can you silence the truth, son of Atreos? How can you turn back the destiny that fate has chosen for you?"

Now Agamemnon trembled, with anger. He hauled himself up from his chair and stepped down to the ground before Poletes.

"Hold him!" he commanded, drawing out a jeweled dagger from his belt.

Two of Menalaos' men gripped Poletes' frail arms.

"I can silence you, magpie, by separating you from your lying tongue."

"Wait!" I shouted, pushing my way toward them.

Agamemnon looked up as I approached, his piggish little eyes suddenly surprised, almost fearful.

"This man is my servant," I said. "I will punish him."

"Very well then," said Agamemnon, pointing his dagger toward the iron sword at my side. "*You* take out his tongue."

I shook my head. "That's too cruel a punishment for a few joking words."

"You refuse me?"

"The man's a storyteller," I pleaded. "If you take out his tongue you condemn him to starvation or slavery."

Slowly, Agamemnon's flushed, heavy features arranged themselves into a smile. It was not a joyful one.

"A storyteller, is he?" He turned to Poletes, who knelt like a sagging sack of rags in the grip of the two burly soldiers. "You only speak of what you see and what you hear, you claim. Very well. You will see and hear *nothing*! Ever again."

My guts churned as I realized what Agamemnon intended to do. I reached for my sword, only to find ten spears surrounding me, aimed at my body.

A hand clasped my shoulder. It was Odysseos, his face grave. "Be still, Hittite. The storyteller must be punished. No sense getting yourself killed over a servant."

Poletes was staring at me, his eyes begging me to do something. I tried to move toward him, but Menalaos' men jabbed their spear points against my leather jerkin.

"Helen has told me how you protected her during the sack of the temple," Odysseos said, low in my ear. "She owes you a debt of gratitude. Don't force me to repay it with your blood."

"Then do something, say something," I begged. "Please. Try to soothe the High King's anger."

Odysseos merely shook his head. "It will be all over before I could speak a word. Look."

Nestor himself carried a glowing brand from one of the dying pyres, a wicked, perverse smile on his wrinkled face. Agamemnon took it from him as the soldiers yanked Poletes' arms back and one of them jammed a knee against his spine. Agamemnon grabbed the old storyteller by his lank hair and pulled his head back. Again I felt the spear points jabbing against me.

"Wander through the world in darkness, cowardly teller of lies," said the High King.

Poletes shrieked in agony as Agamemnon burned out first his left eye and then his right. The old man fainted. The smile of a sadistic madman still twisting his thick lips, Agamemnon tossed the brand away, took out his dagger again, and sliced the ears off the unconscious old man's head.

The soldiers dropped Poletes' limp body to the sand as the High King tossed the severed ears to the dogs scrambling behind his makeshift throne.

"Well done, Brother," said Menalaos, with a nasty laugh.

Agamemnon looked up and called out in his loudest voice, "So comes justice to anyone who maligns the truth!" Then he turned, smirking, to me. "You can take your servant back now."

The soldiers around me stepped back, but still held their spears leveled, ready to kill me if I moved on their king.

I looked down at Poletes' bleeding form, then up to the High King.

"I heard Cassandra's prophecy," I told him. "She is never believed, but she is never wrong."

Agamemnon's half-demented sneer vanished. He glared at me. For a long wavering moment I thought he would command the soldiers to kill me on the spot.

But then I heard Magro's voice calling from a little way behind me. "Lukka, are you all right? Do you need help?"

The soldiers turned their gaze toward his voice. I saw that Magro had brought my entire contingent with him. There were only five of them, but they were Hatti soldiers, fully armed with spears and shields and iron swords.

"He needs no help," Agamemnon answered, "except to carry away the slave I have punished."

With that he turned away and started tottering back toward his cabin, up the beach, his dogs following him. The soldiers seemed to breath one great sigh of relief and let their spears drop away from me.

I went to Poletes and picked up his bleeding, wimpering body. As we started back toward our own part of the camp, I asked Magro, "My sons?"

"Safe with Odysseos' women. I thought you might want us to back you."

I nodded, too angry and relieved and filled with disgust to speak. But after a half-dozen steps, I told Magro, "We leave camp tomorrow."

"Tomorrow?"

"I want to leave this damned place and all its blood far behind us."

"But where are we going?" Magro asked.

I had no answer.

5

I tended Poletes far into the night. We had only wine to ease his pain, and nothing at all to ease the anguish of his mind. I laid him on the cot in my own tent, groaning and sobbing. Magro found a healer, a dignified old graybeard with two young women assistants. He spread a salve on his burns and the bleeding slits where his ears had been.

"Not even the gods can return his sight," the healer told me solemnly, in a whisper Poletes could not hear. "The eyes have been burned away."

"The gods be damned," I growled. "Will he live?"

If my words shocked the healer he gave no sign of it. "His heart is strong. If he survives the night he could live for years to come."

The healer mixed some powder into the wine cup and made Poletes drink. It put him into a deep sleep almost at once. His women prepared a poultice and showed me how to smear it over a cloth and put it on Poletes' eyes. They were silent throughout, instructing me by showing rather than speaking, as if they were mute. They never dared look directly into my face. The healer seemed surprised that I myself acted as Poletes' nurse, but he said nothing about it and maintained his professional dignity.

I sat over the blinded old storyteller far into the night, putting fresh compresses on his eyes every hour or so, keeping him from reaching up to the burns with his hands. He slept, but even in sleep he groaned and writhed.

Twice I ducked out of the tent and checked my sons. They were still sleeping quietly, side by side, wrapped in a good blanket, oblivious to the world and all its pain.

The candle by the cot had burned down to a flickering stub. Through the flap in my tent I could see the sky starting to turn a pinkish gray with the first hint of dawn. Poletes' breathing suddenly quickened and he made a grab for the cloth covering his eyes. I was faster and gripped his wrists before he could hurt himself.

"Master Lukka?" His voice was cracked and dry.

"Yes," I said. "Put your hands down at your sides. Don't reach for your eyes."

"Then it's true? It wasn't a nightmare?"

I held his head up slightly and gave him a sip of water. "It's true," I said. "You're blind."

The moan he uttered would have wrenched the heart out of a marble statue.

"Agamemnon," he said, many moments later. "The mighty king took his vengeance on the lowly storyteller. As if that will make his wife faithful to him."

"Try to sleep," I told him. "Rest is what you need."

He shook his head and the cloth slid off, revealing two raw burns where his eyes had been. I went to replace the cloth, saw that it was getting dry, and smeared more poultice on it from the bowl at my side.

"You might as well slit my throat, Master. I'll be of no use to you now. No use to anyone."

"There's been enough blood spilled here," I said.

"No use," he muttered as I put the soothing cloth over the place where his eyes had been. Then I propped up his head again and gave him more wine. He soon fell asleep once more.

Magro stuck his head into my tent. "Lukka, King Odysseos wants to see you."

I stepped out into the brightening morning. Commanding Magro to watch over my sons and the sleeping Poletes, I walked swiftly to Odysseos' boat and clambered up the rope ladder that dangled over its curving hull.

The deck was heaped with treasure looted from Troy. I turned from the dazzling display to look back at the city. The fires seemed to have died down, but hundreds of tiny figures were already at work up on the battlements, pulling down the blackened stones, working under the rising sun to level the walls that had defied the Achaians for so long.

I had to step carefully along the gunwale to avoid tripping over the piles of treasure spread over the deck. Odysseos was at his usual place on the afterdeck, standing in the golden sunshine, his broad chest bare, his hair and beard still wet from his morning swim. He had a pleased smile on his thickly bearded face.

Yet his eyes searched mine as he said, "The victory is complete, thanks to you, Hittite." Pointing to the demolition work going on in the distance, he added, "Troy will never rise again."

I nodded grimly. "Priam, Hector, Paris—the entire House of Ilios has been wiped out."

"All but Aeneas the Dardanian. Rumor has it that he was a bastard of Priam's. We haven't found his body."

"He might have been consumed in the fire." Like my wife, I thought. But I held my tongue. No sense making an enemy of this man who had taken me into his household.

"It's possible," said Odysseos. "But I don't think it's

terribly important. If Aeneas lives, he's hiding somewhere nearby. We'll find him. Even if we don't, there won't be anything left here for him to return to."

As I gazed out toward the distant city, one of the massive stones of the parapet by the Scaean Gate was pulled loose by a horde of slaves straining with levers and ropes. It tumbled to the ground with a heavy cloud of dust. Moments later I heard the thump.

"Apollo and Poseidon won't be pleased with what's being done to the walls they built," I said.

Odysseos laughed. "Sometimes the gods have to bow to the will of men, Hittite, whether they like it or not."

"You're not afraid of their anger?"

He shrugged. "If they didn't want us to pull down the walls, we wouldn't be able to do it."

I wondered. The gods are subtler than men, and have longer memories.

Odysseos mistook my silence. "I heard about your wife," he said, his voice grave. "I'm sorry you weren't able to save her."

"I found my sons," I replied tightly. "They're safe with my men now."

"Good." He gestured toward a large pile of loot at the stern of the boat. "It's your turn to select your treasure from the spoils of the city, Hittite. Take one-fifth of everything you see."

I thanked him and spent the next hour or so picking through the stuff. I selected blankets, armor, clothing, weapons, helmets: things we would need once we left this accursed place. And jewels that could be traded for food and shelter once we were away from Ilios.

"There are captives down there, between the boats. Take one-fifth of them, also."

I shook my head. "I'd rather have horses and donkeys. Women will merely cause fights among my men."

Odysseos eyed me carefully. "You speak like a man who has no intention of sailing to Ithaca with me."

"My lord," I said, "you have been more than generous to me. But no man in this camp raised a hand to rescue my wife. No man helped to save my servant from Agamemnon's cruelty."

"You expect much, Hittite."

"Perhaps so, my lord. But it's better that our paths separate here. Let me take my sons and my men, and my blinded servant, and go my own way."

"To where?"

It was my turn to shrug. "There are always princes in need of good soldiers. I'll find a place."

The King of Ithaca stroked his beard for several silent moments. Finally he agreed, "Very well, Hittite. Go your own way. May the gods smile upon you."

"And upon you, noblest of all the Achaians."

I never saw Odysseos again.

6

Despite my eagerness to leave Troy, Poletes was in no condition to travel. He lay in my tent all day, drifting in and out of sleep, moaning softly whether asleep or awake.

The camp was bustling, noisy, slaves and *thetes* loading the boats with loot, carrying the trappings from the cabins of the nobles to the boats. Women were lugging cook pots and utensils to the rope baskets that were being used to haul them up to the decks. Stinking, bleating goats and sheep were being driven from their pens onto the boats. The fine horses that pulled the chariots were led carefully up wooden planked gangways while grunting, sweating slaves pushed the chariots themselves up the gangplanks after them. Everywhere there was shouting, calling, groaning, squealing beneath the hot morning sun. At least the wind off the water cooled the struggling workers somewhat.

I put my men to gathering horses and donkeys, and a pair of carts to go with them. I gave them some of the weapons I had taken from Odysseos' boat to use for trading. Most of them were ornamental, with engraved bronze blades and hilts glittering with jewels: not much use in battle, but they fetched good value in trading for well-shod horses or strong little donkeys.

As I stood in front of my tent surveying the Achaians breaking up their camp and preparing to sail back to their homes, I realized that I didn't know where my sons were. I looked around the boats, asked some of the women busily toting loads. No one had seen them since sunup.

The five-year-old's name was Lukkawi, I recalled, named after me since he was the firstborn. I had to search my memory for his younger brother's name. Uhri, I finally remembered.

Where were they? With growing disquiet I went from boat to boat, searching for them, calling their names over the din and commotion of the camp.

I found them splashing by themselves in the gentle

wavelets lapping up onto the beach, under the stern of one of Odysseos' black boats. They looked up and froze into wary-eyed immobility as I approached them.

"Don't be afraid," I said to them, as gently as I knew how. "I'm your father. Don't you remember me?"

"Father?" asked Lukkawi in a small, fearful voice.

"Where's my mama?" Uhri asked.

I took in a breath and squatted on my heels before them so I could be closer to eye-level with them. I realized that their eyes were gray-blue, like mine.

"Your mother's gone away," I said softly. "But I'm with you now and I'll take care of you."

"Yes, sir," Lukkawi said. He was accustomed to receiving orders, and obeying them, even though he was barely more than five.

Their faces were smudged with grime. The smocks they wore were filthy, tattered. I dropped down onto the sand and took off my sword. Both boys eyed it but made no move to touch it. Then I unlaced my boots and placed them carefully next to the sword.

"Let's take a swim," I said, making myself smile at them.

They made no move, no response.

Getting slowly to my feet, I said, "In the water. We'll pretend we're dolphins."

"Mama told us not to go into the water," little Uhri said in his high child's voice.

"Not above our knees," added Lukkawi.

Nodding, I replied, "That's all right. I'll hold you. We'll look for fish."

I scooped Uhri up in one arm; he was as light as a little bird. I looked down at Lukkawi and offered him my free arm. He hesitated a moment, then reached up and allowed me to lift him off the sand. Both boys clutched at my neck and I stood there for a brief moment, my heart thumping beneath my ribs, my sons in my arms.

And my heart melted. These were my sons. They trusted me to protect them, to provide for them, to show them how to become men. I felt a lump in my throat that I'd never known before.

"We're going into the water now," I told them, my voice strangely husky. "It's all right. I'll hold you. You'll be safe."

Slowly I waded into the water. Up to my knees. Up to my waist. When the boys' feet touched the water they both squirmed.

"It's cold!"

"No, no. That's only the way it feels at first. You'll get used to it and then it will feel warm."

I held them tightly and moved very slowly into deeper water. Uhri let go of me with one hand and splashed a wave into his brother's face. Lukkawi splashed back. In a few heartbeats they were laughing and splashing, drenching me and each other.

We laughed and played together. Before long the boys were paddling happily in the water.

"Look! I'm a fish!" Lukkawi shouted, and then he squirted out a mouthful of water.

"Me too!" cried Uhri.

I sat on the sea bottom, only my head and shoulders above the waves, and watched my sons playing in the water. It was strange. I hardly knew these boys, yet once they clung to me, once they trusted me in the water, I felt as if they were truly mine forever. My father had been right. Flesh of my flesh: these boys were my sons and I would protect them and teach them and help them all I could to grow into strong, self-reliant men.

When I told them it was time to get out of the water they both squalled with complaint. But when I said that I was hungry, they quickly agreed that they were hungry, too. They shivered as we walked back to the tents, despite the warm noontime sunshine. I stripped off their wet rags, rubbed them down with woolen blankets and found decent shifts for them to wear. They were too big, of course: Uhri's dragged on the ground until I got one of the women to stitch a hem on it.

We ate with my men: chunks of broiled goat and warm flat bread. The boys drank water, the men wine. There was plenty of meat to be had, since the sacrifices of the previous night.

That made me think of Aniti again, and my guts clenched inside me. I told myself that there was nothing I could do about her. I had tried my best to save her and failed. Now I had my two sons to take care of. What's done is done and not even the gods can unravel it. Yet my insides burned.

Until my mind pictured Helen's incredible face and golden hair. What's happened to her? I found myself wondering. Does she still live?

After our noonday meal I looked in on Poletes. He was awake, lying on his back on my cot, his eyes covered by a poultice-smeared rag.

"How do you feel?" I asked him.

For a few heartbeats he made no reply. Then, "The pain is easing, Master Lukka."

"Good. Tomorrow we leave this wretched place."

"Will you put me out of my misery then?"

The thought hadn't occurred to me. "No. You'll come with us."

"I'll be nothing but a burden to you."

"You'll come with us," I repeated. "We might need you."

"Need me?" he sounded genuinely surprised at the thought. "Need me for what?"

"To tell the tale of Troy, old windbag. When we come to a village the people will gather 'round to hear your voice."

Again he fell silent. At last he murmured, "At least Agamemnon didn't cut my tongue out."

"His knife would have broken on it, most likely."

Poletes actually laughed a little. "I have you to thank for that small mercy, Master Lukka."

I grasped his knobby knee and shook it. "Rest now. Get a good night's sleep. Tomorrow we travel."

"To where?"

I shook my head, although he couldn't see it. "South, I think. There are cities along the coast that might welcome a group of trained Hatti soldiers."

"And a blind old man."

"And two little boys," I added.

I spent the rest of the afternoon supervising my men as they assembled a pair of sturdy carts and a half-dozen donkeys to pull them. I would have preferred oxen, but they had all been sacrificed. We also had horses for each of us. The boys and Poletes would ride in one of the carts, with the food and water we had collected. Our loot and weapons were piled in the second cart.

The boys tagged along with me all the long afternoon, getting underfoot, asking endless questions about where we were going, how long our trip would be—and whether we would meet their mother on our travels. I answered them abruptly, tried to shoo them out of the way, but they never strayed more than a spear's length from my side.

Once the tide came up, several of Odysseos' boats put out to sea, pushed into the water by grunting, cursing men who scrambled aboard once the boats were afloat. I watched them unfurl their sails and head off into the sunset.

At last all was ready. We gathered around the cook fire as the sun went down and had our last meal on the beach encampment along the plain of Ilios. In the last rays of the dying sun I saw that Agamemnon's vengeance on the city was far from complete. Troy's walls still stood: battered and sooty from the fires that had raged in the city, but despite the Achaians' efforts most of the walls still stood.

I brought my boys into my tent and made bedrolls out of fine Trojan blankets for them; they fell asleep almost as soon as they lay down. I stood over them while the shadows of dusk deepened. Their faces were as smooth and unlined as statues of baby godlings. All that had happened to them, all that they had suffered and lost, did not show one bit in their sleeping, trusting faces.

At last I laid out a blanket for myself next to them. It was fully dark now, and tomorrow would not be an easy day, I knew.

But before I could stretch out for sleep Magro called my name. I stepped out of the tent and he said softly, "We have a visitor."

S tanding in the lengthening shadows was Apet, in her black Death's robe with its hood pulled up over her head. I sent Magro to his tent as I stepped up before her.

"You come from Helen?" I asked.

"Yes," she whispered. And without waiting for another word she turned and ducked inside my tent.

A single candle burned beside my cot. It cast enough light to see Poletes lying there asleep, the greasy cloth across his eyes, the blood-caked slits where his ears had been, my two sleeping boys on the other side of the tent.

She gasped. "They talked about it in the camp . . ."

It was not Apet's voice. I grasped her by the shoulders and pulled her toward me, then pushed down her hood. Helen's bountiful golden hair tumbled past her shoulders.

"You!"

In the flickering light of the candle I saw that her face was battered, one cheek bruised blue-black, her eye swollen, her lower lip split and crusted with blood.

"Menalaos?" I asked needlessly.

Helen nodded numbly. "He was drunk. I did what he asked but he was so drunk he couldn't become aroused. He called me a witch and said I'd cast a spell over him. Then he beat me. Apet tried to stop him and he knocked her unconscious. He says he'll kill us both once we get back to Sparta."

"How did you get away from him?"

"He drank himself into a stupor. I told the guard that

I was sending my servant to find a healer. Then I left Apet in the cabin and came searching for you."

Poletes moaned and shifted on the cot slightly.

Helen looked down at him. "Agamemnon did this?"

"With his own hand," I answered, hot anger seething inside me. "Out of sheer spite. Drunk with power and glory, your brother-in-law celebrated his victory by mutilating an old man. And murdering my wife."

"Your wife?"

"One of the victims of Agamemnon's thanksgiving to the gods for his victory."

Helen lowered her eyes. But not before I saw that there was not one tear in them.

"Your husband stood by and watched it all," I said to her, my rage growing hotter. "His men held me at spear point while his brother did his noble deed."

She nodded and turned away from Poletes.

"What do you want of me?" I asked her.

In a flat, almost hopeless voice, Helen replied, "You see how cruel they are. What monsters they can be."

I said nothing, but in my mind I pictured again Aniti's final moments: the terror she must have felt. The pain.

"He's going to kill me, too, Lukka. He's going to take me back to Sparta and kill me, but not until he's had his fill of me. Then he'll have his priests put me on the altar like a sacrificial sheep and slash my throat. Just as they did to your wife."

Her voice was rising, her eyes were wide, but it seemed to me that she was not panicking. Fearful, certainly. But she was not frenzied; instead she was grimly seeking a way out of the fate that loomed before her.

I asked coldly, "What do you expect me to do about it?"

"You will take me away from this camp. Now, to-night, while they are all sleeping. You will take me to Egypt."

I almost laughed. "Is it the Queen of Sparta who commands me, or the princess of Troy?"

Something flickered in her eyes, but Helen maintained her composure. "It is a woman who has nothing to look forward to but pain, humiliation, and death."

Like my wife, I thought. Like Aniti.

"Do you want me to beg you?" Helen said, a tiny hint of a quaver in her voice. "Do you want me to drop to my knees and clasp your legs and beg you to save my life?"

She *was* begging, I realized. In her own way, the most beautiful woman in the world was pleading with me to take her away from her rightful husband, a man who had just fought a war and conquered a powerful city to get her back. She was too proud to admit it, but she was beseeching me to help her escape her fate.

"I have five men with me, not an army. Menalaos will track us down and kill us all."

"He won't know I went with you," she said, her words coming faster now that she felt some hope. "He'll search the camp, the boats. We'll be far from here by the time he realizes what's happened."

"Egypt is a thousand leagues from here."

"But there are cities along the way. Miletus. Ephesus. Civilized kingdoms. Apet told me of Lydia, and of Phrygia, where King Midas turns anything he touches into gold!"

"Egypt," I muttered.

"It's the only truly civilized land in the whole world, Lukka. I will be received as the queen I am. They will treat me royally. Your men can find a place in the pharaoh's army."

I should have refused her. I should have flatly told her it was madness and sent her back to Menalaos. But in my mind a mad tapestry of vengeance was weaving itself. I pictured the fat, stupid, cruel face of Agamemnon when he discovered that his sister-in-law, the woman for whom he had supposedly fought this long and bloody war, had spurned his brother and run off with a stranger. Not a prince of Troy, but a lowly Hittite soldier. Not carried off unwillingly, but run away at her own insistence.

I saw Menalaos, too, he who had his men hold me at bay while his brother mutilated Poletes. He who beat this woman who stood pleadingly before me.

Let them eat the dirt of humiliation and helpless fury, I said to myself. Let the world laugh at them while Helen runs away from them once again. They deserve it. They deserve all that and more.

They would search for us, I knew. They would try to find us. And if they did they would kill me and my sons. And Helen, also, sooner or later.

My sons. It was my duty to protect them. I had come all this way to find them, to save them from slavery. What Helen asked would put them in danger, put all of us in danger.

And there was Helen herself. She was a queen, a woman of the nobility, while I was a common soldier. But she was willing to put herself in my charge, place her life in my hands. Her body, as well?

I shook my head to drive away such thoughts. Madness. I'm just a servant, as far as she's concerned: a professional soldier who can help her to get away. Nothing more. I looked again at Helen's face, so beautiful even though battered, her eyes filled with hope and expectation, innocent yet knowing. She was maneuvering me, I realized, using me to make her escape from these Achaian barbarians. Was she offering herself as my reward for defying Menalaos and Agamemnon? No, I thought. She expects me to do what she wishes because she's a noblewoman and I'm trained to follow orders.

"Very well," I heard myself say to her. "We'll leave at first light."

Helen beamed a smile at me. "I'll stay here, then. With you."

"You can stay here in the tent with Poletes and my sons. You'll have to sleep on the ground."

Helen nodded gratefully. "I'll be back in a few moments," she said, in a half whisper, then hurried out, pulling the hood of Apet's black cloak over her golden hair.

I realized she was attending to nature's call. I turned and looked down at Poletes. He was stirring on the cot, muttering something. I bent low to hear his words.

"Beware of a woman's gifts," he croaked.

I frowned at him. "Now you utter prophecies instead of stories, old man."

Poletes did not reply.

8

I slept poorly, on the ground outside the tent, knowing full well what lay ahead of us. What little sleep I got was filled with fitful dreams of Egypt, a hot land stretching along a wide river, flanked on either side by burning desert. The Hatti had fought wars against the Egyptians, in the land of Canaan beside the Great Sea. But Egypt itself no Hatti soldier had ever seen. My dreams showed me a land of palm trees and crocodiles, so ancient that time itself seemed meaningless there. A land of massive pyramids standing like enormous monuments to the gods amid the puny towns of men, dwarfing all human scale, human knowledge.

It was still dark when I decided I could sleep no more. Egypt. Far-distant Egypt. We would have to travel a long time, through strange kingdoms and hostile territory. To bring fair-haired Helen to Egypt.

Once the first gray hint of dawn started lighting the eastern sky I roused my men and got them ready to leave. After a cold breakfast of figs and stale bread we loaded my boys and Poletes into one of the wagons with Helen, muffled once again in Apet's hooded black robe.

Then it struck me. "What about your servant?"

From inside the hood Helen answered, "I can't go back for her, Lukka. She'll have to remain behind."

"But once Menalaos realizes you've gone . . ."

"Apet will say nothing."

"Even when they put her feet in the fire?"

Sitting up on the wagon's headboard, Helen was silent for a heartbeat. Then, "Apet knows that if I'm not back to her by sunrise I've fled with you. She has sworn to kill herself before Menalaos can even begin questioning her."

I felt my jaw drop open. "And you'll let her die?"

"She's very old, Lukka. She would only slow us down."

"You'll let her die?" I repeated.

"She loves me," Helen said, her voice firm, as if she had thought it all out in her head and made her decision.

I stared up at her. Helen avoided my eyes. "You said you loved her," I said.

With a burst of impatience, she demanded, "What would you have me do? You're a soldier. Will you invade Menalaos' camp and steal my servant away? You and your five men?"

I had no answer for that.

Leaving Helen sitting in her black robe, I straddled the thickly folded blanket that served as a saddle and nosed my horse toward Magro, who was leading a string of three ponies.

"Go drive the wagon," I told him, reaching for the reins he held. "I'll take the horses."

"We're really going to Egypt?" he asked, smiling quizzically at me.

I nodded.

"With your woman?" Magro tilted his head in Helen's direction.

"She's not my woman."

Still smiling, "Then who is she?"

I decided to evade his question, for the time being. "Will it cause trouble with the men? Jealousy?"

Magro scratched at his beard. "There've been plenty of women in the camp. Especially in the last two nights."

"I don't want the men dragging along camp followers."

"The men are satisfied for now. We can move faster without camp followers, that's for certain."

I could see from the look in his eye that he was thinking I was already dragging our little group down with two little boys and a blind old man. And now a woman.

Magro shrugged and let his smile grow wider. "We'll find women here and there as we march, I suppose."

I understood what he meant. "Yes. Our passage to Egypt won't be entirely peaceful."

His eyes locked on mine. "I hope we can leave the camp peacefully."

I made myself smile back at him.

So we started out of the Achaian camp on the sandy beach. Ships were gliding out onto the sea, colorful sails bellying out as they caught the wind, carrying the victorious Achaians to their home cities. Troy still stood, gutted and burned black, its walls battered but still standing, for the most part. The sun rose in the east as it always does while our little procession of two carts and a dozen horses filed slowly through the gate that I had defended against Hector and down onto the strangely quiet plain of Ilios.

A pair of young warriors slouched by the gate, their spears on the ground, gnawing on haunches of roasted lamb. They waved lazily at us as we passed. Helen stayed inside the first wagon, tucked down among the bags of provisions with my two sons and Poletes.

We forded the shallow river and turned south, where the land rose slightly toward distant bare brown hills. I took over the wagon and let Magro take the horses. The rest of the men rode easily, glad to be mounted instead of afoot, as usual.

As we climbed the rutted trail I turned back for one last look at the ruin of Troy. The ground rumbled. Our horses snorted and neighed, prancing nervously. Even the donkeys pulling the carts twitched their long ears and hurried their pace unbidden.

"Poseidon speaks," said Poletes from the depths of the wagon, his voice weak but clear. "The earth will shake soon from his wrath. He will finish the task of bringing down the walls of Troy."

The old storyteller was predicting an earthquake. A big one. All the more reason to get as far away as possible.

Then Hartu, riding at the rear of our little .group, pointed and shouted, "Lukka! Riders!"

I looked in the direction he was pointing and saw a cloud of dust. Riders indeed, I thought. Probably sent by Menalaos to search for his missing wife.

I snapped the reins, urging the donkeys onward. Thus we left Troy.

9

As I had feared, our journey southward was neither easy nor peaceful.

The whole world seemed to be in conflict. We trekked slowly down the hilly coastline, through regions that the Hatti called Assuwa and Seha. Once these people had been vassals of the emperor; now they were on their own, without the armed might of the Hatti to protect them, without the emperor's law to bring order to their lives.

It seemed that every city, every village, every farmhouse was in arms. Bands of marauders prowled the countryside, some of them former Hatti army units just as we had been, most of them merely gangs of brigands. We fought almost every day. Men died over a brace of chickens, or even an egg. We lost a few men in these skirmishes and gained a few from bands that begged to join us. I never accepted anyone who was not a former Hatti soldier, a man who understood discipline and knew how to take orders. Our little band grew sometimes to a dozen men, never fewer than six.

I kept anxiously searching our rear, every day, for signs of Menalaos' pursuit. Helen tried to convince me that her former husband would be glad to be rid of her, but I thought otherwise. There were times when the hairs on the back of my head stood up. Yet, when I turned to search, I could find no one following us.

I did not sleep with Helen. I hardly touched her. She traveled as one of our group, watching after my sons when she wasn't tending to Poletes. She never complained of the hardships, the bloodletting, the pain. She made her own bed on the ground out of blankets and slept slightly separated from the men. But always closer to me than anyone else. She wore no jewels and no longer painted her face. Her clothes were plain and rough, fit for traveling rather than display. It wasn't easy, but I was determined to be her guardian, not her lover; too many complications and jealousies lay in that direction. If my coolness surprised her, she gave no hint of it.

Yet at night as I lay on the cold, hard ground I cursed myself for a fool. I knew that if I wanted her she would yield to me. What choice would she have? But I couldn't take her that way. No matter the urges of my body, I could not force myself on her. Each night I felt more miserable, more stupid. And each night I dreamed of Helen, although sometimes her face changed to Aniti's.

Poletes slowly grew stronger, and began to learn how to feel his way through his blindness. He was very good with my sons, amusing them for hours with his endless trove of stories about gods and heroes, kings and fools.

The boys were a constant source of joy for me. And

worry. Too innocent to understand the dangers we faced, they played rough-and-tumble games whenever we camped. On the march they ran alongside our carts or begged rides on the horses, then returned to their wagon with Poletes or Helen. But even then they kept themselves busy turning empty flour sacks into tents, broken tools into magic swords. It never ceased to amaze me how little boys could turn almost anything into a toy.

I tried to keep them out of sight when we were in a village or town. And I insisted that Helen stay well hidden among the sacks and bundles in the wagons. She grew impatient, of course, as women will.

"But no one knows of me here," she said as we approached the city of Ti-smurna. "We're hundreds of leagues from Troy."

I was sitting on the wagon's highboard beside her, working the donkeys' reins. Behind us, among the bales and baggage, Poletes was spinning a tale about Herakles to my two eagerly listening boys. The men were riding the horses up ahead of us and the other wagon was trundling along in the rear, with the string of extra horses ambling along behind.

I shook my head. "How do you know that Menalaos or some other Achaians haven't come to this city in search of you?"

She was wearing a simple shift, and the long weeks on the road had thinned her face somewhat. Her flawless skin was coated with dust, but her glorious hair shone in the sunlight like a torrent of gold.

Helen laughed at my fears. "We left Ilios before Menalaos realized I was gone, Lukka. He couldn't have gotten here ahead of us."

"Couriers ride fast horses," I said.

"We would have seen them on the road long before this," she countered.

"Ships travel faster still."

That stopped her. She knew that Menalaos had dozens of boats to send in search of her, if he wished. Even though we had traveled along the coast road most of the way, the road cut well inland in several places. A boat could have passed and we would never have seen it.

But Helen replied, "He'd never send one of his precious boats to seek me. He'd never admit I'd gotten away from him once again. No, Lukka, he's telling everyone he killed me and burned my body. He's not trying to find me."

I nodded wearily. It was no use arguing with her. She was determined to believe what she wanted to believe. But I still felt that uneasy prickling sensation that warned me we were being followed.

Ti-smurna was a sizable city, the largest in the land of the Arzawa, who had been vassals of the Hatti emperor until the empire dissolved in civil war. I decided to bypass it. The men grumbled; they had been looking forward to finding a decent inn and sleeping under a roof for a change. With women. Helen became angry at my decision.

"You're being foolish!" she snapped at me. "You're frightened of shadows."

I said nothing. A man doesn't argue with an angry woman. I let her rant. Poletes talked to her that evening, while we camped within sight of the city's walls. I don't know what he said to her, but she calmed down.

Lukkawi and Uhri goggled at the walls of Ti-smurna, and the towers of the citadel that rose above them. To them, it was a magic city of princes and warriors. To me, it was a well-defended city, but hardly impregnable. I could see where a determined army with proper siege equipment could break through those walls and take the city. I wondered what kind of an army they had.

I sent Harta and one of the new men, a Phrygian named Drakos who spoke the local tongue well, into the city to see what they could learn. They returned a day later to report there was no knowledge of the fall of Troy or of Achaians seeking Helen. Yet I worried about being pursued. We skirted Ti-smurna and moved on, southward, still following the coast road.

The rainy season began, and although it turned the roads into quagmires of slick, sticky mud and made us miserable and cold, it also stopped most of the bands of brigands from their murderous marauding. Most of them, at least. We still had to fight our way through a trap in the hills a few weeks south of Ti-smurna.

I myself was nearly killed by a farmer who thought we were after his wife and daughters. Stinking and filthy, the farmer had hidden himself in his miserable hovel of a barn—nothing more than a low cave that he had put a gate to—and rammed a pitchfork in my back when I went in to pick out a pair of lambs. It was food we were after, not women. We had paid the farmer's fat, ugly wife with a bauble from the loot of Troy, but the man had concealed himself when he had first caught sight of us, expecting us to rape his women and burn whatever we could not carry away with us.

He lunged at my back, murder in his frightened, cowardly eyes. Fortunately, Magro was close enough to knock his arm away partially. The pitchfork's tines caught in my jerkin and rasped along my ribs; I felt them like a sawtoothed knife ripping into me.

Magro clouted him to his knees while I sank against the dank wall of the cave, hot blood trickling down my side. The farmer expected us to kill him by inches, and Magro had drawn his sword, ready to hack his head off. But I stopped him. We left him quaking and kneeling in the dung of his animals.

Back at the wagons, Magro helped me take off my leather jerkin and the linen tunic beneath it. The tunic was soaked with blood and badly ripped.

"It didn't go deep," Magro said.

I felt weak, sweaty. "Deep enough to suit me," I muttered, lowering myself to the ground.

Tiwa came up with clean rags and a bucket of water. Helen walked slowly toward me, her eyes wide, her lips trembling.

"You're hurt," she gasped.

"It's not serious," I said, trying to sound brave. "I've had worse."

She knelt at my side and took the bucket and rags from Tiwa. Without a word she dipped them in the water and began to gently clean my wounds. It hurt, but I said nothing. The men gathered around and watched until Helen tied two of the rags around my rib cage with her own hands.

"The bleeding will stop soon," Magro muttered. Then he and the other men turned away, leaving Helen and me alone.

"Thank you," I said to her, my voice half choking in my throat.

She nodded wordlessly, then got to her feet and walked back to the wagon. My two little boys were standing there by the donkeys, staring at me. I waved them over to me.

I could see the fear in their eyes.

"It's nothing," I said to them. "Just a scratch."

Lukkawi made a tiny smile. To his brother he said bravely, "No one can kill our father."

I wished that was true.

10

The rains poured down day after day out of sullen gray skies. We were wet to our skins, our cloaks and clothing soaked, our bags of provisions sodden. The donkeys trudged through the mud slowly, grudgingly. The horses were spattered with mud up to their bellies. We were miserable, cold, our tempers fraying. Some nights it rained so hard we couldn't even start a cook fire.

With the rain came fever. I felt hot and cold at the same time, shivering and sweating. That farmer's dung-coated pitchfork probably carried the evil demons that clamped the fever on me. I grew too weak to drive a wagon, too dizzy even to mount a horse. I lay in the wagon among the soggy, rain-soaked bundles, alongside Poletes.

Helen tended me. She made a tent from horse blankets that kept most of the rain off us. I lay under it, helpless as a baby.

I had crazy dreams: about Aniti, but sometimes she was Helen, and then my two boys were grown men fighting on the battlements of Troy against me. Gods and goddesses appeared in my dreams, and always the goddesses had Helen's face.

Despite all the rigors of our trek she was still beautiful.

Even in my fever-weakened condition I could see that she didn't need paints or gowns or jewelry. Even with her face smudged with mud and her hair tied up and tucked under the cowl of a long dirty cloak, nothing could hide those wide blue eyes, those sensuous lips, that flawless skin.

Slowly the fever left me, until one day I felt strong enough to take over the reins of the wagon once again. Helen smiled brightly at me.

"It's a lovely day," she said. And indeed it was. The clouds were breaking up and warm sunshine made the land glow.

Lukkawi and Uhri scrambled up to sit on either side of me and I let them take turns holding the reins for a few moments. It made them happy.

Poletes was gaining strength, too, and even some of his old quizzical spirit. He rode in our creaking cart and pestered whoever was driving to describe to him everything he saw, every leaf and rock and cloud, in detail.

In truth, the rainy season was behind us at last. The days grew warm, with plentiful sunshine. The nights were balmy and filled with breezes that set the trees to sighing. I felt strong enough to ride a horse again and retook my place at the head of our little column.

Magro nosed his horse up beside me. "You're leaving Helen in the wagon?" A crooked smile snaked across his bearded face.

"She's with Poletes and my boys," I said, knowing where his sense of humor was leading and wishing to avoid it.

But Magro said, "Maybe I'll go back and drive the wagon for a while. Show her my skills at handling stubborn asses."

"Drako is handling the wagon."

"He's just a lad," said Magro. "Why, if Helen should smile at him he wouldn't know what to do about it."

"And you would, eh?"

With a grin and a shrug Magro replied, "I've had some experience with women."

"With a sword in one hand," I said.

"No, no—*willing* women! Back at the camp by Troy I had to fight them off."

I laughed. "I can't picture you fighting off willing women."

"I didn't say I won every battle."

More seriously, I told Magro, "Listen, old friend. She's a noblewoman. She was the Queen of Sparta. And a princess of Troy. She's got no interest in a battle-scarred soldier."

Magro nodded, a bit ruefully. "Maybe so. But she took good care of you when the fever had you down."

"That's because I'm the leader of this troop that's protecting her. She's got no passion for any of us. Her interest is strictly self-protection."

Magro said nothing, but the expression on his face showed clearly that he didn't believe me.

It was two days later that we first spied Ephesus.

We had spent the morning trudging tiredly uphill through a sudden springtime thunderstorm, wet and cold and aching. I was driving the wagon again and Helen sat beside me, wrapped in a royal blue hooded cloak. I had sent two of the men ahead as scouts, and detailed two more to trail behind us, a rear guard to warn of bandits skulking in our rear—or Achaians trying to catch up with us. I still could not believe that Menalaos had given up Helen so easily.

As we came to the top of the hill the rain slackened away as suddenly as it had started. The sun came out; its warmth felt good on my shoulders. One of our scouts was waiting on the edge of the muddy road.

"The city." He pointed.

Ephesus lay below us in a pool of golden sunlight that had broken through the scudding gray clouds. The city glittered like a beacon of warmth and comfort, white marble gleaming in the sunshine.

We all seemed to gain strength from the sight, and made our way down the winding road from the hills to the seaport city of Ephesus.

Magro rode up beside our wagon. "There're no walls around the city!" he marveled.

"Ephesus is dedicated to Artemis the Healer," said Helen. "Men from every part of the world come here to be cured of their ailments. A sacred spring has waters with magical curative powers."

I couldn't help giving her a skeptical look.

"It's true," said Poletes, groping his way up to the front of the wagon to stand between Helen and me. "Everyone knows the truth of it. There are no walls around the city. None are needed. No army has ever tried to take it or sack it. Everyone knows that the city is dedicated to the goddess Artemis and her healing arts; not even the most barbarian king would dare to attack it, lest he and his entire army would fall to Artemis' invisible arrows, which bring plague and painful death."

That reminded me. "Artemis is a moon goddess, isn't she?"

"Yes," Helen said, nodding. "And the sister of Apollo."

"Then she must have favored Troy in the war."

"I suppose she did."

"It didn't do her much good, though," Magro said, with a chuckle. "Did it?" His horse nodded, as if in agreement.

"But she'll be angry with us," I said.

Helen's eyes widened beneath her blue hood. "Then we must find her temple as soon as we enter the city and make a sacrifice to placate her."

"What do we have to offer for a sacrifice?" I asked.

Magro jabbed a finger at the donkeys wearily pulling our wagon. "This team of asses. They're about half dead anyway."

"Don't make light of it," Poletes insisted, his voice stronger than his frail body. "The gods hear your words, and they will punish mockery."

"I will offer my best ring," Helen said. "It is made of pure gold and set with rubies."

"You could buy a whole caravan of donkeys with that," Magro said.

"Then it should placate Artemis very nicely," Helen replied, in a tone that said the matter was settled.

11

Whatever its patron deity, Ephesus was civilization. Even the streets were paved with marble. Stately temples with fluted white marble columns were centers of healing as well as worship. The city was well accustomed to hosting visitors, and there were plenty of inns available. We chose the first one we came to, at the edge of the city. It was almost empty at this time of the year, just after the ending of the rainy season. Wealthier travelers preferred to be in the heart of the city or down by the docks where the boats came in.

The innkeeper was a lean, angular man with a totally bald head, a scrawny fringe of a beard, shrewd eyes, and at least a dozen sons and daughters who worked at various jobs around the inn. He was happy enough to have the ten of us as his guests, although he looked hard at my two little boys.

"They're well behaved," I told him before he could work up the nerve to say anything about them.

A look of understanding dawned on his face. "Your sons?"

"Yes. Treat them well."

"Of course, sir. Of course. My own daughters will watch over them."

Then he glanced at Helen, who had kept the cowl of her robe pulled up over her golden hair. "And your wife, sir?"

"She will require a room of her own," I said.

He nodded and smiled knowingly. "Next to yours."

I smiled back. "Of course."

Gesturing to our two miserable, creaky wagons, the innkeeper said grandly, "Your goods will be perfectly safe here, sir, even if they were made of solid gold. My sons protect this inn and no thief will touch what is yours."

I wondered how certain of that he would have been if he'd known that inside the boxes we lifted out of the wagons there really were treasures of gold and jewels from gutted Troy. I let his four sons handle our baggage, but I watched them closely as they stacked the boxes in the inn's largest room. I chose to sleep in that room myself, together with blind Poletes and the boys. Helen disappeared into the next room, but almost immediately a procession of younger women paraded in, four of them tugging a large round wooden tub, others bearing soaps and powders and whatever else women use in their baths.

I frowned with worry over that. A stranger with an entourage that includes a blind old man and a golden-haired beauty. How long will it take that news to spread throughout the city? How long before it reaches the ears of Menalaos or one his men, even if they are half a world away from here?

But there were more immediate problems to deal with. A bony, sallow-faced girl presented herself and offered to watch my sons. I told her not to let them go beyond the inn's courtyard. After endless days on the road, Lukkawi and Uhri were eager to explore this new and fascinating set of buildings and their yard. They ran off happily with the girl.

The city had whorehouses, of course, and my men were eager to sample their wares. Once we got all our baggage stacked in my room I gave Magro permission to go.

"They'll be back in the morning," he told me.

"You go with them," I said. "Try to keep them together."

His heavy brows rose. "You'll need someone to guard our goods."

"I'll stand guard. You go with the men and try to keep them out of trouble."

Magro couldn't hide the grin that broke across his face. "I'll bring them back in the morning."

I clapped him on the shoulder. "Enjoy the city. You've earned a night's entertainment."

"And you?"

Gesturing to the boxes stacked against the wall, I said, "I'll guard our treasure."

"Alone?"

"I have the innkeeper's ferocious sons." Two of the grown sons were big and burly, the other two slight and wiry, as if they had been born of a different mother. They hardly seemed dangerous to us, not after the fighting we had seen, but they were probably adequate to ward off sneak thieves.

"And I am here also," said Poletes, from the bed where he was sitting. "Even without ears I can hear better than a bat. In the dark of night I will be a better guard than you with your two eyes."

If you don't snore, I thought.

Helen, in the next room, had commandeered two of the innkeeper's young daughters to serve her. I heard them chattering and giggling as they hauled buckets of steaming water up the creaking stairs and poured them into the wooden tub for her bath. None of them knew who we were, of course. Or at least, I hoped that none of them had pieced together the significance of a golden-haired beauty traveling with a gaggle of Hatti soldiers and a blind man. As long as no one from Troy has reached Ephesus before us, I reasoned, we were safe.

Still, I was fretful. I paced my room as I munched on the dried figs and tough strips of dried goat meat that the innkeeper had sent for our early dinner.

I stepped out onto the balcony and saw Lukkawi and

Uhri playing tag together while the innkeeper's daughter sat on the ground by the stables, elbows on her knees, watching them. Their laughter lifted my heart. I realized that there is little in the world as happy as the laughter of children.

"Can you see the city?" Poletes asked, still sitting on our bed.

I nodded, then realized he couldn't see it. "Yes. Right outside our balcony, beyond the window."

"Tell me, what is it like?" He got to his feet, his arms stretched out before him, and stepped uncertainly toward the sound of my voice.

I took his arm and led him out to the balcony. The street on which the inn fronted ran downhill toward the wharves at the water's edge. Poletes could hear the sounds from the street, but he begged me to describe what I saw. I told him of the temples, the inns, the busy streets thronged with people in colorful robes, the chariots and wagons rolling by, the bustling port, the billowing sails out in the harbor, the splendid houses up on the hills. Ephesus was a prosperous city, peaceful and seemingly secure.

"There must be an agora in the heart of the city, a marketplace," Poletes said, cackling with anticipation. "Tomorrow one of the men can take me there and I will tell the story of the fall of Troy, of Achilles' pride and Agamemnon's cruelty, of the burning of the great city and the slaughter of its heroes. The people will love it!"

"No," I said as I came in off the balcony. "We can't let these people know who we are. It's too dangerous."

He turned his blind eyes toward me. The scars left by the burns seemed to glower at me accusingly.

"But I'm a storyteller! I have the greatest story anyone's

ever heard, here in my head." He tapped his temple, just above the ragged slit where his ear had been. "I can make my fortune telling this story!"

"Not here," I said softly. "And not now."

"But Master Lukka, I can stop being a burden to you! I could earn my own way! I could become famous!"

"Whoever heard of a storyteller becoming famous?" I growled.

"You'll be able to travel faster without me," Poletes insisted. "At least let me—"

"Not while she's with us," I said.

He snorted angrily. "That woman has caused more agony than any mortal woman ever born."

"Perhaps so. But until I see her safely accepted in Egypt, where she can be protected, you'll tell no tales about Troy."

Poletes grumbled and mumbled as he groped his way back to the bed. I stayed with him and steered him clear of the stacked boxes of loot.

As the old storyteller plopped down on the dusty feather mattress I heard a scratching at the door. Picking up my sword from the table by the bed, I held it by the scabbard and went to the door, opening it a crack.

It was one of the innkeeper's daughters, a husky, dimpled girl with mistrustful dark eyes.

She curtsied clumsily and said, "The lady asks if you will come to her chamber."

I looked up and down the hallway. It was empty, although anyone might be hiding behind the closed doors of the other rooms.

"Tell her I'll be there in a few moments," I said.

Shutting the door, I went to the bed and sat on it beside Poletes.

"You needn't say anything," he told me. "You're going to her. She'll snare you in her web of allurements."

"You have a poet's way of expression," I said.

"Don't try to flatter me."

Ignoring his petulance, I asked, "Can you guard our goods until I return?"

He grunted and turned this way and that on the soft bedding and finally admitted, "I suppose so."

"You'll yell loudly if anyone tries to enter this room?"

"I'll wake the whole inn."

"Can you bar the door behind me and find your way back to the bed again?"

"What difference if I stumble and break my neck? You'll be with your lady love."

I had to laugh. "She's not my lady love. I'll probably be with her only a few moments. I have no intention—"

"Oh, no, not at all!" He hooted. "Just make sure that you don't bellow like a mating bull. I'm going to try to get some sleep."

Feeling like a schoolboy sneaking out to play, I went to the door and bade Poletes a pleasant nap.

"I sleep very lightly, you know," he said.

Whether he meant to reassure me that no thief would be able to sneak in to rob us, or to warn me to be quiet in Helen's room, next door, I could not tell. Perhaps he meant both.

I belted my sword to my hip and stepped out of the room, closing the door softly behind me. I waited until I heard the bar behind it slide into place. The hallway was still empty, and I could see no dark corners or niches where an enemy could lurk in ambush. Nothing but the worn, tiled floor, the plastered walls, and six wooden doors of other rooms. My men had taken three of them,

I knew, but they were off in the city enjoying themselves. On the other side of the hall was a railing of split logs that overlooked the central courtyard of the inn and its packed dirt floor.

My boys were still playing in the courtyard; I could hear their shouts and laughter.

Very well then, I told myself. And I went to Helen's door.

12

Feeling more than a little uncertain, I scratched at the smooth wooden planks of Helen's door.

"Who is there?" came her muffled voice.

"Lukka," I said, feeling slightly foolish.

"You may enter."

I pushed the door open. Helen stood in the center of the shabby room, resplendent as the sun. She had put on the same robes and jewels she had worn that first time I had seen her alone, in her chamber in Troy. I hadn't realized until this moment that she had brought them with her all this way. She'd probably hidden them under Apet's black cloak that night when she asked me to take her away from Menalaos. In Troy she had looked incredibly beautiful. Here, in this rough inn with its crudely plastered walls and uncurtained windows she seemed like a goddess come to Earth.

I closed the door behind me and leaned my back against it, almost weak with the beauty of her. No one else was in the room; she had dismissed the girls who'd been waiting on her.

"Lukka," she said softly, "you've saved my life."

Somehow I managed to say, "You're not safe yet, my lady. We're still a long way from Egypt."

"Menalaos must be back in Sparta by now, telling everyone how he killed his unfaithful wife with his own hands and burned her body as a sacrifice to his gods."

"Or he could be following our trail, trying to find you."

She shook her head hard enough to make her golden curls tumble about her slim shoulders. "Don't say that, Lukka! You're frightening me."

I stepped toward her. "That's the last thing in the world I want to do, my lady."

"My name is Helen."

My voice caught in my throat, but I managed to half-whisper, "Helen."

She stood before me, warm, alive, breathing, her clear blue eyes searching mine.

"I owe you my life, Lukka," she said.

Like a fool, I replied, "Apet told me about Prince Hector."

Helen sighed. "Hector."

"She told me that you loved him."

"I still love his memory. But he's dead now, in Hades with the rest of the House of Ilios." She slid her arms around my neck. "And we're alive."

I looked down into her eyes and grasped her slim waist in both my hands. Our lips met.

And then I heard my two boys shouting to one another out in the hall. They pounded on the barred door to my room, calling out, "Daddy! Daddy!"

I twitched with surprise.

"Daddy! Open the door!"

Swallowing hard, I released Helen. "They'll get frightened," I said, apologetically.

A strange expression came over her face. She appeared puzzled, then angry, then amused—all in the span of a heartbeat.

Helen broke into laughter. "Go, tend to your little boys," she said, giggling at me. "I can see that my charms are nothing compared to a father's love for his sons."

I felt my face reddening. "My lady . . . they're only children."

"Go, Lukka," said Helen, her laughter tinkling like silver bells. "Do your fatherly duty."

Shamefaced, I opened her door and stepped out into the hall just as Poletes opened the door to our room. The boys turned, saw me, and ran into my arms. And I was happy to hold them—even with Helen standing alone in her room, laughing. At me.

13

I hardly slept at all that night. Poletes snored beside me on the featherbed, Lukkawi and Uhri slept peacefully on the cots that the innkeeper's sons had set up for them. I knew that Helen was on the other side of the wall that separated our rooms. Was she sleeping? Dreaming?

Strange thoughts filled my mind. I desired her, of course I did. What man wouldn't? But did she truly desire me, or was she simply using her charms to keep me bound to her? She knew I could leave her here in Ephesus if I chose to. Leave her alone, defenseless, friendless and helpless in a strange land.

Do I love her? I asked myself. The idea struck me like a thunderbolt. Love her? A princess of Troy? The Queen of Sparta? Then an even wilder question rose before me: does Helen love me?

I lay there on the sagging feather mattress and wondered what love truly is. Women are for men's pleasure. A wife takes care of a man's home, bears him children, rears his family. But love? I never knew Aniti well enough to love her, nor could she have loved me. But Helen . . . Helen was different. What is love? I've put my life at risk, the lives of my men and my sons as well, for her. Is that love? Could she possibly love me? I knew it was impossible. Yet I lay there in the darkness, wondering.

Time and again I thought about tiptoeing out to her room. Time and again I could not work up the courage to do it. Yes, courage. I'd faced armed soldiery and never turned my back. I'd followed the emperor's orders even when they sent me far from my home. But facing Helen was a different matter.

A thousand thoughts raced through my mind. I saw Aniti's face, sad-eyed, watching me from the gray mists of Hades. I had failed her, and now Helen had offered herself to me. The most beautiful woman in the world. What would happen if I bedded her? We still had months of travel ahead of us, through strange and unknown territory. How could I maintain discipline if we were lovers? The men would want women of their own, surely, and our little troop would bog down into a caravan of women. And my sons. It was difficult enough traveling with them. If the men took women we'd soon enough have pregnancies to deal with. And then babies.

Then there was Poletes. He wanted to stay in Ephesus, but I couldn't risk allowing him to tell the tale of Troy to these people. They would soon realize that the Hatti soldiers in their midst were harboring Helen, Queen of Sparta, princess of Troy.

Helen. Was she really offering herself to me? A common soldier? A man with two young sons clinging to him? If I told her that I loved her, would she be pleased? Or would she scorn me? Then I realized that she must be lonely. After the mortal peril she'd been through, after seeing the man she loved spitted on Achilles' spear, after watching Troy and its entire royal family destroyed, she was alone in the world, without a love, without a friend, without even the servant she had known since childhood.

She didn't love me, of that I was certain. She couldn't. It was impossible. But she needed me, and she knew that the best way to keep me loyal to her was through her body. Poletes had been right: she'll snare me in her web of allurements. Or try to.

I watched the nearly full moon sink behind the darkened temple roofs before I closed my eyes in troubled sleep. It seemed merely a moment later when I felt Poletes get out of the bed, coughing and groaning.

"Are you all right?" I asked.

"No," he said. "I'm old." And he reached under the bed for the chamber pot.

Morning came bright and clear, the sky an almost cloudless blue. We were all up early and trooped down to the inn's tavern for a breakfast of yogurt and honey, followed by hot barley cakes. Magro and the men came dragging in, bleary-eyed but grinning and joking to one another about their night's adventures. They joined us for breakfast and ate heartily. Helen stayed in her room and had one of the innkeeper's daughters bring breakfast to her.

I sent Magro and two of the men back into the city to trade our worn horses and donkeys for fresh mounts.

"These old swaybacks won't fetch much," Magro said, as the men walked the animals out of the stable. I couldn't tell which looked the worse for wear, the animals or my men.

"Probably not," I agreed, nodding, "but get what you can for them and buy new ones." I handed him a small sack that held some of the baubles from Troy.

As Magro and the two others left, with the string of animals plodding slowly behind them, the innkeeper came bustling up to me.

"My lord," he said grandly, "may I ask how do you intend to settle your account?"

He'd seen me hand the sack to Magro and now he wanted his own payoff.

I clasped him by the shoulder and walked him back toward the tavern. "I have little coin," I explained, "but this should cover our debt to you, don't you think?" And I pulled from the purse on my belt one of the jeweled rings I'd been carrying.

His eyes flashed wide momentarily, but he quickly covered his delight. Holding the ring up to the sunlight, where its emeralds flashed brightly, he couldn't help but smile.

"This will do very nicely, my lord," he said. "It will fetch a fine price at the agora."

I thought for a moment about going down to the marketplace and converting a few more of our baubles into coin.

"And how long do you plan to stay with us, sir?" asked the landlord.

I made myself shrug. "A few days, perhaps less, perhaps longer."

He bobbed his head up and down. "My inn is at your disposal, sir. Would you like to have one of my daughters tend to your children this day?"

"I think not. I want to see the city, and I know they'll be curious about it also."

"As you wish, my lord."

I could see the thoughts running through his greedy mind. If I could pull a precious emerald ring out of my purse, what other treasures might I have in those boxes that we had carried up to my room? I realized that I couldn't leave my room unguarded.

I detailed Hartu and Drako to stay at the inn and protect our goods. "Wear your swords," I commanded them. "Let these busybodies see that you're armed."

They nodded blearily, their eyes bloodshot. I had to make an effort not to laugh at them. "You can stay in my room with the baggage and take turns napping. But wear your swords when you come out here."

Then Helen came down, muffled in her royal-blue cloak. As if nothing had happened between us the previous day, she asked me, "Are we going to see the city?"

"We are," I replied.

14

We made an odd procession as we walked through the streets of Ephesus: Helen, Poletes, my two children and I—plus Sukku, one of the Hatti soldiers we had picked up along our route from Troy.

Still muffled in her hooded cloak, Helen walked at my side. On my other side Poletes, strong enough now to walk, had tied a scarf of white silk across his useless eyes. He carried a walking stick, and was learning to tap out the ground ahead of him so that he could walk by himself. Still, he never strayed more than an arm's length from me.

Lukkawi and Uhri ran ahead along the narrow, crooked streets, poking their heads into every doorway, chasing after every alley cat they saw, laughing and happy to be able to give free rein to their childish high spirits. Sukku plodded along behind them and never let them out of his sight.

Soon the streets widened into broad avenues paved with marble, which opened onto grand plazas flanked by gracious houses and shops bearing wares from Crete, Egypt, Babylon, even fabled India.

I saw only a few beggars on those avenues, although there were mimes and acrobats and other performers in each of the plazas, entertaining the people who, from their dress, seemed to come from the four corners of the world.

Ephesus was truly a city of culture and comfort, rich with marble temples and centers for healers to ply their craft and even a library that stored scrolls of knowledge. We walked slowly through the plazas and the growing throngs of people crowding into them. Then we came to the city's central marketplace, and passed a knot of people gathered around an old man who was squatting on the marble paving blocks, weaving a spell of words, while his listeners tossed an occasional coin his way.

"A storyteller!" Poletes yelped.

"Not here," I whispered to him.

"Let me stay and listen, Master Lukka," he begged. "Please! I swear that I won't speak a word."

Reluctantly I allowed it. I thought I could trust Poletes' word; it was his heart that I worried about. He was a storyteller, it was in his blood. How long could he remain silent when he had the grandest story of all time to tell to the crowd?

I decided to give him an hour to himself while Helen and I browsed through the shops and stalls of the marketplace. Even with Sukku watching after them, I kept an eye on little Uhri and Lukkawi; they kept disappearing into the crowds and then popping into sight again. Helen seemed delightedly happy to be fingering fine cloth and examining decorated pottery, bargaining with the shopkeepers and then walking on, buying nothing. I shrugged and followed her at a distance, my eyes always searching out my two boys.

The ground rumbled. A great gasping cry went up from the crowd in the marketplace. A few pots tottered off their shelves and smashed to the ground. The world seemed to sway giddily, sickeningly. In a few heartbeats the rumbling ceased and all returned to normal. For a moment the people were absolutely silent. Then a bird chirped and everyone began talking at once, with the kind of light fast banter that comes with a surge of relief from sudden terror.

My sons came running up to me, with Sukku trotting behind them, but by the time they were close enough to grasp my legs the tremor had ended. I assured them everything was all right.

Helen stared at me, her face white with apprehension.

"An earth tremor," I said, trying to make my voice light, unafraid. "Natural enough in these parts."

"Poseidon makes the earth shake," she said in a near-whisper. But the color returned to her cheeks.

The marketplace quickly returned to normal. The crowd resumed its chatter. People bargained with merchants. My boys ran off to watch a puppet show. I could see Poletes across the great square of the market, standing at the edge of the crowd gathered around the squatting storyteller. His gnarled legs were almost as skinny as the stick he leaned upon.

"Lukka."

I turned toward Helen. She was half-frowning at me the way a mother shows displeasure with a naughty son. "You haven't heard a word I've said," she scolded.

"I'm sorry. My mind was elsewhere."

"Watching over your boys."

Nodding, I added, "And Poletes."

Very patiently, Helen repeated, "I said that we could live here in Ephesus very nicely. This is a civilized city, Lukka. With the wealth we've brought we could buy a comfortable villa and live splendidly."

"What about Egypt?"

She sighed. "It's *so* far away. And traveling has been much more difficult than I thought it would be."

"Perhaps we could get a boat and sail to Egypt," I

suggested. "That would be much swifter than travel overland."

Her eyes brightened. "Of course! There are hundreds of boats in the harbor."

I pulled Poletes away from the storyteller and we made our way to the harbor. Heavily laden boats lined the piers while bare-chested gangs of slaves unloaded their cargoes. The breeze off the sea carried the tang of salt air, although Poletes complained of the smell of fish. The boys ran up and down the piers, goggling at the boats, with their high masts and furled sails.

I saw that these merchant ships were different from the black-hulled boats the Achaians had used to cross the Aegean and reach Troy. They were broader in the beam and deeper of draft, built to carry cargo, not warriors; designed for commerce, not for war.

I began to ask about boats that carried passengers and talked with two different captains. Neither of them wanted to travel to Egypt.

"Too far," said one of the grizzled seamasters. "And those Egyptian dogs make you pay a prince's ransom just for the privilege of tying up at one of their stone docks."

Disappointed, I was walking with Helen along one of the piers, searching for a willing captain, when suddenly Helen clutched at my arm.

"Look!" she cried, her eyes staring fearfully out to the water.

Gliding into the harbor were six war galleys, their paddles stroking the water in perfect rhythm. Each of them bore a red eagle's silhouette on their sails.

"Menalaos!" Helen gasped.

"Or his men," I said. "Either way, we can't stay here. They're searching for you."

15

W e fled Ephesus that night, sneaking away like
thieves, leaving a very disappointed innkeeper
who had looked forward to having us stay much longer.

As we rode into the hills and took the southward trail,
I wondered if we could have appealed to the city's
council for protection. But fear of the armed might of the
Achaians who had just destroyed Troy would have paralyzed the Ephesians, I realized. Their city had no protective walls and no real army, merely a city guard for
keeping order in the bawdier districts. Ephesus depended
on the goodwill of all for its safety. They would not allow Helen to stay in their city when Menalaos threatened to bring down the wrath of the Achaian host upon
them.

So we pushed on, through the growing heat of summer, bearing our booty from Troy. A strange group we
were: the fugitive Queen of Sparta, a blind storyteller, a
half-dozen professional soldiers from an empire that no
longer existed, and two buzzing, chattering, endlessly
energetic little boys.

We came to the city of Miletus. Here there were walls,
strong ones, and a lively commercial city. I remembered
my father telling me that he'd been to Miletus once,
when the great emperor Hattusilis was angry with the
city and brought his army to its gates. The Miletians
were so frightened that they opened their gates and offered no resistance. They threw themselves upon the
emperor's mercy. And he was magnificent! He slew only

the city's leaders, the men who had displeased him, and forbade his soldiers to touch so much as an egg.

We bought fresh provisions and mounts in the city's marketplace. From my own hazy knowledge of the area, and from the answers I received from local merchants, Miletus was the last big city on our route for some time. We planned to move inland, through the Mountains of the Bull and across the plain of Cilicia, then along the edge of the Mittani lands and down the coastline of Philistia and Canaan.

But the sounds and smells of another Aegean city were too much for Poletes. He came to me as we started to break our camp, just outside the city walls, and announced firmly that he would go no farther with us. He preferred to remain in Miletus.

"This is a city where I can tell my tales and earn my own bread," he said to me. "I won't burden you further, Master Lukka. Please, let me spend my final days singing of Troy and the mighty deeds that were done there."

"You can't stay by yourself, old windbag," I insisted. "You have no house, no shelter of any kind. How will you find food?"

Poletes reached up for my shoulder as unerringly as if he could see. "Let me sit in a corner of the marketplace and tell the tale of Troy," he said. "I will have food and wine and a soft bed before the sun goes down."

"Is that what you truly want?"

"I have burdened you long enough, my master. Now let me take care of myself. Release me. You can travel faster without me."

He stood there before me in the pale light of a gray morning, a clean white scarf over his eyes, a fresh tunic hanging over his scrawny frame. I learned that even blinded eyes can cry. So, almost, did I.

"No telling of Troy until we are safely away from the city," I warned, trying to make my voice growl.

We embraced like brothers, and he turned without another word and walked slowly toward the city gate, tapping his stick before him.

I sent the others off on the inland road, telling them I would catch up later. I waited half the day, then entered the city. Leaving my horse with the guards at the gate, I made my way on foot to the marketplace. Poletes sat there cross-legged in the middle of a large and rapidly growing throng, his arms gesturing, his wheezing voice speaking slowly, majestically:

"Then mighty Achilles prayed to his mother, Thetis the Silver-Footed, 'Mother, my lifetime is destined to be so brief that ever-living Zeus, sky-thunderer, owes me a worthier prize of glory . . .'"

I watched for only a few moments. That was enough. Men and women, boys and girls, were rushing up to join the crowd, their eyes fastened on Poletes like the eyes of a bird hypnotized by a snake. Rich merchants, soldiers in chain mail, women of fashion in their colorful robes, city magistrates carrying their wands of office—they all pressed close to hear Poletes' words. Even the other storytellers, left alone once Poletes began singing of Troy, got up from their accustomed stones and ambled grudgingly across the marketplace to listen to the newcomer.

Poletes had been right, I had to admit. He had found his place. He would be fed and sheltered here, even honored. And as long as we were far away, he could sing of Troy and Helen all he wanted to.

I went back to the city gate; my horse was still there, tethered at a hitching rail with several others. I gave the corporal of the guards a few coppers, then climbed onto my chestnut mount and nosed her up the inland trail. I would never see Poletes again, and that made me feel the sadness of loss.

Time and distance will soften your sorrow, I told myself. You have two little boys to look after. And the fugitive Queen of Sparta.

It was evening by the time I caught up with our two carts and my men. Lukkawi and Uhri ran up to meet me, and I swung them up onto my horse, laughing at the sight of them. Helen sat in one of the carts, watching with eyes that never wavered from me.

We made camp by the roadside as the purple of evening deepened into night's darkness. We had a long, long road ahead of us. Deserts and rivers and mountains stood between us and distant Egypt.

The campfire slowly guttered into embers. My boys went to sleep in one of the wagons; Helen had the other to herself. The men rolled themselves in their blankets while I sat by the dying fire, on watch.

The night was chill. A solitary wolf howled in the darkness while the sad, lopsided face of the moon rode high above among scudding clouds. Stars twinkled up in the black bowl of night, like the eyes of the gods watching me.

"Lukka."

I was startled to hear her voice, and cursed myself for a fool for letting her steal up on me. Some guard!

Helen was wrapped in that dark robe again, although she had let the hood down. Her hair glowed like gold in the pale moonlight.

"I'm glad you returned," she said, sitting beside me.

"You knew I would."

"Still . . ." She let the thought hang in the air. At last she said, "I was afraid that maybe . . . something could have happened . . ."

"Nothing could keep me from my sons," I said.

"Yes. Of course."

There was something in her voice, a questioning, a seeking. She lapsed into silence, her chin down, her eyes avoiding mine.

I heard myself admit, "And nothing could keep me from you."

"No," she whispered, her face still downcast. "Don't say it. Don't even think it. I bring nothing but death and ruin. I'm cursed, Lukka, cursed by the gods."

"The gods of Egypt will love you better."

"But Egypt's so far away. I thought we could stay in Ephesus, but he's searching for me! He's after me!"

"He won't find you. He doesn't know we were in Miletus." But then I thought of Poletes spinning his tale in the marketplace. Menalaos will know we were there soon enough.

"I'm afraid, Lukka. I'm frightened!"

Without thinking, without worrying about the consequences, I took her by the shoulders and pulled her to me. She buried her face in my chest, sobbing like a child. She wasn't the Queen of Sparta now, nor a princess of Troy. She was a frightened woman fleeing for her life, dependent on my protection. She was the most beautiful woman in the world and she was in my arms, trembling with fear, needing me as much as I wanted her.

I got to my feet and lifted her into my arms and carried her to the wagon. There, amid the blankets and bags and boxes we made love. Not in a palace, not amid royal trappings on a beautifully decked wedding bed. On a cart that smelled of donkeys and sweat and the dust of long, hard travel.

The stars peeked through the tattered clouds and Artemis' silver moon sank down behind the western hills while Helen and I made love, all other thoughts, all other cares, driven from my mind completely.

But in the gray half-light that preceded true dawn, as Helen slept in my arms, I knew that I would cross deserts and rivers and mountains for this woman. That I would carry her to the ends of the earth to keep her safe, to protect her against the vengeful Menalaos.

Thus our journey from Miletus began.